WESTERN

Rugged men looking for love...

Her Hometown Christmas
Anna Grace

Once Upon A Charming Bookshop
Heatherly Bell

MILLS & BOON

HER HOMETOWN CHRISTMAS
© 2023 by Anna Grace
Philippine Copyright 2023
Australian Copyright 2023
New Zealand Copyright 2023

First Published 2023
First Australian Paperback Edition 2023
ISBN 978 1 867 29539 6

ONCE UPON A CHARMING BOOKSHOP
© 2023 by Heatherly Bell
Philippine Copyright 2023
Australian Copyright 2023
New Zealand Copyright 2023

First Published 2023
First Australian Paperback Edition 2023
ISBN 978 1 867 29539 6

MIX
Paper | Supporting
responsible forestry
FSC® C001695

Published by
Harlequin Mills & Boon
An imprint of Harlequin Enterprises (Australia) Pty Limited
(ABN 47 001 180 918), a subsidiary of HarperCollins
Publishers Australia Pty Limited
(ABN 36 009 913 517)
Level 19, 201 Elizabeth Street
SYDNEY NSW 2000 AUSTRALIA

Cover art used by arrangement with Harlequin Books S.A.. All rights reserved.

Printed and bound in Australia by McPherson's Printing Group

Her Hometown Christmas
Anna Grace

MILLS & BOON

Anna Grace justifies her espresso addiction by writing fun, modern romance novels in the early-morning hours. Once the sun comes up, you can find her teaching high school history or outside with her adventure-loving husband. Anna is a mediocre rock climber, award-winning author, mum of two fun kids and snack enthusiast. She lives rurally in Oregon and travels to big cities whenever she gets the chance. Anna loves connecting with readers, and you can find her on social media and at her website, anna-grace-author.com.

Twitter: @AnnaEmilyGrace
IG: @AnnaGraceAuthor
Facebook: Anna Grace Author

Dear Reader,

Welcome back to Outcrop, Oregon! Enthusiastic, outgoing Hunter is everyone's favourite Wallace sibling, and he finally meets his match when Ani Blaisedell comes breezing into town.

Hunter is the ultimate hometown boy, dedicated to his community. Ani is a free spirit, dedicated to a life on the road. The mismatched pair is stuck together as they prepare for a holiday gala. Can they survive the countdown to Christmas and keep their hearts in check?

My husband refitted an old Sprinter van, opening up a world of adventures for us. Sometimes (okay, most times) when we're out on the road, we're tempted to leave all our responsibilities behind and keep travelling. But inevitably we start to think about the friends, family members, pets and yes, even the responsibilities, we would miss. This book explores the balance between a love of freedom and the need for community.

I'd love to hear what you think of *Her Hometown Christmas*! You can find me on social media and at my website, anna-grace-author.com.

Happy reading!

Anna

DEDICATION

To Ann Hettick,
For cheering on all my literary dreams
and then fact-checking the equestrian details
as those dreams came true.

CHAPTER ONE

NOTHING BEAT SNUGGLING under a cozy quilt on a cold winter morning. Except maybe snuggling under a quilt with coffee.

Ani wrapped the blankets around her shoulders and sat up on the raised bed in the back of her van. She pulled back the rear window curtain. Stars retreated in the early morning light as a line of pink grew stronger along the crest of the Cascades. Pressing a finger against the window, she shivered. It was colder than she'd expected in Outcrop, and the heating unit in her Sprinter could only crank out so much warmth.

Either that or your solar-powered battery has finally died.

No, it was just cold. She could do this. She *liked* living on the road. Or at least it beat the alternative. And it was going to be glorious today. Anticipation shot through her: a sweet commission and a cold, sunny day in a brand-new place awaited.

But first, coffee. There was probably time to climb up on top of her van and watch the sunrise as she sipped.

Coffee. Sunrise. New place.

Life is good.

She'd seen a little of the town of Outcrop when she'd driven in the night before, but it had been dark. She'd get her rooftop view before meeting... *What was the guy's name again?* Ani reached up to the shelf above her bed and found her notebook.

Hunter Wallace.

But right now she had to get out of bed.

Ani loved every inch of the van she'd remodeled: the clever storage, the functional kitchen, the solar power system, the extremely comfortable bed. It was a perfect home, and perfectly mobile. She'd earn money here in Outcrop then head to Tucson before the holidays hit. This year, she planned to be safely out of Oregon when the mayhem began.

Ani glanced toward her little kitchen. She'd tried to make coffee without getting out of bed once. That had not gone well. She steeled her will, took a deep breath and threw off the covers.

"Hey!" an angry voice outside the van barked. The pounding of a fist reverberated throughout the Sprinter.

Ani groaned. Nothing like a local parking vigilante to take the thrill off a perfect morning.

The banging continued. "You can't park here."

"Already did," Ani muttered, pulling an old puffer jacket from its cubby. She slipped the jacket over her pajamas.

The banger/yeller seemed to be working at the slider door. Ani smiled to herself as she gripped the handle. There were few things more satisfying than confusing people by opening the door they were banging on.

Why anyone would be so passionate about where she parked—or didn't park—her van overnight, she could never understand. But by now, she knew how to deal with them. Her grin widened and she flung the door open.

So, she was smiling as she met the eyes of the most ridiculously good-looking man she'd ever seen.

It was like he'd been ripped out of a men's outdoor clothing catalog. His dark brown hair was a little too long for him to be straight-laced, but too short to be flaky. Complex hazel eyes glared at her from under long lashes. The man was tall and carelessly fit. He dressed in the standard Oregonian-cowboy ensemble of jeans, work boots, flannel shirt, puffer vest and Stetson. *And, man, it looked good on him.*

He lifted his hat and ran a hand through his hair, looking as startled as she was.

Okaaaaay. Deep breath. It was time to fight her way out of a ticket, not speculate about why this banger/yeller looked so unreasonably handsome in a plaid shirt. She crossed her arms over her chest and nodded toward the back of the restaurant.

"Sign says Eighty Local parking."

"It's seven a.m.," the hottie replied. "Restaurant's not open."

"Actually, I think it's closer to seven thirty."

"I'm sorry, but you can't park here."

Ani reached for her phone to confirm the time. She tapped the screen, but nothing appeared. *Weird.* The phone was plugged into its charger.

"It's private property." Even his voice was attractive, a low resonance sparking a response from her belly. Ani didn't look up as she checked to make sure the charger was plugged in correctly. "Look, I don't mean to be rude, but there's no overnight parking here."

"Yeah, you've been pretty clear about that." She flipped the light switch over the induction stove. Nothing happened.

Ani let out a breath and could see it. The battery *was* out, and with it went her heat and power. No wonder she'd been so cold.

"There's a Walmart in Bend. You can park overnight

there." He nodded, like this was new and useful information. "And there's national forest land to the north of here, where you can camp for free."

She met his gaze. "Thanks. I'm not sleeping at Walmart, and I know where the forest is. I have a meeting—"

"You need to move off this lot."

"Oh, I intend to move off this lot as soon as possible, but I have a meeting—"

"I'm going to ask you to leave now."

Ani stilled herself. On instinct, her core muscles tightened, her shoulders relaxed, her breath steadied. She looked straight into the man's beautiful eyes. He took a step back.

This was her personal nightmare. Her power was out, it was cold, and she was being yelled at by an intolerant, gorgeous, central Oregon lug nut. And she'd lost the capacity to make herself a cup of coffee.

The crunch of gravel pulled Ani's attention away from the man. A pearly white, hybrid SUV bumped up over a curb and into the lot. Doors opened and slammed as two identical women jumped out, jabbering and laughing.

The man turned back to Ani. He looked like he could possibly be apologetic if he had another ten minutes, and existed in an alternate universe.

She didn't need an apology. This man and this parking spot meant nothing to her. The world was full of people trying to enforce their own particular set of rules. Ani would park her van on the street in front of Eighty Local and never see this man again for the rest of her life.

What she needed was her freedom and the job she was in Outcrop to do would fuel that freedom.

"Excuse me," he said, as though his departure would in any way inconvenience her. "Those are my sisters. I didn't mean to be rude, I just don't want this lot to become a campground."

"Yes, you are vigilant in protecting this patch of gravel."

"Hey—"

"Look, I have way bigger problems than this." She gestured between them then flipped the light switch again.

Because it was her ability to flip a switch, right? Not the battery that had been on the fritz for the last month. *Keep flipping the switch and the power will miraculously restore itself...*

The man's gaze connected with hers as he touched his fingers to the rim of his Stetson and took one step away, then another. The gesture was unexpected, like the first warm breeze in early March.

Ani pulled her focus from the cowboy and got back to the problem at hand—no heat. She heard his boots crunching across the gravel then exclamations of greeting as he neared the women. Ani could feel the veneer of ice around her heart start to thaw as she listened to the man greet his sisters. She caught herself turning to take one last look. He really was the most attractive man she'd ever seen. *Would it hurt, another look?*

Point of fact, she was never going to see him again. She *should* take another look, because the whole point of life was to experience new things, and the experience of a man this good-looking wasn't going to come around again. Ani grinned to herself and glanced over her shoulder.

And there he was, looking right back at her as he pulled a set of keys out of his vest pocket. He replaced his own smile with a look of stern disapproval, but he wasn't quick enough. The damage was done. That smile was enough to make her want to stay illegally parked here forever; his attitude was enough to make her want to hit the road immediately. He was gorgeous, but maddening, and probably thinking the exact same thing about her.

And he was unlocking the door?

Judging from the keys, and his strong feelings about the gravel surrounding Eighty Local, she'd just met Hunter Wallace.

"Do YOU LOVE your Christmas present?" Clara was jumping up and down as they entered the restaurant. Piper clapped her hands.

Hunter let the door fall shut behind them. He had so much to do today. Why had he let his sisters talk him into an 8:00 a.m. meeting?

Because there is literally no other time in the day.

He loved his sisters and, by the way they were bouncing off the walls, they were pretty stoked about the present. Why it couldn't wait another month until Christmas, he didn't understand. He looked around the room.

"My Christmas present?"

Clara pointed at the parking lot, her bright, dimpled smile lighting up her face. Piper's matching smile flashed as she said, "Ani!"

Hunter looked out the window. The admittedly beautiful—but freeloading—woman circled her van.

"Ani?"

"Yes!" Piper cried. "She's your Christmas present!"

Hunter shook his head. His sisters were highly successful matchmakers and had been trying to set him up for the last five years. Surely, they hadn't...

Had they?

"You got me a hippie chick for Christmas?"

"She's not a hippie," Clara protested.

"She lives in a van," Hunter reminded her.

"With zero bumper stickers." Clara widened her eyes.

"Because everyone with an alternative lifestyle sticks pithy sayings to the back of their vehicle?"

"Basically," Piper confirmed.

Hunter looked back out the window. The woman, Ani, had climbed up onto the top of her van and was examining the solar panel.

"She paints murals," Piper said. "We know how stressed out you've been about the expansion and the Bend Equestrian Society Gala."

"And we know how you keep complaining about how dull this building looks when you approach from the east," Clara cut in.

"So, we hired her!"

"She can finish it in time for the gala. She'll paint whatever you like—"

"—but we do have a few suggestions."

Hunter scrambled for an excuse. "I don't have the time—"

"You literally don't have to do anything," Piper said. "Just be all *'looks great!'* if she asks, then go marinate something, or whatever you do in the kitchen."

"And I can totally help with anything," Clara said. "We one hundred percent didn't make more work for you. I promise."

"Merry Christmas!"

Hunter stared at his sisters. He was touched by their thoughtfulness, annoyed by their interference and now trapped with an inconsiderate, inconceivably attractive woman.

Family.

Hunter's gaze drifted to the ceiling then circled through his restaurant. Eighty Local was his life. He'd bought the condemned building with money he'd earned sweeping floors, waiting and busing tables, and cooking in dive restaurants.

Rescued lumber, third-hand appliances and repurposed materials came cheap, and Hunter had collected what he'd needed over time. While continuing his work on the family ranch, Hunter had built this place board by board. "Stylish and sustainable," was what *Central Oregon Living* had said in its write-up. At least eighty percent of everything he served was local. Fruits and vegetables came from Oregon's Willamette Valley, grain was shipped in from the eastern half of the state. He bought from small, family-run farms, like the beef he sourced from his brother-in-law's ranch a few miles up the road.

After being a daily disappointment to his parents for most of his life, Hunter was finally successful.

Or at least he had been until he'd gotten it into his head to expand. Hunter had sunk every penny he'd had, and every penny he could get the bank and friends and family to loan him, into an events hall. With the location and the surprising success of his restaurant, it had seemed like a sure bet. Hunter's lungs constricted as he thought of everything he still had to do to get the space ready for the Bend Equestrian Society Gala. If the space and the event weren't perfect, the women of BES would flood the internet with bad reviews. Eighty Local would be finished. He had twenty-seven days. Six-hundred, forty-nine-and-a-half hours to go.

A beautiful, mural-painting woman was the last distraction he needed. She'd caught him at his worst, then caught him staring at her.

What could he possibly say to his sisters? They were both so busy with their matchmaking business. Clara was newly married. Piper had rallied for Clara's wedding, but still hadn't snapped out of the funk she'd been in since a painful breakup last summer. Yet here they both were, bouncing with excitement about the possibility of a mural for Eighty Local.

"Thank you." Hunter held out his arms. His sisters came in to hug him and he found himself worrying a fifteen-second family hug would take up too much time. Along with finishing the events center, he had to help with the family's Mistletoe Festival, participate in the town business fair, and host the gala. All while running the restaurant.

And somewhere in there he needed to celebrate Christmas with his noisy, loving family.

The bells on the front door jangled and Hunter felt the gust of cold air. He looked up to find Ani fully dressed, long hair piled artfully on her head, eyes sharp and determined.

"Given the way my morning is going, can I assume you're Hunter Wallace?"

CHAPTER TWO

"I'M SORRY, but I'm not going to work for him." Ani kept her shoulders relaxed and her voice steady as she looked first at one of the women then the other. She didn't love backing out on these two. They seemed nice. But spending two weeks working for a grumpy, rule-following hottie? Not gonna happen.

"I appreciate the commission, and hate to back out like this," Ani continued. "But after a quick conversation with Hunter in the parking lot, I don't think this is a good fit. I have the freedom to choose when and with whom I work."

Ani met Hunter's gaze. It wasn't entirely a lie. She did get to choose whom she worked for. Unfortunately, she was desperate for money, and returning the down payment for the mural to the sisters was an additional problem.

"But you promised…" The more smiley of the two twins started to complain as the more sophisticated one turned on her brother and demanded, "What did you say to her?"

"I asked her not to park in the lot." Hunter gestured toward her van.

"Asked?" one of the women questioned.

"Look," Ani interrupted the siblings. She needed to get out of there and away from the unreasonably handsome parking lot monitor. "I know you hired me for this job in good faith, but I won't work here. Life's too short to take jobs that aren't fun or at least interesting."

"Must be nice," Hunter muttered, running a hand

through his slightly-too-long hair. What was it about men who couldn't make time for a haircut that she found so attractive?

Ani did her best to ignore him. "I do need to work right now. The lithium-ion battery in my van is out."

"That's...awful?" the smiley twin asked.

"It's two thousand dollars of awful. I need to earn enough to replace it. It's a lot to ask, but it would be incredibly helpful if you could point me in the direction of other work in town. I have a lot of skills and I work hard." She looked carefully into the eyes of one twin then the other. They seemed so nice, and so disappointed. "I'm sorry, but I won't work here."

The moment stretched out. The sisters looked at one another, communicating without making a sound.

"Okay, so, I'm Clara," the smiley one said, holding out a hand.

"I'm Piper. We spoke on the phone."

"Clara and Piper," Ani repeated. There was no reason she should take the time to remember which was which, but found herself looking for defining characteristics anyway.

"And you pronounce your name Ah-nie, not Annie, right?"

"Correct. I know it's confusing."

The sisters exchanged a glance. Then Clara surprised her by gently resting a hand on her arm. Ani looked at the hand and then into Clara's smiling face. She couldn't remember the last time someone had touched her.

Piper leaned in and said, "Our brother can be such a crank sometimes, but, honestly, he's super sweet."

Hunter had his hands on his hips and was studying the floor, like he was counting the seconds until everyone left.

"I'm totally curious about your van." Piper's eyebrow quirked up.

"Do you live in it full-time?" Clara asked.

At this Hunter groaned and stalked over to an espresso machine. He flipped a switch and the grinder cranked up, flooding the room with an intoxicating aroma. Ani's nervous system snapped to attention and began begging for coffee.

"I do live in my van full-time." Ani wrenched her attention away from the attractive man at the caffeine delivery system and focused on the sisters. "It's great. I did the remodel myself, so it's exactly the way I want it."

"Seriously?" Clara's eyes widened. "You did all the work yourself? Like the van life videos?"

The sound of steaming milk filled the room. Was he trying to torture her?

"Yep. Then I did all the work a second time to fix the mistakes I made the first time."

The sisters laughed. Ani felt a little more comfortable, then a little worse about backing out on the job. They were so nice.

"For the most part, it's fantastic, but this morning I'm kinda freaked out," she admitted. "The lithium-ion battery stores all the electricity from the solar panels. I can still drive the van, but until I get a new battery, I have no heat and I can't cook."

"You must have been freezing last night," Piper said.

"And then, let me guess." Clara connected the dots. "Our brother woke you up by banging on your door and demanding you remove your van from his parking lot."

"I don't want people parking overnight, and leaving trash, and asking to use the restroom," Hunter said.

Ani turned so she didn't have to look at him. Unfortunately, she could still smell the coffee.

Clara stepped closer, like she was sharing a confidence, but spoke loud enough so anyone in the room could hear.

"He's been super touchy. Hunter helps run our family's ranch *and* has this restaurant."

"Our brother takes on way more than he should," Piper said loudly, looking over her shoulder at the offending sibling. "Normally, he's a great guy. The best."

"Now he's expanding this place and there's this big gala coming up a few days after Christmas."

"This isn't about the gala." Hunter took a big, delicious-looking swig of coffee. "I'm trying to run a nice establishment here. This isn't a truck stop."

"I don't drive a truck," Ani said.

Hunter spoke over her. "I don't need rich kids parking in my lot." He looked out the window and shook his head. "Spending their parents' money on hundred-thousand-dollar vehicles so they can pretend to be dirtbags for a few months. Get real."

Ani gripped the back of a chair. *Get real.* That had been her dad's line whenever Ani's opinions differed from the family's. Her fingers tightened around the chairback, adrenaline flooding her body, blurring her vision as she imagined hurling the chair across the room. Pain radiated up her arm from gripping the wood too tightly.

Anger won't help me.

The twins were talking. They were like two birds flitting between her and Hunter. Ani managed to fill her lungs with air. The static anger subsided. These people meant nothing. Hunter's opinion held no significance in her world.

Hunter was coughing out some forced apology.

Ani spoke over him. "I'm out." She took decisive steps toward the door.

"Wait!" Clara cried. Something seemed to click through her mind and she settled. "Please. Have you had any coffee?"

"No." Ani's voice was sharper than she would have liked. "My power's out."

"Seriously? Hunter!" Piper gestured at the espresso machine.

For one brief, beautiful moment, Ani allowed herself to get excited about coffee.

But no. The line had been drawn and she wasn't backing down.

"No, thanks. I'm sure I can find a truck stop with something just as good."

"Let me make you coffee," Hunter grumbled. He pulled off his vest in a move so smooth Mick Jagger could learn something. Seriously, Hollywood actors should have to take a class in vest removal from Hunter Wallace.

Because what was more popular in romantic comedy than a grumpy Oregonian battling his way out of Gore-Tex and goose down?

"I'm not taking your handouts."

"You. Move," Clara said to her brother. She tamped out Hunter's grounds and then flipped the switch on the grinder. Piper rounded the counter and rummaged around, coming up with a scone.

Ani weighed her options. On one hand, every part of her being was desperate for coffee, and the scone appeared to be a buttery, flaky masterpiece of pastry. On the other hand, she had a point to make with Hunter.

On the other hand—if she had another hand—coffee.

"Here you go." Clara slid a big, steaming mug of espresso and foamed milk onto the bar, next to the scone. "Please?" She turned a radiant smile on Ani.

"This scone is the best scone you'll ever have. I'm serious." Piper crossed her arms and leaned back against the counter.

The room quieted. Ani could feel the lack-of-caffeine

headache coming on. The thought of weak truck-stop brew made her stomach turn. She glanced at Hunter. He had a clipboard in his hands and was scribbling something at the end of a long list.

"I'm sorry." He kept his focus on the clipboard. "My behavior was, and continues to be, rude." He looked up then. His eyes were a rich mix of brown and green, as though the landscape of his home were reflected in them. "Have some espresso."

Ani moved toward the counter. Of their own accord, her fingers reached for the cup and brought it to her lips. The scent enveloped her. She took one small sip then another. Smooth and nutty, with an unexpected kick, it was the most incredible coffee she'd ever experienced. World religions had been founded on experiences similar to the one she was having with this beverage.

The twins were staring at her, grinning.

Hunter cleared his throat then muttered, "Nothing you can't find at a truck stop."

Ani set the coffee down deliberately. Hunter met her gaze. Maybe it was just the coffee talking, but was it possible she'd misjudged him?

She refocused on her mug. It didn't matter. What mattered was earning money and getting out of the state before her family started pressuring her to come home for the holidays. Since Oregon was her official residence, she had to come back every so often to tend to her adulting chores: check her PO box in Portland, see a dentist, deal with her taxes, vote. But she'd learned early on in her van life adventures that the best way to avoid Christmas with her family was to be a good two thousand miles away from them at the time.

"I'd love to find work here in Outcrop." Ani turned to address the sisters. "I can do basic car repairs. I'm competent with finish carpentry and basic masonry. I've done all kinds of service jobs. I learn quickly, so I'm confident taking almost anything."

"Carpentry?" Hunter asked.

"Carpentry is my favorite. Not having my own band saw is the only drawback to my lifestyle."

Maybe not the only drawback, but these people didn't need to know how lonely it could get being free.

She felt rather than saw Hunter moving toward her. Something seemed to shift in the mood of the room.

"My sisters hired you. You came here to work." Hunter drew in a breath. "If you're looking for work in Outcrop, you've come to the right place. Please, don't let me being rude run you off."

"I'm not running off. I'm choosing to leave because I don't like you."

"Look, I'm normally a good boss. Ask anyone. This month I have a lot going on and when I saw your van I thought—"

"I was some rich hippie kid from Eugene freeloading off your hard-won patch of gravel?"

His shoulders dropped; his exhalation brushed her cheek. "Something like that. I'm sorry."

Ani ran her hand across the glossy wood-slab bar. Her gaze ran to the ceiling then around the stylish room: reclaimed wood, artfully unmatched seating, older, rebuilt appliances. The dining room had an eclectic, soulful feel, and she was beginning to get a sense of whose soul had been poured into Eighty Local.

"Did you build all this?" she asked.

Hunter ran a hand through his hair. "Yep."

The guy looked like he was at his rope's end. She was feeling substantially better as she made her way to the bottom of the coffee cup, and the scone wasn't doing any harm, either. The restaurant felt like a good place. Painting a mural was easy money, and there was no way she could set off over the Rocky Mountains without electricity in her van.

She looked up and found Hunter studying her. His eyes did seem sorry, but also deeply troubled. It was likely her van in his gravel lot was the last straw for this guy. They might never be best friends, but that didn't mean she couldn't do honest work in return for reasonable pay.

Man, how long had she been staring into his eyes?

"Let's see how the morning goes," she said.

"Sweet! Thank you. High five for Christmas." Clara held up her hands for a double high five, which Piper returned, whooping and cheering.

Piper winked at Ani. "You have no idea how hard he is to buy for."

The faintest smile misted across Hunter's face. He nodded but didn't say anything.

A gust of cold washed across Ani's back, accompanied by the sound of the bells jangling from the door handle. A string of complaints followed.

"Is that parking lot ever going to get fixed? If I were you, I'd be worried about a lawsuit, particularly with this weather."

"Is there no mercy?" Hunter implored under his breath.

Ani studied Hunter for a moment longer before glancing at the door.

Apparently, there was no mercy at all whatsoever, because Holly Banks was in the house.

"HI, HOLLY." It took some effort for Hunter to push himself back from the counter, out of Ani's gaze. "What brings you—"

"It's freezing in here," Holly interrupted him, pulling her long down jacket closer.

"We're not open yet. I turned on the heat—"

"I'm only here to check out the events venue," she said.

The events venue. The massive void looming on the other side of the dining room.

"I'm sorry." Hunter scrambled for an excuse to keep Holly out of the unfinished room. "The inspector hasn't signed off on it. I can't take customers in yet."

"I'm not a customer. I'm an events planner."

Hunter noticed a silent exchange between his sisters. The most subtle eye roll from Clara met with a twitch of the lips from Piper. Holly was no more an events planner than he was an astronaut, even if she was in charge of this year's BES Gala.

"It's not safe," Hunter said. "There are tools lying all over the place, and I'm halfway through the finish work. I couldn't live with myself if someone got hurt."

Holly used two fingers to adjust her hair then addressed Clara. "Did he let you see it?"

"It's going to be perfect for the gala," Clara said.

Hunter's eyes flickered to where Ani had been enjoying her coffee, but she'd abandoned her perch on the stool. She was snooping behind the counter, investigating his espresso machine. For some reason, she'd pulled the hood of her sweatshirt up over her head.

"You do realize how big this is?" Holly focused her gaze on Hunter. "The BES Gala is one of the three major events of the season, according to *Central Oregon Living*."

Piper turned sharply and Hunter would bet good money she was trying not to laugh.

"We have a month," Hunter said.

"We have twenty-seven days. We've always held it at the country club in Bend, and it's always been successful. But Shawna wanted it here, and I'm stuck planning. If it fails, everyone will blame me." Holly held eye contact with him, trying to impress upon him the seriousness of the situation.

Like it hadn't occurred to him.

Hunter ran a hand through his hair. He knew the stakes. If he didn't get the hall ready, it would be catastrophic for Eighty Local.

He also knew Eighty Local served far better fare and was considerably more hip than the country club. The Bend Equestrian Society couldn't have chosen a better place to have their gala. Hunter just had to make sure that *place* existed by the big night.

"Forget it." Holly stamped her foot and tossed her hair back. "You know what? Forget it. I don't even want to look at it—it will probably give me nightmares. I'll have a double skim latte."

Holly shifted from insult to drink order so fast that Hunter didn't register it until he heard the portafilter tamping out behind the bar. He glanced over to see Ani at the espresso machine. Her hood was still up and she'd grabbed an Eighty Local apron to throw on over her jacket. *What the...?*

"How's Shawna?" Piper asked.

Hunter mentally thanked his sister for distracting Holly then moved quickly toward Ani. Her scent, something spicy with an underlying sweetness, pulled him closer.

Yeah. Bad idea. He did not need to waste his time trying to decipher why she smelled so good.

"You know how to make espresso?"

"I'm not sure yet," Ani said as she located the correct switch to start the espresso shot. "But I watched you and then Clara. It's not rocket science."

Hunter crossed his arms, watching as she repeated the

movements that had become natural to him in the years since he'd started the restaurant.

"And, if I happen to make a mistake and poison her, oh well." She grinned at him. Her smile raced down his spine and radiated through him. "Is this the skim milk?" She held up a container of half-and-half.

Hunter nodded. His pulse kicked up as Ani caught his eye in conspiracy.

"Yes. Yes, that is the skim milk."

"New employee dress code?" Holly interrupted, looking for the first time at Ani.

"I'm in training," Ani said, keeping her eyes averted from Holly as she reached for a to-go cup. The pitch of her voice sounded different, higher than before.

Hunter cleared his throat and leaned in closer. "Thank you for giving this a chance. I need a lot of help right now."

She shrugged one shoulder. "I need a lot of money right now. And I'll park somewhere else."

"No." The word leaped out of his mouth like an ambitious trout. "Park here. Use my dumpster. I even have a shower." He gestured to one of the charging stations he'd set up for patrons. "Feel free to plug your phone in over there."

She gave a dry laugh. "I do understand property rights and parking laws." She looked up at him. Hunter steeled his body's response to her. "I just didn't want to be late for the meeting this morning."

Hunter groaned, leaning against the counter. "I'm such a jerk."

She grinned as she held the frothing pitcher under the steam nozzle. Hunter reached over and adjusted the dial. "You keep the nozzle low in the milk until it comes up to temperature, then pull it up to create the froth." She nodded, placing a palm on the outside of the pitcher to check the temperature.

"I take it you're under some stress?"

Hunter held up his clipboard. The to-do list ran down the entire page and covered everything from setting up a brine to installing outlets in the addition.

She set down the pitcher and took the clipboard. Hunter studied her as she studied the list. Her clothes were the highest quality but well worn. There was a patch of duct tape on the elbow of her puffer jacket. Her skin and eyes glowed as though she were healthy, rather than made up. She moved with the ease of someone who was completely comfortable with herself.

"This is quite a list," she said. "What's the Business Fair?"

"Outcrop, Outside. All the local businesses set up on Main Street. It's fun. There are lights and music, and everybody turns out for it. I'm making a special holiday sandwich, and we generally do good business."

"And that's on Friday?"

Hunter's lungs constricted. "Yep."

"How much do you pay?"

"It depends on the work. All my employees start at a dollar over minimum wage and get a raise once they can function without my direct supervision."

"Sounds good. Three weeks? I can help out around here and, if that goes well, I'll do the mural." She looked thoughtful, as though the mental math was running through her brain. "Yeah. That should buy a battery and have enough of a cushion left over to get to Tucson."

Ani poured the espresso shots into a paper cup then picked up the frothing pitcher. Hunter took a spoon and held back the milk foam as she poured. He placed a touch of foam on top before Ani put a lid over the drink.

"I'll take it to go," Holly said, not noticing Ani had already made that decision for her. "I'm heading down to Outcrop Hardware, Tack and Feed to take a few shopping pictures for Insta, then stopping in at Second Chance Cowgirl." She addressed Piper and Clara, gesturing with spread fingers across her neckline. "I'm thinking of a topaz lavalier for the gala."

"Oh, Second Chance Cowgirl is closed this week," Clara said, a guilty smile lighting her face.

"No, it's not," Holly said.

"Um. It is. And it's kind of my fault."

Hunter warmed to hear Clara say this. It was a good reminder of the world existing outside of Eighty Local.

"Is Christy off with Coach?" Hunter asked.

"Yep! He bought the tickets to Aruba the minute the doctors cleared him to go." Clara clapped her hands, like she did whenever a match she'd made was going particularly well.

Holly wasn't feeling her joy. "Look, I know Christy Jones. And she would not close down her store the first week in December."

Clara checked her watch. "Welp, Christy Jones took off yesterday for Aruba, which is four hours ahead of us. My guess is by now she's engaged to a very happy Coach Kessler."

"You have it wrong," Holly barked, walking over and picking up the latte. "Christy Jones wouldn't marry some local coach."

Clara's face folded sharply. The look she exchanged with Piper was not subtle. Hunter had always wondered if there was a limit to Clara's goodwill and kindness. This was it. "Yeah. Well. You're wrong. Good luck with your shopping."

"So, I've just wasted my day?" Holly asked. Hunter

glanced at the clock; it was only 9:00 a.m. Holly took a long drink of the coffee. Her expression shifted. "At least you've finally hired someone who can make a decent latte."

The collective sigh of relief was audible as the door swung shut after Holly's exit. Ani pulled the hood off her head and shook her shoulders loose. A few strands of hair fell forward and framed her face. She visibly relaxed, wandering into the kitchen and leaving him alone with his sisters.

It was weird. She'd taken him on and been prepared to walk even though she'd clearly needed work. But Holly had her retreating behind her hood and the espresso machine. She must have that effect on everyone, because there was no way this beautiful drifter could know Holly Banks, was there?

Piper pulled a pale green folder out of her bag and handed it to him.

"Just a few design ideas for the mural."

Hunter raised his brow. Clara pushed the folder more firmly into his hands.

"You don't have to look at them now. Ani can get set up with whatever she needs and start when she wants to."

"I'm heading back to Portland, bro," Piper said, dropping a kiss on his cheek. "I'll see you in a week and a half when we have the family meeting for the Mistletoe Festival."

Hunter's stomach tightened. The Mistletoe Festival was the family's big sales and advertising event of the year. He could barely spare time for the meeting, let alone the entire day the festival would take.

But he didn't have a choice. He'd failed his family in the past and wasn't ever going to let them down again.

CHAPTER THREE

"LET'S START WITH you putting down my clipboard." Hunter turned from the door as his sisters exited. Ani had commandeered his favorite spot behind the bar where the morning sunlight created a patch of warmth. She clutched his clipboard and studied the to-do list.

"Is it private?"

"No, it's just my clipboard."

Ani looked up and met his gaze. Then she took the tip of his Bic soft-feel, medium, black pen, and chewed on it.

It was horrifying, and so cute he nearly forgot where they were.

Hunter moved quickly, taking the clipboard and the pen.

"Please don't chew on my stuff."

She surrendered the pen and list that constituted all order in his world.

"Got it. Rule number one, no chewing in the restaurant."

Hunter shot her a stern look that generally worked on his employees. She bumped her hip against the counter and brushed past him, stretching her arms over her head.

"Can I start in the events venue?"

"No. You can start…" He glanced around the room then back at his clipboard. Delegating was not his strong suit.

Ani leaned over his arm and pointed at the list.

"You've got baseboards to go in, trim around the bar, hardware for the cabinets—any of that would be easy for me."

Right. Like he was going to let a stranger slap on drawer pulls and finish the trim. He'd sooner hand his firstborn child over to a tattoo artist for practice.

Ani drifted into the kitchen, picking up cooking utensils and examining vegetables as she went. Hunter followed.

"Can you wash your hands? Let's start there."

"Okay."

Ani pulled off her jacket, leaving her in a long-sleeved fitted T-shirt, leggings and stretchy skirt. She moved with the grace of a dancer, mesmerizing him as she drifted across his kitchen right up to—

"Not that sink!" Hunter body-blocked the vegetable-scrubbing station. "Hands are washed over here."

Ani rolled her eyes. "Sure thing, Captain Clean."

Hunter tilted his head. "That's not a very good insult."

"It's a fine insult," she contradicted him. "I'm mocking you. I've washed my hands twice today and you're worried I'm going to spread giardia just by existing."

"No, I like it. Captain Clean. He'd be a great superhero to teach kids about not spreading germs."

Ani laughed, her head full back, and several more long strands of hair fell loose. Her face lit up; her sparking laugh filled the kitchen. His heart reacted fast, all signals instructing him to let Ani work wherever she wanted in the restaurant, wash her hands in any sink she came across. Captain Clean would never approve.

It was going to be a long three weeks.

"You know what? We're going to start with a food handler's permit." Hunter pushed away from the counter. "It's online. You can use your phone, or I have a computer in the back."

"That sounds—"

"Boring. I know. But my employees will be here in ten minutes. I'll take their input on the best place for you to fill in today. Whether it's in the kitchen or not, having your food handler's permit will be handy."

Ani gave him a sullen glare, reminding him of the look he got from his mom's favorite horse, Bella.

"I'd be much more use to you helping out with your events venue."

Hunter's stomach turned. He was behind as it was, and he didn't have the time or mental energy to fix anyone's mistakes. Plus, there was no way he could focus on construction with Ani in the same room.

"As far I know, you can't get a contractor's license online in less than half an hour. If you can help pick up the slack here, it'll free me up to get my work done."

"You like your licenses, don't you?"

"Love 'em." Hunter crossed his arms over his chest. "My food service license, my music license, my liquor license, these are some of my favorite things."

Ani shook her head. "If that sentence ever comes out of my mouth, shoot me."

"And don't even get me started on permits. I have a fine collection of all the classics—health, sign, dumpster placement."

Ani shuddered theatrically.

"Oh, you'll see. Get your food handler's permit, and you'll be hooked. It's what I like to think of as a gateway document." Hunter stood with his hands on his hips, like Officer Harris used to at school assemblies warning kids about drugs. "You start with something that seems harmless and pretty soon you're into hard-core papers, like a certificate of occupancy."

"Which, I'm guessing, you still don't have for the events center?"

Hunter dropped his stance, his eyes drifting to the clipboard. Time to stop talking to cute hippie chick and get to work.

"Fine. I'll get my food handler's permit." Ani sauntered over and unplugged her phone from the charging station. Something she saw on the screen wiped the smile from her face. Her eyes clouded. For a brief moment, she looked lost and sad.

"Everything okay?" Hunter asked.

Ani's gaze lifted from her phone and met his, raw and vulnerable. She gave a barely perceptible shake of her head. Then she relaxed her shoulders and the smug little grin returned. "Siri, I want to apply for a food handler's permit."

"IT'S GOT TO be next week. We clear?" Hunter's voice snapped Ani to attention. She looked up to see him ending a phone call as he emerged from the back room.

She'd done her best to be a useful worker bee in the frenetic hive of Eighty Local. But Hunter kept thwarting her efforts at helping by trying to put her in one box or another: washing dishes *or* waiting tables *or* prepping food. He didn't see she was the most helpful filling in where his regular employees seemed to need her at any given moment. And he refused to put her in the box she was most interested in: the events venue.

He surveyed the orders resting on the counter and asked his backup chef Caleb, "Where are the—"

"Sweet potato fries?" Ani suggested. "Right here."

Hunter spun around. His eyes ricocheted from her face to the fries, to the fryer behind her, over to Caleb and then, as though bouncing off him, to her again.

Ani tried not to laugh.

"Do you even know how to use a fryer?"

"Yes." Ani moved past him and shook the fresh fries

into a basket. Hunter reflexively picked up a massive pepper grinder and ground out a sprinkling of pepper over the fries.

"Since when?"

Ani looked up at the clock. "Eleven thirty?"

"Caleb, did you tell her she could use the fryer?"

Caleb delivered a dry look.

"Sorry. The question implied she would ask." Hunter shifted his posture, glowering down at her. "You could get seriously hurt. Please wait to be trained before using the fryer."

"It doesn't make any sense to wait to get trained on things when I can figure them out myself."

"Unless you can't figure it out and set the place on fire."

"I'm not going to—"

"Look, there's no rush for you to learn all this."

"There is, too, a rush." Ani gestured to the dining room. "There's like a million people in there waiting for their lunch. Are you always this busy?"

Hunter shifted, stress, fatigue and pride swimming across his face. She poked further. "And someone's waiting on those fries."

Hunter grabbed the sweet potato fries and a couple of orders. "I'll take these out." He peered into the dining room. "You need to take a break. When you return, we can talk about what are, and are not, good places for you to fill in."

"Okay." Ani turned around and muttered, "Bossy."

"Thanks, Vagabond," he shot back.

"No problem, Local."

Hunter paused with his back to the swinging door.

"You really need to work on your insults. 'Local'?"

"Local's a great insult."

"Local in Outcrop, Oregon, is about the highest compliment someone can get."

"That's just the sort of thing a local would say."

Hunter pushed through the door. His demeanor changed abruptly as he entered the dining room. The brilliant smile emerged, he greeted customers, stopping to chat and soak up their compliments.

He headed to a table of men about his age where he deposited the fries and a couple of sandwiches. Backslapping and loud guffawing commenced.

Locals.

Ani wasn't sure if she'd ever met anyone so connected to a place. Hunter knew everyone and seemed to be related to half the town. He had the ability to completely focus on his work, but the minute the faintest acquaintance came into the room, Hunter would speak to them like there was nothing more important in the world.

Like he was doing right now.

One of the men popped a fry into his mouth then began enthusiastically gesturing at the basket. That made her boss happy.

Sometime during the morning, Hunter had lost the flannel shirt. Now he stood in an Eighty Local T-shirt and jeans, looking more appealing than a fresh batch of sweet potato fries.

Ani let her gaze rest on him again.

This was not a good habit, and she really was going to have to quit before she got...

Caught.

Hunter was looking straight at her. She picked up a cloth and began wiping down the already-clean counter.

"Ani," he called out from the dining room. "Take a break."

"I'm fine."

She was fine. Restaurant work was surprisingly fun. And she wanted to earn as much as she could as quickly as possible and move on. The latest barrage of texts from her mom made it clear; so long as she was in Oregon, her family would not leave her in peace. Blaisedells weren't quitters.

Hunter rested his hands on his hips and widened his stance.

"It's not about you. It's the law. You get a half-hour lunch and two fifteen-minute breaks. Take a break."

"Ooooh, it's the law?" Ani asked, widening her eyes and clutching the cloth.

Hunter crossed his arms. "I'm not interested in getting shut down because you feel like you're having fun now, then go complaining to the Oregon Labor Commission behind my back. Take a break."

Ani held eye contact as she pulled her apron over her head. "Okay, Boy Scout."

"Thanks, Drifter."

Deliberately, Ani drifted out of the kitchen and into the back room.

Maybe she *was* ready for some downtime. From the minute she'd started on the latte for Holly Banks, Ani had been working. An involuntary shiver ran through her. It'd been at least five years since she'd competed against Holly at an equestrian competition, but she would have recognized her anywhere: the pinched expression, the demands, the arrogance. She was the type of person to whom nothing was more important than being in the *right* crowd, and like it or not, Ani had led the crowd everyone had wanted to be in with. She absolutely could not risk being recognized by Holly or any of the other women from the Bend Equestrian Society. Fortunately, most people saw what they expected, and not one of those women would ever expect to see Stephanie Blaisedell living in a van, working at Eighty Local.

Ani shook her shoulders loose. There was no reason to dwell on the past. She had the opportunity to explore Hunter's restaurant, and that was even better than figuring out how to use a deep fryer.

The back rooms of Eighty Local were pure Hunter. Everything appeared to be repurposed or recycled, but in such a smart way, you'd think a designer had planned it all from the onset. The massive walk-in freezer was tucked in next to an industrial refrigerator along one wall. An ancient oak table dominated the center of the room. Shelves lined the walls, holding bins of grain, canned goods and other provisions. It smelled good. Actually, it smelled like Hunter, earthy and warm.

Ani pushed through a small door into an office. Or office-slash-weight room. A lifting bench and assortment of weights dominated one corner, and a chin-up bar was attached to the wall. That, apparently, was where all the muscles came from.

Hunter's spartan desk was piled with papers. Above it was a messy mosaic of mementos: an aerial view of Outcrop, thank-you notes written on napkins, family pictures. Ani leaned in and looked at the photographs. The twin sisters, smiling, with a ranch spread out behind them. Happy parents. A recent picture of a radiantly happy couple and a teenage boy, all wearing red sweatshirts with Outcrop Eagles Football splashed across the front.

Ani honed in on a picture of two identical little boys. They stood on the muddy bank of a pond and appeared to have made good use of the mud. You could feel the sheer childhood joy radiating off them; big smiles and a huge mess of mud all over their clothes.

So, Hunter had a twin. And somehow had had the joy

of life knocked out of him between now and whenever that picture had been taken.

Ani lifted her fingers to the picture then dropped her hand. Hunter's life—joy or absence thereof—was his own affair. She squared her shoulders and exited the office.

An opening covered with a tarp ran along the north wall. Ani slipped through. Her breath caught at the sight.

This is what had Hunter so stressed out.

HAVING TRIED THE back room, the parking lot and even his office, it didn't take Hunter long to realize Ani was exploring the addition. He pulled his flannel shirt back on and then his vest. With a deep breath, he steadied the cup he carried and pushed into the void.

Weak winter light poured in from the windows, illuminating the vaulted ceiling and pine walls. Ani stood, staring up at the exposed rafters.

"Hey," Hunter said, hoping to avoid startling her.

"Hey," she called, not looking at him but keeping her eyes up. "This is beautiful."

"This is an unending, unfinished mess that will probably kill me."

"But beautiful." She drew her gaze from the ceiling and focused on Hunter. More specifically, she focused on the coffee in his hand.

Hunter held out the drink. "Can we talk about what you're going to do here? As much as I appreciate you jumping in this morning, ideally you would get trained then work."

"That coffee's for me?"

"It's a honey latte with cardamom. And, yes, it's for you."

She eyed the drink with suspicion. "Why?"

Why? He hadn't stopped to examine his motivations.

He'd just made the coffee. And now she was staring at him like he'd made it on purpose, to be nice. Like he was a pet dog offering their person a favorite stick. Time to come up with an excuse.

"Because it's your break. And I am grateful you stayed." She didn't take the cup. He tried again. "And I'm still mad about your comment about truck-stop coffee."

She smiled and reached out for the cup. Her hair fell forward as she touched her lips to the drink. Lids slid down over her eyes.

Hunter warmed. He might not be perfect, but he made a good latte.

Ani took another drink. "Your own invention?"

He nodded.

"Thank you for taking the time to make this for me."

Her words crept in and settled in his chest. She understood. His time was in short supply, but he had unconsciously chosen to dole out several minutes for her coffee. It wasn't something he should be doing, but was probably going to do it anyway.

Ani walked over to the bar. He'd installed a wood-slab counter. Coordinating tall tables would be delivered next week.

"Your sisters hired me to paint a mural, but I get the sense public art is the least of your worries."

"I need to be working on this." He gestured to the space. "But since it dumped snow on Mount Bachelor two weeks ago, I've had a steady stream of out-of-town skiers on their way to and from the mountain, along with the regular customers."

"And they'll be picking up with the holidays," she predicted.

"They will."

Ani glanced over her shoulder toward the dining room.

Keeping her eyes averted, she asked, "You have some kind of gala coming up?"

"Yes. The Bend Equestrian Society Gala. It's a huge holiday fundraiser, attended by the wealthiest families throughout central and western Oregon. If it's successful, Eighty Local will become a major destination for events like this."

Ani nodded, rubbing the back of her neck. "When is it?"

"December twenty-seventh."

She met his gaze with an unreadable expression in her eyes. "I'll be gone by then, but I'll help you get everything ready. It's going to be a huge success. Horse ladies are going to love this place."

Hunter chuckled. Ani was the exact opposite of the women in the Bend Equestrian Society. "How do you know so much about horse ladies?"

Ani looked away. "Have you got your list?"

"My clipboard? It's in the kitchen."

"How about this?" Ani leaned over the bar, her long hair falling forward. "How about I show up when you do, and I'll pitch in around the restaurant when it's busy." Hunter opened his mouth to interrupt. Ani held out a hand to stop him. "I'll try not to fry anything without permission. When there's a break in the kitchen, I'll work through the things on your list I can help with. If we have time for the mural before the BES Gala, great. If not, just pay me for the work I do."

"I work long days."

"I'm sure." She met his gaze. "I like to make money. You have work, you pay well, and then there's the coffee." Her slow smile emerged and Hunter knew he'd be making her a different espresso drink every day of her sojourn in Outcrop. "What's first? Baseboards? Window trim?"

"I'm kind of picky about the finish work," Hunter admitted. He didn't want to upset her, but he wasn't going to let just anyone slap together the final pieces of the events center. "You are clearly capable, but I need this room to be perfect. No offense."

A spark lit up her eye. "What if I could show you something that would help you trust me with your nail gun?"

Hunter grinned at her bravado. "It's worth a try."

"Great." Ani took a few steps away from the bar. "Until then, can I start by installing the last of these outlets?"

"You know how?"

"Not yet."

"Then no."

She started to complain but he cut her off. "I have three calls in to an electrician and I'm hoping he'll be by tomorrow morning. It's not legal to have a unlicensed person install them."

"I don't think that's true."

"You can think whatever you want. In cases like these, I, as the building owner, or any member of my family, or an electrician, can install them. But the inspector isn't going to sign off on an itinerant hippie for the installation."

"Fine, Rule Follower."

Hunter caught her eye. "Okay, Rubber Tramp."

"Hometown Boy," she countered.

"Van-lifer."

"Hayseed."

"Trust-funder."

Her gaze dropped. It felt like the blade of a guillotine had fallen between them and cut off the fragile connection they'd built.

"You can't say trust-funder," she said, turning her back to him and heading toward the door.

Hunter scrambled to keep up.

"I can call you a hippie, a rubber tramp and accuse you of being a van-lifer, but not a trust-funder?"

"Yes."

"Because?"

Ani stopped walking. She drew in a breath and met his gaze.

"Because I don't have a trust fund."

"And I *am* a hayseed?"

She reached up and picked a piece of…yes, it actually was hay…off his vest.

She twirled it between her fingers.

"Little bit." Her smile was back, setting Hunter off kilter. He was a rule follower by nature. And that was going to be difficult with someone like Ani, who kept changing the rules as she went along.

CHAPTER FOUR

"Mom!" ANI HEARD Hunter call. He came bounding out from behind the counter and wrapped a woman, presumably Mom, in a bear hug. "When did you and Dad get home?"

"Our flight landed at one o'clock." The woman emerged from the hug and examined her son. "You look tired."

"I look tired? You're the one who just flew in from Jakarta."

Ani leaned over the counter as she watched mother and son try to outworry each other. Her money was on Mom.

"You've been here for thirteen hours," the woman accused.

"How do you know that? You weren't even in the western hemisphere when I left for work this morning."

"My point exactly."

Ani glanced around for a clock. Thirteen hours? She'd had a lunch break around one but had no idea how much time had passed since then. Restaurant time seemed to function outside of the rest of life. By now the crowd had thinned and mostly consisted of customers lingering over their meals, sharing slices of chocolate torte or wrapping up with an espresso.

"It's after eight o'clock." The woman rested her hands on Hunter's arms and looked him in the eye.

He nodded in response. "I know."

"Is this Ani?" The woman abruptly redirected her attention.

Ani started then looked at Hunter. Why would his mother know who she was? A flash of fear shot through her before she settled her shoulders against it. No one in this tiny town had any idea who she really was.

"Right, sorry. Mom, this is Ani. Ani, Mom."

"Hi... Mom?" Ani stepped out from behind the counter.

"Lacy." The woman had a warm smile, like the twin sisters. "But 'Mom' is fine. My girls told me about the adventure you had this morning." She gave Hunter a look that could have shut down the power grid.

Ani raised her left shoulder. "Technically, I was parked illegally. And Hunter didn't know I was coming."

"That's very generous of you," Lacy said.

Ani laughed. It was probably the first time anyone had accused her of generosity. "I've been making money and eating sweet potato fries all day. I'm feeling pretty generous."

"Thank you," Hunter said to Ani. "Did I say that yet? Thank you. I'll grab a W-2 form and we can get settled for today."

"I had fun."

Eighty Local *was* fun. W-2 forms, on the other hand, were not. After "Mom" was gone, Ani would see if she could convince Hunter to pay her under the table.

"I hear your solar battery is out and there's no heat in your van," Lacy said.

"Right." Ani had managed to put that particular piece of information out of her mind for most of the day.

"It's now five degrees outside and getting colder. We'd like you to stay in our gardener's cottage. Or, if you're not comfortable there, we'll get you a hotel room."

"I'll be fine—"

Lacy interrupted her. "Was it the 'five degrees' you misunderstood or 'getting colder'? It doesn't make sense for you to sleep in your van, and we have an extra cottage on our property."

Wow. The woman had a way of making you feel cared for *and* totally clueless at the same time. No wonder Hunter acquiesced so quickly to his mother's authority.

"The gardener's cottage?" Hunter asked.

"Where would you have her stay?" Lacy addressed her son. "In the house with your older brother and his teenage son? Or in the guest apartment with me and your father? Perhaps the bunkhouse with you and Bowman?"

"Wait." Ani grinned. "You still live with your parents?"

"I live on a ranch," Hunter said.

"With your parents."

"I live with my brother, and I work on the ranch, because my parents like to travel and they've earned the luxury." He reddened. "Plus, I own property adjacent to our family's. And this restaurant."

"And judging by the cot, bench press and shower in the back, you probably live here part-time," she muttered.

"You live in a car," he shot back.

"It's a van."

"At any rate," Lacy interrupted them, "we'd love for you to stay with us. The gardener's cottage is small but very cozy. It has a woodstove. I think you'll like it."

Ani scratched at a spot on the counter. She didn't have to take it. She could get a hotel room. Or she could spend a very cold night in the van. She probably wouldn't freeze to death, but she wouldn't sleep very well, either.

"I would feel much better if I knew you had a warm place to stay this evening," Lacy said.

Ani studied the woman. She had the honey-blond hair of her daughters, with ribbons of white coming in at the temples. Her eyes were the same deep hazel green as

Hunter's. Kindness wafted from her, but with a steely resolve underneath.

"Okay. One night. I can find something else for tomorrow."

"Your staying won't bother anyone." Lacy glanced at Hunter. "You'll drive her home?" It wasn't a question.

"Of course," Hunter responded.

"I can still drive the van," Ani said. "It just doesn't have any heat."

"We live out of town," Lacy said. "There's no need to drive two vehicles. If it's okay with Hunter, you can leave the van here."

Ani clamped her lips together to keep from smirking. She looked up at her boss. "Is it okay with Hunter?"

"I said it was fine to park here this morning," he shot back.

"I realize this is a classy establishment. Not a truck stop."

He turned to her, leaning close enough for her to catch his scent. "As demonstrated by the superior coffee."

"Great," Lacy interjected, checking her watch. "I'll head back and get the fire started. Caleb can lock up?"

"Yep."

"I expect to see you there before nine o'clock."

"Okay," Hunter said without hesitation.

Lacy headed to the door. She stopped to chat with a young woman sitting alone at a table. Ani had noticed the girl earlier. She looked to be about thirteen years old, and had been at the small table for a couple of hours, shuffling through a pile of books and homework assignments. The girl seemed relieved to have someone to talk to, and Lacy focused on her in the same way Hunter focused when he wanted to make someone feel comfortable in the restaurant. Then Lacy patted her shoulder and headed for the door. The girl watched her leave before reluctantly return-ing to the books spread out on the table.

Ani shook her head. "Fascinating."

"What?"

"Mom." Ani gestured toward the door.

"You mean the offer of our cottage?"

"More how she swept in here and got us both to do what she wanted in less than ten minutes."

"She's efficient." Hunter headed for the kitchen. "And reasonable. I finally figured out she rarely tells me what to do, but when she does, she has a good reason for it."

Ani nodded. It was the exact opposite of her relationship with her mom. All these years later, Ani still got texts with unreasonable requests. Her mother's greatest wish was for her daughter to become an entirely different person.

As a child, Ani had been the model daughter, literally posing for the happy family photos lining bookshelves and gracing gold-foil Christmas cards. She thought everyone learned the basics of social manipulation by age five and knew better than to ask for a hug if there wasn't a camera snapping your picture.

No, the problems hadn't started until Ani had thought to question the status quo. Did all parents fight like this? Did all families discuss other people's social failures over the occasional but mandatory dinner? Did she have to hate her body the way her mother and sister did, or could she just…not?

Her questions had infuriated her family, but she'd given them the one thing they'd craved: bragging rights. She was a star on the hunter/jumper circuit. That meant Ani could have whatever she'd wanted, so long as she kept bringing home the trophies, kept climbing higher in the national rankings. There was no plan for college when Ani graduated high school, no gap year, no self-discovery; nothing but the relentless circuit.

By the time Ani was twenty-one it was clear the family would get along a lot better, or at least fight a lot less, if Ani had her own space. Because competition required so much travel, her parents had agreed to a Sprinter van. Ani could still remember the thrill of completing the interior remodel with the help of YouTube and online van life discussion forums. It was the first thing she'd done entirely on her own. Her parents' utter belief that she'd fail to create a home out of the van had made succeeding all the more fun.

But traveling on her own to competitions and parking on the expansive property surrounding the stables still hadn't changed the fact that her parents were bankrolling her life, and that money came at a cost. That was made all too clear when she'd asked the question that ultimately forced her to tear loose from the family: Did she have to compete?

That question wasn't met with a sneer, or condescension, but with the full force of her parents' rage. If Ani didn't compete, she couldn't win. Blaisedells were winners. They wanted an Olympian, and Ani was Olympic material.

When she'd refused, they'd hit back with the worst punishment imaginable. The trusting gaze of her horse was seared into Ani's mind. She had underestimated her parents and sealed Rabiana's fate.

The rage Ani had felt as she'd driven away from her parents' house for the last time was still fresh and raw, all these years later. The humiliation to her parents was extreme, but their disapproval no longer held any power over her. They'd already done their worst. For years now, she'd dodged bribes and threats, pleas and promises. Apologies. But she was never going back, and certainly not to stand in front of a massive fake tree pretending to care about a selfish, angry group of narcissists as someone snapped a picture.

Ani shuddered then glanced up to see Hunter studying her with those deep, brown-green eyes. She shook out her shoulders and gave him her best snarky grin. "I guess if she's going to make me stay in a warm cabin, I can handle it."

Hunter nodded, gesturing toward the kitchen. "Can you help me set up a brine for tomorrow? Then we can take off."

"Yes! Brine. Sounds fun."

Hunter laughed as they rounded the counter into the kitchen. Ani warmed. She had to admit that as much as she mistrusted personal connections, she loved making Hunter laugh. He was under so much pressure, complicated by his never-ending to-do list and inability to delegate. Each time one of her jokes landed and he smiled, Ani could feel a little of his pressure release. And this request to help set up the brine felt sweet, like he sincerely wanted her help.

That was ridiculous. Hunter needed to get his work done, and she was a willing accomplice. Plus, brine had to be the least romantic substance on earth. *Help me set up brine* was probably some type of Outcrop, Oregon, code for telling a woman you're not interested.

Ani slowed her pace, so her shoulder would not bump against his as they walked into the kitchen. She was here to make money, not attachments. The flood of texts from her mother rattling her phone as the holidays approached was all the reminder she needed. She could enjoy, and learn from this experience in Eighty Local, but the sooner she got out of Oregon, the better.

Ani glanced up at Hunter. He was still smiling. It was going to take at least three weeks to earn the money she needed. She just had to keep reminding herself that if

Hunter and his family had any idea who she was, there was no way they'd be so kind. She might be critical of her family, but she was a Blaisedell through and through. Her childhood had been a master class in the calculated manipulation of others. She had learned to act appropriately in the years away from her family, but she feared her ugly, selfish impulses would come out in time, and she'd prefer to be somewhere else when they did.

HUNTER SWALLOWED AND looked over at Ani again. She'd said little on the way home as she'd watched the town roll past, taking in everything with her intelligent gaze.

He shifted his eyes back to the road, annoyed with himself. Why was he so conscious of her? She was beautiful, yes, but also confusing. And capable on a level he didn't know existed. There didn't seem to be anything she couldn't figure out and do well. One day into her three-week sojourn at Eighty Local and he couldn't remember how he'd functioned without her.

His heart lifted as he pulled off the main road onto Wallace Creek Drive, just outside the limits of Outcrop. Returning to the haven of his family's property always felt right, no matter what had gone wrong in the outside world. The truck bumped over the white-gravel drive, crested the rise, and the ranch spread out before them.

Ani breathed in sharply. Moonlight illuminated rolling hills. Clusters of aspen and Oregon oak were interspersed with the pastures, giving way to pine forests. The big pond lay frozen behind the barn. Christmas lights twinkled on the outbuildings and house, echoing the bright stars above.

"This is beautiful."

"Yeah, we're lucky."

"Do you…" She paused and scanned the property. She sat straighter, her brow knitting. "Do you have horses?"

"Yeah. We raise—"

"Canadian Horses," she finished his sentence. She shivered, and Hunter could tell she was trying to keep her voice steady. "This is Wallace Ranch, isn't it?"

"Heard of us?" he asked.

She exhaled and leaned back in her seat, silent again. It was an electric, focused silence as she stared out at the property.

He always forgot how famous his family ranch was in the horse world. Canadians were, in many ways, the perfect family horse. They were sturdy, calm, hearty animals with a lot of personality. A Canadian might never win the Triple Crown, or place in an elite dressage competition, but if a family was looking for a good horse to ride and work, there wasn't much better than a Canadian.

Hunter's parents had realized this and started the seeds of a horse-breeding operation that now supported the family. Throughout his childhood, they'd worked tirelessly, both teaching at the small high school in town and raising horses. Their work, the ranch and five children bound them to Outcrop. As a child, then a thoughtless teenager, Hunter had never noticed how hard his parents had worked.

It was funny, how things shifted. They'd retired from teaching just as Hunter's oldest brother Ash came home to take over the ranch. With the property paid off and a tidy profit coming in from the sale of horses, his parents had the time and money to travel all over the world. They were now carefree and having fun, while Hunter worked harder than he'd ever known was possible.

He had to work like they had, so he could provide the same feelings of stability for his family in the future. And so he could make up for the humiliation his family must have felt when he was such a problem as a kid.

"This is the gardener's cottage." He pulled up in front of

the cabin next to the massive garden. "We've never actually had a gardener, unless you count me and Mom. This used to be a potting shed, but then my sisters got a hold of it and turned it into a guesthouse. They're matchmakers, and we have a lot of weddings here. I guess the brides have to have a fancy place to get ready."

A ghost of a smile passed over Ani's lips. She seemed distracted. If Hunter hadn't been witness to her courage and self-assurance all day, he would have called her nervous.

The door to the cottage opened and Mom stood in the light. "Welcome!" She waved them in.

Ani gripped the door handle and then hesitated. "Your mom is really nice."

"My mom is the nicest person on earth. Clara is a close second."

"And what about you? Where do you fall on the nice scale?"

"Trying to get back on it at this point."

She laughed, warming Hunter as he jumped out of the truck into the freezing air.

"Get inside, it's cold," Mom demanded.

Ani climbed out of the truck and walked slowly up the steps into the cottage. Her brow furrowed as she studied her surroundings. The cottage had a small kitchen area at one end, a little table, and a woodstove with two comfy wingback chairs facing it. At the far end of the room was an old-fashioned canopy bed. Lamps spread pools of light throughout. Hunter noticed a winter bouquet of roses and fir branches on the table, and a stack of books on the nightstand from his mom's personal collection. She really was the nicest person.

"Woodstove," Mom said, pointing. "You should have

plenty of wood to get you through the night, but call Hunter if you need more."

Hunter looked at Ani with the intention of nodding at this statement but got so lost in her eyes, he just stood there.

"You brought her something for dinner, didn't you?"

"What?" Hunter looked up, startled to find his mom addressing him.

"You brought something from the restaurant for Ani to eat?"

"Yeah, of course." Hunter nodded. "Be right back."

In two strides, Hunter was out the door. The cold hit him and he was grateful for the bracing air. He pulled in deep breaths, relishing the burn in his lungs.

This was not going to work. Ani had been enough of a distraction at the restaurant all day. Now with her staying not fifty yards from the bunkhouse, Hunter wasn't going to get any sleep at all.

He rummaged in the jump seat and pulled out a to-go bag.

He may as well go back to work tonight. Caleb had the kitchen under control, but Hunter could work on the addition. He drew up a mental image of his list. Baseboards still needed to go in. If he stuck to the east side of the addition, none of his patrons would be bothered by the hammering. Bracing cold and baseboards would go a long way toward keeping his mind off Ani.

Mom was still talking when Hunter stepped back into the snug cabin, showing Ani where coffee was and discussing extra blankets. Ani seemed to get more uncomfortable with each simple, thoughtful gesture his mother made. His mom either didn't notice, or more likely, didn't let it bother her.

Ani, who had been brave and adventurous all day,

seemed to shrink back from Mom. It was almost as though she felt trapped.

"Hey," Hunter said, setting the bag on the small counter. "Here's dinner. Mom, let's let Ani settle in. I think she's had enough of me for one day."

Ani, by this point, seemed completely deflated. She had to be exhausted. They'd been working hard for thirteen hours straight.

"Thank you," Ani said quietly. The color had drained from her face. "I am pretty tired."

Hunter felt a rush of tenderness, an overwhelming urge to get her settled into a comfy chair by the fire and bring her soup.

But he would not be sharing dinner with her tonight, or any other night. The best course of action was to get back to work.

"Rest up," he said. "We've got a big day tomorrow."

THE DOOR SHUT, leaving Ani alone in the little cottage. She dropped onto the bed then flopped backward.

Who were these people?

First, Hunter, gorgeous guardian of the parking lot and all things Eighty Local.

Then his adorable sisters, who loved their cranky brother so much they'd pulled out all the stops to keep her there. Who on earth even cared about having a nice mural on the exterior wall of someone else's business?

Now, Wonder Mom, setting up this perfect little cottage for her and being so concerned about her freezing to death.

Ani was certain her own mother had never once worried about her freezing, other than some concern over how it would reflect on the family were she foolish enough to do so.

Apparently, there were other Wallaces. Two brothers

and a dad, probably running around being excruciatingly good, responsible people at this very moment.

Ani shook her head. There was no sense comparing these people to her family. She was here now, in this warm, cozy little cabin stocked with books, food and coffee.

Ani stood, stretching as she crossed to one of the windows. Cold air slipped through the casing, whispering across her face as she held the curtain back and peered into the clear night. Stars blanketed the sky and a huge moon shone down on the ranch.

Acres of beautiful property spread in all directions, but all she could focus on were the snug red stables and riding arena. Christmas lights twinkled along the roofline and ran down the pine pillars of the open arena. She could almost hear the soft huffs of breath coming from the horses, smell the earthy rich scent of the barn.

Ani loosened her grip on the curtain then dropped it, wiping out the view with the swath of calico muslin. She stalked away from the window.

Cute cabin. Books. Dinner. Three weeks of interesting work ahead of her. This was all good. She would not let herself get distracted by the horses.

Ani picked up the stack of books Lacy had left and sorted through them, finding a political thriller, a historical romance, a couple of classics and a biography of Diego Rivera.

Hunter's mom had dug around, found a book about a famous muralist, and brought it out to the cabin.

Seriously, who are these people?

The ranch certainly explained Hunter Wallace. She'd be a hometown kid herself if she had a home like this. Great family, supportive community, spending all day doing what he loved. Hunter was completely in his element here, and she'd never even known what her element was. Or rather, she had known. But it had come with a price far too high. Walking away had been the only option.

Ani drifted to the window again, feeling the shift in temperature. The barn still waited. Maybe tomorrow morning she could poke her head in before work?

No. She couldn't get too comfortable. She was here to make money. In offering her this cottage, Hunter's family ensured a competent worker who could help their son as he counted down to an important event. That was what this was.

Ani picked up the romance and flopped into one of the wing chairs.

An image of Hunter, settled into the chair next to her popped into her mind. Ani pushed the thought aside. She didn't do casual relationships. It was all or nothing for her. And inasmuch as she was leaving Outcrop in three weeks, that wasn't possible.

A knock and rattling of the door startled her. A blast of cold air hit her as Hunter came in.

Had she summoned him?

"Sorry to barge back in," he said, his smile lighting up the room. "I know you're sick of all of us by now, especially me."

"N-no," she managed to respond.

"But I forgot to leave the beer." He set a mason jar of dark beer on the counter. "I didn't know what you like, so I went out on a limb and grabbed an espresso stout."

She stared at him. They'd had one brief interaction during the day when Ani asked had him about how he chose the beers he served. From that, he'd managed to pick her very favorite adult beverage the world had to offer.

Beer was a luxury she rarely enjoyed. Living and traveling on her own, Ani wasn't in a position to let her guard down. If something went wrong with the van, or she found herself in an unsafe situation, she had only herself to rely on. A woman didn't need drunk frat boys pounding on the side of her van more than once to decide she didn't have the mental space for relaxing with a beer.

"I hope it's okay." He looked nervous now.

"Thank you. This is all so—"

"It's nothing."

Ani blinked. *Nothing?* To these people, this was nothing. A perfectly cozy home stacked with books and food and now beer was just what you did for the itinerant muralist.

She let her eyes rest on Hunter. Did he feel any of this connection? Or had he just been raised to bring dinner and beer?

"I'm going to head back in," he said, gesturing toward the door.

Ani relaxed her shoulders and breathed in. The cowboy wasn't going to be sharing dinner or even the next fifteen minutes with her.

"To the restaurant?"

"Yeah." A sheepish grin lit his face.

"You're a little obsessed."

"If I can get through the BES Gala, I'm golden."

As though he could possibly shine any brighter.

Hunter cleared his throat. Ani realized she was staring again.

"Thank you for this." She walked decisively to the little kitchen and opened the bag he'd left for her. "For feeding me all day long."

"Eighty Local employees should eat Eighty Local food."

Ani nodded. Pretty much everything she'd eaten in the last fourteen hours would go down in her personal food hall of fame. The buttery scone for breakfast. Lunch was a grilled veggie sandwich crowded with sweet potato fries. Then a biscotti with her cappuccino in the afternoon.

"What do you normally eat when you're out on the road?"

Ani peeked into the bag and pulled out a container. "Not this."

"That's the beef stew you helped make this morning," he said as she continued to unpack the bag. "And I put a couple of rolls in, with some butter. And a cookie."

Ani lined the food neatly on the counter.

The great thing about living alone and completely free is that there were never moments like these, times when someone was incredibly kind, and she didn't know how to react.

"Cool." She didn't look up from the food.

Hunter took a step back toward the door. "So, yeah. I'm planning on getting in later tomorrow. We don't need to leave until eight."

Ani's gaze jumped to Hunter.

"How will I possibly make use of the time?"

He grinned. Ani felt the tension resonate between them. *Okay, so he did feel this.*

Her smile widened.

Stop flirting. Getting involved with the ultimate hometown boy was nothing but a bad idea. Hunter probably saw a reasonably attractive woman who would be hitting the road as soon as her van was up and running. A perfect fit for a man married to his business.

Ani refocused on the food.

"Well, thanks for the weirdest day I've ever had," she said.

"Welcome. Coming from you, I take it as a point of pride."

Ani gave Hunter one last glance. He was leaning against

the doorjamb, watching her. Delicious food, gorgeous man, horses not one hundred yards away… This place was dangerous. She needed to hit the road as soon as possible. If her parents had any idea how close she was, they'd never let her be. Not because they had any desire to actually see her, but because having a daughter who refused to come home didn't project the image they were going for.

No, she needed to get moving as soon as she could replace the battery in the van, no matter how tempting this place might be.

CHAPTER FIVE

IT WAS STILL dark when Hunter pulled a shirt off the top of his dresser. He hesitated. Maybe he should put some thought into what he wore? He scoffed and stuffed his arms through the sleeves as he moved toward the kitchen. No one cared what he wore, and all his shirts said Eighty Local somewhere on them anyway.

A press pot of coffee stood on the counter, along with toast crumbs and a mug. Hunter set his hand along the side of the pot. Cold. He looked out the window to see if his brother's truck was still there. It was only 6:30 a.m., but Bowman could have been up for over an hour by now. Probably out running up a mountain with Maisy or doing chin-ups on a tree branch.

His eyes drifted to the gardener's cottage. No lights. He'd half expected her to disappear in the night, like a dream. Hunter looked back down at the remains of Bowman's coffee. An espresso was much more appealing than Bowman's thoughtless brew. He'd get his chores done then head in and have coffee at Eighty Local.

Not that he had any interest in trying to impress a free-spirited woman with his skills involving a portafilter and steam.

Hunter threw an insulated flannel on over his shirt then added a down vest.

The first faint rays of sunlight crept across the property as Hunter left the bunkhouse. Short-cropped grass was white with frost, and the air was bracing. He felt fantastic despite the short night of sleep and looming to-do list.

Hunter started to jog, then ran, enjoying the burn in his lungs. He leaped over an irrigation ditch and headed into the greenhouse.

"Listen up," he addressed his radicchio and arugula starts as he entered the warm space. "You've got three weeks to get some growth on." Hunter walked down the rows of salad greens. Plants seemed to wilt at his voice.

"I'm not joking," he told the watercress. "You're not just garnish. I need to fill some high-class bellies with you two days after Christmas. So, get growing."

The watercress did not respond.

Fortunately, kale, which never failed him, was growing robustly in the back corner. Hunter snapped off a few stems and wondered if he had enough potatoes in storage for a potato, kale and bacon soup.

But did Ani eat bacon?

Hunter stopped cold at the door. *What did it matter if Ani ate bacon or not?* He wasn't making this soup for her. Hunter went back and picked enough kale for the entire town of Outcrop to have a bowl of his soup.

The plan was to keep the positive Yelp reviews pouring in while creating a premier events center for central Oregon. Ani was here to help him, and he would not be distracted by trying to impress her. She'd be on the road as soon as her van was up and running anyway.

A light winked at him from the barn. Bowman must be cleaning out stalls. Since Hunter had started the addition, his family had been generous about picking up the slack. They'd been generous about everything. His dad helped with the books for Eighty Local. Piper found repurposed materials for the events center online and sent him links.

Hunter's stomach turned as he thought about the massive check his brother-in-law Jet had handed him.

"It's an investment," Clara's new husband had said casually, as though everyone had forty-thousand dollars lying around to dole out as they were so inclined.

But no one had done more to help out than Bowman. His twin had been at his side since the day they'd broken ground. With the exception of a few climbing trips with his fiancée, a day rarely passed where Bowman didn't stop by and put in hours of his own time. Once they'd gotten to the finish work, Bowman's skills ran out. Now he supported his brother by doing more than his share of work with the horses.

Hunter could only pray the day would come when he could repay his brother. For now, he'd head over to the barn and help him with their mom's devil horse. The Mistletoe Festival, coming up in a few weeks, would be a chance to pay the rest of his family back for some of what they'd done. The huge holiday event designed to introduce people to the Canadian breed always needed all hands on deck, and Hunter was determined to do more than his share this year.

A small forest of kale stashed safely in the cooler in the back of his truck, Hunter headed over to the barn to catch Bowman. His brother wouldn't want any fuss about doing more than his share of work. He would, however, be willing to cast light on the Ani situation. There hadn't been the chance to speak the night before, and Hunter wanted to catch his opinion.

Because every fiber of Hunter's body screamed that letting the beautiful, strange woman get her hands on his to-do list was a very bad idea.

Thank God for Bowman. Throughout his childhood, Hunter had taken having a best friend and partner in crime for granted, but over the last few years he'd realized just how lucky he was to have his twin brother. Bowman was reserved, and focused in a way that eluded most people. But he had Hunter's back, every step, every day.

Hunter jogged over to the barn, slipping in the open bypass door.

Where he stopped.

Ani leaned over a railing into a stall, scratching beneath the mane of an elderly stallion. The gentle horse snorted and nuzzled her neck.

And Bowman—quiet, reserved, introverted Bowman— was talking. To Ani. Without stopping.

"Canadians were bred to be work horses," Bowman said. "They're beautiful, and you won't find a more resilient horse. Stan here is the best."

Ani turned her mischievous smile on Bowman as she continued to commune with Stan, the retired stallion.

"I love this guy." She leaned in and dropped a kiss on the horse's nose.

Jealousy coursed through his body and Hunter wanted to hurl his twin out the door. And the horse.

Bowman looked up, as though he'd known Hunter was there all the time, which he most likely had.

"Hey," Bowman said, conveying a world of information in one word. Things like *Settle down* and *You remember I'm in love with Maisy Martin, right?* and *Man, you've got it bad.*

"Hey," Hunter responded with a look attempting to wipe out the idea that he had anything for Ani, bad or otherwise. He ran his hands through his hair and breathed in. If he needed any confirmation, this was it. This woman was trouble, and the sooner she got her van fixed and herself out of Outcrop, the better.

"Morning, Boss Man," Ani said, still fully focused on Stan.

"Morning," Hunter responded. "You doing okay after spending a full twenty-four hours in one place?"

She grinned at him. "I'm managing."

A low nicker sounded behind him and Hunter glanced into the opposing stall. Dulce watched her colt scamper over to the stall door. Hunter reached in and rubbed the colt's nose. "Good morning, Spinach."

The colt flailed his front legs up to get closer. The foal had been born late, toward the end of summer, and in his attempt to acclimate the animal to people, Hunter had made a lifelong friend.

"He's a friendly one," Ani noted.

"Yeah, the irony is, we were all trying to love him up so he'd be used to people and easier to train, but now no one's willing to part with him."

Ani laughed as Dulce gave him a knowing look. Hunter grabbed a flake of hay and threw it into a stall, then threw another to Stan.

"Stan hasn't had this much attention since the Bush administration," Bowman said.

Hunter moved to join Ani at the horse. "You can ride him if you want, while you're here."

Ani's face shifted. Yearning then resolute.

"No. We've got work to do. I'm planning on making as much money off Eighty Local as I can in the next few weeks."

"You got somewhere you need to be by Christmas?" Hunter asked, trying for a casual off-the-cuff tone that he completely missed.

Her expression shifted. "I don't really celebrate holidays. And, yeah, I need to be not-in-Oregon."

"You don't celebrate holidays?"

"I don't buy into over-commercialized, materialistic,

false-promise calendar days to distract from the narrowness of life. No."

Hunter turned to Bowman, who looked as horrified as he felt.

"Do yourself a favor," Bowman said. "Do *not* say those words around our mother."

"Unless you want the world's longest lecture on human connection, the sacred nature of eating together, commitment to family and the value of giving thoughtful gifts to those you live in community with."

Ani shivered. "Sounds like quite the lecture."

"Yeah," Bowman said, "then Dad will hear the word 'community,' and start in on your responsibilities."

Ani stepped away from Stan's stall. "The only thing I'm going to say to your parents is thank you."

"Good call." Bowman nodded. "Hey, Hunter, can you help me with Bella's stall while you're here? And I hate to bring it up, but she's looking pretty ratty."

"I know." Hunter grabbed a halter off the rack. "Let's get it done. I don't want Mom thinking we can't handle her."

"What's up with Bella?" Ani followed them down the corridor of stalls.

As though responding to the question, Bella kicked the front then the back of her stall, before walking up to the gate to glare at Bowman.

"Well, she hates Bowman. And she likes me even less."

Bella tossed her mane and turned her back on the humans.

"Is she the lead mare?" Ani asked.

"Yeah." Hunter was surprised Ani knew about a lead mare. Most people thought stallions led the herd, but it was a mare who called the shots. Bella could defend this group of horses from a cougar, lead them to shelter in a storm, and would fight anything for the privilege of doing so. Including the people who ran this place.

"She's mean," Bowman said.

Bella lifted her head to glare in contempt. Hunter felt a prick of uncomfortable anticipation. He knew Bella could sense his hesitation, which only made matters worse.

"Easy," Bowman said. Bella braced her front feet and slammed her back hooves into the stall. The other horses shuffled uneasily.

Hunter held an arm out instinctively to shield Ani, as though his forearm could protect her from the incarnation of hellfire that was Bella.

Ani responded by taking the halter from his hands.

Bowman sent a questioning look to Hunter.

Ani squared her shoulders then relaxed. She fixed her gaze just above Bella's eyes. Bella snorted and shook her head. Ani remained absolutely still, relaxed and in control of herself.

Bella kicked the stall again. Ani didn't even flinch. In fact, she looked a little bored. The horse blew out a breath then raised her gaze to meet Ani's.

Ani stepped forward, unlatched the door and walked into the stall.

"Bella, is it?" Ani ran her hand along the horse's neck. Bella dropped her head and Ani slipped the halter on her. "Pretty name for a pretty horse."

Bella gave Ani an exploratory nip on the shoulder. Ani relaxed, delivering a warning look. Bella morphed the nip into a nuzzle.

"Where do you want her?" Ani asked, looking up at Bowman.

Bowman never had a lot of words, but right now he didn't have any.

Hunter spoke for him. "How'd you do that?"

Ani ignored the question and kept her focus on Bella. "You are looking crunchy, my girl. Let's get you cleaned up."

Bowman pointed out the tack room. Ani walked calmly down the aisle, chatting with Bella. She hooked the horse to crossties, then selected a currycomb. Moving to Bella's side, she began her work. Easy, unthinking motions loosened the dirt and gave Bella an expert massage at the same time. The horse leaned into her attention.

Hunter had never seen anyone so easy and confident with a horse, not even his mom, who had spent her life with the animals. A stable was clearly Ani's natural habitat.

He grabbed a brush and started on the opposite flank. "You know horses."

She lifted her shoulder in a half shrug. "I like horses."

"No one likes Bella."

"I like Bella," she said to the horse, leaning her head against Bella's nose.

"Then you should probably stay in Outcrop," Bowman said from the stall he was cleaning out.

Ani laughed.

"I'm serious. That was impressive."

"I'm sure your mom can handle her," Ani said.

"That's part of the problem." Hunter shifted so he could see Ani as he brushed the horse. "Mom's always dealt with the lead mare. But when my parents retired from teaching, they started traveling."

"They're gone almost as much as they're here," Bowman said.

"So, there's no consistency?" Ani guessed.

"There's plenty of consistency." Hunter glanced at Bowman. "Our brother Ash runs this place."

"Very consistent, Ash." Bowman grinned back at him. "Named after a tree, and slightly less mobile."

"But he doesn't have time for this nonsense?" Ani ventured.

"Right. And no one wants to tell Mom, because then she'd feel compelled to stay."

Ani nodded. She rubbed Bella's withers in short, efficient circles.

"So, you two try to figure it out." Ani glanced up and met Hunter's eyes. A flash of attraction sparked. "Even with everything else you have to do?"

Hunter swallowed then nodded.

"You Wallaces are quite the family," she said.

She had no idea. He was lucky to have such a great family. It was living up to them that was the problem.

ANI'S HEART BEAT HARD, thumping against her rib cage. She felt energized and genuinely happy for the first time in a long time. The worries pressing in on her seemed to lift, and all she wanted to do was to stay in this barn.

That meant it was absolutely time to step away from the horse.

As though reading her thoughts, Bella nudged Ani's shoulder.

Okay, one more minute.

Ani ran her hand along the sleek neck of the animal. Bella twitched then pushed her nose more firmly against Ani.

"You're all cleaned up," she told Bella. "Want to go back to the stable, or are you ready to head outside today?"

"You want to take her for a ride?" Bowman asked.

"No." The word shot out of her mouth. "No, thanks." She glanced from Bowman to Hunter, wondering exactly how weird she sounded. Fortunately, she had a great excuse. "I have this really cranky boss who expects me to get into work this morning."

"It's fine by me if you want to take her out," Hunter said.

"No, I—"

"I mean, this is incredible." He gestured between her and the horse.

Bella met her gaze and suggested they go for a ride. Ani ran her hand along Bella's muzzle and tried to communicate that she couldn't get back on a horse, ever again. Bella didn't believe her.

"Lacy will probably want to ride today, don't you think? How long was she away?"

"Six weeks. And, yeah, you're right." Ani was conscious of Hunter's eyes on her as she led Bella back into the stall. "But you can ride her anytime."

"Anytime," Bowman concurred.

Ani nodded, keeping her face away from the brothers so they couldn't see how difficult this was for her.

Bella stepped into the stall, glossy and clean. Ani pulled off the halter and scratched her ears. "I bet you're happy Lacy's home."

Bella twitched her tail in response. Ani forced herself out of the stall and closed the door, then took long steps away, calling to Hunter, "Let's get in to work. I need to make some cash and get out of town."

Hunter trotted after her. "We don't have to get in super early today—"

"Because you stayed super late last night?" She turned and walked backward, grinning up at him. She was flirting and she knew it, but she'd give herself the distraction to get away from the horses.

Hunter glanced down at his boots, color rising in his face. "Something like that."

She spun back around so she was walking next to him. "You know what's at Eighty Local?"

"What?"

"Really good espresso."

Hunter laughed. Ani kept talking, kept moving, so she wouldn't turn around and throw a saddle on Bella and go tearing out into the arena. "I want to take some time before work to think about the mural. You've got your sisters' sketches, and I want to check out the wall. Coffee would help."

"I'm happy to do my part," Hunter said.

Hunter turned back and nodded at his brother. "See you, man."

Bowman returned the nod. "See you. Thanks, Ani."

Ani looked over her shoulder, intent on giving him a big cheerful wave. Bella caught her eye then shook her mane.

"No problem," Ani choked out.

But it was a problem. The biggest problem. Ani absolutely could not risk coming back into this barn again.

CHAPTER SIX

ANI WRAPPED BOTH her gloved hands tightly around the coffee. She wanted to wrap her whole body around it. She hadn't been warm since exiting the barn.

You are not going back in that barn again.

She was here to paint a mural, and this glorious morning was a good time to get started. The sun hit tiny crystals of ice lodged in the fields surrounding Outcrop, making the whole town seem like a fairy kingdom.

What they were staring at, however, was far from magical.

"This is it." Hunter gestured to the thirteen-by-twelve feet of boring space. "The east wall. It's not that big, but, man, is it ugly."

"Yeah. I'm beginning to understand why it was so important to your sisters to get some paint on this."

Hunter chuckled. "I've always planned on putting a mural here. I even got the wall prepped and primed last spring. But then I decided to move ahead with the addition, and you have a sense of what it's been like."

"Absolute insanity?"

"Yeah. That. But I'm glad my sisters hired you now. We'll get a lot of potential customers at the gala, and the mural will make this place easy to find when they come back."

Ani nodded, moving forward to run her fingers along the smooth cinder-block wall.

"You did a nice job of prepping it."

"Good. That means you'll have to spend less time out in the cold painting. I'll set up the propane heaters I use for outside seating."

"You will?" Ani spun around and looked at Hunter. Then she spun right back and studied the wall. She was not going to read the look in his eyes as someone who cared about her. He might like what he'd seen of her so far, but he didn't *know* her. Hunter was a busy guy and probably just didn't want a frozen body to deal with on top of everything else.

"Have you looked at your sisters' designs yet?" Ani asked.

Hunter let out a breath. "No."

Ani laughed at his tone. "How bad could they be?"

"My sisters are awesome, but they get a little carried away with their own cleverness. You might want to work from your own inspiration."

"But they know you, and Eighty Local, a lot better than I do."

"That's what I'm worried about. I'll go grab the sketches and you can tell me what you think."

Hunter disappeared through a side door into the restaurant. Ani jumped from foot to foot, sipping her coffee. *What would look good here?* It needed to reflect the ethics of Eighty Local and also fit with the town of Outcrop. "Something outdoorsy…definitely needs grain, maybe garden rows. An eagle? Several eagles."

"Hi."

Ani jumped at the voice. The young woman she'd seen sitting alone in Eighty Local the day before had materialized in the parking lot.

"Hi," Ani said. "Was I talking to the wall?"

The girl nodded.

"I'm sorry. It's a little early for 'strange lady talking to a blank wall.'"

The girl's face lit up with a close-lipped smile. She took a step closer. "Do you live in that van?"

"I do. It's awesome. Did I see you studying in Eighty Local yesterday?"

"I was doing my homework. My brother works here."

"Who's your brother?"

"Caleb."

Ani studied the girl. Her clothes were ill-fitting, not shabby, but cheaper imitations of the styles other girls wore. She looked uncomfortable in her skin, as though she were afraid of taking up too much space. And Ani had no idea why, but the girl seemed to want to connect with her.

"Well, I work here too. I'm supposed to paint a mural, but I have no idea what to paint."

The girl pressed her lips together. Her eyes flickered to Ani's face then back to the gravel. "I like to draw."

The side door opened and Hunter came striding out, holding a pistachio-green folder marked with multicolored tabs. "This is so much worse than I thought. Hey, Maia."

"Hey."

"You're early today."

Maia dragged her toe through the gravel, creating a perfect arc. "I was just heading to school."

"You got time for a chai tea?"

She shook her head. "I don't need any."

"But I got some new chai in, and I need to know if it's any good." Hunter held his hands up, like he was stuck and Maia was the only person who could get him out of it. She smiled, exposing an incisor painfully overlapping another tooth. "I'll be right back." Hunter deposited the folder in Ani's hand. "You two can try to decide which of these is the worst."

Ani opened the folder and burst out laughing.

"Told you so," Hunter called over his shoulder.

"Can I see?" Maia asked.

Ani held the folder at Maia's eye level. The first sketch was of Hunter, arms crossed, cape waving in the background, surrounded by a group of happy people holding forks.

"Hard pass," Maia said.

Ani flipped to the next picture and started laughing even harder. Hunter again, center stage with a floppy hat and overalls, leading a team of marching vegetables.

Maia giggled. "Zero out of five stars."

"Could we give it negative stars?" Ani asked.

"Black holes."

"Yes!" Ani nodded, keeping her eyes on Maia. The kid was really clever.

And hanging out in a cold parking lot before school.

"One chai latte," Hunter said, reemerging through the side door. He handed Maia a large to-go cup and a pastry bag. Maia took both, her smile aimed at the ground. "What do you think of the chai? Three stars? Four stars?"

Maia took a sip and glanced cautiously up at Hunter. "All the stars."

Ani looked from Maia to Hunter then back again. Hunter was so busy but found time to help out his employee's younger sister. His restaurant was always packed, but a table was reserved all afternoon and evening for a girl who didn't purchase anything.

What was Maia's story? And why did Hunter help her out like this?

The second wasn't even a question. Hunter just did kind things. It's who he was. His generosity illuminated Ani's own failings in stark contract. Since leaving home, she'd avoided permanent connections, believing most people were as self-involved as the family she'd grown up with. Hunter challenged her assumptions, and that made her uncomfortable.

It didn't matter if he was truly kind and generous, because she certainly wasn't. When she was Maia's age, she would have tormented a shy girl with off-brand clothing. Ani cringed with the memory of her behavior as a teen. How many nice kids like Maia had she made miserable just because she could? No, no matter how far she ran, Ani would always be the self-centered Stephanie Blaisedell her family had raised. There was no escaping her true nature, and if she could hide it from Hunter for the next few weeks, that would be enough.

"WELCOME," ANI CALLED. "Have a seat anywhere and I'll be right over."

Hunter shifted so he could watch her interact with the new customers. Ani finished up a coffee-to-go for a skier on his way to Mount Bachelor, then headed to where Jet and Clara's good friends, Michael and Joanna Williams, were tucked up in a booth together.

Today was running significantly smoother than the day before. He had Ani take the orders and he brought out the food. This would work until Janet came on at eleven thirty. Once Janet and Caleb, along with the rest of the staff, arrived, he could finish the prep for the local business fair then get to work on the addition.

He'd been nervous about Ani's attitude, but so far, so good. Better than good; she was fantastic. And having her out front was easier than letting her get into his space in the kitchen.

A burst of laughter rippled through the restaurant. Hunter glanced over to see Ani, head thrown back, hair cascading around her shoulders, laughing at something Michael had said.

Yeah. Definitely better to have her out of the kitchen.

"Hey, Boss Man."

Hunter tried to keep his focus on the breakfast sandwich he was building rather than get lost in Ani's golden eyes.

"What's up?"

"That woman wants to know if you're serving cornmeal blueberry pancakes."

Hunter glanced over at the table, his gaze tangling and tripping over Ani on the way. "For Joanna? Sure."

Ani rested her forearms on the counter and leaned toward him. "That's nice of you, to make her a special order."

"Michael and Joanna are good people."

"You think everyone is good people."

"Aren't most people good?"

Ani raised her brow. "You have *not* spent much time outside of Outcrop."

Hunter dropped the spatula he'd been using. "No, because I've been working my behind off since I was old enough to work."

Ani held her hands up. "Sorry. I just meant there are a lot of selfish people on this earth. Apparently, they don't show their dark side while eating in your establishment."

Hunter shifted. "I do see the good in most people."

"Because you spend your days filling them with food. Most people are innately selfish and always act in their own best interest. You make it in their best interest to eat here." She gestured toward Joanna Williams.

Hunter cracked an egg onto the griddle. "No one acts in their own best interest all the time."

Ani tilted her head. "I disagree. From the minute we're born, most people are out for themselves. If helping someone is in their best interest, they'll do it."

Hunter picked up his spatula and flipped the egg. "Is that why you were being nice to Maia this morning?"

"I don't mean people can't be polite—"

He set down the spatula and leaned toward her. "Ani, you weren't just being polite. You were talking with her and asking for her ideas on what to paint."

"Because those sketches your sisters made were ridiculous!"

Hunter gave Ani a sideways glance to call her out.

"Whatever. My point is chatting with a kid in the parking lot is no big deal."

"And my point is you saw a kid wandering through the lot a full hour before school starts on a cold morning, instinctively understood she needed your kindness and gave it to her."

Ani pulled her hair over one shoulder and glanced to where Maia generally parked herself after school. "What's her story?"

"I don't know. She comes in after school and stays until Caleb leaves. She orders a cup of hot water and brings her own tea bag, which she uses for the five or so hours she's here. A few times a week, she drifts by in the morning and I make sure to come out and say hi, and if I can figure out how to get her to take some food or a drink, I do."

Ani nodded. Then a spark lit in her eye as she said, "Maybe I was being nice because it made me feel good, so it actually was in my best interest."

Hunter scoffed. "For a hippie chick who lives in a van, you're pretty harsh. Where's the peace, love and Grateful Dead?"

Ani shook her head, strands of hair falling against her cheeks. She looked at him. "I'm not a hippie. I'm just a woman who likes to travel. I believe people are selfish, and attachment to anything leads to heartache."

Hunter glanced around the room. He couldn't be more attached, to his family, to the people of Outcrop, to his restaurant, even the spatula he was using. All of it had been hard won.

Ani gazed at him, daring him to contradict her.

Yeah. He got attached way too easily.

"I disagree. Attachment is healthy, and most people are good once you get to know them. Even you."

Ani's laugh hit him like kryptonite. Hunter melted toward her. His forearms collapsed next to hers on the counter. He leaned in, her lips in sharp focus and very close.

"You sure about that?" she asked.

Hunter pulled himself up. "Seriously, you've been a big help this morning. First with Bella—"

Ani turned away sharply. She started to speak then shook her head. Hunter didn't push it. She'd been pretty clear on the ride in she didn't want to discuss her magic with Bella.

"Then with Maia. And in the last hour, I've forgotten how I cover the midmorning shift without you. So, yeah, I think deep down inside, everyone is good."

A cold breeze floated in from the door as someone held it open for an unusually long time. Hunter glanced over.

Ani followed his gaze. "Everyone?"

He flexed his brow. "Almost everyone."

Holly Banks and her crew crowded just inside the door, assessing whether or not they were going to stay. Cold air swirled in and around them as they looked at the specials, scanned the clientele and generally drew focus to themselves. The lead mares of the Bend Equestrian Society had arrived.

He might not be great with Bella, but these women Hunter knew how to handle.

"Hey, welcome!" He smiled and walked out of the kitchen. "I wasn't expecting you all today."

"We just came for coffee," Shawna Hains said.

"We know we're 'not allowed' in the events venue," Holly said, engaging air quotes.

"It's great to see you!" Hunter faked his enthusiasm. He addressed Holly. "The inspector will be here next Thursday." His heart pounded as the words came out. He had until Thursday. Fortunately, Ani had showed up. Even if she was a maddening distraction, this morning she'd proved herself capable of holding down the fort out front. When the rest of his employees arrived, he'd get back to work in the events center.

The women shuffled through the dining room, prancing in their big fuzzy boots. They pulled long down jackets tighter around their bodies, jabbering about the coffee options.

"Are we still on for a tasting on the fourteenth?"

"Yes," Holly said. "And remember about the menu. We need some low-carb options, and a lot of it should be gluten free."

"It's all on the list." Hunter gave her the most charming smile he could. Once he got through Outcrop, Outside on Friday, he'd put together the tasting menu for these women.

"Let's get you some coffees, it's cold out. Ani, can you get set up?" Hunter glanced at the espresso machine, where he'd assumed Ani would have stationed herself. She wasn't there. Hunter swiveled his body, scanning the restaurant. She was nowhere in sight. The woman had the curiosity of a cat with an extra set of lives, so why would she bail on this? "Ani?"

"Be right out." Her voice drifted from the far end of the kitchen.

"I want a grande hazelnut latte," Shawna said then turned to Holly, explaining, "I didn't have breakfast."

"Ani?" he called again.

"I want a latte like that girl made last time." Holly nodded.

Hunter took one last look into the kitchen. Ani was not coming out. Annoyance flashed through him. *What was she thinking?*

"I'll get those started for you." Hunter stepped to the espresso machine. The women fired orders at him in quick succession. *Where was Ani?*

He moved efficiently, setting up cups and getting the shots brewing. The women's conversation flowed from gossip to carbohydrates to horses. Hunter noticed Ani skirt the group, the order he'd been working on for table five in her hands.

"Ani, you want to take over here?" he asked. She didn't respond. "Ani?" She set the orders down at table five and began an animated conversation with the customers. He was pleased with how she connected with the patrons, but right now he needed her help with these women.

"I'm going to have to sell Olive," Holly said.

"But she's so beautiful," a woman responded.

"I know. But I think I can get twelve thousand out of her. And she will not work with me or my trainer."

Hunter looked up. "You having trouble with a horse?"

Holly seemed surprised at his interest. Her eyes ran to Shawna, then she actually smiled at him. "I am. She's a strong jumper, but I don't trust her."

"You know who could help is Ani." He gestured to where Ani stood with her back to him.

Holly gave Ani what had to be the briefest, most disinterested glance on human record. "The waitress?"

"She's amazing. I've never seen anyone take on a mare like her."

"Oh, I always forget you're Wallace, like Wallace Ranch." Holly wrinkled her nose. Then her expression flipped to one of suspicion. "Wait, are you dating her?"

"No." Hunter chuckled. Then shook his head. Then crossed his hands in an X toward Ani.

Because if you deny something enough, that means you don't want it, right?

Hunter cleared his throat. "She took on my mom's horse this morning, had Bella eating out of her hand in seconds."

"Canadians aren't exactly the same thing as a Dutch Warmblood."

"Hey, Ani," Hunter called. She did not turn to face him. "Holly's having trouble with her mare. You should tell her about how you dealt with Bella."

Ani glanced over. "I don't really know much about horses."

Hunter laughed. "Right." He looked up at Holly. "I'd call her the horse whisperer, but she doesn't even need to speak."

Ani stepped behind the counter, keeping her back to the women. It was rude in the extreme and she knew how important it was to keep them happy. Hunter masked the anger rumbling in his chest.

"I just got kind of lucky," she said then focused on Michael and Joanna's table. Her voice was tight and strangely high-pitched as she called out, "I'll get started on those cornmeal pancakes for you."

Shawna glanced at Holly, a smirk riding across her face. "I'm sure she's better with horses than she is with people."

"Yeah, she's not going to be working our event, right?" Holly asked.

How could Ani do this to him? And why would she be

so charming and funny with every other customer then completely dismiss a group of patrons she knew was important?

It didn't matter. Ani did what she wanted, when she wanted and he'd known that from the start. Minutes earlier, she'd flat-out told him she only acted in her best interest. At a different time, he might be willing to help a new employee along, but right now? No. Particularly not one who kept distracting him from the task at hand. He needed to get the events center finished and host a perfect gala for these women, and not embarrass his family with another failure.

"No, she's not working the gala."

Or even one more day at Eighty Local if she kept this up.

ANI HAD FOUND CORNMEAL, flour, baking powder, blueberries and what she'd assumed were the rest of the ingredients for cornmeal pancakes. It was all stacked around her like a protective wall, but she knew she'd need more than dry goods to save herself from the blast of Hunter's wrath.

The bells on the door jangled as the horse ladies exited the establishment. Ani glanced at the recipe she'd pulled up on her phone. Hunter's footsteps fell fast and angry.

"What was that?"

Ani shrugged her left shoulder, going for casual. "You seemed to have it, so I jumped in back here." The lie flopped between them like second-rate rat bait.

Hunter didn't bite.

"You bailed on a group of important customers for no reason."

"I didn't bail. I'm working." Ani gestured to the ingredients.

"In what bizarre fantasy of yours do you make the special orders while I make coffee?"

In what bizarre fantasies did Hunter make coffee? Hers. Only, in that particular fantasy, he was pulling espresso while grinning at her from under his Stetson.

She glanced at him. He was furious, his pulse visible in his neck.

"I'm trying to help."

Hunter picked up her phone and eyed the recipe, then scoffed as he dropped it facedown on the counter. Ani pulled her hands back from the cornmeal mess she'd created.

"Just when I think I can trust you."

Ani focused on the counter. She didn't want to hurt Hunter. This was good work in a nice place. But he would never understand why she couldn't serve coffee to Holly Banks, Shawna Hains and the rest of their crew.

Fortunately, she'd been raised to know how to turn the tables in an argument, even when you were clearly in the wrong. *Time to go on the defensive.*

"I don't like those women."

"You don't like a lot of things. You don't like rules." Hunter ticked off the list on his fingers. "You don't like to follow simple directions. You don't like homes attached to the ground."

"I choose to live unencumbered by society's small-minded rules. I choose freedom and honesty over pandering to small women for the Yelp reviews."

Hunter's eyes flashed. "Yelp puts money in my pocket, Ani. Yelp keeps everyone here employed, it pays the mortgage on this place and it's responsible for the tips you'll stash in the glove compartment at the end of your run here."

Ani rolled her eyes. "People come here for the freakishly delicious food."

"How does anyone know about my food?" Hunter crossed his arms.

"Everybody in town knows you."

"Everyone in town could eat here twice a week and I would fold. Half of my business is made up of skiers, climbers and hikers who drive from the Willamette Valley to central Oregon. They get outdoors, they get hungry, and they look for a good place to eat. Yelp brings them here. If I have bad Yelp reviews, Eighty Local will close. It's that simple."

Ani kept her gaze on the tiled floor. There was no way she could have stayed in the same room with those women. And there was no way she could tell Hunter the truth. Any idea he had of her as capable and independent would fly right out the window. She'd just be some rich girl, pretending to be a dirtbag in a hundred-thousand-dollar vehicle she'd bought with her parents' money.

"I'm sorry I didn't deal with those women the way you would have liked me to. At the time, it seemed like the best option."

"Being rude was the best option?"

Ani set her hands on the counter and met Hunter's angry gaze. He would never understand where she was coming from, not with a family like his. But she was not going to play games with Holly Banks and Shawna Hains ever again.

Manipulating others by being mean was an art form, and Ani had studied at the feet of a master. She knew how to draw people to her then slap friends down frequently enough to keep them on their toes. She'd studied how to groom inferiors into sycophants. She'd become a master at using fear and flattery to manipulate any social situation.

Women like Holly and Shawna brought out the worst in her. Ten minutes in their company and Ani's inner mean girl was already starting to show.

"I'm not going to pretend to like anyone, ever. So, if that's a prerequisite of this job, I'm out."

"I'm not asking you to pretend anything. I'm asking you for basic civil behavior. We don't get to pick and choose who we serve here. I'm not going to put up a sign and ask people to take a personality test before they place an order."

The counter blurred before her, fury and shame storming in her chest. "I'm not going to lie—"

"Actually, you did lie. You said you don't know much about horses, which we both know isn't true."

A lump wedged in her throat. She never should have gone into the barn this morning. The minute she'd taken the harness from Hunter's hand and stepped up to Bella, everything got irrevocably complicated.

"You can't take on Bella then expect me to pretend you didn't because you don't feel like talking to a few customers."

Ani swallowed hard. *Don't let him see you cry.*

"You don't understand."

"I sure don't." Hunter stormed toward the addition. He stopped in the door frame, his shoulders expanding and contracting with his breath. When he turned back to her, his earthy brown eyes were tired. "What I really don't understand is why you would humiliate me like that. You might not like those women, but they took a chance on Eighty Local. They booked the events center before it was even built. Yeah, they're hard to work with." Ani started to speak but Hunter held up a hand. "You had a chance to help me out by connecting with them over horses. But you're so selfish you couldn't even stay in the same room with them for ten minutes. Great lifestyle you've set up for yourself."

CHAPTER SEVEN

"HERE YOU GO." Ani set a fresh block of Tillamook ched-dar next to Caleb then glanced at the door to the addition. It was only a matter of time before Hunter stormed back in and fired her.

"Thanks." He didn't look up as he reached for the knife. "You're a lifesaver."

"Ani?" Janet stuck her head in the kitchen. "Can you bus dishes for a second? Katie's backed up."

"Sure." Ani spun from Caleb and headed to the din-ing room.

"You came at just the right time," Janet said. "I'm not supposed to say it out loud but I'm really glad your van is having problems. It's almost impossible for Hunter to find good help."

Ani nodded. *Good help* might not be the first words he'd use to describe her at this point.

"I can't even believe he's left the place to us for the lunch rush."

Ani continued her bobbing nod. Hunter had slammed the door to the addition behind him the minute Caleb ar-rived and hadn't emerged from the room for the last three hours.

"And it's so good for Caleb to get experience in the kitchen on his own." Janet was still talking. Ani started to feel like a bobblehead. Caleb had the kitchen to himself because his boss was so furious with her, he couldn't even run his restaurant while she was in it. "Table eight." Janet gestured to a vacant table and then headed off to take the orders, blissfully ignorant of the storm Ani had stirred up.

Great. Now she was going to disappoint Janet on top of everything else.

Ani stacked dishes in the bin. This was why she didn't get attached. It was fine to appreciate people. It was fine to enjoy the experience of a new place. But any attachment led to misery. Yet, here she was, not even forty-eight hours into Outcrop, and she was already letting people down.

Hungry patrons watched as she worked, ready to pounce on the table the minute she was finished. Ani propped the bin on her hip and carefully wiped the table. Captain Clean would be proud.

Who was she kidding? Captain Clean couldn't look at her. And why would he? He'd called her selfish. *Self-important* was the term her mother used to use. Ani would come trotting off the field with another heavy trophy. Her father snapped pictures to document the family's success. Her mother would float over and brush her cheek with a kiss, whispering, *Don't get self-important.*

Ani shifted the dish bin and pulled up a smile as she waved the waiting party over: a man in his sixties with a passel of grandkids. "Janet will be right with you."

"We're just here for the cocoa," the man said, sending the kids buzzing.

"Cocoa, is it?" Ani surveyed the children, pretending to be perplexed. "I might be able to make cocoa."

"With marshmallows!" one of the children clarified.

Ani blinked hard. *God, when had she last had cocoa with marshmallows?* She could sure remember the time *she didn't.* Her mother had reached out and taken the cup from a little ten-year-old Ani, saying, *Consider your figure.*

A week later, that little ten-year-old Ani had thrown the same words in the face of a friend at a slumber party.

Ani shook her shoulders loose. She focused on the excited faces of the children.

"Cocoa with marshmallows? It's never been done."

"Yes, it has." The oldest boy spoke with authority.

"Everyone puts marshmallows in cocoa," his sister said with some concern, like Ani might refuse the request.

"I'll see what I can do. How many marshmallows do I put in each cup? One?"

"Noooo!"

"You put in a lot of marshmallows, as many as you can," the boy said.

Ani exchanged a smile with the grandpa. "I'll do my best."

She took a few steps away then turned back to the table. "What about candy canes? Do you think anyone has ever put a candy cane in hot cocoa?"

A little girl began dancing in the booth. "Try it!"

Ani's gaze met the grandpa's. "Do you think a shot of espresso might work in your cocoa?"

"Yes, ma'am. Thank you for thinking of it." He nodded. "We're going to walk down and see Santa at OHTAF. It's going to be a long afternoon."

Ani laughed. "Two shots?"

"That'll do it."

"I'll run these dishes back, wash up, and get started." Hunter probably had some plan for the candy canes that didn't involve her doling them out in cups of cocoa. But she was getting fired at the end of the day, anyway, so might as well live large.

Ani was three steps toward the kitchen when a group of rock climbers flagged her over.

"Sorry to bother you," a woman with a smudge of

climbing chalk on her cheek said. "Can we have some of the sauce?"

"The 8L sauce?" Ani guessed.

"That's it," one of the men said, a grin cracking his wind-tanned face. "She sent Chain Reaction this morning." He held out his phone to show Ani a picture of the woman climbing what looked to be an impossible route. "My wife needs all the calories she can get."

Ani surveyed the table, which was crowded with burgers, cheese chili soup, nachos and sweet potato fries.

"Have you all been climbing in this weather?" she asked.

"We got to Smith at six a.m. The friction on the rock is better when it's cold."

"I'm going to bring you a whole bowl of sauce. You need it!"

The group cheered and Ani hustled back to drop off the dishes, wash up, get the sauce out and the cocoa going.

She paused at the dishwashing station where Katie, an earnest teenager, was powering through the dishes. The busy energy of the kitchen offset the cheerful hum of the dining room. Beyond the door to the addition, Hunter had music playing as he worked on the beautiful space.

Fine, she was a little attached. There was a lot to learn here. Plus, it was too cold to sleep in the van, and the gardener's cottage was so cozy. She needed money and this was a good place to earn it.

She just had to fix things with Hunter. Ani washed her hands carefully then eyed the dining room. How could she make this up to him? Or, if not make it up, help him understand she hadn't meant to hurt him or his business. She looked at the hungry climbers, who desperately needed to replace the calories they'd lost climbing in the cold. She took in the children, bumping and buzzing in the booth, waiting for their cocoa.

A plan began to take shape. Some calories, an apology and just enough truth to buy her two weeks in this place.

THE HAMMER CONNECTED with the head of the nail in a satisfying thunk. Doing delicate finish work while angry wasn't the best idea, but it was better than being in the restaurant with Ani for one more second. Hunter reached over to his phone and tapped up the volume a notch further. A Jeffrey Desoto playlist could get a man through a lot.

Hunter sat back on his heels. The trim around the exterior door was acceptable. He should have used the nail gun, but something about that morning had made him reach for an old-fashioned hammer. Besides, if he did his job in the kitchen right, patrons would be full and happy when they left, and not stop to examine the molding around the exit.

Acceptable was going to have to do. Caleb had the kitchen covered, Janet was out front and knew to get him if anything went wrong. So long as Ani hadn't burned the place down, they were fine. He fished another nail out of the can. At the end of the day, he'd cut her check and suggest she look for work in Bend, or Redmond, or anywhere but here until she could afford a new battery for her van. He'd stop thinking about her, stop craving her presence, stop listening for her warm voice to come floating across the restaurant.

"It's cold in here."

Hunter dropped the nail back in the can. He didn't look up. Ani's high-tops padded across the room, barely audible over a ballad about broken trust.

"I brought you some hot chocolate." The phrase sounded apprehensive, almost rehearsed.

He exhaled then stood. Ani and her cocoa could head

straight back into the restaurant, or better yet, into her van and on the road.

His movement stopped her. She hesitated, like he was an angry stallion she was approaching. Light shone in from the high windows, illuminating the dust mites dancing in the air around her. Her frame seemed smaller, vulnerable, in this big unfinished room.

Hunter started to speak. Ani held out the cup and interrupted him.

"I'm sorry."

Hunter shook his head. He had too much going on: the gala, the business fair, the Mistletoe Festival. Ani's erratic behavior, disregard for rules and propensity for trouble, all wrapped up in an inconceivably beautiful woman, was more than he could deal with right now.

"We gave it a good try," he said with all the generosity he'd ever bothered to cultivate. "It's not a great time for it, but I'll cut a check at the end of your shift—"

Ani crossed to him. She released one hand from the cocoa and took his fingers in hers, still warm from the cup. She placed the hot chocolate in his hand and stepped back.

"Look, I know you need this job, but I can't deal—"

"I want this job. I want to help."

Hunter shook his head. "Ani, I can't do this."

"Please, drink your hot chocolate."

Hunter glanced at the cup then furrowed his brow. "What's with all the marshmallows?"

The spark returned to her eyes. "They represent how sorry I am."

Hunter unhooked a candy cane from the side of the cup and poked through the marshmallows. "You have like twenty marshmallows in here."

"I'm really sorry."

Hunter glanced up. A hopeful smile played across her

face. This would be so much easier if he didn't want to kiss her all the time.

"The candy cane is functional. I intended you to use it just as you are, to push marshmallows aside so you can actually drink the cocoa."

Hunter tried to clamp down on a smile. Ani stepped closer and he lost the battle.

"Over time, the marshmallows will melt, as will the candy cane, making a rich, delicious cup of peppermint cocoa." Hunter started laughing as Ani continued to unveil her plan. "And you'll drink it and have the sugar, fat and protein running through your system, and it will put you in a good mood, and you'll forget what an ungrateful brat I was this morning." Her golden eyes met his. "Please?"

"Ani, I cannot afford to insult those women."

"I know. Please. Drink your cocoa and let me explain."

Hunter brought the cup to his lips, using the candy cane to navigate the flotilla of marshmallows. The hot chocolate was rich and smooth, darker than expected.

"Butter," Ani answered his questioning look. "There's like a billion calories in that cup, which you need, because it's freezing in here."

Hunter took another drink. There were worse things than make-up cocoa. He refrained from looking at Ani because there were also better things than make-up cocoa.

And they weren't going to make up. They could part on good terms, but he could not risk having her in the restaurant.

Ani put her hands in her jacket pockets and took a few steps into the center of the room. She glanced up at the exposed pine pole rafters then turned back to him.

"I'm not good at following rules."

Hunter sputtered out a laugh. "You think?"

She wasn't laughing. Ani's shoulders rose and fell as

she pulled in a breath. "I come from a place where there were a lot of rules, spoken and unspoken. I've spent most of my life disappointing other people."

Hunter took a step toward her, stilled. If she was going to open up with her bizarre ideas about not getting attached and people being self-serving, he wanted to hear it.

"What was so hard…" She pulled in a breath and shuddered. "What was so hard was constantly doing the wrong thing without even knowing it. I broke the rules just by being myself."

She trembled and seemed, for the moment, fragile. Then she straightened her shoulders and exhaled.

"When I was twenty-one, I chose to live my life authentically." She met Hunter's gaze. "I decided I would always live honestly and without attachment. I would only do good work that doesn't hurt anyone, and explore the world." She nodded, as if she had to convince herself of this over and over. "Hunter, I want to work here. I like the work, and this is a good place."

He met her gaze, his eyebrows raised.

"Yes. Fine. I'm a little attached." She looked away. "The food is incredible."

His resolve was melting away like the marshmallows.

"Ani, there have to be rules in a restaurant. You get that, right?"

"I know. Can I just…" She stopped and drew in a breath. "Keep drinking your cocoa and let me explain one more thing."

Hunter stirred the marshmallows aside and took a long drink. When his gaze returned to Ani, her face was serious.

"Horses are like crack to me."

Hunter chuckled. Ani held out her palm to stop him.

"I mean it. I'm one of those people. My heart rate goes up if I so much as smell saddle leather."

"So, stop traveling. Get a horse."

Ani shook her head, her lips pressed tight together. She threw her head back, eyes closed. "No." She opened her eyes and looked at him. "I'm happy when I'm traveling to new places. I love the freedom of never ever having to be someone I'm not. I'll never fit in anywhere. This life-style works for me."

Hunter shook his head. "I don't get it. How can you be happy without your family, or friends, or community?"

She gave him a wry smile. "If you knew my family, you'd get it."

Hunter started to contradict her but stopped himself. He didn't know what it was like to have an unsupportive family. A highly supportive family that you'd failed over and over was more his wheelhouse.

Ani continued. "I don't want anyone to have expectations of me. I want to be myself and not have everyone wish I was someone else."

"Who wants you to be someone else?"

"Um, you? You've known me for less than forty-eight hours and already you can't stand me."

The sincerity in her expression felt like a slap across the face. *Had he really been that rude?*

"Ani, I'm sorry. Yes, I was mad earlier, but I don't dislike you."

"It's okay. I'm hard to like. I know."

Hunter stared. Where had she gotten that idea? "Everyone likes you. You're always laughing with the customers, and you get along with everyone who works here. You even got Bowman talking, which puts you in the top one percent of likable people."

Ani pressed the tip of her sneaker against the floor. She

nodded, her focus directed toward her toes. "You don't like me."

"That's not true." He took a step forward. "It's also not fair. This restaurant is my life. When you threaten my work, I'm going to get angry."

She met his eye. "Okay, so I don't get *that*. I don't know why you're so afraid to fail, or how you even think you could fail with this place."

Hunter stirred his candy cane through the cocoa. Maybe if she knew his family a little better, she'd get it.

Ani reached up and pulled a band out of her hair. She caught the long strands falling around her shoulders and twisted her hair into a new knot as she spoke. "I can't be around the women from the Bend Equestrian Society. I just can't. I will chop your vegetables, clean your floors, do whatever you need. But I can't serve them."

"What are you afraid of? That you'll envy them?"

She met his eye and spoke clearly. "I'm afraid I'll become one of them." He started to laugh, but her tone stopped him. "The horse world has all types. Some nice folks like your family. And some mean, backstabbing, petty people, like Holly Banks. I know myself, Hunter. If you throw me in with women like that, I will battle my way to the top."

"I wasn't asking you to hang out with them, I just wanted you to make them coffee."

She shook her head. "The last time I made coffee for Holly, I replaced the skim milk with half-and-half. This time, I probably would have put in dish soap."

Hunter laughed.

"It's not funny. I can get mean. I don't like that side of myself, so I try to never be in situations where it might come out."

"I don't believe you."

She met his gaze frankly.

"Well, you're snarky," Hunter conceded. "But I'd never call you mean."

"I hope you never see me get mean. I don't want to upset you. You and your family have been good to me. If my battery was working, I'd save you the bother of firing me and be on my way. But I have to earn a lot of money fast, and I like it here." Her gaze met his, open and vulnerable. "Let me stay."

He exhaled then shook his head. Ani kept talking. "You have rules for a reason. I get it. I don't want to break them, but I know myself well enough to admit I probably will. Please let me stay anyway. I can make it up to you."

Frustration rose in his chest, crowding his lungs. "What do you want to do, then? You put my whole collection of permits and licenses at risk when you don't follow the rules."

An unexpected grin broke out across her face. "I can do any of the work in here. I'll show you my van—I did the entire remodel myself. Let me help."

Her golden eyes met his, sending his heart thudding up against his rib cage.

"Trust me. I can help you."

Hunter's chest constricted. Accepting help wasn't his strong suit, and any combination of trust and Ani seemed like a terrible idea.

But his family had the Mistletoe Festival coming up, and he had to make time for the family planning meeting on Monday. Outcrop, Outside was the following Friday. And this space had to get finished.

Hunter took another sip of his drink. Could he blame bad decision-making on really good cocoa?

"Okay, Outlaw. You got your way."

"Yeeessss!" She spun and took in the room. "Gimme your nail gun."

"But you've got to follow the rules."

"Hunter, I promise to do everything I can to act in the best interest of Eighty Local."

"That's not what I asked."

"It's all I got." Her eyes connected with his. Ani sobered as she made her final request. "Just don't ask me to be someone I'm not. I think I can be a big help to you, but I'm probably going to tick you off occasionally."

"Occasionally?" he asked.

"Daily?"

"More like hourly."

She glanced up at him, raw gratitude evident in her expression. She really wanted to stay. And as much as he didn't want to admit it, he wanted her to stay too.

CHAPTER EIGHT

"OKAY, EXACTLY HOW late did you plan on being?" Piper questioned, or rather accused. It was a certain tone and inflection only his sister seemed to manage. Bowman called it a "quackusation."

"Am I late?" Hunter asked, glancing around the dining table in the family home. Mom, Dad, Bowman, Piper, Clara and Jet, her new husband, Ash and his fiancée, Violet, and even Ash's son, Jackson, were already seated around the table. The one family member missing was Maisy, Bowman's fiancée, and since she was the only doctor for forty miles in any direction, it was likely she had a solid excuse. Hunter pulled his Stetson off and sat next to Jackson.

"Um, yeah," Piper said. "And I did not save you one cranberry jumble cookie, so that's what you get."

Hunter shook his head. "Piper, I know you live a hundred miles away in the big city, but have you forgotten how things go around here? I made the cookies. I created the recipe."

"Unless that's why you're late, I don't want to hear about it," she snapped. "Clara, where were we in our discussion?"

Jackson, arguably the best sixteen-year-old kid in the universe, took a cranberry jumble off his plate and offered it to Hunter.

"Don't encourage him!" Piper snapped.

Jackson laughed then grabbed the carton of eggnog and

poured himself what seemed to be a second glass. "You're not late, Uncle Hunter."

He *was* late, and he knew it. The Mistletoe Festival was the family's big event of the year. People came from all over to enjoy the festivities and learn about the horses they raised. It was vital to the family's income. But he'd gotten stuck in the kitchen and then allowed himself to laugh with Ani as she'd pulled out his sisters' designs again and started planning for the mural.

He and Ani had gotten an incredible amount of work done over the last week and a half, and that was awesome. But he couldn't let her distract him from the work he still had to do.

"Okay, I hate to interrupt, but we have a festival to plan," Clara said. She shot her new husband a grin. "Jet and I have an idea for a fun addition this year." Clara placed both her hands on the table and grinned. "A Christmas emu!"

The table erupted. Predictably, the parents thought it was fantastic. Ash and Bowman brought up every reasonable concern a person might have given Jet's track record with the emus. Violet just wanted to watch the emu annoy Ash like only a large, curious bird could. Piper defended emu participation as though having birds at a Christmas festival was a human rights issue.

Hunter met his brother-in-law's eyes from across the table. "This was not your idea, I'm assuming?"

Jet chuckled and peeked at Clara. "No, but I am supportive. And Larry would love it." That Larry was a large bird with a beak for trouble didn't seem to factor into the evaluation.

"Where's Ani?" Clara asked.

Hunter looked up sharply. "She's working on the mural today."

"Why didn't you invite her to join us?"

"Why *would* I invite her to join us?"

"Because she's awesome," Piper said. "She'll help out with the Mistletoe Festival, won't she?"

"She's great with the horses," Bowman added. "We could use her help."

"Plus, she's super beautiful," Clara said.

"Right? We had no idea she was so pretty when we hired her." Piper turned to Hunter and said pointedly, "You're welcome."

"Uh…" Hunter shook his head, trying to think about anything other than how pretty Ani was. "I didn't notice."

The family silenced. Then several throats were cleared and Jackson wasn't successful in repressing a laugh.

"What?" Hunter asked. "She's helping out at the restaurant and I'm grateful she's here. That's all."

Mom pressed her lips together, stealing a glance at Dad. "It's just kinda funny you haven't noticed how gorgeous she is."

"Yeah," Bowman agreed, "especially since you're staring at her all the time."

Hunter stood and pushed his chair in. "Are we done here? Because I have a lot going on and really don't have time for this."

Dad rose and rested his hand on Hunter's shoulder. Hunter dropped back into his chair and raked his hands through his hair. He had so much to do. The tasting for the Bend Equestrian Society was coming up. Outcrop, Outside was Friday night. The Mistletoe Festival would take up an entire day. How could he possibly get it all done?

But he didn't have a choice here. He *had* to help out with the family business. And he had a real chance with Eighty Local to finally make his family proud. He just had to do everything, perfectly, between now and December 27. It shouldn't be too hard since his siblings had been doing everything perfectly since they were born.

Hunter hadn't been an easy kid from day one and having a twin to get into trouble with had intensified the issues. It was one thing when he was four years old and had a few hundred acres to go tearing around on, but school was a disaster.

From his first day in kindergarten, Hunter had hated it. The teachers had expected him to sit at a desk, sit in the lunchroom, then sit outside the principal's office when he couldn't sit in the first two places. He'd been constantly held back during recess to finish his work, so the one place he might have been able to run around was practically off limits. His parents had been called in to meetings, everyone trying to find a solution to his problems. Hunter had been tested for every learning disability in the book. But he'd always known he didn't have a learning disability; it was a sitting-still disability. He just couldn't do it.

High school had been a little better and also a lot worse. He'd had PE, woodshop and culinary class. He'd signed up to take journalism when he'd found out they needed a photographer, and was allowed to wander around the school with a camera.

But his parents were Bob and Lacy Wallace, Outcrop's star teachers. When he'd entered school each morning, he passed a case holding their teaching awards. When he'd come home at night, he'd pass them sitting together over his abysmal grade reports, worrying. He could learn the material fine, it was the endless worksheets, review packets and poster projects that had turned his stomach.

Hunter had scraped through in high school, while his siblings were straight-A, advanced-placement kids. Clara, Piper and Ash all went to college on academic scholarships. Bowman had opted for EMT training, and now

served as part of the fire department. His twin was a hero
by trade and Oregon Firefighter of the Year.

Hunter had barely graduated, then taken a job sweeping
floors and washing dishes in an old, run-down restaurant.
He'd spent years of working two or three jobs at a time,
and now he owned the building in which he'd had his first,
low-paying job. Eighty Local was successful.

And these people he'd failed over and over again were
asking one thing of him: to help out with the family business for one day.

Dad seemed to read his thoughts. "Hunter, for the festival this year, I thought you could manage the horseback
rides in the arena. You're great with kids, and their parents."

"I can help there too," Jackson offered.

"If Ani wants to join us, she's welcome," Mom said.
"But we can easily manage without her."

Hunter nodded. He heard what his family was offering here. A simple job where he could show up, help, and
then get back to work. To run the rides, all he needed was
to be focused and sociable. He'd intended to do more than
his share this time, but here he was with his family letting
him off the hook, again.

"Great," Dad said. "Now, Outcrop, Outside is Friday
night. Who can help at the Eighty Local booth?"

ANI GLANCED AT her sketch then back at the blank wall.
It was two o'clock in the afternoon and, according to the
weather service, it was as warm as it was going to get
today. She and Hunter had a solid plan to finish the events
center and, all impending crises aside, Ani might actually
find time to paint the mural that had brought her to Outcrop in the first place.

Working in the events center with Hunter had been

more fun than either of them had expected. Together they'd installed the pine trim and would varnish it next week. Her creative thought process and his propensity for doing everything by the book made a surprisingly productive combination.

Ani couldn't remember the last time she'd laughed so much or felt such joy in making someone else laugh. She needed to be careful.

So today, she'd start the mural. A nice, solitary job that she could execute without the company of a handsome cowboy chef. He had a meeting with his family and she was alone and free to create.

The sun shone brightly, reflecting off the fields of stubble beyond Eighty Local. She jumped from one leg to the other and then did fifteen jumping jacks. Moving her limbs while wearing every piece of clothing she owned was less than optimal, but it got the job done. Her blood began to flow and warm her body.

Ani took one last look at the sketch and stepped up to the wall with her pencil. Most muralists had systems for translating their work from sketch to wall. Ani preferred to start with an idea and then let it develop as she went along. Her pencil sailed across the bumpy cinder-block wall, leaving a dark trail of graphite in its wake. Mountains took shape, the fields below them. Ani focused, drifting deeper into the work.

"Hi."

Ani started at the voice, the tip of her pencil breaking off as she pressed too hard into the wall.

"Hello," Ani said. It was Maia, arriving for the afternoon. "How was school?"

"Good. I don't mean to bother you. I just wanted to say hi."

Maia might not want to bother her, but she clearly

wanted to talk. Ani smiled. "It's okay. My pencil broke, so I have to stop anyway."

"Do you want to use one of mine?" Maia pulled off her backpack and rummaged inside, coming up with a well-used plastic zip bag. She held it out to Ani. It was packed with pencil nubs, all well sharpened, with varying states of erasers at the ends. It was as though Maia was afraid of not having a pencil when she needed one.

"Thank you." Ani selected a pencil then held up her sketch. "What do you think?"

Maia took the sketch and looked at the wall. A slow smile spread across her face. "It's all of Oregon, isn't it?"

Ani felt ridiculously pleased the thirteen-year-old could see her vision. "It is."

Maia traced her finger across the paper. "These are all the places Hunter gets his food. Then they come here." Her finger stopped at a cluster of buildings in the shadow of Smith Rock. She looked up at Ani, her rare smile shining. "I love it."

"Stars?" Ani asked, knowing Maia's habit of rating everything on a five-star scale.

Maia nodded. "Yeah. You should put them here, over the ocean. Five stars, so the people eating here know how to rate the place."

Wow. The kid had immediately picked up on what Ani was trying to do with the mural, then added a really nice detail for subliminal advertising. Plus, she had what looked like an unlimited supply of pencils.

"Maia, how much homework do you have today?"

"Not much." She studied the ground for a moment, rubbing her wrists together. "Not any, actually."

A mix of unfamiliar emotions ran through Ani. She'd been taking care of herself for so long, and protecting herself from her family, she didn't have much experience helping others. But right now, Ani had an overwhelming urge to help Maia tap into what seemed to be a natural talent.

"Okay then. If you have some time, what would you think of helping me with this? It's cold out, but I bet we could convince your brother to bring us some tea to warm us up."

Maia's smile said it all. And Ani had to agree. Working on a mural on a beautiful day, with good company and hot tea? That was an experience worth having. And, who knew? Maybe she'd help Maia tap into this talent and the girl would do something with it someday. Ani was pretty sure she'd never been a good influence on anyone, ever. But she could try today.

Time flowed as Ani and Maia sketched out the mural. Caleb brought out hot tea, liberally sweetened. Ani engaged the music app on her phone and Maia picked the station, a mix of 1980's pop music. Ani didn't think she'd ever listened to so much Duran Duran and Wham!, but she had to admit it was great mural-painting music.

She was so deep in her work, laughing and chatting with Maia, she didn't notice the temperature dropping. She wasn't aware that the light had started to fade, or even hear Hunter's truck when he returned.

"What's going on out here?"

Ani looked down from her perch on the ladder as her gorgeous boss came striding over. She wobbled but caught herself against the wall. That Stetson was going to be the death of her.

His eyes ranged from her, to Maia, to their work, then to the mountains where the sun was starting its decline. "Ani, what are you thinking?"

Ani instinctively glanced at Maia. Maia shivered but kept her pencil to the wall.

He shook his head, muttering something about her sanity as he stalked toward the restaurant.

Maia's face fell. "Y-you don't like it?" she managed to cough out, but Hunter was already gone, the back door slamming in his wake.

Not exactly the reaction Ani had been expecting.

But her disappointment was inconsequential in light of Maia's. Ani climbed down off the ladder and approached Maia, realizing for the first time how cold it had gotten. "It's okay. He gets grumpy. You don't see it as much, but I bet Caleb could tell you stories."

Maia's lip trembled as she examined the mural. "I thought he'd like it."

"He will," Ani reassured Maia, and herself. "He can barely even see it, since we've just sketched it in."

The back door banged against the wall as Hunter kicked it open. He carried a seven-foot-tall…something. Maia looked at Ani, her brow creased. Ani shrugged in response.

Hunter set the piece of equipment down and started fussing with it. "Next time, let me know when you're working outside."

"I told you I was working on the mural today."

"I thought you were sketching ideas, *inside*, where it's warm."

"Well, I'm outside, getting started." She lowered her voice, adding, "With a helper, who was super excited for you to see this."

Hunter closed his eyes and rubbed one hand across his chest.

"I'm sorry." He shook his head, glanced at Maia then back at Ani. "It's been a rough afternoon. I didn't expect to come back and find you two working in the cold." He stared at her, his eyes conflicted under the rim of his Stetson. Everything got a lot warmer. "Please don't work out here without heat. I'm never too busy to set up a heater."

Oh. That's what the thing was, a heater. And he was mad because they were working in the cold. The sudden flush of warmth she felt was totally because of the heater, not the way he was looking at her.

Hunter fiddled with a knob then straightened. Somehow, he found a big smile for Maia. "I can't have my girls freezing out here. Now, let's see what you're working on." Hunter stepped back to view their work. Maia had a huge grin on her face as she talked him through the plan.

Ani closed her eyes briefly. *His girls.* Not an itinerant muralist and a middle schooler with nowhere else to go. Not his employee and his backup chef's little sister. But *his girls.*

"I like the stars over the ocean," Hunter said, nodding at the wall.

"There are five." Ani stood next to Hunter. "Maia's idea."

He nodded. Maia's face flushed with pride. Ani flushed for a whole different reason.

"It's perfect," he said. "I've had a hard day, and this makes everything better. How long will it take?"

"It depends on how much time I can have out here. What have we got this week?"

"Well, Friday is Outcrop, Outside. I'd love it if you could help out there."

"If you're paying, I'm working."

He nodded. "The BES tasting is next Tuesday." Hunter looked up, thinking through his list. "Those are the last two big-work hurdles. Then I've got this thing with my family." He gazed down at her. "So, other than finishing the trim in the addition, and helping out when we're busy, you're free to work out here. As long as you have heat."

"Can I keep helping?" Maia asked.

"I'd love that." The words flew out of Ani's mouth before she could think it through. She enjoyed working with Maia, but she was getting in too deep here in Outcrop. She was making friends. These weren't the casually pleasant work relationships she normally developed, but good friends.

She glanced at Hunter, the one friend who was beginning to feel like so much more.

CHAPTER NINE

"YOU'RE COMING, RIGHT?"

Ani startled at Hunter's voice. Normally, she heard the side door bang open when he came charging out to interrupt her as she worked on the mural. This time she must have been too deep in thought to notice.

Oh, but she was noticing now.

On most days, Hunter's style was that of a casual, functional rancher: layers of flannel and waffle weave he shed throughout the day. The slightly shaggy hair, the bright friendly smile, the worn-in blue jeans were all Hunter to the core.

But today he was wearing a scowl, along with a bright red sweatshirt featuring an eagle in a Santa hat with the words Welcome to My Ho-Ho-Hometown scrawled across it.

"You want me to come to the outside thing?"

He put his hands on his hips, which made him look even more ridiculous. "We just talked about it this morning."

"No, I know. Let me rephrase the question. You want me to go somewhere in public, with you, in that sweatshirt?"

In response, Hunter lobbed a matching sweatshirt her way.

"Oh, no—"

"City council's orders. Every representative of local business wears a sweatshirt, so we're easily identifiable."

"Easily identifiable and mockable."

"As of nine thirty this evening, Outcrop, Outside will be over, and we can cross it off the list. You'll never have to wear it again."

Ani held up the horrific article of clothing. "This sweatshirt is an insult to eagles, Santa Claus and hometowns around the world." A thought occurred to her. "Did one of your sisters design this?"

"It's possible. Put it on, let's go!"

Ani glanced longingly back at the mural. It was starting to take shape, in no small part due to Maia's help. Over the last week, they'd established a routine. Ani was on the clock with Hunter in the restaurant until midafternoon. Then he'd make her some kind of fantastic coffee drink before heading into the addition while she and Maia worked on the mural. When it started to get dark around five, Maia did her homework and Ani would fill in wherever Hunter needed her. The pace was intense, but she was making money, and staying away from the horses at Wallace Ranch.

And that's why she was here, to make money, so she could get out of Oregon before the holiday, and possibly forever.

Hunter had spent most of the last forty-eight hours preparing for Outcrop, Outside. Turkey was roasted then slow-cooked in a cranberry barbecue sauce for sandwiches. Ani prepped an excessive amount of kale for something Hunter called "kaleslaw" he swore his community was addicted to. And now they'd head over to the town square to meet Bowman and Hunter's other brother, Ash, who were helping run the booth.

"Why are we doing this again?" Ani asked Hunter as she followed him into the back room.

"Because it helps support the community. Can you grab the sandwich baskets?"

"One second." Ani pulled some kitchen shears out of a drawer and laid her sweatshirt on the oak table. She focused on the sweatshirt as she spoke. "You support your community every day, just by being here. Couldn't you skip one festival?" Ani took the shears and cut out the banded collar at the neckline of the sweatshirt. She held it up by the shoulders. *Still boxy, and not in an attractive way.*

"Couldn't you just follow one rule without arguing about it?"

Ani glanced up and caught his eye. "Why would I do that?"

"Exactly my point." He grinned.

Seriously, this guy made the world's most horrible Christmas sweatshirt look cute.

"I'm going to make your coffee while you finish mutilating your sweatshirt. How's a caffé breve sound?"

Ani sliced through the seam on the bottom band. "Sounds fantastic." She held the sweatshirt up again. Aside from removing the entire front, there wasn't much more she could do to improve it. "Wait." She dropped her voice. "Is Maia here yet?"

Hunter nodded.

"She's got that big project for her science class. Do you want to make my order wrong, so you have to give it to her?"

He raised a brow. "Are you suggesting giving up your coffee for someone else, out of the kindness of your heart?"

"No. I'm suggesting you accidentally make an Earl Grey tea with steamed milk and honey, which I won't drink, so it has to go somewhere." She snipped the other side seam. "*Then* you make my breve."

Ani pulled the sweatshirt over her long-sleeved T-shirt.

When her head emerged through the top, she caught the smug expression on Hunter's face.

"I'm not being nice," she said. "You're the one messing up drink orders."

Hunter raised his hands in mock surrender as he took steps back toward the espresso machine. "I wouldn't want to accuse you of supporting the community by helping a kid channel her inner artist."

"I'm getting some much-needed help. Plus, you always make such a fuss about setting up the heaters when she's out there. It's completely selfish on my part."

"Say what you like. I see a woman in a community-themed sweatshirt helping out a kid. That's Local behavior if I ever saw it."

Ani shook her head, trying to tamp down the conflicting emotions rising within her. She picked up the scissors and spun them around. "Do you want me to start running with scissors? Because you seem to need a reminder of the kind of woman you're dealing with. I've done it before and won't hesitate to do it again."

Hunter laughed, his bright smile lighting the room. Ani's heart knocked against her rib cage, nearly leaving her winded. She needed to stop flirting, fast.

What's the least romantic thing in this place?

"Sandwich baskets?" she asked.

Hunter seemed to snap out of the moment too. He shook his head. "Yeah, the bag's ready to go in the storeroom. Meet you out front?"

Hunter set the tea in front of Maia, ignoring her suspicious look. "Ani rejected the Earl Grey."

"Earl Grey tastes funny to me," Ani told her, following him out of the kitchen with the sandwich baskets.

Hunter kept his smile to himself as Ani masked her generosity. Over the last week, he'd watched her connect with

Maia. He was getting to know Ani well enough to call her bluff at this point. She wasn't incapable of caring, rather, she cared about others far too deeply for her own comfort.

"Are you coming to the outside fair thing?" she asked Maia.

Maia nodded, her hands wrapped tightly around the tea. "I like your sweatshirt."

"Really? That's weird, because it's horrible."

"It's so ugly, it's pretty," Maia said. Ani laughed, her head thrown back, her long hair coming loose from its knot.

"Sadly, you only get one if you're working tonight," Ani told her.

Maia turned her gaze on Hunter. "I wish I could work for Eighty Local."

"Maia, I promise to hire you as soon as you're old enough to work in the State of Oregon."

"You better," she said earnestly.

Hunter crouched down so he was eye level with Maia. "There will always be a job for you at Eighty Local. Your brother too."

A deep flush ran up Maia's face.

"Do you want to walk down to the festival with us or stay until Janet locks up in about an hour?"

"I should finish my homework," Maia said. "Then I'll come and see the tree lighting."

"How's your science project coming?" Ani asked, peering over Maia's shoulder. Maia slipped a worksheet over the paper she'd had out.

"Fine."

Ani leaned in closer. "That didn't look very science-y to me."

"No, I was taking a break."

Ani lifted the worksheet to uncover a sketch, reminiscent of the one Ani had done for the mural. This one featured a series of stylized women engaged in various activities: hiking, working, studying, shopping. In the center was a stylishly dressed woman with a lasso. Hunter couldn't stop himself from picking it up. "This is another mural, isn't it?"

Maia pressed her lips together and nodded.

Ani leaned over his shoulder to look at it, a strand of her hair brushing against his knuckles. It was unfair how incredibly *right* she smelled.

"It's for Second Chance Cowgirl," Maia said quietly.

"It's fantastic." Ani turned her bright smile on Maia. "What's Second Chance Cowgirl?"

Maia cleared her throat. Hunter could tell she was starting to feel embarrassed, so he said to Ani, "The fact that you've been here this long and haven't been to Second Chance Cowgirl is remiss on my part. Let's get downtown and I'll point it out to you."

Ani took the paper from him and gazed at it then at Maia. "This is really good. It fits with our mural, which would be nice cohesion for such a small town."

Maia nodded, hope radiated in her eyes. Hunter knew what the girl was thinking. Maia wanted Ani to pitch this to the store's owner, and the two of them could complete another mural. What he didn't know was if Ani could open up to the possibility of staying.

"You have an eye for this," Ani told her. Maia shrugged, took the paper from Ani and tucked it back into her notebook.

"Let's go," Hunter said. "Outcrop, Outside doesn't start until people have their sandwiches."

Ani threw the sack of sandwich baskets over her shoulder, imitating St. Nick. "We wouldn't want to disappoint all the good boys and girls in your ho-ho-hometown."

Maia laughed. Ani pretended to lumber to the door then gave Maia a big wave. Hunter grabbed Ani's coffee and followed her, like he'd been doing since the day she'd arrived.

Readying for Outcrop, Outside was always a challenge and the work, once he got there, was intense. But no matter how much he dreaded the quarterly festival, Hunter was always struck by the magic when he arrived.

Sparkling lights were strung across Main Street. The storefronts were all decked out in garlands of fir, juniper and holly. Over the last ten years, Outcrop had experienced a lot of positive growth. Old brick buildings that used to sit vacant were now leased to thriving businesses. Booths had been set up along the sidewalk all the way down to the town square where a massive Douglas fir would be lit at the end of the evening.

Normally, the lighting of the tree got Hunter excited, as it meant it was almost Christmas. Tonight, his heart constricted. Only eighteen days until Christmas meant twenty days left until the BES Gala.

"Is that Ani, the girl with the van?" The question shook Hunter out of his thoughts. Mr. Fareas stood on a ladder, fixing one of the hundreds of bulbs on the old-fashioned Christmas lights he had running along the porch of Outcrop Hardware, Tack and Feed.

Ani waved. "Hi, and yes, I'm Ani."

Mr. Fareas kept his eyes on the lights. "You can come work for me if you get tired of Hunter."

Hunter took half a step in front of Ani. "Don't even think about it." Arguing with Mr. Fareas was never a good idea, but Ani's help was worth fighting for.

The curmudgeonly keeper of OHTAF chuckled. "I pay well and could use the help."

Somehow, Hunter's arm slipped around Ani's shoulder in a wildly unplanned move. But rather than shake it off,

Ani stepped closer as she looked up at OHTAF. Her hair brushed against Hunter's cheek and he caught her scent. *Could he wrap both his arms around her, and then maybe ditch this whole festival?*

"I believe you," Ani told Mr. Fareas. "But will you serve me sweet potato fries?"

"Hunter's got me there," he said, giving Ani one of his rare smiles. "Looks like you're pretty happy where you are."

Ani blinked then seemed to realize she was tucked up under his arm. Her gaze met his. Hunter knew he *had* to drop his arm but kissing her seemed like a much better idea.

Get it together, Wallace. He had to knock some sense into his own head. Ani would be gone before Christmas. She'd said it a hundred times. She didn't believe in community or permanent connections. There couldn't be a woman less suited for him.

But Hunter couldn't seem to get that irrefutable fact through his titanium skull. There was something about Ani. She managed to lift the weight of expectation, the fear of failure, that had always rested so heavily on him. She made him feel free. It was her very impossibility that made him feel like anything was possible.

Hunter pulled his arm back. Something between relief and regret flashed across Ani's face. Then she stepped back, grinning wickedly as she pointed at him.

"You've got competition!"

"You've got a lot of nerve thinking you'd last two days at OHTAF. You think I'm grumpy? Mr. Fareas smiles three times a year."

"And I got one of the three smiles. How special am I?"

"You're special all right…" he muttered.

"Uncle Hunter!" Jackson was waving at them from the

Garcias' tamale booth. Hunter waved back and dove into the crowd, greeting people and introducing Ani. She would be gone before Christmas, but the least he could do was make sure she had the best memories of Outcrop.

By the time they made it to the Eighty Local booth, his brothers Bowman and Ash, and Ash's fiancée, Violet, were already there. Caleb had the digital register set up, along with a cashbox.

"What do you think?" he heard Ash ask Ani.

She shook her head. "I'm not sure I've ever seen this much Christmas crammed together in one place."

Ash chuckled. "We like our holidays in Outcrop."

What had her experience with Christmas been like before this?

"Hey, speaking of which," Bowman said, "our family's got this thing next weekend. Can you help out?"

Hunter spoke over his brother. "Ani's got a lot going on. It's not fair to ask her to help on the ranch."

"Of course, I'll help," she said.

Hunter wrapped his hand around her arm and drew her toward him. "You don't have to help. You've done so much already."

"Your parents are letting me stay on their property. You're supplying all my meals. I can help for one day." Ani's eyes connected with his. She had no idea what they were asking of her, and when she realized what the Mistletoe Festival was, he suspected she'd balk.

She leaned in toward him, keeping her eyes on the ground. "I don't want you or your family to think I'm freeloading."

"No one thinks that."

"I'm just not community-oriented, like you are. But I'm willing to admit Outcrop is a pretty special place, and if I can leave it a little better than I found it, I'm in."

"Great," Bowman interrupted.

Ani glanced up and Hunter allowed himself to gaze at her. *Leave it better.* She would be leaving. She'd always planned on leaving and she was going to follow through. His heart sank another notch as he continued to stare at her.

That meant he caught her entire expression as Bowman said, "The Mistletoe Festival is a lot of work, but it's important to the ranch. We put you with Hunter. You two are in charge of the horses."

HORSES? MISTLETOE? Could not one of these people have thought to mention these land mines before asking her help?

Bowman continued to explain the festival, but Ani wasn't tracking his words. She would be working with Hunter and those magnificent horses. She could still feel Bella's gaze, the soft pressure of her muzzle against her shoulder as the horse suggested they take a ride, go tearing across the fields and over fences in what had once felt like the ultimate freedom to Ani.

She couldn't risk it. This place was tempting enough as it was. And it didn't take much to play the scenario out to its natural end. She would get tangled up in Hunter, in the horses, in the false comfort of his perfect family. Then they would all realize just how imperfect she was. In order to stay, they'd want her to change, and she'd never be the person they wanted her to be. It would be like her own family but so much worse because she actually cared what these people thought. In the end, she'd have to walk away, but with her heart even more attached than it already was.

"So, yeah, thanks. It means a lot," Bowman finished. Ani nodded. Hunter was still watching her, gauging her reaction. She shook out her shoulders and tried to act casual.

"No big deal. I'm happy to help."

"You really don't have to," Hunter reiterated. "Caleb, would you prefer Ani's help at the restaurant that day?"

Caleb shook his head. "I got it."

Yeah, that was the expected answer. Ani knew Caleb was itching for solo time in the kitchen. He was a talented chef and enjoyed the challenge of holding down Eighty Local on his own.

"You know what would be great," Caleb continued in an overtly casual tone that suggested he'd been wanting to bring something up for a while, "is if Maia could help out at the festival. It's kinda hard to fill her time on weekends and I know she'd love to see the horses."

All of Ani's selfish, petulant thoughts came to an abrupt halt. Here she was, indulging her inner drama queen, while there was a kid who would love a day of mistletoe and horses at the ranch.

"Sure," Hunter said. "I'll let my mom know. She'll find a job for Maia."

"It will be fun," Ani attempted to convince herself. She glanced back at Caleb, with so many questions about Maia. But Caleb was now focused on the customers who were arriving. From the snippets Maia had offered while working on the mural, Ani had learned that their mom wasn't in the picture and their dad had to travel a lot for work. This left Maia in Caleb's care, which was a lot for the young man. Ani got the sense he didn't like asking for help but, like Maia, was appreciative when it was offered. "Okay, what do I do here?"

That turned out to be a ridiculous question. A line quickly formed as people ordered the seasonal cranberry turkey sandwich, and everyone in the booth just tried to keep up. They functioned as a team, hands and banter flying as they assembled baskets. Ani found herself laughing with Violet as they took orders and cash. Occasionally, other members of the Wallace family would drift by the back of the booth, picking up messed-up orders, asking if they needed any help.

"Ani needs to walk around Outcrop, Outside." Clara was trying to convince her brother.

"I'm good," Ani said.

"You only say so because you are ignorant of the bliss that is Three Sisters Chocolatiers," Violet told her.

Ani laughed. "I can check it out another time."

"Yes, but calories don't count tonight." Clara's brown eyes were wide and serious. "It's a town ordinance. Also, you look adorable in that sweatshirt."

Hunter rolled his eyes.

Talk about adorable in a ridiculous sweatshirt.

"Fine," Clara conceded. "But you one hundred percent have to come to the tree lighting."

"We'll be there," Hunter told her.

"Thank you." Clara pointed at Ani. "Text me if you want to take a break and get some chocolates."

Clara drifted into the crowd and slipped under the arm of a tall, handsome cowboy. He wrapped both arms around her and kissed the top of her head. Beyond them, the town festival swirled.

Over time, the line receded then disappeared, giving way to a trickle of people coming back for seconds or thirds. Caleb left to join Maia. Bowman slipped off to find his fiancée at the medical tent.

It was about nine o'clock when the lights overhead blinked out then came back on, like someone had tripped on an extension cord. Excitement rose in the crowd and everyone started moving in one direction.

"Has the mother ship arrived?" Ani asked.

"It's time for the lighting of the tree," Ash said. "You guys should head out. Violet and I can hold it down here."

"Don't you want to watch the lights with Jackson?" Hunter asked.

Ash looked down the street at a group of teenage boys joking around. One of them was attempting something that might be called dancing, but Ani wasn't sure the meaning of the verb stretched that far. "My son is having fun with a good group of kids." He smiled at Violet as he slipped his hand around her waist. "I think I can leave it at that."

"Good call. Ani?" Hunter turned to her. "You're way overdue for a break. Let's go check it out."

She wrinkled her nose. "It's not really my type of thing."

"You've never been to the tree lighting in Outcrop. How would you know?"

"I've been to a tree lighting."

Growing up, there had been any number of public holiday events she'd been expected to attend. Dress up, show up, try not to think about the massive fight her parents had had in the car on the way there. Yeah, she'd been to a few tree lightings, and watched the anger of her family smolder in the glow.

"This takes less than thirty seconds," Ash said. "Humor me and keep an eye on Hunter."

Ani gave her head a small shake. "All right. Let's go honor the birth of Jesus by putting twinkle lights in a tree. Totally makes sense."

Hunter grabbed his Stetson and handed Ani her jacket. Cool air rushed in all around them as they left the warmth of the booth. Ani tucked her hands deeper into her coat pockets. She could create her own heat. There was absolutely no need to lean into Hunter as they walked together.

Hunter took half a step closer to her, smelling all warm and Hunter-y. Ani glanced back at the booth to distract herself, just in time to see Violet catch a football and launch it toward Jackson and his friends. Hunter followed her eyes then chuckled. "She's the head football coach at the high school, and one of the most competitive people I know."

The kids scrambled toward the ball and a young woman in their midst hopped up to catch it. Ash grumbled something about the tree lighting. The kids took off in a pack, jogging toward the park, leaving Violet and Ash alone in the empty street under the fairy lights, which seemed to be exactly what they'd wanted.

Hunter nudged her elbow with his, recalling her attention. Ani nudged back.

"Help me out with your not-celebrating-holidays thing," he said. "I don't get it."

She shrugged her left shoulder. "You don't have to get it."

"But I want to."

Ani sighed. "In my experience, holidays are about pretending to be happy, to 'feel the magic.' For a lot of people, holidays are about consuming more food than they want, more presents than they need, and more family than anyone can stand. That's not fun, it's just wasteful."

Hunter took her arm as they neared the crowd, indicating she move to a small rise in the park. He kept his eyes off her, but his hand on her elbow.

"For some people, there's not enough food, no presents, and no family. I'm inclined to celebrate what I have, and help others find what they need."

Yeah. That was Hunter: first-rate human and excellent reminder of how petty she was.

Ani glanced around then asked, "What will Maia do on Christmas?"

Hunter leaned closer and spoke quietly. "Caleb has a bonus coming, and he'll be off on Christmas Eve and Christmas. He'll take care of her."

Ani nodded, feeling an uncomfortable pressure in her

throat. Sometimes the world seemed so dark and the people in it so very alone. Then someone like Hunter did what he could to shine some light in the darkness.

"Look up," he said.

Ani glanced at Hunter, but he nodded to the tree. She turned in time to see the magnificent fir light up with thousands of fairy lights. It shone against the dark, cold sky, and reflected off the faces of the crowd. The tree didn't just look beautiful, it felt beautiful.

She looked at Hunter to see if he felt it too. He was smirking.

"You said 'Awww!'"

She stepped away. "No, I didn't."

"Yes, you did. The lights went on and, with everyone else around here, you said, 'Awww!'"

Ani scoffed. "I was yawning." She gave an exaggerated stretch. "Super boring, huge tree being lit up."

"You like the tree. Admit it."

Ani stared up at Hunter, falling a little deeper into his sparking brown-and-green eyes. There were a lot of things to like around here.

"Fine. I like the pretty tree."

"And you realize you made it through the entire festival without breaking, or even challenging, one rule."

"Um. Not true. Pretty sure Clara said I *had* to eat chocolates."

Hunter nodded, mock serious. "That's my fault. We've probably got five minutes before they lock the doors on Three Sisters. Wanna make a run for it?" He held out his hand and readjusted his Stetson as he prepared to sprint to the chocolate shop.

Did she want to hold Hunter's hand and run toward chocolate? It was a terrible idea, but also a really good one. His brilliant smile broke out, warming her like a long, hot summer day. That smile was the one flaw in Ani's plan. Yeah, she wanted the work, and the cozy cabin, and everything she could learn at Eighty Local. But no matter what she told herself, what Ani really wanted was to make Hunter smile. That type of attachment could only end in heartache.

Ani slipped her hand into Hunter's. "Just so you know, I'm going to break a major rule next week."

"The women from the Bend Equestrian Society are coming for their tasting on Tuesday. If you could wait until it's over, I'd appreciate it."

"You're making a rule about when I can break rules? That's a new bar. I'm almost impressed."

Hunter laughed and tugged at her hand. Ani followed. Apparently, the only rules she'd be breaking tonight were her own.

CHAPTER TEN

ANI MADE IT to Tuesday with any number of minor infractions, but she didn't manage to break a major rule. That was a bit of a disappointment. Currently, she was poised to bail on the kitchen and give some knives a much-needed sharpening. It would annoy Hunter, but it wouldn't have the full effect she was hoping for.

Tomorrow is another day.

Ani clutched the bundle to her chest, walking quickly to the rear exit.

"Ani?" Hunter called after her.

She didn't pause in her stride. "It's hardly going to take any time at all."

"Are you sure?"

Ani met Caleb's eye and tried to keep from laughing.

"It's six knives," she called out over the hum of the dishwasher. "They desperately need to be sharpened. I'm parked thirty feet from the kitchen. If there's some slicing emergency, Caleb can come get me." Ani put her hand on the back door, ready to bolt.

Hunter's steady footfall came from the kitchen and then his frame filled the doorway. *Not helpful.* The man somehow got better looking as each day passed. She wouldn't have thought it possible, but every morning when they hopped into the truck, there he was, more handsome than the day before.

Over the last week, she'd learned that getting out of

his presence was the best way to ensure she didn't break even more of her own rules and start kissing the man in the middle of his restaurant.

"You need this done, and I can do it." It was hard to keep her eyes off him when he leaned against the door-jamb, stretching his biceps against the frame. But Ani could do hard things.

Hunter tilted his head. "Yeah. Or not. We still have so much to do, and both of us will miss work Saturday for the Mistletoe Festival."

"There is a reasonable load of work to do before the gala," she corrected him. "Maia and I will have the mural finished early next week."

He shook his head and glanced back into the kitchen. "Gotta be honest, I'm glad it's taking your battery so long to get here. I couldn't have done this without you."

She nodded, clutching the knives she'd wrapped up in a series of kitchen towels to her chest. He could have done it without her, by working himself into a pulp. The pace of the restaurant was intense, even without the pressure of finishing the addition. But more shocking than the pace was Hunter's reaction to it. He thrived in the blur of work, his focus sharpening with each new crisis. It was as though he needed the world around him to move as fast as his thoughts.

Outcrop would definitely go down as a favorite adventure. The work, the people, the smell of sage in the air. The complicated, driven man with earthy brown-green eyes. It was enough to make her dread the arrival of her battery.

That meant she absolutely had to get moving as soon as it arrived.

Hunter cleared his throat. "Hey, speaking of the gala, do you remember that some women from the Bend Equestrian Society are stopping by this afternoon for a tasting?"

Like she'd forget.

Ani held up the bundle of knives. "I'm trying to get out of your hair."

The realization finally dawned on him. "Oh. Great idea. Right. Get out of here, go sharpen my knives, Rubber Tramp."

Ani laughed. "Sure thing, Local."

He shook his head in mock disappointment. "How many times do I have to tell you Local's not an insult?"

Ani shrugged one shoulder and turned to the door. "Like you're some master of insults yourself? Some of the greatest people in history were rubber tramps. Marco Polo. Ibn Battuta."

"I don't think rubber was invented in the Medieval period."

"Same concept, less technology." Ani pushed open the door. Then she glanced back at Hunter. "Can you find out if she sold Olive?"

Hunter's face fell blank. "What?"

"That woman, Holly...or something. Last time she was here, she said she was thinking about selling her horse because she couldn't get it to do what she wanted. I'm just curious if she sold it."

Hunter nodded. He was clearly confused, but he nodded. "You want me to ask about it?"

"No. Of course not. If it comes up." Ani shrugged her shoulders so many times there was no way it could come off as casual. "It was just funny. Like, who has trouble training a Dutch Warmblood?" Hunter shot her a look. Way too many words had fallen out of her mouth. "I'm gonna go sharpen these."

Ani pushed the back door open and trotted out into the cold. Within minutes, she was back in her van, pulling on extra layers for warmth, about to embark on a task in the quiet privacy of her home.

It felt kinda weird.

Ani pulled out the honing steel and set the knives in a row on her counter. Somehow, the cold seemed to make the world quieter. Either that or she was so used to the noise of Eighty Local, any relative quiet felt conspicuous.

The knives Hunter provided were American made. She studied the angle of the blade then imitated the movement she'd watched on a YouTube video moments before. Ani's breathing slowed and minutes stretched out as she focused. She drew the blade across the steel then repeated the action.

Time flowed. Ani gave each knife her full attention. They were beautiful, each gleaming in the cold sunlight as she restored them to their original function.

Gravel crunched as a car pulled up next to her van. Ani snapped out of her focus. Hunter's sister Clara parked poorly and climbed out of the driver's side.

Clara examined the angle of her car. "I have got to learn how to park."

Ani smiled. "Do you?"

Clara gestured to her vehicle, which skewed awkwardly between spaces.

"Tell me that's acceptable."

"It's so bad, I'd almost think it was intentional." Ani set a knife aside.

"Right? I'm literally the worst parker in the world."

"But your outfit matches your car." Ani gestured between Clara, dressed in a cream wool coat, camel-colored scarf, cognac boots and gloves, and her pearly-white SUV with its honey-colored leather interior.

"So satisfying." Clara looked down at her coat then at the car. "How are you? And what's this?"

With the Wallace family, Ani had learned conversation flowed fast and outsiders just needed to keep up.

"I'm sharpening knives," Ani said, holding up a cleaver.

"Oooh! Does that mean Hunter's calming down about the gala?"

"Or it could mean I came out here with as many knives as Hunter would let me get my hands on to escape."

Clara smiled and poked her head in the slider door. "Can I check out your van? I've been dying to."

"Come on in. This is my kitchen," Ani said, looking around at the four-by-three-foot space. "Kitchen-slash-yoga studio."

Clara laughed. Ani ran her hand along the counter.

"Induction heating unit, fridge and sink." Ani pumped the pedal by the water jugs with her foot. "Water is pulled from this jug—" she indicated one of the five-gallon containers "—then empties into the other." She pulled back a curtain to expose shelves. "And this is food storage. Which is looking pretty bleak."

Ani showed Clara her bedroom, with the cozy bed flanked with cubbies, then explained her system for everything kept in deeper storage under the bed.

"I'm so impressed."

Ani soaked up the compliment. "I'm proud of it. I was very young and naive when I started. I had to do a lot of things over, but I finally got it right."

"What about, like, an address? For taxes and voting and everything. Do you use your parents' home as your residence?"

"No. Absolutely not. I have a PO box in Portland. I check it every few months. It ties me to Oregon, which is kind of a pain. Sometimes I think I should set up residency right in the middle of the US, so I have more options."

Clara shuddered. "How can your home be a post office box? Don't you get lonely?"

Ani raised one shoulder. "I am alone, yes. And it can get lonely. But I'm free."

"Free from what?"

"Everything. Free from expectations, commitments, letting people down. Free to be who I want, go where I want to go."

Clara shook her head. "I really hope you get that I respect you, but I'm confused. I can't imagine *wanting* to be alone."

"I can't imagine wanting to be tied down."

"My job, my whole life, is about helping people open themselves up to love. Like, I seriously think I'm making the world a better place, one relationship at a time. That's my goal."

Ani nodded. "I can respect that. I don't understand it, but I respect it."

"You don't want a relationship?"

An image of her parents, crisp with hatred, squaring off against each other in the entrance hall came into her mind. How tragic to imagine something like that evolving between her and Hunter.

"No, I don't."

Clara tilted her head, questioning her. Ani continued. "It's not relationships I have a problem with, it's permanence. You know what I mean?"

"I honestly have no idea."

"I don't want to get trapped into something awful."

"What if you got trapped into something wonderful? Like, what if you got trapped in a place with unlimited coffee and scones and puppies?"

"Puppies grow up."

"Into *dogs*! Literally the only thing better than a puppy is a good dog."

Ani laughed. As much as she disagreed with Clara, she could see she truly believed in relationships. And being around Hunter was almost enough to make Ani want to believe in relationships too. But that was never going to happen. He was the ultimate hometown boy and she lived on the road.

Another car pulled into the lot. Clara looked over Ani's shoulder and visibly tensed. Holly Banks emerged from the Escalade. The other women followed, with large sunglasses and long down jackets.

"The Bend Equestrian Society has returned," Ani said.

"That's why I'm here." Clara eyed the women.

"Are you part of the Equestrian Society?"

Clara laughed. "Oh, no. I love horses. I love my horse, Shelby. But I am not interested in competitive horsemanship."

The words *competitive horsemanship* shot through her. Ani's nervous system quivered, like a high-strung Thoroughbred.

"But Piper and I did Equestrian Youth Competition when we were younger. I've known those women most of my life." Clara examined the pack sharply.

Ani picked up a knife and turned it in the sunlight. Neither Clara nor Piper had seemed at all familiar. But, given their sunny, generous nature, it was unlikely they would have risen the ranks in EYC. And given Ani's nature, she never would have noticed a couple of happy sisters competing in the lower echelons. The hunter/jumper girls at Ani's level had been intensely competitive, and cutthroat.

"And that one has her eye on Hunter." Clara gestured at Holly.

The knife slipped from Ani's fingers, clattering as it hit the counter.

"Th-the snotty one?"

Clara crossed her arms and nodded, her focus still on Holly. "Piper and I try not to interfere with Hunter and his haphazard approach to dating. But I am not going to let Holly Banks get her hooks into my brother."

Ani swallowed hard. "But she's so rude to him."

"She's rude to everyone. It's her natural state of being. But she has found every and any excuse to stop by Eighty Local once or twice a week for the last four months." Clara looked up at Ani. "Have you not noticed that my brother is super good-looking and, like, a really creative and hard-working person?"

Um, yeah. The thought crossed my mind.

Ani picked up the knife and resumed her work. "Right. So, it's unlikely he'd go for Holly."

"Men can be incredibly clueless."

Ani started. The words sounded so harsh coming from the optimistic, cheerful matchmaker. Clara quickly amended the statement. "In my professional opinion." Ani laughed, and Clara went on. "Women can be clueless too. Most people are when it comes to love. Even matchmakers."

Holly had paused at the door and pulled out a compact to check her makeup. Ani set the knife down carefully.

"I don't see Hunter going for Holly," Ani said. "I mean, the woman can't even handle a Dutch Warmblood. She's not strong enough for Hunter."

Clara narrowed her eyes and studied her. Then her smile reappeared and Ani felt as though she could see directly into her soul. "Right. I think he needs someone smart, resourceful, hardworking and funny. Someone who loves everything about him but is willing to call him out when he needs it."

Ani pressed her lips together and nodded.

Hunter is deeply attached to this town, these people, this patch of ground. I live on the road. He is not your man, and Holly is not your problem.

"Holly's not really interested in Hunter, she's interested in the idea of Hunter." Clara focused on the group of women. "She would try to change him. Get him out of the kitchen, into a business suit, franchises, that sort of thing. Hunter would hate it."

Ani snorted. "Good luck to her then. Hunter won't give up cooking. I don't see him changing for any woman."

Clara tilted her head, debating this. "My brother struggles with Love Rule Number Two."

"There are love rules?" *These Wallaces literally have rules for everything.*

"I'll print you out a copy." Clara snapped open a leather notebook and made herself a note. She continued speaking as she did so, "Love Rule Number Two. *To find love, love yourself first.* Hunter feels like he's a failure, which couldn't be farther from the truth."

Ani gestured to the full parking lot, getting fuller by the minute with hungry patrons. "How can he possibly think that?"

"Sometimes people get stuck. My brother was desperate to prove himself to this community when he was younger. He felt like he'd failed academically and let our parents down. Then he just got into the pattern of trying to prove himself, over and over again." Clara shook her head. "He's got to be exhausted."

"But your parents are so supportive. And he's done so much. I mean this place is incredible."

"Exactly." Clara grinned at Ani. "So, he doesn't need someone to change him. He needs someone to kick him in the behind and get him to realize how awesome he is."

Ani swallowed hard and refocused on the knives. She didn't need to save Hunter. She needed to keep herself from getting stuck among people who would grow to resent her. On the road, she was often lonely, but she was free. *You can't disappoint someone if they don't expect anything from you.*

"I'd better get in there," Clara said. Her dimples disappeared and she narrowed her eyes. "I'm here to make sure those women treat my brother with respect."

"THANKS FOR TAKING time out of your day for this tasting," Hunter said.

Shawna and Holly did not pause in their conversation as he spoke, and another woman was deeply engrossed in her phone. The fourth nodded and then looked around blankly.

"Can I have a latte?" the fourth woman asked.

Hunter glanced up and around the room. He and Ani had finished nearly every detail of the events hall in anticipation of this meeting. Over the last two days, he'd prepared a sampling of six different hors d'oeuvres, and created a specialty drink for the occasion. He'd been working nonstop to get ready for the tasting today. He had not factored in espresso.

"It might work best for me to take you through the tasting first then grab coffee drinks while we finish up with details."

"I would totally love a coffee," Shawna said. "Do you have any holiday drink specials? Like a peppermint latte?"

Hunter shuddered at the thought of peppermint anywhere near his tasting menu.

"Hello!" Hunter looked up sharply to see Clara enter the room. "Sorry I'm late."

Hunter sent her a look suggesting that she hadn't been invited and therefore couldn't be late. She hugged him.

"Look how cute you are!" Clara said to someone in the group. "I love your sweater!" They all jumped on the compliment bandwagon and swung nice words back and forth for a good three minutes. The espresso problem had been averted.

"So whatcha got?" Clara redirected the conversation back to Hunter once everyone's ego was appropriately placated. His sister really was brilliant.

"I thought I'd start you all off with the signature drink for the evening, the Madras Mule." Hunter moved toward the bar where four copper cups with his new invention waited.

"I think it's called a Moscow Mule," Shawna said.

"If it were an ordinary drink, it might be," Clara chirped. "My brother probably invented something special for your big night."

"I did." Hunter approached the table with his tray. "House-made ginger beer, a lime wedge, and wheat whiskey sourced from New Basin Distillery in Madras."

He set a drink in front of each woman then looked at Clara. "I forgot to make a mule for you." *Because I didn't know you were coming.* "Let me get one started."

"No, I'm good."

"You sure?" His sister enjoyed his cocktails but was careful not to drink alcohol when her anxiety flared. *Was everything okay with Jet?* Hunter couldn't have been happier with her choice of husband, but he knew change could be hard for Clara.

She must have read his thoughts because she placed both hands on the table before her and gave him a big grin. "I'm fabulous."

Hunter bent down and kissed the top of her head. "Good."

"I cannot stop staring at your ring," Holly said to Clara. "When I get married, I want something similar."

Hunter managed to turn his back before rolling his eyes. The thing was so big, it should have planets orbiting it. When he'd told Jet that, the man's response had been that his world revolved around Clara. It was still hard to keep from hurling.

"How's the mule?" Clara asked.

The ladies sipped then smiled. It was a very good drink.

"Love!" one woman said.

"Is this on the normal menu? I've never seen it before." Holly took a second long drink.

Hunter cleared his throat. *Did they not know what they were paying for?* "I created it for this event. It goes with your menu."

"Seriously?" Shawna asked. Then she looked at Holly. "I told you we should have it here."

"What's on the menu for the gala?" Clara redirected the party, again.

"Did you make up the whole menu?" Holly asked, suspicious.

"The whole thing!" Clara said, sparkling like only his sister could. "What's up first?"

The menu was a thoughtful pairing of low-calorie canapés and rich comfort foods. As he'd expected, the women reached for the cranberry, wild rice and radicchio wraps first, but polished off the mini grilled-cheese sandwiches sooner.

Forty minutes and a lot of canapés later, Hunter pushed his way through one of the swinging doors into the kitchen, only to find Ani listening up against the other.

"Anything interesting going on in there?" he asked.

"Fascinating." Ani stood and crossed her arms. "How do you stand them?"

Hunter placed his hands on his hips and studied the floor. "My parents always said most people are doing the best they can with the tools they've been given. I try to remember that."

"Generous of you."

"It helps that Clara showed up to keep me from lumbering around and offending everyone."

Ani's eyes met his. "She's got your back."

"She does. Clara's always been there for me, even when it was hard. I…" Hunter stopped. This was getting deeper than he meant to.

Ani held his gaze, questioning.

"Let's just say I wasn't the easiest Wallace kid, and Clara always shows up to help me be my best." Hunter cleared his throat. "You have any brothers or sisters?"

Ani nodded. Hunter raised his brow, inviting her to talk about it. She shook her head. "It's a situation."

Hunter didn't push. There was a lot to Ani's home life she wasn't sharing.

"What do they want now?" Ani nodded to the events hall.

"Presently, they're a little tipsy and requesting holiday-themed espresso drinks."

Ani laughed.

It had been a long afternoon, and Hunter gave in and stared at her.

"Let me get the coffee."

"Are you sure?" Hunter asked. "You seem pretty busy listening at the door."

"I can take a break."

"But can you keep from putting dish soap in someone's cappuccino?"

Ani tilted her head and grinned. "I think I can. But I might go a step worse and make them all decaf."

Hunter laughed. Without thinking, he reached out and

took her hand. "Thanks. Can you do a café Borgia? It's a mocha with orange zest and whipped cream."

Her eyes lit up at the challenge. "I'll google it."

"Thank you."

Ani nodded. He almost thought he saw her blush. Hunter forced his fingers to release hers and took a step toward the events center.

"Can you come grab them in a few minutes?" she asked a little too casually.

"You don't want to bring them in? There's some fine quality gossip getting slung around."

She shrugged.

"Fine," he said dramatically, pushing back into the events hall. "Thank you."

"No problem. I've got your back."

He shook his head. "Five minutes into the Mistletoe Festival and you'll probably regret those words."

She lifted one shoulder in what looked like feigned confidence. "How bad can it be?"

She had no idea.

CHAPTER ELEVEN

THERE WAS MISTLETOE EVERYWHERE. Everywhere. Like, Ani hadn't been aware there was so much mistletoe in the entire world. In the barn, it hung from the rafters, the railings, over stall doors and along the arena walls. It adorned the wagons for the hayride, was suspended from tents for the wreath making, and garnished the hot cocoa table.

Did they think someone might find refuge under the table, so they took precautions and made sure you could kiss there too?

"You doing okay?" Hunter asked.

Inasmuch as he had that Stetson on, and was looking down at her with a concerned smile, and they were literally, completely surrounded by suggestions to kiss, the answer was no. She was very much at risk of grabbing her boss by his puffer vest and giving in.

"I'm fine." She shrugged one shoulder. "I'm a little worried about the world-wide shortage of mistletoe you all have touched off with this. But other than that, I'm fine."

Hunter laughed, which was not helping the situation. "Bowman's responsible for it. Mistletoe is a parasite, it's not good for our Oregon white oak trees. He starts collecting it in November. This stuff has been piling up in the bunkhouse for a month and a half."

Ani glanced at the bunkhouse, imagining Hunter and a whole pile of mistletoe. Was he trying to kill her?

"Ani! Hunter, hi there!" Lacy came trotting across the

arena on Bella. Hunter's mom looked perfectly in her element in a pair of blue jeans, boots and a cozy red jacket. The tack and Western saddle were high quality, but not flashy. Bella carried her proudly and gave Ani a look reminding her the offer of a ride still stood. Ani steeled herself. This was not her life. She could enjoy the day, and the experience, but this was not her life.

Lacy swung out of the saddle and handed her the reins. Ani's hand instinctively closed around them. Bella pressed her nose against Ani's shoulder.

"She likes you," Lacy said. "Bowman said as much, but this is impressive." Lacy ran a hand down Bella's muzzle and spoke to the horse. "You're normally such a picky girl."

Bella gazed into Lacy's eyes, suggesting that *selective* was a better word. Ani gave in and scratched Bella's ears.

"You and Hunter are in the arena. Hunter knows the drill. We've got two geldings saddled up, you help each child onto the horse, walk them twice around the arena, and try not to step on the parents while they snap a million pictures, then move on to the next kid. If the parents have questions about Canadian Horses, Ani, you can refer them to a family member. This is a community event, but it's also a sales event. People may not buy today, but if they consider buying a horse anytime in the future, we want their first thought to be Wallace Ranch."

"Got it." Ani nodded. It was unlikely anyone she'd known from the horse world would be here. Canadians were too practical of a choice for the crowd she used to hang out with.

Lacy continued. "And Hunter, I know it's a lot for you to take this day off, what with the big gala coming up. We really appreciate it."

Hunter stiffened. "It's nothing, Mom. I wouldn't miss this."

Lacy looked him in the eye. "You're doing too much."

Hunter tried to interrupt her, but she spoke over him. "No one expects you to run a restaurant and a ranch full-time."

Hunter stared out over the arena. "You and Dad had full-time jobs, and you ran this place. I can manage."

"Your dad and I had jobs that allowed us flexibility in the summer, and this ranch started with two breeding mares and a big mortgage. It was nothing like it is now."

"You built it from the ground up. The least I can do is keep it running."

Lacy sighed and Ani could tell this wasn't the first time they'd had this discussion. "Your siblings can handle the ranch."

"I'll do my fair share," Hunter shot back.

"Why are you so driven?"

Hunter turned away, heat rising in his face. *What was going on here?* In Ani's experience, most parents complained their kids weren't doing enough. This was the exact opposite problem.

The noise of a trailer backing up caught her attention. Hunter's posture changed and a low groan escaped from his chest. "You have got to be kidding me."

Ani and Lacy followed his gaze to where Clara was wheeling a recycling bin out of the back of a horse trailer.

"I tried to talk her out of it," Lacy said.

"What is it?" Ani asked.

"Larry," Hunter said dryly.

Clara's husband carefully tilted the recycling bin and lifted the lid. A beak peeked out, followed by a scrambling mass of feathers and legs.

"Larry!" Hunter's nephew Jackson called out and raced up to the bird. Larry squawked then pecked at Jackson's boots. The teenager laughed and helped Clara settle a sort of wreathlike collar/harness around the emu's chest.

"The Christmas Emu," Lacy said. Then she gave a sigh and smiled. "It's amazing to see Clara so relaxed."

Hunter nodded and wrapped an arm around his mom as they watched Clara lead the bird from the trailer.

"Do not let that thing near the horses," Ash warned.

"He's fine!" Clara called back.

"He's not gonna be if he spooks the herd."

"Speaking of horses," Hunter said, gesturing to the arena, "Ani and I better get started. People are arriving."

"Is Maia here?" Ani asked.

"She should be soon. I've asked her to take pictures for the website."

"Is she a good photographer?" Hunter asked.

"Who knows?" Lacy grinned. "I just hope she has fun today."

Ani warmed at Lacy's comment. Maia deserved a fun day on the ranch.

Ani, however, needed to be careful about how much fun she had and not become even more attached to this place. But if a person was trying to avoid fun, they really shouldn't watch Hunter Wallace help little kids on horses. He was always at his best in the middle of a crowd, but here he was like Cowboy Santa.

"Up you go!" he said, swinging a little girl onto a horse. The child giggled, bouncing in the saddle.

"What's his name?" she asked.

"This is Hopper," Hunter told her. "What's your name?"

"Fatima."

"Okay, Fatima, you ready?"

She gave a big, wide-eyed nod of her head. Hunter's grin flashed as he backed up, holding the reins and keeping a watchful eye on the child.

"We're riding!" the girl cried out.

Hopper, a patient and steady horse, walked slowly

around the arena with little prompting from Hunter. The girl's mother snapped dozens of pictures, and Ani was fairly certain some of them included the handsome man in a Stetson leading her daughter on the horse. He chatted easily with everyone, so happy to be there, on his family's ranch, with horses and kids.

Ani pulled in a deep breath and patted the gentle horse named Midnight she'd been assigned. Midnight gave her a comforting nuzzle. She could do this. She could help out with the horses and not completely unravel all the work she'd done over the last few years to get used to not being around them.

"Is it my turn?"

Ani glanced down to see a boy in jeans and boots, miniature versions of what his father wore. Hunter would have a son like this someday, dressed just like dad.

"Yes," she said, gesturing to the stool next to her horse. "Step right up."

The boy studied her then got a shy smile on his face. "Aren't you the marshmallow lady?"

It was the little boy who'd been at Eighty Local with his grandpa. *Perfect*. If there was one kid on earth willing to give her leeway, it was this little man. "I am. That makes you the Marshmallow Kid!"

"Yes, ma'am!" The boy's cowboy hat slipped over his eyes as he nodded in approval of the name.

His dad laughed. "That's a pretty good title for this guy."

"Let's get you on your steed," she said. "The West won't be safe until the Marshmallow Kid is in the saddle."

She gave the horse a gentle tug, but Midnight didn't need a lot of urging. He walked carefully around the edge of the arena. The child's father fell in next to her, asking about the Canadian Horses. Ani found she had plenty to say. She knew about the responsibility and empathy a child learned in caring for a horse, could approximate the costs and wholeheartedly recommend a Canadian over the flashier, high-strung breeds.

The day flew by as Ani gave horseback rides and avoided clumps of mistletoe. Occasionally, she caught a glimpse of Clara as she led her emu around the property, Piper giving instructions in the wreath-making tent, or one of the other Wallaces keeping the festival running. For the most part, though, she was lost in the moment of sharing these magnificent horses with others. Bella, still saddled, stood at the side of the arena, watching. As the humans decided whether or not to buy a horse, Bella was taking note of which humans were worthy of the honor.

"Ani." Ash stood at the side of the arena and gestured to her.

She helped a little girl from the saddle and trotted over to Hunter's oldest brother. He pointed to a family talking to his parents at the information booth. "That's number five."

Was she in trouble?

"That's the fifth family that's walked straight from your ride over to the information booth and put down money to buy a horse."

"Oh." Ani straightened. The family Ash was pointing to was a great fit for a Canadian. "They're nice people. I think they're ready for a horse."

Ash chuckled. "And after talking to you, they feel the same way. Most people come here and just get a feel for Canadians. Our sales take place throughout the year. Not many people put money down on this day."

Ani warmed. Ash wasn't the most effusive of the Wallace family, not by a long shot. His sincere appreciation felt like a gift.

"What's she done this time?" Hunter asked, sauntering over.

"She just covered Mom and Dad's next vacation. Ani's
selling horses while you're over there messing around."

Hunter shook his head. "What are you even doing
today?"

"I'm in charge."

"If you're so 'in charge,' why is there an emu running
around?"

Ash glowered at Hunter then turned around to where
a group of kids had gathered around Larry. In the background, a familiar car caught Ani's eye. A big shiny Escalade. Holly exited the car, nose wrinkled, searching for
something. Then she turned, looked straight at Ani, and
waved.

THE BLOOD RUSHED from Ani's face so quickly Hunter was
worried she might pass out. She stared at the parking area
like she'd been slapped. Ash furrowed his brows. Hunter
shook his head in response. He didn't know what was going
on any more than Ash did.

Ash cleared his throat. "You two had a break yet?"

"No," Hunter said more loudly than necessary. "Let's
go grab something to eat."

"I'm not hungry," Ani whispered.

"Then let's go for a walk."

"Go take a ride," Ash said. Hunter made eye contact
with his brother and tried to communicate that Ani was
being weird about riding. Ash, after serving eighteen years
with the National Guard, was not inclined to understand
fears that didn't involve mortal danger. "What? She obviously loves horses. Go for a ride. I can cover this for
an hour."

"I thought you were busy being in charge?"

Ani looked over her shoulder then up at Hunter. "Um. I don't…"

"Exactly," Ash said. "So, get out of here. We'll see you back at four o'clock." Ash stalked away yelling over his shoulder. "Bowman! Maisy! You're on rides. Ani needs a break."

Bowman glanced at Ani and immediately nodded. Maisy gestured to the line of kids and Bowman broke into a big grin. "Is that Captain Kai out there?"

Kai Larsabal was a regular fixture at Wallace Ranch ever since he'd been to Cowboy Camp the previous summer. Now he spent every second he could helping out at the stables. He'd already taken three rides today because every time he hopped off the horse he went to the back of the line and waited again.

"Get up here. You're gonna help Maisy lead Midnight."

Kai kept his head down, but Hunter could see his huge smile.

"Ani, we've got this covered." Bowman said. "Go take a break."

Hunter took Ani's arm and led her out of the arena, back to the stables. Her breathing steadied and the color returned to her face as she walked down the aisle between the stalls.

"You want to tell me what's got you so upset?"

Ani looked tired for a moment, and truly frightened, as she glanced over his shoulder toward the arena. Then she rubbed the back of her neck and the spark reappeared in her eye. "Nope."

Hunter leaned against a stall. Questions piled up in his chest, but he knew Ani well enough not to push it. "Was it the Christmas cheer? A little too much holiday joy send you over the edge?"

Ani barked out a laugh. "It was probably too much mistletoe."

Hunter glanced cautiously at the rafters. You never knew where you were or were not safe at this time of year.

"You know what you need?" Ani quirked her brow in question. Hunter grinned back at her. "A ride."

"In your truck?" she asked.

Hunter shook his head slowly. Ani picked up on his intention and glanced toward Bella. Bella shuffled her feet.

"I don't think I should…"

"But you want to?"

Temptation wrestled across Ani's face as she looked from Hunter to Bella and back again. "You don't understand."

"Sure don't. You like horses, they like you, and there's something happening at the festival that's got you upset. A ride seems like the perfect idea."

Time seemed to expand as Ani pulled the elastic out of her ponytail and gathered her hair into a new knot. Finally, Bella exhaled and stomped one foot.

"Fine." Ani walked briskly to where Bella stood waiting, saddled and ready. "Let's do it before I change my mind."

Her hesitation was brief, one hand on the horn of the saddle, one hand resting on Bella's neck. Hunter almost thought she was going to bail. Some communication passed between her and Bella then, in one fluid motion, Ani mounted the horse and the two of them were out the door. All he could do was hop on Beau and follow.

Ani had a light hold on the reins, directing Bella with her legs and core muscles. She flew past the arena, headed west, away from the festival, toward Old Wallace Creek Road. Hunter didn't have time to point out one of the riding trails his family maintained, but just watched as woman and horse sprinted off in the direction of his property.

The winter late-afternoon sun was already starting to fade. A line of Aspen trees ran along the creek to the north, their bare branches reaching up to the cloudless sky. In the distance, Fort Rock marked the border between the property he owned with Bowman, and the family place.

Ani and Bella flowed over the frostbitten landscape. He'd expected her to be an adept rider, but this was something more. Bella thundered across an open field with Ani easy and in control. Ani's hair fell out of its knot and flowed on the wind. Her face was serene and focused, like this was the one thing she was born to do. Watching her felt like the only thing he ever wanted to do.

She finally slowed as they approached the outcrop he and Bowman had named Fort Rock, then she turned the horse and called back to him with a brilliant smile, "You coming, Wallace?"

He gave his mount a squeeze with his calves, and Beau seemed to realize he'd been staring too. Hunter was a solid rider, and Beau was a fast horse, but they were both way out of their league here.

"Having enough fun?" he asked as they trotted up.

A flush filled her cheeks as she patted Bella's neck. He'd never seen anything more free than Ani on a horse.

"We're doing okay." Then she glanced over at him. "Thank you."

What had she seen back at the festival that had upset her? Why had she been so hesitant to ride? And where had she learned to ride like that?

"Any time," he said, holding her gaze.

Ani shifted her body and Bella began walking along the outcrop. She gestured to the rock. "This is cool."

"This was Bowman's and my fort growing up. Now it's the border to our property."

"You own this?" she asked.

"Yep. Bowman and I bought it together. He's planning on building a house for Maisy here by Fort Rock. Someday I'll fix up the old house the property came with."

"Sounds like another never-ending Hunter project."

"You'll get it when you see it."

They rounded the end of the outcrop and Hunter's spirits kicked up. His land spread out before them, soft shades of brown that would turn green as spring came. The weak winter light gave the landscape a pearly sheen. Five ancient, leafless oaks stood guard around the old house.

Ani stared at the house then back at him. "Whoa."

"You like it?"

"It's stunning." She and Bella trotted toward the house.

Hunter chuckled. Very few people had that reaction. Sure, the house was gorgeous, over a hundred years old, soaring up three stories. A multi-gabled roofline and expansive porch oriented the building, and weathered windows hung in proudly. The siding had been worn to a dove gray decades ago. A new red tin roof protected the old building, but that's all Hunter had done so far to fix the place up. No one could accuse it of being in good condition. *Dangerous* was a better word.

Ani swung out of the saddle and walked to the wrap-around porch. She glanced up and saw how the underside of the porch roof had been painted a robin's-egg blue. She turned back to Hunter with a brilliant smile on her face.

"I'm in love."

And he was really trying not to be.

But when a woman could look at a sagging porch and see the same potential he did? He should be sending up flares.

Instead he said, "That's one of my favorite parts of the house."

"Can you imagine having your whole family over here in the summertime? They're going to love this."

Hunter smiled. He'd thought of the same thing. Someday he'd have his own family. He and his wife would have everyone over, and the whole, big, noisy crew would hang out on this porch.

He rubbed a hand over his chest. It was getting harder and harder to want a future without Ani by his side.

"THAT WAS THE first thing my mom said when we bought it," Hunter said. He looked down, his Stetson obscuring most of his face, save the brilliant smile.

"It's perfect. Or it will be once you fix the termite damage and the dry rot."

Hunter laughed then rubbed his hand across his chest a second time. He lifted his head and gazed at her.

Blood pulsed through Ani's system, warming her as she got lost in Hunter's eyes, imagining a summer evening with his family. Kids running amok, laughing and reckless. Conversation flowing between Hunter's siblings. Hunter at a grill, fussing with something that would be incredible whether or not he got the timing right.

Her wild thoughts froze.

This was not her front porch and she would not be spending summer evenings here with anyone.

Not your porch. Not your house, not your family.

Not your man.

Hunter would marry a local woman, someone his family had known for years. The kind of woman who would never operate a deep fryer without instructions. She would fit in. They would have a lot of nice kids, and the Wallace family would continue to roll along in their happy, perfect family lives.

Any thought of staying and taking a place among these people was pure fantasy. Few things led more quickly to pain than delusion. She had to get moving.

The way she'd fled at the sight of Holly Banks was all the reminder she needed.

Holly hadn't been waving at her, obviously. She'd been waving at Hunter. Clara was right: Holly, and any other woman with sense in the State of Oregon, was going for the handsome cowboy chef. Holly was looking to replace her Dutch Warmblood with a Canadian and her last name with Wallace.

But her wave had been *so* familiar, a stilted gesture of insecurity masked with unwarranted confidence. Ani could still remember Holly trying to ingratiate herself on the competition circuits. She hadn't liked Holly's behavior at the time but, looking back, it was her own behavior that was disgusting. She'd toyed with Holly, making her think they were friends then gossiping behind her back, not because she had anything out for Holly, but because it made her feel superior.

Ani closed her eyes against the hardest memory. Holly competed in dressage, perfecting the delicate, complicated maneuvers of English riding. She'd complained to Ani of a new girl sweeping the circuit, stealing what could have been Holly's trophies. Ani had laughed at Holly's concern, carelessly suggesting she sabotage the girl's horse.

Judges in dressage were fastidious, going over a horse's sensitive areas with white gloves to look for traces of blood that could suggest mistreatment. A little cherry juice near the mouth would look like blood, disqualifying the girl instantly. Ani hadn't thought twice in suggesting it, and the next morning Holly was sneaking into the stall, feeding the horse a handful of cherries.

An hour later, the two of them had watched as a judge pulled back her hand and examined the faint spots of red. Holly had snickered, turning to Ani for approval. Ani hadn't been able to pull her focus away from the quiet, rasping sobs of the girl as she'd pleaded with the judge. *I would never hurt my horse. Never.*

The judge, who'd heard it all before, had just shaken her head and walked away. Ani never saw the girl again. She'd ruined her career in competition, and encouraged Holly to new lows, for nothing. It was the type of careless cruelty Ani had engaged in over the years.

If Holly recognized her as Stephanie Blaisedell, the whole pattern would start again. Ani was always at her meanest when part of the elitist group that made up the highest levels at a riding competition. Her worst side would come out; she'd be mean just because she was good at it. Then Hunter and his family would see her for her true self. There was no way Hunter would like her, or ever respect her, if he knew about her past.

Ani pulled in a deep breath. She had to get out of Oregon and stop whatever this growing feeling was with Hunter. She would head to Arizona as soon as her battery arrived, then set up a new permanent address. She could leave Oregon, and all her ghosts, forever.

"Want to see the inside?" Hunter asked. "It's even worse."

Did she want to walk through this intriguing building and fantasize about a life with Hunter? *Absolutely.* But it was beyond time to get herself under control.

"We should probably head back, shouldn't we?"

"I guess so." Hunter seemed disappointed.

Ani went for a joke. "Who knows what Clara's emu has gotten up to by now."

"Right." He gazed into her eyes, calling her bluff. She tightened her core and relaxed her shoulders, but it didn't help. He nodded. "Let's go."

Ani took one last, long look at the beautiful house. It was unlikely she'd ever be here again.

She swung onto Bella's back. The horse twitched in anticipation. Ani's instinct was to let her fly. Instead, she ran her hand along Bella's neck, letting her know they had to settle down and act like a normal horse and rider. Bella snorted. She didn't agree but was willing to go along.

By the time they got back to the arena, the sun had set. Christmas lights sparkled against the darkness and music floated out from inside.

"What's this?" Ani asked.

She could barely make out Hunter's expression in the darkness, but she could imagine it by the way he sighed before saying, "Mistletoe dance."

"Your family does not hold back, do they?"

"Not even a little bit."

Bella picked up the pace as she headed to the stable. Without direction, she walked right in and parked herself next to the tack room.

"You ready for a good scrubbing and a blanket?" she asked the horse as she dismounted.

"She won't take a blanket." Ani looked up to see Lacy walking toward her. Lacy scratched Bella's ears and addressed the horse. "She won't take a blanket even if she needs it."

"Stubborn lady." Ani unbuckled the girth then pulled the saddle from her back. "In here?" she asked, gesturing with the saddle to the tack room.

"Yep. Put it anywhere. I'll get in and organize tomorrow."

Hunter followed her into the tack room with Beau's saddle. The room was open to the arena over the half wall. Music played and everyone—children, parents, grandparents—all danced. Ani saw the Marshmallow Kid bopping to the beat. Maia stuck to the edge of the arena, snapping pictures, a huge smile on her face. Jackson and his friends joked around, confident enough to draw attention to themselves but too shy to ask anyone to dance.

"Looks like fun," Ani said.

"It can be." Hunter joined her at the opening and scanned the room. "Do you dance?"

She loved dancing. And dancing with Hunter, having an excuse to snuggle up to his flannel shirt? The answer would be an embarrassingly loud *Yes!*

Ani drew in a deep breath to keep herself from speaking, but since Hunter was standing right next to her, it turned out to be a deep breath of warm Hunter-y scent. *Not helpful.*

"Hunter!" Piper saw them from the dance floor and came clipping over. "Holly Banks was looking for you. She's gone now, but she wanted me to let you know she stopped by. Super insistent. I *don't* want you to call her."

"Did she need to talk to me about the gala?"

"No."

"Then why was she here?"

Piper delivered a dry look to Hunter then addressed Ani. "My brothers are literally hopeless. Like, I have zero hopes at this point."

Ani laughed, surprised at the relief that flushed through her. If Hunter's sisters were intent on keeping Holly away from him, they'd succeed.

Bowman came trotting over. "Is it true? Are you finally giving up on us?" He held a hand up and Hunter returned the high five.

"Never," Piper snapped, eyeing Bowman. "What are you wearing?"

Bowman looked down at his outfit. "Clothes?"

She took Bowman by the shoulders and turned him to see the dance. "This is a family sales event. No one is going to buy from someone who looks like they've been lost in the woods for three weeks. Go change your shirt."

Bowman just laughed. "Ash is right. You sound just like one of his old drill sergeants."

"The only sound I want to hear right now is you walking to the bunkhouse to change your shirt."

Bowman began to weave his shoulders in a dance move and then his feet followed. He was surprisingly agile.

"You are not going to dance your way out of this."

Bowman spun, winked at Maisy, looking like something out of *Footloose* as he reached for his fiancée's hands. Smooth dance moves were the last thing Ani would have expected from Hunter's quiet twin brother.

"I mean it, Bowman. Go change."

Hunter glanced at Ani, a conspiratorial gleam in his eye. He pointed to the open door leading to the aisle. "We should get out of here before she sees what *we're* wearing."

They left Bowman and Piper to their argument/dance-off and returned to see Lacy tenderly brushing Bella with a currycomb.

"I'm sorry," Ani addressed the horse. "I was supposed to be getting you cleaned up."

"I can groom her if you want to go join the dance," Lacy said.

"I'd like to help." Ani selected a brush. Hunter grabbed Beau's reins and led him to his stall, leaving her alone with Lacy. "Thank you for letting me ride her."

Lacy paused in her movements and looked at Ani. "You ride well."

Ani pressed her lips together and nodded. Anyone else might be willing to accept that Ani was just a decent rider, but she couldn't hide her level of technical skill from Lacy.

Hunter's mom turned her attention back to the horse and kept her voice low as she said, "If I'm not mistaken, I've seen you ride before."

Ani's hand froze midstroke on Bella. Her heartbeat crashed in her ears.

"It's okay," Lacy said. "I just wanted to be honest. You seemed familiar, but it wasn't until I saw you ride that I put it together."

Ani swallowed hard then nodded. How much would Lacy remember about her? How much would she have known?

"Would you hand me a hoof pick?" Lacy asked.

Ani grabbed one and handed it over. Lacy ran a hand along Bella's shin and Bella lifted her foot for Lacy to clean. "The last time I remember seeing you compete was at the Western Oregon Classic, five years ago."

Ani shivered. Rabiana had had such a tough time that day, but had still done her best. They'd won, neither of them aware it would be the last time they'd walk off a competition field together. Ani closed her eyes against the tears building in her throat.

"You don't ever think of going back to competition? I don't mean to pry, but you were so talented, so natural on a horse."

Ani blinked back tears. She'd never considered herself talented. People had called her a phenomenon and lined up to watch her ride, hoped to catch her secrets. But there were no secrets. She'd just wanted to spend every moment of every day with the magnificent, intuitive creatures. The time and passion translated into success.

But her success had come at the cost of her horse's

health. She would never push a horse like that again. She would never compete against other women that way. She would *never* put herself in a position where her worst side came out and she hurt others simply because she could.

"I'm not really that person anymore," Ani said.

Lacy didn't respond. The sound of her cleaning Bella's hooves mingled with the music from the dance and the low tenor of Hunter's laugh as he joked with Bowman. Ani let her love and regret flow as she groomed Bella, as though by attending to this horse she could make up for the hurt she'd inadvertently caused Rabiana.

"No woman is the same person she was at twenty-one," Lacy said. "You had a reputation as a serious competitor."

"That's one word for it," Ani muttered. "'Mean girl' was the term most people used."

Lacy chuckled. "You're a strong woman, and yes, sometimes we strong women can hurt others when we don't want to put up with their nonsense."

Bella pressed her nose against Ani's shoulder, agreeing with Lacy. Ani couldn't help but laugh. Lacy was the best kind of strong woman: caring, and using her strength to bring out the best in other people. Ani was strong but had used her strength to pull others down. And Bella, also a strong female, really didn't care much about the feelings of humans one way or another.

"The horse world can be cutthroat, but it doesn't have to be. Give yourself some credit for growing up and changing since you were young. I'd hate to see you turn your back on your natural talents." Lacy looked up from her work. "You belong with horses."

Ani smiled weakly. She didn't want to contradict Lacy, but she didn't belong anywhere.

Heavy boots *thunked* along the plank floor. Ani glanced

up to see Hunter smiling at her. He gestured over his shoulder toward the dance.

"Clara threatened to let Larry the emu onto the dance floor if I didn't ask you to dance, and I *do not* want to see that thing shake its tail feathers. Please help me out?" He held his arms out, like he did with Maia when he handed her a chai tea and needed an excuse to help her take it. He wanted to dance with her. And Ani really, really wanted to dance with him.

Ani ran her hand along Bella's neck.

"I've got this," Lacy said, her voice pleasant, a current of steely resolve underneath. "You go have fun."

Ani took one step toward Hunter then another. The music drifting in from the arena sounded like Jeffrey Desoto, Hunter's favorite artist.

"Are you a better or worse dancer than Larry?"

"Way worse," Hunter said. "But I cause less damage."

"Yeah." Ani shook her head. "We'll see about that."

Hunter's grin sent her heart skipping then her feet got in on the action and she recklessly grabbed Hunter's hand. "I love dancing, but no one would call me good at it," she said. "Let's go show 'em how it's *not* supposed to be done."

Hunter laughed, following her to the dance floor. He held his arms wide and her body stepped up to his on instinct.

"This is a two-step," he informed her.

"You say that like those words can form any kind of meaning in my brain."

He laughed again, his right hand closing around hers, his left coming to rest at her waist. Her endorphins, already warmed up from her ride, kicked into overdrive.

"But you can figure out anything." His voice was soft, his lips so close to her ear. Soulful music washed around them, along with the hum of conversation. In the moment, it felt true, like she could figure out anything. She glanced up into his rich brown-green eyes. *Almost anything.*

He took a step forward and she moved with him. Ani was surprised by her body's reactions to Hunter. He put the slightest pressure on her waist and she spun under his arm.

"We are not terrible at this," he said.

Ani had no idea if what they were doing looked good, but it felt amazing, like We-Should-Be-on-*Dancing-with-the-Stars* amazing.

"We could absolutely be worse."

The beat shifted and slowed. She glanced over to where Ash and Violet were playing DJ, the Christmas emu doing its best to wedge its large fluffy body between them. Ash pushed the bird's beak away and spoke into the microphone. "This is a request and a dedication—" The emu leaned his long, wobbly neck over Ash's arm and pecked at the microphone. Ash made the mistake of engaging the bird and soon the delighted emu had all of Ash's attention. He tried to push the bird away, grumbling as the emu bopped around with a wild grin on its beak.

Violet took the microphone from his hand, unable to stifle a laugh as she said, "And since the song is 'Love Story' by Taylor Swift, we all know the dedication goes out to our own Dr. Maisy Martin, from Bowman."

Ani joined in the general "Aww!" but sobered quickly when she realized she'd gotten considerably closer to Hunter. Her body had used the distraction as an excuse to practically hug her boss. Her right arm was fully wrapped around his waist and the soft flannel of his shirt brushed her cheek. He glanced down at her then looked away as he pulled her even closer. She could feel his heartbeat quicken and knew hers was keeping up a similar pace.

Hunter readjusted his hand, looping his fingers through hers. Ani closed her eyes and let her cheek rest against his chest as they moved to the music. For one, beautiful song, Ani let herself rest in the shelter of Hunter's arms. If she was going to break her own heart over Outcrop, she may as well take a cue from the Wallace family and go all-in.

CHAPTER TWELVE

"BYE, MAIA!" ANI CALLED, waving as Maia exited through the back door of the events center. "You sure you want to leave before Hunter brings us coffee?"

Maia made a face. "He brings *you* coffee. I get tea." She glanced at the clock then back at Ani. "My dad will be home by two, he said. I want to get there first."

Ani nodded. Maia's dad was home for a solid three days over Christmas and she was excited to spend time with him. "Have fun."

"Merry Christmas!" Maia's bright smile warmed Ani to the core. "And don't work on the flower buds without me."

"I wouldn't dare."

Maia waved again and moved quickly across the parking lot toward her home. When she got to the mural, she stopped and admired their work with pride. Ani was pleased with how the mural had turned out, but even more excited about Maia's reaction to it.

Ani closed the back door to the events center and looked around. It was finished too. The press of customers at Eighty Local had lessened as people finished their holiday shopping and settled in with their families. Hunter didn't really need her anymore.

She and Maia were planning decorations for the gala. They'd come up with a gorgeous plan and were looking forward to surprising Hunter with it. But when that was done, well…she'd be done.

"Ani?" Hunter called into the events center.

She forced herself to take a deep breath. Memories from the Mistletoe Festival swam in her head. Watching Hunter help children ride. The sprint with Bella. Lacy's revelation. The soft flannel of Hunter's shirt against her cheek as they'd danced.

That night cemented their friendship. And while Hunter hadn't made a move to create something more, he'd definitely stepped up his espresso game where she was concerned. Since the first week, he had been religious about bringing her coffee when it was time for her break, but the drinks had become sweeter and more elaborate each day since the Mistletoe Festival. Yesterday he'd created something out of espresso, eggnog and a dusting of spicy ginger so delicious she didn't think she'd ever fully recover.

No, she *knew* she'd never recover, not from this sojourn in Outcrop. Leaving would be devastating, but she could enjoy the coffee, and Hunter's brilliant smiles, while they lasted.

Ani closed her sketchpad and looked up. Would there be chocolate involved in today's coffee?

Hunter stood at the door to the events center, but without the satisfied grin of a man still salty about a truck-stop coffee comparison. Instead of a cup, he held a box. His deep brown-green eyes connected with hers then he nodded to a box. A good-sized, heavy-looking box, just the right shape for a lithium-ion battery.

"You're free." He cracked a weak smile. "You can pop in the Willie Nelson mix tape and get back on the road."

"Oh. That's my battery?"

"Looks like it."

Ani waited for the flutter of anticipation that generally accompanied the thought of hitting the road. Nothing fluttered.

Hunter cleared his throat. "I don't know how I'm going to manage without you."

Ani met his eyes and that's when things started to flutter. She looked back at the battery and willed herself to get excited about it.

Hunter continued. "You've done so much around here."

Ani nodded. It was an employee he'd miss. *Good to remember.* He liked having a hardworking problem-solver on hand for all the trouble he got himself into.

"I'm sure you can find yourself another inconsiderate drifter to boss around." She followed him into the dining room.

"Right." Hunter set the box on the counter. "Because there's a million women like you rolling through Outcrop." She met his gaze as he gave her a forced smile. "It's creating a traffic problem."

Ani ran her hand over the top of the box. She absolutely had to get out of here before the gala. When those women finally recognized her, Hunter would realize what she was. If she left now, they'd have wonderful memories of each other to cherish. The *almost* in their case would be so much sweeter than the reality of a relationship.

"You want me to finish this first?" She gestured toward the events center. "Maia and I had some ideas for decoration."

Hunter's shoulders relaxed. "Yeah. That'd be great. I was also hoping…" His voice trailed off.

Ani forced herself to keep looking at the battery.

"I was hoping you might be willing to work late with me tomorrow night, for Christmas Eve."

"Sure." Relief spanned her chest. She could take a few more days.

"I know you originally wanted to be out of Oregon before Christmas."

Ani waved her hand, pushing the comment aside. It felt so immature now. Like she couldn't handle being in the same state with her family for one day of the year? "I'm happy to work tomorrow."

"Great. I can give everyone else the evening off. It won't be busy, but we stay open until ten."

The anticipation that hadn't bubbled up over the battery now came dancing out. Her, Hunter, this place and a few regular customers. She glanced at Hunter. He was studying his clipboard with an adorable furrow in his brow. *Maybe no customers?*

Okay. Enough. Ani grabbed the battery. "I think I'll take my break."

Hunter looked up from the clipboard. "Why don't you take the afternoon off?"

"Seriously?"

"Yeah. I'll make your coffee to go. Tomorrow is Christmas Eve—you could probably use the time."

"You're giving me time to prepare for a holiday I don't celebrate?"

He headed to the espresso machine. "I've got to run a few errands myself. Things are slow, and you haven't even had time to check out the town."

Ani glanced out the windows. She and Hunter had spent almost all their daylight hours in Eighty Local for the three and a half weeks she'd been there. She glanced back at Hunter. He was stirring a heavy spoonful of rich chocolate into espresso. It looked like caramel would follow.

Her battery sat on the counter, challenging her. Technically, she could hit the road this afternoon. Hunter began to steam the milk for the rich chocolate-caramel-espresso combination he had in store for her.

Freedom or coffee?

"You can't come to Outcrop and never walk through OHTAF."

"Is that the law?"

Hunter widened his stance and crossed his arms over his chest. "Yeah. I think there's a local ordinance to that effect."

"Honestly, you can come up with a rule for anything."

"What would you have to break without me? Now, get out of here." He grinned as he handed her the coffee. "You're driving me up the wall."

Ani grabbed her jacket from its peg and headed for the door. If anyone was driving anybody to distraction, it was Hunter. "Maybe you're driving *me* up the wall."

"Hmm." Hunter pondered this then shook his head. "I don't think I can drive someone up the wall, if they're already so far *off* the wall."

Ani sighed in mock frustration. "That's it. I'm out of here. I'm not working for the rest of the afternoon."

Hunter laughed, his brilliant smile lighting up the dining room of Eighty Local.

Ani fled out the door.

The afternoon was glorious, bright and cold. Ani kept warm by hustling from one shop to the next. As much as it annoyed her, Hunter was right. OHTAF was charming. She spent a full hour there, reverently examining everything from birdseed to camping gear to Post-it notes.

But nothing could prepare her for Second Chance Cowgirl.

"Hello," a voice called out as Ani walked into the store. As a rule, Ani did not like being greeted, or even spoken to, by store employees. She felt if some sort of relationship was established, she'd feel obligated to buy something. And if there were two things Ani did not like, they were spending money and feeling obligated to do anything.

Yet something about this voice caught her attention.

A stunning woman stood behind the counter. She had pale skin, blonde hair streaked with gray, and a radiant smile. She was the sort of woman who made you feel like you couldn't wait to be fifty.

"Hi," Ani said, wandering farther into the shop. A thoughtfully curated selection of vintage dresses hung on a pipe rack. Ani drifted closer.

"That rack is twenty-five percent off," the woman said.

"Oh, I…" Ani started to speak just as her fingers fell onto the collar of a gorgeous calico-print dress. She steeled herself. "I don't actually need anything."

"Then just enjoy. Vintage finds are up front, and I sell a few small designers in the midsection. Boots are in the back."

Ani approached a jewelry case. Rather than the haphazard jumble found in many vintage stores, each piece of jewelry was carefully displayed, and all of it looked extraordinary.

The woman smiled at Ani. "I'm Christy Kessler, and I won't pretend not to know who you are. Everyone in Outcrop is grateful you showed up to save Hunter when you did."

Ani grinned. "It's been quite an adventure."

"Will you be heading home for Christmas?"

"No." The word dropped out cold. It was the wrong answer. Everyone "headed home for Christmas." It was what was done. Her family still got aggressive around the holidays. Blithely texting and calling with messages about making plans and hoping to see her.

But each year there were fewer attempts at contact. Eventually, the messages would end altogether and everyone could breathe a sigh of relief.

Ani added, "I need to install the lithium-ion battery in my van. I can't spend the night in it until I have heat."

It was a weak excuse. Installing the battery would take ten minutes. Eugene was less than three hours away. Ani could hop in her van right now and be home before dark, even without the battery.

"Well, I hope you make the most of your time here in Outcrop."

"Oh, I am. You know I get all my meals at Eighty Local while I work there."

The woman laughed. "That is my husband's dream, unlimited food at Eighty Local."

Warmed by the woman's laughter, Ani relaxed. She didn't need anything, but the soft music and the scent of roses made her feel like she could stay forever.

A rack of vintage concert T-shirts caught her eye. Ani brushed the age-softened fabric of a Fleetwood Mac tank top then an artfully shredded Brittany Spears.

"Those are all authentic," Christy said.

"Where did you find them?" Ani asked.

"Here and there. Some are from my own closet. I love concerts, always have."

Ani's hands stilled. *Duran Duran.* The T-shirt had been well loved back in the 1980s. Someone had cropped it and cut the sleeves off. Simon and the boys were fading across the front, but still recognizable.

It had been years since Ani had bought anyone a gift. Gift-giving had been a complicated and ultimately futile process in her family. Everyone'd had more stuff than they could possibly use and bought anything they wanted at a moment's notice. But everyone expected presents and judged gift-giving like a dressage competition. It had gotten to the point that Ani had hated the whole concept of gifts.

But there was no way she was leaving Second Chance Cowgirl without buying this T-shirt for Maia.

"I know someone who needs this." Ani looped the shirt over her arm and opened a zippered pocket inside her jacket to see if she had any money on her.

"Please tell me you're not thinking Hunter."

Ani burst out laughing at the image. "No, although it wouldn't be any worse than the Ho-Ho-Hometown sweat-shirt."

Christy shuddered theatrically.

Ani grinned. Christy was *awesome*.

"There's a girl who's been helping with the mural, and I think she'll love this." Ani sobered, thinking of the mural Maia had designed for this very store. She glanced at Christy and back at the shirt. Could she pitch the project and then stay another month?

No. She had to get out of here before she took one step closer to Hunter. They'd both wind up hurt. She'd made peace with playing roulette with her own heart, but she couldn't stand the thought of hurting Hunter.

"You should try these on."

Ani looked up from her meditation on the T-shirt.

Christy was holding out the most beautiful boots Ani had ever seen. Golden brown, the boot shaft was embroi-dered with a subtle decoration of leaves, ending in two simple flowers at the top, reminiscent of Art Deco. The heel was low, but substantial. The stitching looked to be hand done. Ani's fingers reached out.

"These were custom-made as part of a woman's trous-seau in the early 1960s. She came from an oil family in Texas. They've barely been worn. A woman who came from that kind of money wouldn't be doing her own rop-ing on the ranch."

Ani took the boots and sat on the wooden bench.

Ani didn't value money, or displays of wealth, or expensive clothing.

But good craftsmanship? *That* she could respect.

The boots slid on easily. Ani stood and walked a few paces.

What the heck?

Her walk changed in these boots. She was more confident.

Ani paced along the back wall.

The boots felt as though they'd been made for her.

"Those will last a lifetime," Christy said.

Please, her feet begged. *Please let us have the boots.*

Ani placed a foot on the bench and looked at the price tag tied to the bootstrap.

Nope.

Her greedy consciousness began to beg, and wheedle, and browbeat her into buying the boots.

Ani closed her eyes and focused on all the human misery that came from the thoughtless accumulation of material goods. She worked because it felt good to work. She worked to fuel a life of freedom. The minute she gave in to her greed, she would be trapped in an endless hedonic cycle.

Ani opened her eyes and took another peek at her feet.

But, dang, these were nice boots.

HUNTER SHUFFLED THE torte he'd made into his other hand as he pushed open the door to Second Chance Cowgirl. Then he sent up a prayer that in all the excitement, Christy would still help him with last-minute Christmas shopping for his sisters.

"Welcome home!" Hunter called out.

"Thank you, Hunter." Christy smiled at him, and Hunter

had no trouble imagining why his old football coach was so smitten with this woman.

"I brought a chocolate hazelnut torte for you and Coach. My sister tells me congratulations are in order."

"That is so sweet of you."

Hunter had never paid much attention to engagement rings until Jet had placed the ridiculous diamond on Clara's hand. He glanced at Christy's left hand, only to find a simple band of gold.

"Is that your engagement ring?"

"This is my wedding ring," she said. "We changed the flight and stopped by Vegas on the way home."

"No way!" Hunter yelled, startling the customer at the back of the shop. He turned to apologize.

And there was Ani, looking, if possible, more beautiful than ever. Time stuttered. The room seemed to narrow until there was nothing but Ani. His eyes ran down her body.

Oh, my.

"Nice boots."

"I'm not going to get them." Ani took a few more steps.

"Seriously? They look like they were made for you."

Ani paced the length of the bench. She always walked with confidence, her head high, easy gait. But in those boots? There really ought to be a law.

"She's just enjoying them," Christy said.

Hunter stared as Ani moved through the back of the store. As a rule, he didn't care much about what women wore. But he liked Ani's style, functional with a creative kick to it. The boots were pure Ani.

Christy cleared her throat.

Okay, time to stop staring.

"Would you like to see what you're getting your sisters this year?" Christy asked.

Hunter used all his brainpower to focus. "Yes. I'm in your hands."

"For Clara, I have these new raincoats in." Christy walked over to a rack with a small selection of bright-colored raincoats. "I thought the classic yellow would look good on her, and she could probably use something practical on Jet's ranch."

Hunter took the yellow coat from Christy, examining the lining and fit. He tried to be interested, but the even sound of boots clacking on a hardwood floor approached.

"She'd be adorable in that," Ani said.

Hunter kept his eyes on the coat. "We could probably put Clara in a burlap sack and she'd look adorable."

"Piper, on the other hand, would make a burlap sack look like high fashion," Christy said.

"Pretty sure she's tried that." Hunter grinned at Christy then snuck another quick look at Ani. He took the jacket up to the register.

"How do you feel about going in with Bowman on a gift for Piper?"

"Sure."

Christy opened the jewelry case at the front of the store. Hunter heard the soft tap of the boots as Ani followed to see what Christy had in the case. Her scent hit him. With no thought other than *gorgeous woman in boots*, Hunter gazed at Ani. He'd sent her out of the restaurant this afternoon because he'd nearly kissed her twice then had to stop himself from throwing the expensive battery in the trash.

"It's made by a designer out of Coos Bay. He does high-detail, heritage-inspired work."

Hunter willed his eyes to look at the necklace; a large piece of turquoise framed by delicate silver.

"Wow," Ani said.

"I think she'd love it. Your mom bought her a white blouse that would set this off perfectly."

"Great," Hunter said. "Let's wrap it up. Does Bowman know?"

"Bowman does his shopping at four thirty on Christmas Eve," Christy reminded him.

Hunter laughed. "Thank you."

"I heard Piper and Clara managed to get you the perfect gift this year." She nodded toward Ani.

"We finished the mural," Ani said then pressed her lips together, as though there was something else she wanted to say. "All I need to do now is decorate the events center." She glanced at him. "Maybe Christmas Day would be a good time? You'll be closed, right?"

Hunter allowed himself to imagine a full day with Ani in Eighty Local.

No customers. No interruptions. Best Christmas ever.

He shook his head. "Yeah. No. I gotta…"

Christy came to the rescue. "We're all anxious to see Eighty Local succeed, and I know your help couldn't have come at a better time."

Ani glanced down. "It's been fun." She stared at the boots for a moment longer and then walked to the bench and started to remove them.

The action felt very wrong.

"I'd better get back to exploring the town." Ani let out a little sigh as she placed the boots back on the shelf and grinned wickedly at Christy. "I have this mean boss who is always on me about following all the rules, and he told me I have to go exploring before I leave." Christy laughed. Ani laced up her high-tops. "Thank you for letting me enjoy your store and walk around in your boots."

"Any time," Christy responded. "I like to think of this store as a gallery."

Ani nodded. She pulled some cash out of her coat and set it on the counter. Hunter sent her a questioning look. She held up a T-shirt with a picture of five guys wearing more than their share of hair gel and said, almost shyly, "Duran Duran. For Maia."

Something shifted in his chest and any resolve he had for not falling for this woman melted like snowflakes on a streetlamp.

She readjusted her grip on the shirt and moved to the door. "See you back at the ranch, Jefe."

Hunter cleared his throat. "See you."

Ani shot him a smile as she waved and left the store. She moved quickly across the street, her head up and alert, examining the Christmas decorations, observing the kids out for winter break. A light snow began to fall.

Hunter glanced at her feet. The high-top sneakers looked as though they'd seen better days.

He turned to Christy, but she was no longer behind the counter.

A moment later, she emerged from the back room with an old, perfectly kept box that looked like something out of the 1960s.

"Hey, can I see those boots again?" he asked.

Christy smiled as she slipped the boots into the box. "I got you covered."

Hunter felt a silly grin coming on.

"It's just, you know…" He stuttered a little. "Sh-she's been such a huge help."

"Right."

"It's the least I can do."

Christy set the box on the counter. "The world will be a more beautiful place with that girl walking around in these boots."

Hunter blushed then ran a hand through his hair. He handed his bank card to Christy.

"Cards, scissors and ribbons are set up in the back room," she said. "You know what to do."

CHAPTER THIRTEEN

"WE'RE OPEN FOR another three hours," Hunter heard Ani say. "Linda kick you out of the house?"

"She said I was getting the grandkids too riled up. Sent me here for takeout."

Hunter looked over the counter to see Ani standing on her toes, trying to find Dean's truck in the parking lot.

"Sneak any out with you?"

"A few," he admitted with a grin.

"The Marshmallow Kid?"

"He was the first to jump in the truck."

"Bring 'em in. I'll get the cocoa going. Let me know when you're ready to order."

Ani turned back and caught Hunter watching her. He didn't look away.

Hunter had sent the rest of his staff home. On Christmas Eve, he kept a simple menu and closed up early. He and Ani could handle the place.

The bells on the front door jangled and the voices of Dean and Linda's grandkids rang through the restaurant. He listened in as Ani interacted with the children.

"How many marshmallows this time?" she asked. "Ten? I don't know if ten will fit in the cup." She dramatically began to float marshmallows on the hot chocolate.

The crowd was smaller tonight, but festive. Hunter grabbed his clipboard and went over the night's list. He planned to clean and decorate the events hall after they closed. He'd get the linens and service ready. Basically, have everything set up for the gala, so he could at least try to relax tomorrow.

Ani might be interested in staying late and helping. He looked up to see her popping candy canes into the cocoa while Dean's grandkids bounced around the room in anticipation. His heart was bouncing around in anticipation along with them. He had a long evening ahead in a quiet restaurant, with Ani.

Yeah, he had a long evening ahead in a quiet restaurant, with Ani, and so much work to do the two of them could stay up all night and not finish it.

Hunter shook his head. Her battery had arrived, she would install it and hit the road in a few days. He glanced over the counter. Dean's youngest granddaughter beamed as Ani handed her the cocoa. Ani straightened, her long hair falling out of its knot, a few strands drifting across her shoulders.

A low rumble sounded from the back room. Hunter took a step toward the noise then remembered he was sautéing mushrooms. "Ani, could you go check—" The lights dimmed in the dining room, but Hunter could still see the confusion on Ani's face. Then, with a sad *pop*, the restaurant went dark.

Voices in the dining room buzzed in confusion. The sizzle of mushrooms quieted as the stove burner went out. Hunter ran into the back room, pulling out his phone for light to check the circuit breaker.

"Hunter?" Ani's voice drifted to him.

"I'll have it right back on." He fumbled with his phone to illuminate the circuit board.

"Hunter!" She was closer now. The room was incredibly dark. "The power's out on the street as well."

Hunter groaned and leaned his head against the fuse box.

"Linda just texted. It's out at our place too," he heard Dean call from the dining room.

"Looks like it's out all over town," someone else noted.

"I've got so much to do tonight." Hunter's chest tightened.

Ani's scent, the mysterious spicy tones with a hint of sweetness, hit him as she came closer.

"It's okay," she said quietly. "We'll get it done."

"We can't work in the events hall without heat at night. I can't prep food so we're ahead for the twenty-seventh. I can't even wash the dishes without power."

She placed a hand on his arm. Her fingers slid along his bicep; a tendril of hair brushed his shoulder.

The panic in his chest dissipated at her touch. He placed his hands on her arms then pulled her into a hug. Her warmth and calm self-assurance ran through him. He tucked his head into her hair and breathed in. He could feel her heart beating.

"We can do this," she said.

"I don't know."

"We can." She reached up and rubbed his back. Hunter leaned into her touch. Maybe they could wait out the power outage in the back room?

No. There were customers out front and half-filled orders on the counter. Hunter reluctantly stepped away from Ani. "Let's go assess the damage."

The dining room of Eighty Local was cheerful. People continued to eat by the light of the candles on each table. The kids were running around in the dark with their cocoa, laughing.

"What have you got that's already cooked?" Dean asked.

"Today's soups were tomato basil bisque and elk stew. Can I send you home with a couple of pots of soup and some dinner rolls?"

"Sounds good to me," he said.

"Hunter, we're ready to cash out," a woman called from a nearby booth.

"Well, the card reader won't work without power. Looks like tonight's meals are on the house."

A cheer went up throughout the restaurant.

"If they can't pay, does that mean we're not working?" Ani's pirate smile broke out, even more mischievous in the candlelight.

Hunter gave in and stared at her, his heart blithely ignoring every command his head made about looking away. "I guess so."

"Sweet. I'm starving. What do we need to eat up?"

He let himself drink her in. Her long hair was falling out of its knot, loose wisps clinging to her neck. She wore an Eighty Local T-shirt tied at her waist and a jersey skirt over leggings.

"The beer. We should drink up the beer. I'm sure it will go bad."

Ani laughed, once again confirming he had zero willpower when it came to a capable, free-spirited woman in an Eighty Local T-shirt.

"I'll help you out with that," Dean said.

"You want marshmallows?" Ani asked.

"I'm going to see what I can grab for us, Ani." Hunter next addressed the patrons. "Everyone, the heat will probably dissipate in about an hour. No rush, but you might want to finish up before it gets cold in here."

Hunter ducked behind the counter then stopped to grab one last look at Ani. She was stretched up on her toes, getting glasses. She must have felt his eyes on her, because she turned to him. The challenge he normally met in her eyes was gone for a moment, and although the candlelight could be deceiving him, he thought he saw her blush.

ELK STEW, HOUSE-MADE tortilla chips, guacamole and half a coconut-cream pie in a dark, rapidly chilling room made an unexpectedly good meal.

Eighty Local had emptied out as people learned the power was down throughout Outcrop. Patrons hurried home to check on animals, make sure they had wood for fires, and see to it that loved ones were safe and comfortable. Ani felt perfectly warm in the candlelight and Hunter's gaze.

"Do you miss anything about having a home?" Hunter asked.

"I have a home."

"You know what I mean." He leaned forward and used a tortilla chip to serve himself a bite of guacamole.

Ani was probably staring at his lips a little too hard.

"No. The van allows me to live in accordance with my values. You saw me in Second Chance Cowgirl the other day. I'd have bought out the entire shop if I had a place to put everything."

Hunter laughed. "Those were some nice boots."

Ani remembered the feel of the leather encasing her feet, the way her walk felt in the boots.

"There are nice things everywhere. I can appreciate them, but I don't have to have them."

Hunter met her gaze and she took some time to appreciate him. She leaned back and propped her feet up on the other side of the booth. Next to Hunter.

"Candlelight is definitely helping this meal," he said abruptly.

"I think this meal would be delicious no matter what kind of lighting we had."

"Because everyone loves lukewarm stew with chips?" he asked.

Because everyone loves everything you make. He put

so much soul into creating this place and this food for his community. Hunter just naturally did good in the world. He didn't buy local products because it was trendy, he bought them because he knew and liked the people who produced them. He wasn't a chef because he had some power complex, but because he genuinely loved feeding people.

"When did you start cooking?"

Hunter studied his plate then looked back up at her.

"I don't know. I was always interested. Following my parents around in the kitchen, you know how it is."

"No. My parents didn't really cook."

"Oh?"

Ani shook her head. No sense in ruining a wonderful evening talking about her parents. Hunter didn't push it.

"Well, we always ate together. I figured out pretty fast that if I helped in the kitchen, I got a say in what we had for dinner."

Ani grinned. "What were your favorite meals?"

"Um, you know. Stew." He gestured to the meal. Ani laughed. "I liked everything. I like food."

"I like your food."

"And then…" He paused, let out a breath. "I figured out that cooking is a good way to care for others. Clara had a pretty tough time when she was younger. Cooking for her was the one way I could help out."

"Clara had a tough time? She and Piper seem so perfect."

Hunter shrugged. "Everyone has their story."

Ani nodded. When she'd had a tough time, neither her brother nor her sister had ever thought about doing anything to help.

The bells on the front door jangled. Hunter and Ani both turned as a tall man entered the room in a few long, confident steps.

"Hey, Jet."

"Hey." The man removed his Stetson and shook the snow off it.

"Ani, I don't think you met Jet at the Mistletoe Festival. He's Clara's husband."

"Hi." She smiled up at the cowboy.

"Nice to meet you," Jet said. "I'm sorry to interrupt."

Ani and Hunter spoke at the same time.

"Oh, you're not—"

"No problem, we were just—"

Okay. That sounded pathetic.

Hunter cleared his throat. "It's all good."

"Power's out at your parents' place," Jet said.

"Is everyone okay?"

"Yeah." Jet nodded. "Most everyone is at our house. I rigged the solar power to run to the house in case of an outage, so we're fine."

"Seriously?" Ani sat up. She liked this guy already. "Aren't most solar-powered homes plugged into the grid?"

"They are. But I figured out a way to make it work."

"And the power company let you do that?"

Jet laughed. "Had a heck of an argument about it, but they get their share."

"That's cool."

Jet's expression turned serious. "I've sat in a cold house more than enough times in my life. My kids will never be cold in their own home."

Ani felt tears prick her eyes at the power of the statement. She was a little surprised to see Hunter toss a wadded-up napkin at him.

"You don't have any kids," Hunter teased.

Jet pulled a lump of snow off his coat and dropped it down Hunter's collar. Hunter fished it out and lobbed it back at Jet.

"Just wait," Jet said. "I'm gonna train all our kids in snowball tactics. You and Bowman won't stand a chance."

"They're going to have a lot to learn."

"I'll start 'em early."

Ani watched the men banter back and forth. A twinge of envy threatened at the thought of participating in a Wallace family snowball fight.

She shook her shoulders against the cold. The guys seemed to remember she was still there.

"I stopped by to ask, are you okay with cooking Christmas dinner at our place?" Jet asked Hunter.

"Absolutely. It's about time someone made good use of that kitchen of yours."

"I cook," Jet said.

Hunter turned to Ani. "Sandwiches."

"Legendary sandwiches," Jet clarified. "Anyway, the house is warm and we're happy to have everyone stay with us. Your parents, Ash and Jackson arrived tonight. Violet and Maisy will be there too. Piper's been with us since Friday."

"I can stay at the ranch, take care of the horses." Hunter thought for a moment. "It's going to get well below freezing. Mom will have blanketed the horses already. We'll insulate their water buckets and probably do a live feeding in the middle of the night. It's not fun but it works."

Jet surprised Ani by turning to her. "You're welcome at our house."

"Oh, I'm good," she said. "The gardener's cottage has a woodstove. It's cozy."

"Offer still stands," he said.

"Thank you," she responded.

"I'll come out around ten tomorrow to start cooking," Hunter said.

"Great. Clara's stoked about hosting."

"I'm sure she is."

"Are you cool with Michael and Joanna joining us?" Jet asked.

"Of course." Hunter looked across the table and gestured. "And Ani."

The cold, which she'd somehow kept at bay, came rushing in. She shook her head. "I don't celebrate Christmas."

Hunter's face constricted. "It's just dinner."

"No, I know. Thank you." She reached across the table to take his hand then remembered this wasn't a hand-taking sort of relationship. "Thank you," she said to Jet. "I appreciate the invitation. Honestly, I'm looking forward to a good book and a day off from this guy," she tried to joke, but it fell flat.

Jet, a man she had known for less than six minutes, focused on the floor and looked like he was trying to wrap his head around the rejection.

"Okay." He nodded at Ani as though he'd accepted the wrong side of a bad deal. Then he spoke to Hunter. "I'm going to run over to your place to pick up a few things for your mom. I'll help Bowman get started with the horses while I'm there."

"Thanks," Hunter responded. "See you tomorrow."

"See you. Nice to meet you, Ani. Don't work too late." A gust of cold swirled through the room as he left.

Hunter turned his beer glass on the table. Then he looked at Ani. "Do you know how much time I've spent trying to understand you?"

She laughed. "I'm very simple."

Hunter leaned back, a competitive spark in his gaze. "Oh, that's a lie."

"Seriously, I've spent the last five years trying to live simply. I'm a simplicity poster child."

"You are the most complex woman I've ever known."

Ani ran her finger along the grain of the wooden table-top. She liked the idea of having Hunter Wallace off kilter.

"You know, this Christmas might be different from what you're used to," he said, grinning at her. "Just a thought."

Ani traced the wood grain back to where her finger had started. Christmas was crass gluttony and greed, discarded piles of foil wrapping paper and foam packaging. Christmas was being trapped in a dysfunctional household, posing for pictures in front of a fake tree with people who wanted nothing more than for you to change.

She looked up at Hunter. He leaned toward her, resting his elbows on the table. The briefest moment of fantasy closed in on her.

Showing up to Christmas with the Wallace family, her fingers interlaced with Hunter's. Fast and funny conversation, the best food imaginable, a simply wrapped present under the tree that Christy Kessler helped someone pick out.

A blast of cold hit her back as the bells on the door jangled again. Ani shook off the daydream and ordered her heart back into her rib cage.

"Hi." Jet strode back into the room. He sat decisively in the booth next to Hunter and leaned across the table to speak to Ani. "Look, I'm about to do something very selfish." He took a breath and looked straight into Ani's eyes. "This is the first year of my life that I—" He stopped speaking as though his throat had constricted. He swallowed, then continued. "This is the first time I will really celebrate Christmas. I didn't have a family, like other people do, until—" he cleared his throat "—until now. The whole Wallace family is coming to my house. I know you probably can't comprehend what a gift that is, but believe me, there are kids across this country who would give anything for a family like this one."

Jet's jaw clenched, as though he had a process for holding back tears when he needed to. "All I know about you are the funny stories Clara's been telling me, and you probably have your reasons for wanting to spend tomorrow alone…"

He ran out of words. Ani glanced at Hunter. His hand rested on Jet's back, like a brother. It occurred to Ani there was a lot going on here that she didn't understand, for all she considered herself to be observant.

"But if I'm alone," she guessed, "you'll worry that I'm lonely."

Jet looked up at the ceiling then back at Ani. "I just hate for people to have to be alone on Christmas."

Ani smiled at Jet. "You're a legit good person, aren't you?"

He grinned, and Ani caught a flash of his joy. She could allow herself to attend one Christmas dinner with these nice people. For Jet's sake.

"Okay." She shrugged dramatically. "I guess I can stomach Hunter's holiday cooking."

Jet jumped up from the booth. "Great. Can we get anything special for you? Kombucha? Nutritional yeast?"

Ani laughed. "Do I seriously look like that much of a hippie?"

"We have sriracha," Jet told her.

"That would be a yes."

Ani glanced at Jet. "Please don't do anything special. But so I can be prepared, will there be massive amounts of foil wrapping paper?"

Hunter exchanged a look with Jet. "Are you kidding?"

"With Mr. Wallace in the house?" The two men laughed.

"Mr. Wallace hates foil?" Ani asked.

"Mr. Wallace hates waste," Jet said.

"I assume you've been initiated into the boxes?" Hunter asked Jet.

"That was one of your mom's wedding gifts. Nesting boxes."

Hunter shook his head slowly.

"When we got back from our honeymoon, Clara spent about a week straight-ironing the ribbons from our presents and assessing the boxes."

"My family is ridiculous," Hunter told Ani. "Sad, but true."

Ani looked from one man to the next. Boxes and re-used ribbon?

These guys had no idea what ridiculous was.

CHAPTER FOURTEEN

"Whoa." Ani glanced at Bowman then back out the window of his truck. "I wasn't expecting this."

A long tree-lined drive branched off the highway. It felt a little too fancy for Bowman's beat-up truck. Ani's brief interaction with Jet the night before had led her to believe he was a down-to-earth, central Oregon rancher. She'd imagined Christmas would happen in a simple tract home. The driveway was more elaborate than she would have expected.

Bowman nodded. "Wait till you see the house."

"Thanks again for driving."

Hunter had left the ranch earlier to prepare Christmas dinner. Bowman had offered to drive her when he came, many hours later.

He glanced over at her and smiled. "Our family is a lot."

Ani grinned back.

"You can leave any time." Bowman redirected his gaze toward the drive. "I gotta stay for the whole thing. But I'll leave my keys in the truck if you want to escape."

This family. Did Bowman realize how incredibly thoughtful he was being? Or did everyone around here just have the good manners to plan for every contingency regarding the wandering muralist.

"I'll be fine. It's just a—"

The house came into view, putting an end to any reassurance that she was going to be fine.

The elegant, brand-new, slate-and-timber structure was situated in the heart of Jet's acreage. A powerful creek rushed by on one side and the Cascade Mountains rose majestically in the background. The dusting of snow gave everything a fresh, clean feel.

Ani breathed in deeply as Bowman put the truck in Park. There was nothing to be afraid of. Jet and Clara owned a nice house. That didn't make them bad people. She would walk in the house, be polite, eat the meal. She eyed the keys Bowman left in the ignition. She could leave any time she wanted.

A blast of cold met her as Bowman opened the driver's-side door. Ani clutched the bouquet she'd made and stepped out of the truck.

"Hello!"

Ani looked up to see Clara waving from the front door. Piper scooched in next to her sister and yelled, "It's freezing! Merry Christmas!"

They looked like a Christmas card. Ani felt Bowman's eyes on her. She turned around to see him give her a reassuring nod.

"They're not going to bite. They might try to decorate you, or fix you up with someone, but they won't bite."

Ani grinned at him then mounted the steps.

"Welcome to my home." Clara clapped her hands and jumped. Ani suspected she might do this every time she remembered she lived here.

"Isn't it amazing?" Piper asked.

Ani stepped over the threshold. The house was light and warm. Vaulted wood ceilings reflected light from the windows. Radiant heat came from the floor. A huge Shasta fir tree dominated the living room.

"It's gorgeous. Your tree…"

"You have to ignore the bald spot." Clara gestured to a bare patch near the top.

"No, you have to embrace the bald spot," Piper said. "It makes the décor seem authentic."

"It *is* authentic. I just wish we'd cleared a better-looking tree from the emu pasture."

"I love it," Ani surprised herself by admitting. Little white lights twinkled throughout the tree, but there were very few decorations. It was the tree of newlyweds.

"Hello." Jet stood from one of the leather sofas and came jogging over. He took Ani's hand. "Thank you for coming."

She smiled. This was the right decision.

"Thank you for insisting. I was being weird about the holiday. Here." She held up the greens. "I put this bouquet together." She knit her brow as she handed it over. "There are no flowers. Can we still call it a bouquet?"

"It's lovely," Piper said.

"I wandered along the path on your parents' property and picked things until this emerged." The bouquet had cedar boughs, holly and a few sparse aspen sticks. She had to admit, it looked pretty good.

"It's honestly the most perfect bouquet ever," Clara said.

Ani frowned. It wasn't *that* good.

"These people are not afraid of hyperbole," Violet said from where she sat snuggled up under Ash's arm on the sofa.

Ani laughed. "Then we should probably talk about sweet potato fries while I'm here."

"The. Best. Food," Maisy confirmed.

"Hello," another voice called out from the living room.

"It's you!" Ani recognized a couple of Eighty Local regulars. "I don't know your names but, cornmeal pancakes, right?"

"I'm Michael," the man said, pushing his thick-framed

glasses up on his nose. "This is my wife, Joanna. We know you're Ani, even though Hunter hasn't gotten around to ordering you a name tag yet."

"How do you fit with this?" Ani waved her hands to indicate the whole Wallace family.

"Jet was, and remains, my best friend. Clara was our matchmaker."

"We love her," Joanna said.

Ani looked from one of them to the other. These perfectly sane-seeming people had actually hired someone to get them into a permanent relationship.

Huh.

"Ani, can you come help us with a thing?" Clara asked. She set the bouquet on a coaster on the coffee table.

"We're kind of running behind," Piper told her.

"Sure." Ani smiled at Joanna and Michael. "Nice to see you."

Clara, as though pulled by some type of magnet, walked over and kissed her husband before leaving the room. Jet got a hazy look on his face then had to shake his head before he could refocus on his previous conversation.

"Hi, Dad," Clara chirped as she led Ani through the dining room. A wiry man in the Wallace-male uniform of a plaid shirt and jeans was setting the table.

"Hello, Wallace parent," Ani said.

"Hello, Ani," Dad said warmly. "How was your morning?"

"Very nice. Cold, but nice."

"You want to say hi to Hunter?" Piper asked as they passed an open door into the kitchen. Ani caught a glimpse of Hunter's broad shoulders. Lacy stood beside him, chopping greens and making commentary on Hunter's cooking. His nephew set out spices on the countertop.

"No."

No, I don't want to go say hi to the gorgeous man cooking something incredible and communing with his perfect family.

The sisters were eyeing her. She forced her gaze off Hunter.

"I just came because it seemed so important to Jet," Ani said.

Piper glanced at Clara and a world of communication Ani would never be privy to was exchanged.

Clara started walking again. "Okay. Number one, I'm so sorry he did that. But, number two, I'm kinda not sorry, because I'm really glad you're here."

"Also, we totally need your help."

Clara led them into what could only be described as the world's most beautiful laundry room. Bowls of bath salts sat out, surrounded by little jars and different colored ribbons.

"We made bath salts!" Clara said.

"Manly bath salts. Smell."

Ani dipped her nose to the bowl Piper held out. "Very manly."

"Every guy in this family is constantly complaining about sore muscles but does nothing to make it any better."

"So, bath salts."

"We made some with a rose scent, too, for the women," Clara added.

"And now we need to get them in jars, with tags on them, and under the tree, before dinner."

"Where can I help?" Ani asked.

The women exchanged another glance and Piper said, "We feel like you might excel at tying bows."

Ani stepped up to the ribbon. It was clear they'd fabricated something for her to help with, which was the kind of weirdly thoughtful behavior these Wallaces got up to.

"Clara?" a masculine voice called from around the corner, accompanied by the sound of familiar footsteps. "Where's your salt grinder? Oh. Hey."

Everything in the room seemed to go wonky as Hunter entered. *Had he gotten better-looking since he'd left that morning? Or was the lighting in this laundry room that good?*

"Hey," Ani said with way more eye contact than the situation warranted. Hunter seemed to struggle for words.

Could you get more awkward than staring into your boss's eyes, in his sister's laundry room, at his family's Christmas dinner?

As hard as she worked to keep herself free from social expectations, in Outcrop, Ani found herself in the thick of them. She didn't want to be beholden to other people or fail to meet their unspoken expectations.

But ever since meeting Hunter and this whole family, she was constantly trying to reciprocate all the nice things others did for her. She knew there was no way she was keeping up or doing it right. It was like she'd bought a first-class ticket on the bullet train to Awkward Family Interactions.

Then there was Hunter. In the last week, Ani was unable to stop herself and gave in to wild bouts of uncontrolled flirting. Last night had been the worst. She'd sat laughing with Hunter in the cab of his truck for an hour after they'd pulled up in front of the cottage. Everything was funny, every sentence an excuse not to hop out of the truck, every look could have been misread as an invitation to kiss.

And now they were staring at each other in the laundry room.

"Did my sisters press you into service?" he finally asked, looking past Ani to Clara and Piper, who were weirdly jumping and clapping. Clara kept pointing to the ceiling.

Hunter returned his gaze to Ani, as though she might know what all the excitement was about. She shrugged.

"What?" Hunter demanded of his sisters.

"Mistletoe!"

Hunter's gaze shot to the ceiling, as if Clara had just told him there was a bobcat about to pounce from the lighting fixture. Then he looked at Ani. If Awkward Family Interactions had a grand central station, she had arrived.

"Why in God's name do you have mistletoe in your laundry room?" Hunter asked.

"That is not something you want to know the answer to," Clara said primly. "Kiss."

Ani looked up at Hunter. He froze. There were so many things about this man she couldn't figure out, but right now, one thing was clear. He needed saving.

She reacted. A light kiss wasn't going to kill either of them. The quicker she moved, the more control she had over the situation. Ani placed a hand on Hunter's cheek and stood on her toes to lightly peck his lips. As her face neared his, she was acutely aware of his scent.

Time narrowed. Hunter inhaled sharply as her lips brushed his. Her hand pulled his face closer at his response.

The kiss was light and fast, but it was enough to re-arrange the entire universe. As her lips pulled away, her entire body resonated with a deep, urgent request. *More.*

"I don't have a salt grinder," Clara returned innocently to Hunter's question. Apparently, she hadn't felt the stars reversing course and realigning with the kiss.

"You *do* have a salt grinder because I gave you one for your wedding." Hunter's hands drifted to Ani's shoulders. He picked up a lock of her hair and set it down behind her back. It was a deeply intimate act that he seemed to be unaware of.

"Ooooh." Clara looked at Piper. "Right. *That* salt grinder. Um…?"

Hunter glanced down at Ani and saw his hands on her. He stepped back. Ani managed to keep herself from grabbing him and pulling his hands back onto her body.

"Is fresh-ground salt really any different from regular salt?" Piper asked.

"Yes," Ani and Hunter said in unison.

"Totally," Clara said. "Which is why I know exactly where the salt grinder is and I'm going to get it."

"I'll come with you," Piper offered.

And that's how Ani came to be alone in a laundry room with the most gorgeous man in the western hemisphere.

"Sorry," he muttered.

Ani faked a casual shrug.

"It's all good," she said, aware of an annoying fluctuation in her voice. "You need help in the kitchen?"

"Uh." Hunter stared at the ceiling. Then he shook out his shoulders and continued. "Yeah. Yes. Help me with the roasted Brussels sprouts." Hunter turned and headed into the kitchen, instinctively reaching a hand out to take hers.

Ani stared at his hand. The powerful fingers that could wield a hammer or dust the perfect amount of cardamom onto a latte.

She slipped her fingers into his.

"We're roasting them? Not steaming?"

"It's Christmas."

"Right," she attempted to muster up some snark, but her hand snuggling into Hunter's was dulling her edge. "Because you can't celebrate the birth of Christ with steamed vegetables."

"We're not heathens," he muttered.

HUNTER SEATED HIMSELF as far away from Ani as he could. First the kiss, then the irrational hand-holding incident? *What was he thinking?*

That was the problem. He *wasn't* thinking. He was trotting after Ani like one of Jet's brainless emus, curious and gullible, as she led him to certain destruction.

The night before had felt so much like a date. Well, not like any date Hunter had ever been on. It had felt right. It had felt like music. Somehow, she was easy to be with, but kept him on his toes. He couldn't wait to find out what was going to happen next with Ani.

Even though he already knew what was going to happen next. Ani's battery had arrived. She would decorate the events center then she would hop in her van and head off for the next adventure.

Hunter glanced across the table. There she was, being beautiful and intelligent again as she listened to Mom detailing their plan to visit Mesa Verde. Ani seemed to know when to make a comment and when to ask someone else for their opinion.

Piper leaned in close to him. "You know it's okay to like her."

Hunter glared at his sister. "We're just friends."

"Right."

Ani brushed her hair back from her face and smiled at Mom, then looked at Michael to take in whatever he was saying about the Grand Canyon.

"It wouldn't matter if I did like her. She's leaving."

"Really?" Piper narrowed her right eye.

Hunter exhaled a breath. "Yes. Said it her first day at work."

Piper nodded, keeping her eyes on Ani. "And nothing has happened at all to change her mind in the last month?"

Hunter's heart kicked up at Piper's suggestion. He firmly stuffed the emotion back down.

"Nothing."

"What'd you get her for Christmas?" Piper asked.

Hunter's stomach turned. He shouldn't have wrapped the boots and brought them here. He should have handed them to her as she'd left, a generous thank-you for all she'd done.

"Nothing," he said a little bit louder and a lot more sullen.

Piper looked at him and arched her brow.

Hunter couldn't help but smile. Piper started giggling.

"Just admit that you like her." Hunter scowled and Piper gave him the puppy-dog eyes she'd never been very good at. "Please? I've been in such a rotten mood ever since—" She didn't finish the sentence, but Hunter knew where it was going. He also knew her well enough not to try to offer her comfort.

"He missed out," Hunter said.

"Right. And that means you don't have the option of missing out. Look at her." Piper gestured to where Ani sat at the other end of the table in easy conversation. "You have to admit, she fits in."

Everything about Ani fit with Hunter's life.

"What are you whispering about?" Clara called them out from the other end of the table.

"I'm not whispering."

"I was whispering," Piper confirmed.

Hunter pulled his napkin from his lap and whipped it at Piper's shoulder.

"Not at Christmas dinner," Ash warned.

Most days, Hunter could take his older brother's bossiness in stride. Right now? It felt ridiculous. He should be allowed to hit his sister with a napkin if she deserved it.

"Are you guys going to let him get away with usurping your authority?" Hunter appealed to his parents.

Mom and Dad looked at one another, confused.

"Absolutely," Dad said.

"I don't intend to ever break up another fight for the rest of my life," Mom concurred.

"We are now in the spoiling stage." Dad looked at Jackson, his only grandchild. "I hope that works for you."

Jackson gave him the thumbs-up, setting the table laughing.

"Wasn't that Robert Smith's defense?" Michael asked.

"Who is Robert Smith?" Clara asked.

"You know, the doctor from Eugene who embezzled… What was it? Ten million dollars?"

Dad laughed. "That's right. The guy embezzled ten million dollars from a children's hospital and said it was so he could afford to give his kids the childhood they deserved. The spoiling defense."

Everyone was laughing now. Hunter looked up at Ani to share the joke.

But Ani was staring at the tablecloth, her face gray.

"Maybe if you'd stolen ten million dollars from the school district, we wouldn't have had such miserable childhoods." Clara giggled.

"The school district didn't have ten million dollars," Mom said dryly.

"Twelve," Ani said.

The family quieted and turned to Ani.

She cleared her throat. "Bert Smith embezzled twelve million dollars." Ani drew her eyes up from the table.

"Are you from Eugene?" Clara asked.

Ani nodded.

Clara and Piper looked at one another, communicating like only they could.

"Wait." Piper stared at Ani. "What's your last name?"

Ani's hands trembled against the table. It took her a moment, but eventually her shoulders dropped and she looked Piper straight in the eye.

She didn't have to speak.

"Stephanie Blaisedell," Piper said.

Ani lifted her left shoulder in half a shrug.

"Oh. Wow," Clara said. "We didn't recognize you—"

Ani finished the sentence with an edge to her voice, "Without a two-thousand-dollar riding helmet?"

Hunter glanced around at his family. Was he supposed to know who she was? And what did her being Stephanie Whatever have to do with an embezzling doctor?

"You had that incredible Shagya Arabian."

Ani's eyes dropped. She pulled in another breath.

"Rabiana." Ani looked happy for about two-thirds of a second. "She was—" Her voice broke. She cleared her throat and finished, "She was a good horse."

Hunter raced to keep up. Ani had owned a horse. That wasn't a surprise. But expensive riding equipment?

"What happened?" Piper asked. "You were so good. We assumed you'd be in the next Olympics."

Ani stared down at her plate. "Things. Things happened. You know."

Mom reached over and took Ani's hand. Ani didn't pull away but gripped Mom's fingers more tightly.

"Did you guys compete against each other in that horse club?" Bowman asked.

Clara rolled her eyes. "To suggest we competed against Stephanie Blaisedell would be like saying a five-year-old with a Nerf ball and a whistle were competing with Violet for coach of the year."

"Stephanie was on one level—" Piper held her right hand up above her head.

"And we were on another." Clara completed the thought, holding her hand down below the table.

"I always thought you guys were pretty good," Bowman said.

"We were okay. But Stephanie Blaisedell—"

"Please don't call me Stephanie," Ani said quietly.

Hunter started to stand, to go to Ani. Piper placed her hand on his shoulder.

"Did you know Robert Smith?" Piper asked.

"Dr. Bert was my pediatrician. And a family friend."

"I'm so sorry," Michael apologized. "I always say the wrong thing."

"No." Ani shook her head, turning her clear gaze on Michael. "Don't apologize. The man embezzled twelve million dollars from a children's hospital. He deserves to be made fun of. He deserves a lot worse."

"But?" Mom asked.

Ani pressed her lips together.

"But—" she traced her finger along the swirling pattern of the tablecloth "—it's complicated. I loved Dr. Bert. Everyone did. He was a popular pediatrician before he became chief of staff. He was greedy, but he wasn't all bad."

"Your family must have been devastated when they found out."

Ani looked around the table, her gaze clicking from one person to the next. Her eyes landed on Hunter.

"My parents were the people everyone else had to keep up with." She drew in a shaking breath. "My parents were the type of people that inspired a good man to embezzle millions of dollars. They knew all along. It wasn't a problem until he got caught."

Around the table, his family shifted in chairs, leaning toward Ani. *This* was why she didn't want to go home, or even trust the legitimacy of the concept of home.

Ani drew in a breath and sat straighter. "I'm sorry." She looked at Michael. "I hadn't heard his name in so long, I just reacted." She wiped at a tear then gave a dry laugh. "Did I just ruin Christmas dinner?"

Hunter's body reacted with no conscious thought. He stood and walked to the end of the table, resting his hands on Ani's shoulders. Her silky hair brushed his fingers, but she didn't look up at him.

"It's honestly not possible to ruin Hunter's cooking," Clara said. "And we just like you more now."

"There have been zero arguments and Ash was only a little bossy," Piper noted. "Best holiday ever."

Hunter cleared his throat. "Let's put the food away then have dessert in the living room."

"Great idea," Dad said, hopping up and taking his and Ani's empty plates.

Hunter felt Ani's shoulders rise as she filled her lungs. Then she stood and shook off his hands. Without even a glance at him, she began to help clear the table.

"HEY." HUNTER CAUGHT up to her as she walked a dish of mashed potatoes from the table. He wrapped his fingers around her arm and she fought the urge to lean into him. "Can we talk about—"

"That incredibly weird confession I dumped on your family at Christmas dinner? Sure."

The kindness in Hunter's smile made Ani feel slightly more comfortable then wretchedly uncomfortable. *What are these people doing to me?*

"Come here." He turned her body, keeping his hands on her arms as he guided her from behind. He opened a door off the kitchen and Ani stepped inside.

"The pantry?" she asked, eyeing the even rows of canned and dry goods lining the walls.

"This might be my favorite room in the whole house." Hunter shut the door behind them.

"Jet and Clara will certainly never go hungry."

"Jet will make sure of that."

"Or cold." Ani remembered Jet's powerful statement about keeping his future children warm in their own home. She'd grown disgusted with the massive homes of the rich she'd known in her childhood, but this one felt different somehow. "You know, I'm not really one for big houses—"

"Or houses actually attached to the ground."

She acknowledged that with a lift of her brows, running a hand along a row of jars holding a selection of grains.

"But this is nice."

"Jet worked hard to build a home like this."

"What's his story?" Ani asked.

Hunter sat on a stepladder, so his eyes were a few inches below hers. He took her hands in his.

"I'm interested in *your* story. Who are you?"

She raised her left shoulder. "I'm the middle child of Ted and Evie Blaisedell. I grew up in an outrageously wealthy home." Her gaze met his. "Just like you thought on the day we met."

He shook his head, concerned eyes searching her face.

"I'm sorry I unloaded on your family like that. The whole thing with Dr. Bert was so confusing. It *is* confusing. I've never really come to terms with it."

He nodded, waiting for more.

Ani bit her lip, seriously tired of fighting the urge to kiss him. If they were kissing, she could get out of this difficult conversation.

Plus, kissing.

She pulled her gaze away from his lips and studied the row of canned tomatoes above his head.

"They have sixteen cans of tomatoes," she said.

Hunter tugged at her hands and she refocused on his face.
One kiss?

One, long, warm kiss?

"By Blaisedell, I assume you mean Blaisedell Manufacturing."

"That's us."

"And you're some kind of horse phenomenon?"

Ani closed her eyes at that word. *Phenomenon.* It was loaded with expectation and grief.

"I love horses." Her voice cracked. Hunter pulled her into a hug, running a hand along her shoulder blades then cradling the back of her head.

She meant to push away, but her arms wound tighter around him. Tears began to flow, relief and sadness washing through her.

"I did *not* intend to wind up crying in your sister's pantry today," she said, resting her cheek on top of his head.

Hunter rubbed her back, pulling her between his knees. "It's okay."

"I haven't been Stephanie Blaisedell for years. She's horrible. You'd hate her."

"Oh, whoa." Hunter pulled back and looked at her. "So, you know all those women in the Bend Equestrian Society?"

Ani gave him a wry smile. "I have *never* liked Holly Banks. She brings out the worst in me."

"And she can't even handle a Dutch Warmblood," Hunter quipped.

Ani grinned down at him, allowing her arms to rest on his shoulders. "The horse ladies aren't all bad. Like any group, there are some good people—"

"And some Holly Bankses."

"And some Stephanie Blaisedells, encouraging the worst in everyone else."

Hunter shook his head and brushed a strand of her hair back. *A long kiss really would be just the thing right now.*

"That's why you pull your hood up or leave when they show up. You don't want to be recognized."

"Yes." Her fingers twitched at his collar. "I'm terrified. You don't want to see me become what I was. Stephanie Blaisedell is the mean girl everyone's climbing toward."

"I can't imagine that."

"Can't you? You've said it yourself. I'm selfish, thoughtless." He tried to speak over her, contradicting her. He didn't know what she was capable of. "Let's just say Bella's got nothing on me when it comes to leading the herd."

Hunter laughed again then asked, "Do you remember my sisters from your competitions?" he asked.

"No. I'm sorry."

"You were on a different level?"

"I was."

"You were really good?"

Ani drew in a deep breath. "Yes."

"Then why'd you quit?"

She looked into his warm, hazel eyes. The heartbreak and terrifying anger were fresh and ready, washing through her like it was yesterday.

"I competed as a hunter/jumper. Do you know what that is?"

"It's like the Olympics, right? Jumping over those high fences."

Ani nodded.

"Did you get hurt?"

"No. Not at all. I love jumping. I could hop on Bella this afternoon and go tearing over the fences on your property. I wasn't afraid." Ani glanced up, forcing herself to continue. "Competition can be hard on the horse."

"I bet. Did…did your horse get hurt?"

Ani pressed her lips together and nodded.

"Did she break something?"

Ani shook her head. "She developed ulcers. It's not uncommon. She was so stressed out all the time on the competition circuit. My parents—" Ani swallowed against the fury rising in her chest. "My parents and my trainer tried to convince me to put her down. I couldn't keep riding her for competitions, and they wanted me to put my energy into another horse."

"But you wouldn't give her up?"

"No." Ani let her gaze connect with his. "No. Rabiana and I were a team. The way I saw it, if she was done competing, so was I. But, as my father reminded me, Rabiana didn't belong to me. He bought her. She was his property."

Hunter's face shifted, confused as he reached up and brushed away her tears.

"We had a huge fight. Which was, whatever, I fought with my parents all the time. But they had a point. At the level I'd reached, this was what happened. You wear horses out, one after the next. They break bones or get injured or get ulcers. The answer, in his words, was for me to get real and deal with it."

The lump building at the back of her throat made it hard to continue.

Hunter wound his fingers through hers. "What happened?"

Ani nodded, more tears spilling down her face. "By that time, I hated everyone in the competitive horse world, except my horse. I didn't want to go to the next level without Rabiana, and certainly not if it meant putting her down. If Rabiana wasn't forced to compete, her ulcers could be treated, and then I could just ride. I had a lot of options. I was twenty-one, and had built a name for myself. I could train, give lessons, or just have a horse like a normal person. I didn't have to compete, and honestly, I didn't want to." Ani forced her shoulders to relax then looked at Hunter. "I left the barn on a Tuesday afternoon, after telling my trainer I didn't want to compete anymore."

"How'd your parents take it?"

"We didn't talk about it. I was an adult and I didn't need their permission. I figured they'd cut me off financially, but I was itching to be on my own. The van was in my name, so I had a home. I could have gotten work at any high-end horse operation. Or low-end operation, for that matter. I just wanted my horse, and my freedom."

Ani paused, pulling in a deep breath before reliving the worst of the story.

"When I returned to the barn Wednesday, Rabiana was gone. A jittery Thoroughbred was standing in her stall, along with a note from my trainer." Ani's voice cracked. She swallowed against the pain. She had to finish this. "A note from my trainer that said, *You need to toughen up and do this.*"

Hunter stood and pulled her against his chest. Ani let the fresh pain wash over her as she pressed her cheek to him.

"They put her down?"

"I don't know. No one ever told me what they did with her. She was an expensive horse, and even with the ulcers, they could have gotten good money for her. But I think my dad's vindictive nature might be stronger than his greed." Hunter wrapped his arms more tightly around her. "I miss her so much sometimes."

"I'm so sorry."

Ani snuggled closer against his chest. She hadn't talked about Rabiana, or her family, in years. It felt like she'd slipped out from under a yoke to rest, like Hunter had taken on part of the pain, and she'd taken his comfort in return.

"In my family, there are many, many strings attached to everything. All the expectations tangled around each other, and I was never going to be the daughter they wanted. They couldn't forgive me for dropping out of competition. And I will never forgive them for—" Ani pressed her lips together against the sob rising in her chest. "I will never forgive them."

Hunter's gaze moved across her face. "You get more amazing by the minute."

"No." Ani dropped her eyes. She wasn't amazing, or even particularly interesting. Another few weeks with her and he'd know the truth. "I'm a spoiled rich girl pretending to be a dirtbag in a van she bought with her parents' money."

Hunter shook his head and raised his hand to cradle her cheek. Ani shut her eyes against the tears. He had no idea how horrible she could be. How horrible she was being at this moment. Her parents had tried to apologize over the years. She knew her leaving had shaken them to the core and rearranged something in their warped worldview. Her mom, in particular, texted and emailed and called. Christmas was always the worst. But nothing was simple with her family. They might be sorry about the horse, but they were also embarrassed by her absence. The only way Ani could control the raging feelings of betrayal and loss was to walk away completely.

"Presents!" a voice called out from the kitchen, followed by a hesitant knock on the pantry door. "And dessert?"

Ani pulled away from Hunter. "Bowman said I could take his truck if I wanted to leave early. I think I'll stop ruining the family Christmas now and head back."

Hunter grabbed her hands and smiled. "But I've got a good bottle of cognac and hand-dipped chocolates for dessert." Ani bit her lip. Hunter pulled a napkin from the shelf and wiped her tears. "You know you want hand-dipped chocolates."

"If we serve your family enough cognac, do you think they'll forget my meltdown at the table?"

"Nope," Hunter said. "But they might start talking about something else."

HUNTER PATTED THE space on the floor next to him, by the tree. Ani set the remaining chocolates on the table and joined him. His heart began to do some terrible imitation of the hustle. Her confession had been an important key in understanding her. But more than that, he was honored to be the one she'd shared it with.

In their absence, his family had pieced together much of the story. His sisters had heard some rumors about the horse Ani used to ride and apparently her abrupt departure from the competition circuit had led to a lot of talk at the time. But true to form for his family, Ani got a couple of hugs and then the focus was redirected to gift-opening.

"Let me have that," Clara said, reaching her hand out for a ribbon Jackson had untied from a package. She returned to her perch on Jet's lap, smoothed the ribbon neatly and wound it around her fingers.

Ani turned her head so Clara couldn't see her speak. "You weren't kidding about your family and the recycled boxes and ribbons."

"This is just the tip of the iceberg."

The light feeling of peace Ani inspired flooded through him. He hadn't given Eighty Local, or the gala, a thought in hours. He was sitting under a tree, sharing secrets with a beautiful woman. She'd finally opened up and, from the way the last twenty-four hours had gone, he could almost hope that Piper was right; something had changed over the last few weeks and Ani might consider staying.

"Mom." Hunter looked up at Ash's grumbling. "Put your phone away."

His mom smiled blithely as she set her phone face-down on the table next to her. "Just responding to some holiday wishes."

Ani watched the exchange then met Hunter's eye, clearly trying to keep her smile to herself. "Parents these days," he muttered under his breath.

Ani turned her gaze on Clara and Jet. Clara, finished with her ribbon, had both arms around her new husband. Jet seemed to have forgotten that anyone else was in the room or that the room itself existed. Clara leaned down, sniffed his glass of cognac, and grabbed a second chocolate from the plate.

"Does your sister drink alcohol?" Ani asked. "I've never seen her drink."

"Yeah. I mean she's careful about it. She's prone to anxiety and doesn't drink when she's feeling anxious." Hunter studied his sister more carefully. She'd been in a good mood recently, but as Ani had pointed out, she hadn't had a glass of wine with dinner and had dodged the Moscow Mule he'd served the BES ladies. "But normally, when she's feeling stressed, she'll forget to eat and go for these long runs."

"Well, she was certainly packing it away at dinner."

Hunter grinned. "Yeah, I noticed. She was eating enough for two…people."

His eyes met Ani's as she came to the same realization.

Hunter turned on his brother-in-law and yelled across the room. "Could you two move any faster?!"

Clara gave him a guilty smile then buried her face in Jet's neck.

"Nope," Jet said. "This is max speed. We've got a big house to fill up."

"You're pregnant?" Mom asked, exploding out of her chair like a woman…well, like a woman who was about to get another grandchild.

Clara exchanged a look with Piper, who must have known.

"We were waiting until after presents to tell you." Clara shot Hunter a look. "But, yes. Eight weeks."

Hunter waited until Mom and Dad had hugged and congratulated the couple to their heart's content. Then he said, "You know I was your matchmaker."

"Um. No, you weren't," Clara said.

"Um. Yes, I was." Hunter mocked his sister's tone. "Think about it. Think about all the times you saw Jet last summer. Where were you? And who invited you there?"

Clara glanced at Jet as she thought through the summer, then she placed a hand over her heart. "Hunter, I had no idea."

"You're welcome," he said, gesturing at the house and family all around them.

Clara stood and walked across the room to him. She pulled on his hand and Hunter rose and hugged her. "Thank you."

"You and Piper aren't the only matchmakers in this family." Hunter grinned as she returned to Jet's lap. Time to push his luck. "So, you gonna name the baby after me?"

The family groaned. Bowman reached into the box of carefully rolled ribbons and threw one at Hunter, the red-and-green plaid unfurling as it sailed across the room.

Hunter retaliated with a pine cone from the bowl on the coffee table. Piper caught it and launched it straight back at Hunter. Within seconds, there were ribbons, pine cones and accusations flying in every direction.

"Knock it off," Ash growled. "We're not even done with presents."

"I hope somebody gave you some throw pillows," Dad said. "These pine cones scratch."

"Says the sixty-five-year-old man who was throwing them at his own grandson." Clara rolled her eyes.

Dad turned to Mom and then Jackson, a huge grin lighting his face. "Pillow fights are going to be so fun when there are more grandkids! Jackson, you ready to lead the next generation?"

"Mom, phone," Ash snapped, grabbing the phone from Mom's hands. She snatched it back then whispered to Ash as she gestured at the screen. They both glanced at Ani.

Eventually, Clara directed everyone's attention back to the presents. Hunter's heart beat harder as they made their way through the gifts. Ani watched, detached but interested, like they were an anthropological study. Clara loved her new coat. Piper was thrilled with the necklace, and asked Bowman to thank Christy for picking it out. Hunter felt sweat prick the back of his neck.

"One last present!" Piper said, picking up the old, old box. She looked at the tag attached to the clumsily tied ribbon.

Hunter swallowed. *Time to man up.*

He took the box from Piper and handed it to Ani. Her reaction was exactly what he'd feared.

"I don't need any presents," she said.

The room quieted.

"It's something to remember us by," he said, holding out the box. He could feel his heartbeat throughout his entire frame.

Ani took the box and, for the first time, her eyes left his face and settled on the present. She looked sharply back at Hunter. He was pretty sure he looked pathetic.

Ani unknotted the ribbon and set it on the coffee table.

Clara snatched it up as Ani lifted the lid. Her hands shook as she reached into the box.

"Oh. Wow," Piper said as Ani lifted one boot then the other out of the box.

"Okay, those are the most beautiful boots on the planet," Clara said.

Ani looked up at Hunter with an unreadable expression. He cleared his throat.

"I thought you could take a little Outcrop with you when you go," he said. "There will always be some dust on your boots that belongs here."

Ani met his gaze then gave him the most brilliant smile. Did she realize yet that she belonged here too?

CHAPTER FIFTEEN

"You READY?" Hunter asked her, gripping the handle to his door.

Ready to get out of the warm truck with Hunter and sprint through the cold to spend some time in the freezing barn? Not really.

"Do I have a choice?" Ani prepared to open the passenger door.

"Nope. Let's go."

Hunter opened his door and icy air poured in. Ani jumped out and started running. Their flashlight beams bounced before them as they rushed the barn.

"I've got Stan!" she yelled, ducking into the old stallion's stall.

Stan stood waiting for her, completely unbothered by the cold, the erratic glow of the flashlight or Ani's fussing. *Such a good horse.* Even though Bowman had wrapped padded insulation around the buckets and filled them with warm water earlier in the day, a film of ice had frozen over the top. Ani cracked the ice with a stick and topped off the water. She laid a hand over Stan's untrimmed coat.

"Does he need a blanket?"

"He won't take one," Hunter replied from another stall. "Canadians can do pretty well in the cold if they haven't been clipped."

Ani patted Stan's thick coat. The hair hadn't been trimmed and stood up in places, creating a nice level of insulation. She dashed into the next stall, broke the ice on the gelding's water, and ran a hand under the blanket he wore. Nice and cozy; he would be fine.

She heard Hunter breaking ice across the way.

Hunter had volunteered to head out and take care of the horses. Ani told herself the decision to join him was based entirely on the fact that she would be more comfortable back in the gardener's cottage, rather than in Jet and Clara's home. It had nothing to do with being on the ranch with a beautiful man who'd just given her the most thoughtful gift she'd ever received.

Nothing at all whatsoever.

Oddly, she felt lighter after her confession at Christmas dinner. Rather than feeling horribly embarrassed for doing the wrong thing, she felt more comfortable with the family.

We just like you more now, Clara had said.

That was ridiculous. These people were ridiculous. Very nice, but ridiculous all the same.

"Do you want help with Bella?" Hunter called out.

Ani grinned in the darkness. "Nope. Bella hates you."

She opened the latch and stepped into Bella's stall. Her coat had been clipped, as she was still saddled regularly. Yet she'd refused a blanket.

"How's your water?"

Bella snorted. She'd broken the ice herself and drank most of her bucketful.

"Here you go." Ani topped off the water and then ran a hand over Bella's back. She was not warm to the touch.

"I'd like to get a blanket on you." Bella glared at her. Ani gave the horse a bored look. Bella returned to her water.

"She won't take it," Hunter said.

Ani jumped from foot to foot to keep warm as she studied the horse. Bella shivered then flared her nostrils.

What does Bella want?

She was strong and brave, a magnificent leader. She could tolerate humans but she didn't want them interfering with her business as lead mare. Ani pressed her forehead against Bella's, trying to give the horse some of her warmth.

"It's okay to take a blanket," she whispered.

Bella twitched against the cold, as though she were fighting the entire weather pattern. If they were out on the tundra, she would round up the herd and they'd huddle together for warmth. She didn't want a blanket; she wanted the challenge of leadership.

Ani put her hands on the sides of Bella's nose. "I know you can handle the cold, but it's okay to be warm and comfortable." Bella dropped her gaze and stilled. "You can trust us. We're looking out for you and the whole herd."

Bella let out a huff of breath and shivered. Hunter backed out of a stall and looked at them. Ani held her hand out to him and mouthed the word "Blanket."

She ran her hand along Bella's withers, quietly reassuring her as Hunter stepped into the stall with a blanket. Working together, they slipped it over her. Bella flinched but didn't resist. When they had the blanket settled, Bella relaxed, her eyelids drooping as she leaned her nose against Ani's neck. "It's okay," Ani told her again. "You can rest now."

Feeling his eyes on her, Ani looked up at Hunter. He stepped closer and she could feel his warmth as he said softly, "You're amazing."

Ani shook her head. "I think I just understand Bella a little better than you do."

"No doubt. That's still amazing." He held her gaze then glanced around the barn. "Everybody's got hay and water.

I'll come back and do another feeding around one a.m. Ready to get back to your cottage?"

Ani shivered. "It's going to be so cold."

"I'll help get the fire going. Sound good?"

Ani was tempted to resist. She could handle the fire on her own. She didn't need Hunter's help. Bella caught her eye, as though reminding her of her own words. *I know you can handle this, but it's okay to be warm and comfortable.*

"It sounds…fantastic," Ani admitted. "Let's go."

HUNTER'S HANDS WERE so cold, he could barely turn the doorknob. When he and Ani finally got inside the cottage, it was just as bad as the barn. Colder, in fact, because it wasn't filled with large animals.

"I have never been this cold," Ani said, grabbing several madrone logs off the woodpile.

Hunter knelt before the woodstove and took them from her. Ani aimed her flashlight so Hunter could see what he was doing. He laid logs, kindling and paper in the woodstove without the patience a good fire requires, then peeked over his shoulder. Ani was jumping in place, making her the cutest cold person alive. Hunter shook his head and tried to focus on anything else.

"You know this is heartbreak wood."

"What's that?" Ani asked through chattering teeth. He could hear her jumping, her new boots tapping the floor as she landed.

"When Jet thought he'd lost Clara, he chopped wood for a week straight."

Ani giggled. Encouraged, Hunter noted, "His woodpile is a half mile long."

The rhythm of Ani's jumping changed as she hopped from one foot to the other, giggling harder. Hunter struggled to light a match.

"After he proposed and got it through his head that she wasn't going anywhere, he delivered truckfuls of firewood to everyone he knew."

Ani laughed harder then started to wheeze. "It hurts to laugh."

He gave in and turned from the woodstove to look at her. Hair fell around her shoulders, and she shook from the cold, jumping and laughing. She was so beautiful, like a sky full of stars.

"I think it's stripped," she said.

Hunter stared blankly.

"The match. I think you stripped it."

Hunter looked down to see every bit of red was gone from the head of the match. He started with another and quickly stripped it too. He should probably stop staring at Ani if he wanted to get the match lit.

"Let me have that." She took the matches from his hands.

"Is this another skill you possess? Lighting matches with frozen hands?"

A flame illuminated Ani's face as she struck the match and handed it to Hunter. He touched it to the paper in the woodstove and a fire roared to life. Ani pulled her hair up as she leaned forward to blow gently. The fire crackled before them, a welcome heat in the cold, dark room.

Hunter sat back. Ani scooched close to him. Without hesitation, Hunter wrapped an arm around her, his heart beating newly warmed blood to every corner of his body.

Ani pressed her cold nose into his neck.

"Whoa."

"Sorry," she mumbled, pressing her face further into his neck. "But you are saving my face from freezing."

The warmth of her breath against his skin made up for

almost all the cold he'd endure that evening—and his entire life.

Hunter placed his frozen fingers under her chin. Ani yipped then laughed.

"Did you soak your hands in the water buckets while we were at the barn?"

"Are yours any better?"

Ani stilled. He couldn't read her expression in the dark.

She shifted and brought one incredibly cold hand to the side of his face. Her fingers spread out against his jaw; her thumb brushed the tender flesh under his eye.

Her soft, cold touch unleashed every emotion in Hunter; he wanted to kiss her, to laugh with her, to beg her to stay. He turned his head, lips brushing her palm. She leaned in closer. Tentative, she met his eyes then let her gaze return to his lips.

Hunter's hands closed behind her head and pulled her into his kiss. Every tamped-down, pushed-back moment of longing focused into one long, beautiful kiss.

"Hunter," Ani whispered against his lips.

He hadn't thought it was possible to care for a woman more than he already did, but his name, on her lips, in that tone, did it. Fuses blew in his brain in a chain reaction as he wound his fingers into her hair. Heavy and soft, her hair felt like silk against his fingers. He wound his hands in tighter, deepening the kiss.

Ani pulled back and looked up at him, her golden eyes questioning.

"Is this a good idea?" she whispered.

Hunter scrambled through his few remaining synapses to figure out what she was talking about. She gestured between them.

Her face was even prettier in the flickering firelight. *Was this a good idea?* She was going to break his heart, completely shatter it. He was already in love, and that had started sometime around the first three seconds he'd spent in her company and was cemented with the illegal operation of a deep fryer.

She'd probably known how he'd felt before he did. But if that was the case, why was she trembling? Besides the cold, obviously. She looked scared, but she also kept glancing at his lips. And she had one hand intertwined with his and the other at the back of his neck.

"It's either the best or worst idea I've ever had," he said. "But we might freeze to death if we don't keep kissing."

Ani laughed. Hunter was mesmerized by her joy.

"Did I express how much I love these boots?"

Hunter leaned in to kiss her again then kept his nose against her cheek as he said, "These boots are a selfish gift. I gave them to you because you look so good in them."

Ani laughed, relieved at the joke. Hunter leaned closer and kissed her forehead. "Best Christmas ever."

She flushed. "Employee making a scene at your family dinner and then running around in the cold dealing with horses?"

He shook his head. "Spending the day with you, and my family. Good food, the best company and kissing you? What else could possibly be on my list?"

Ani studied his face. Something like doubt flickered across her expression. She shifted again. Her mischievous smile emerged. "It has been the best Christmas ever. So, we should make the most of it while we're here?"

Hunter leaned in to kiss her again.

"Definitely."

IT SOUNDED LIKE a synthesized harp. A super annoying, super loud synthesized harp, and it had been strumming for some time when Hunter finally addressed it.

He sat back, eyes closed, and took in a deep breath as he pulled out his phone. "It's time for the feeding."

"Noooo!" Ani snatched his phone to check the time. "Impossible. We've only been here five minutes."

The alarm blinking 1:00 a.m. disputed her assessment.

Hunter stood. "If this concerned anything other than the horses' well-being, I would ignore it."

Ani stood, as well, realizing she was literally weak in the knees. "Want company?" The woodstove was pumping out heat now, making the cabin toasty warm, but all she wanted to do was to follow Hunter out into the cold.

He pulled his hat off the hook next to the door. "*Want* company? Yes. Accept it? No. You get some sleep."

Ani shook her head slowly. "Not sleepy."

He grinned back at her. "Me neither."

Ani felt heat rise up her neck.

"But," Hunter continued, "I need to check on the horses, and a walk through the bracing cold is not a bad idea for me right now."

Ani followed him to the door, unable to repress her smile as she reached for his hand. He stilled as her fingers brushed his then he spun and caught her in his arms. "I already miss you."

Ani rose on her tiptoes, the boots flexing with her feet as she stretched to meet Hunter's lips.

The synthesized harp blared again, louder and more aggressively calm than before. Ani dropped back onto her heels.

"You tell Bella she owes me."

Hunter brought his fingers to the tip of his hat and winked in a move so adorable she could barely refrain from yelling *Do it again!*

Hunter jogged a few steps out the door then turned

around. "Hey, want to hang out tomorrow? I was thinking maybe we could... I don't know, go work in my restaurant for twelve hours straight?"

Ani laughed. "It's a date."

"Great. Pick you up in—" Hunter checked his phone "—seven hours?"

Ani leaned out the door frame into the cold night air. "Can't wait."

Hunter grinned, his smile lighting the cold, dark night. He gazed at her, finally saying, "Good night, beautiful."

Then he turned and trotted off toward the barn.

Ani spun, swinging her arms, feeling light and free. How had four hours passed so quickly? One minute Hunter was leaning in for their first kiss and the next his alarm was going off.

Maybe his clock was wrong? Ani fished her jacket off the floor and pulled her phone out of the pocket to check the time. Her fingers swiped across the screen. She froze.

Six texts.

She dropped the phone facedown on the table and walked to the window. Hunter jogged to the barn, visible in the glow of the Christmas lights.

This was what mattered. Any Christmas ultimatums from her parents meant nothing. She didn't have to read them, didn't have to spoil this moment by looking at her phone.

Hunter disappeared into the barn. Could she do this? Stay here, explore whatever was happening with this incredible man? Maybe. It would be a challenge. But, wow, was she feeling motivated.

Her phone buzzed again. Ani closed her eyes against the ache in her chest. 1:00 a.m. and her mom was still texting.

Ani gave up and looked at her phone.

2:15 p.m. Mom: Merry Christmas, Stephanie! I guess you aren't going to make it? If you want to stop by, we're here. We'd love to see you.

5:35 p.m. Mom: Your sister just arrived. Her little Della has your eyelashes. I know she'd love for you to meet your niece.

7:10 p.m. Dad: Pls text your mother. Merry Xmas.

8:23 p.m. Dad: It would mean a lot to her.

11:40 p.m. Mom: It's late. I know you're not coming. I know you can't stand us. I don't know how many times you want me to say I'm sorry. I am sorry. I don't understand why you keep punishing us. You don't like our lifestyle, and I don't understand yours, but we are still family. Anyway, it's Christmas night and I miss you. Please text back and let me know you're doing okay. That's all I'm asking.

1:03 a.m. Mom: Would you please text me this week sometime and let me know you're okay?

Ani wiped at the tears. It was always like this. The first few times Mom had sent texts like this, Ani had responded. But responses led to conversations, which led to arguments. They had excuses for their behavior. She couldn't forgive them. They still thought she had a future that could include horses.

But, deep down inside, Ani didn't respond because she was self-absorbed, just like her mother had always accused her of being. Had her parents changed, like they'd claimed?

Perhaps. But she hadn't, not in her heart. She didn't respond because it was too hard to be connected with them.

And here she was, tangling up again with another family. They would love her until they got to know her, the real her, an angry, selfish person who held on to old hurts. Someone who could have dealt with her parents as an adult years ago, but still clung to her twenty-one-year-old heartbreak.

Hunter liked her, a lot. But he was simply too good for her. They might have two months of bliss then her true nature would shine through. She wouldn't be able to keep it together. And she would never get over disappointing Hunter.

CHAPTER SIXTEEN

WHY WAS LIGHT streaming through the windows? Hunter propped himself up on his elbows. He couldn't remember the last time he'd slept past dawn. He couldn't remember the last time he'd felt so incredibly good. The BES Gala was less than forty-eight hours away and Hunter wasn't even nervous.

The events of the previous day flooded him. Hunter leaned back on his pillow and grinned.

Because of Ani. With her by his side, there was no way he could fail. The grueling work of Eighty Local was fun now. Any corner he backed himself into, Ani created a fresh new way to get him out. She was the most amazing woman. And she was here, on the property, probably ready for coffee.

Hunter sprang out of bed.

In minutes, he was dressed, out the door and heading to her cottage. It was warmer this morning; the cold spell had snapped. Or maybe *he* was just warmer. He wished he had flowers for her, but there wasn't anything blooming at this time of year.

Hunter scanned the property. Could you take a woman a bouquet of kale?

Technically, yes, but is it a good idea?

There would be plenty of time for flowers. He'd ask Clara to grab a bouquet and drop them off at Eighty Local today. Then, when the first primrose starts arrived at

OHTAF, he'd line the walkway to the cottage with flowers for her.

And when they were married, he'd plant every bulb imaginable around their house and seed whole fields in wildflowers for her.

Hunter jogged up the front steps of the cottage. Ani opened the door, hesitated for a moment, then stepped into his arms. Hunter grinned against her hair.

"Good morning," he whispered. This was the best morning.

Ani hugged him tighter. He hadn't thought things could get any better, but now she was a fraction of an inch closer.

"I know you need to get to the restaurant." Her words were muffled against his chest. "I'm just not ready for this to be over."

Hunter kissed her cheek. It had to be almost eight. He was going to be late to work for the first time in his life. When he got there, nothing would be ready for the day. There would be cleanup from Christmas Eve, and a ton of prep for the gala to finish. But Ani wanted a few more minutes.

Fine by him. By his calculations, he'd be begging her to marry him within the week. Babies, life insurance, joint checking accounts, he was ready. Hunter responded with a long kiss to stop himself from saying any of this.

Ani sighed. "I'm going to miss you so much."

"I was hoping you'd head into work with me." He kissed her again. "I don't want to spoil this, but I have a ton of work to do today."

Ani blinked. A tear snuck out and rolled down her cheek.

"You okay?" Hunter moved his hand to cup her face. "We don't have to go right now."

Ani pulled back and glanced behind her into the cabin.

Cool air rushed in around him as he followed her gaze. The cabin was very tidy. Too tidy.

"What's going on?" he asked before realizing he wasn't sure he wanted to know.

Ani closed her eyes, tears lacing her lashes together. Panic started to rise in his chest. He laid his hand on her face and brushed at a tear with his thumb. Her cheek felt so right in his palm. *This* was right. Everything would be okay.

She trembled but didn't open her eyes to look at him as she said, "Hunter, I should get ready to leave."

The words shattered around him like a thin sheet of ice over a dark, cold pond.

"Ani..."

"My battery is here."

He let out a breath and stepped back, falling into the icy, lonely hurt. He opened his mouth to speak but nothing came out.

Ani stepped close to him again and rested her cheek against his chest. Reflexively, Hunter wound his fingers through hers.

"Don't go."

She placed a hand against his chest and stepped back to look up at him. Her eyes held a complicated mix of determination and regret. She took a second step back.

She was actually going to do this. Everything he felt was nothing to her, everything they'd experienced.

"Is this the part where I pretend like I don't care?" he asked.

"No. We shouldn't have to pretend anything. That's the point. I don't want to pretend like we can—"

"Like we can what?" he asked, shifting to look into her eyes, daring her to say it.

"My life is moving from place to place."

"Why?"

"Because it's how I've chosen to live."

"Choose something else. Choose this."

Her eyes clouded then closed at his words. "I have to go. I'm sorry."

Hunter stepped away from her. Reality went better with cold air. "So, this is just nothing?"

"Of course it's not nothing."

What had he expected? He'd known from the start she was leaving.

"This has been—" Ani cleared her throat and looked back up at him. "This has been incredible. It doesn't change who I am."

It changed who he was. Every stubborn impulse was gone. The panic, the daily fear of failure, was gone when Ani walked into any room.

"Ani, don't go. I can't even think about facing the day without you."

"Hunter, I couldn't survive here. Within a few months, you'd hate everything about me."

"That's not true."

"I think I know myself better than you do."

"Do you? Because you keep talking about this mysterious self-centered woman lurking inside you, and I have yet to see her."

"I won't survive here."

"I won't survive if you go." He held her gaze and could see her resolve waver.

She crossed her arms as she threw down a dare. "Okay, then. Leave with me. Leave Eighty Local. Lock the door and come with me."

He shook his head. "Ani, I can't—"

"Exactly," she snapped. "You can't leave. Eighty Local is your life."

"I'm asking you to be a part of that life."

"What if I want you to be a part of my life? Don't think I haven't thought about it. How fun it would be to pull into an entirely new town with you next to me. The two of us, moving from place to place, seeing the world together. Yeah, I'm selfish enough to want that."

"It's not the same. I have commitments. I owe people money."

"If you wanted to leave, you could make it happen. But I'm not worth it."

"Don't say that."

"I'm not, Hunter. I'm not worth it, admit it. You have your family and your community. You like it here. You like connecting with your patrons, and hanging out with your siblings, and making cakes for your old coach and his new wife. That's who you are. I would never ask you to change. Don't ask me to change."

Hunter's legs buckled and nausea swept through him. He sat on the front steps, open to the cold wind picking up from the east. Ani sat next to him.

Instinctively, he wrapped his arms around her, running his hands through her hair, down her back. Of course she was leaving. He'd been so naive to think this relationship could work. He failed at everything. That's just what he did. No one expected anything better.

Hunter leaned his forehead against hers. Her fingers wound into his hair as she pulled his lips to hers. Salt tears flavored the kiss with grief. He wasn't going to get over this. There was no way he could pull off running an events center without her.

Ani kept her hands in his hair as she spoke, her breath whispering across his face. "I'll install the battery this morning, then come in and clean and decorate the hall."

She shuddered, pulling in a breath. "I can stay in the van tonight, then leave tomorrow morning."

Hunter pulled back. "You're leaving tomorrow?"

"I have the battery."

Hunter shifted quickly from pain to panic to anger. "You're not going to help with the gala?"

ANI OPENED HER mouth to apologize then stopped. *The gala. That was what mattered here.*

He stared at her, incredulous that there might be anything more important than an event at Eighty Local. "I've got everything riding on this event and you have to leave the night before? If you'd sat down and calculated the best way to hurt me, you couldn't have done a better job."

"You know I can't stay for the gala," she whispered.

"Why? Because you might fall off the free-spirit wagon and revert to your former, bourgeois self?"

His anger flattened her. It felt like being bucked off a horse. There was nothing that made her madder than being bucked. A flash of anger washed her conflicting emotions clean. Ani moved away from him, shaking her head. "That's what this really is, in the end. You like having an attractive, helpful woman around Eighty Local."

"I do. I love having you here. I love—" He stopped speaking. Hunter stood and stalked to the end of the porch, staring off toward the barn.

"I get it. This matters to you. And I'm so glad I was here to help. But I am not going to pretend like I'm anything more to you than a really great employee."

Hunter stood with his back to her. "How can you say that? How can you possibly say that?" He turned, examining her with fresh eyes. "You show up, you get exactly what you want, we have—" Hunter struggled to get air in.

He gestured between them. "We have this. Then you act like I'm the one being selfish?"

"The gala matters to you, fine. But—"

"It does matter to me," he said. "The good opinion of my community, my family…it matters."

"You care about the opinion of the Bend Equestrian Society," she snapped.

"I care about my restaurant succeeding."

"Your restaurant is fine. You're so busy you can barely keep up." He started to interrupt her. Ani held up a hand. "I know the drill. You complain about how you think you're going to fail, but that's not going to happen. Eighty Local is a great restaurant. The events center is beautiful. The BES Gala and every other gala you throw for the next fifty years will be a huge success."

"It's not that easy."

"I didn't say it's easy. I'm trying to tell you you're too invested in the opinions of others."

Blood rushed to Hunter's face. This was the side of her he needed to see; the side of her that could make people seethe with anger. He crossed his arms and glared at her. Ani could feel the tender kisses he'd placed on her cheek evaporate in his contempt.

"You have no idea how the finances of a restaurant work."

She tried to respond but he spoke over her. "You don't know a single number involved with running a restaurant. I bought Eighty Local with money I earned. I took nothing from my family."

She blinked hard. "Right, and I'm just a rich girl who doesn't understand anything."

"I didn't say that."

"Yeah, well, Hunter Wallace, not everyone lives in your perfect world."

"Everyone's invited."

She met his gaze. All of the want came flooding through her. *This man, this place, this family.* They made her want to flatten her own tires with a freshly sharpened steak knife. She wanted to wake up a local. But that wasn't going to happen, because all this emotion wasn't going to change who she was.

"I am trying to be realistic. We might have…what? A couple of great months? Then we'll start fighting and, suddenly, we're trapped together, resenting one another, and *then* I leave? Believe me, it's a lot less painful this way."

"That's not how all relationships go."

"Name one long-term couple who doesn't secretly hate each other."

"My parents?"

"Your parents aren't normal."

"No, they're not. They actually take the time to care."

"It's not that I don't care," Ani cried. Hunter started to move toward her. She could not let him touch her again; one touch would tether her to this place, and they'd be trapped. She stood and paced into the yard of the cottage.

"Look, any relationship is going to have problems." His voice caught, softened. "You happen to be really good at solving problems. It's like your superpower."

She gave him a weak smile.

"And I work really hard at things that matter to me."

"Hunter," she said, unable to stop herself from drifting toward him. "You could lose all of this. The gala could fail and, yes, somehow those horrible women could convince the world not to eat your amazing food. But you would still have your family and your friends. You would still have a beautiful place to live and people to cook for. My life has been, and continues to be, so radically different from yours. Please don't ask me to be something I'm not."

"How do you know this isn't you? If I'm judging from the last month, I'd say you fit in pretty well." He reached out and took her left hand. He held her fingers lightly, staring down at them. This thumb brushed across her fingers. "You fit perfectly."

Ani allowed the temptation to wash through her.

But, no. Everyone responded to her this way. She knew how to be social. She'd been trained to charm.

She gazed up at Hunter. While leaving now was hard, it could get a lot worse: falling more deeply in love with him, coming to depend on him, imagining herself a part of this community. Then Hunter realizing she was unlovable. Realizing she'd manipulated him into loving her.

Hunter dropped her hand. "You're leaving because you think we might fail."

"I'm leaving because I know we'd fail."

Hunter crossed his arms and stared at her, anger darkening his face. "Well, that's what I do when you're not around. Fail."

She threw her arms up in frustration, new tears threatening. "Think about it. What happens when we get comfortable and our worst selves come out?"

"This *is* my worst. Getting ready for the gala, freaking out at every turn, working myself into the ground, snapping at you and everyone else. This is it. Most of the time, I'm a pretty good guy."

Ani shook her head. There was nothing to say. Naturally, he had a hundred beautiful moments up his sleeve. He'd become a better person with each passing day. But Ani knew this was her very best. Every creative, fun, interesting part of her had come shining out to greet Hunter Wallace over the last month.

He'd never seen her worst, and he needed to. Now. She'd

let him know just how low she'd learned to strike. Ani relaxed her shoulders and steadied her breathing.

"I'm not going to stay here and follow your small-town rules. Work hard, get married, pretend you're not miserable until you die."

She met his eyes, tilting her head like she'd learned to do when shutting someone down.

He widened his stance. "No. You're going to leave and live within your own narrow set of rules."

"You're accusing me of living within the rules?" Ani scoffed. "You, Hunter Wallace, are accusing *me* of having a narrow set of rules?" Ani shook her head against the sickness rising in her stomach. "I'm free. You're the one chained to this place."

"You can tell yourself that, if it makes you feel better. I never met anyone with so many rules." Ani tried to interject but Hunter spoke over her. "Don't stay in one place too long. Don't buy anything. Don't celebrate holidays. Stay away from horses. Stay away from anyone who has ever owned a horse or might be thinking of riding a horse. Don't listen to anyone who might challenge your worldview."

Ani held up her hand to stop him from talking. This wasn't how the argument was supposed to go. He took a step toward her.

"Don't get attached."

"That's not—"

"I'm heading into work." He took long, heavy strides off the porch.

"Hunter, you don't know me. You have no idea who Stephanie Blaisedell is."

He stopped in the yard but refused to look back at her. "You're right. Because the woman I'm falling in love with would never walk away."

CHAPTER SEVENTEEN

ANI'S FINGERS TREMBLED against the steering wheel as she parked her van in front of Eighty Local. She pulled in another breath. She could do this. She just needed to go inside, face Hunter, say goodbye to Maia and hit the road.

She reached into the passenger seat where the Second Chance Cowgirl bag sat. She tried to imagine Maia's expression when she saw the Duran Duran T-shirt but could only picture her face when Ani told her she was leaving.

Ani finally gave in to the pressure building in the back of her throat. The sob that escaped startled her as she cradled her head in her hands, tears falling through her fingers.

Why had she allowed herself to get attached? She'd known what she was doing and yet she'd walked straight in, every step of the way.

She tried to tell herself that Hunter didn't care, or cared a lot more about Eighty Local and his standing in this community than he did about her. She just happened to be able to help him. It didn't matter who had showed up, Hunter would have been grateful.

Ani wrapped her arms tight around her middle and gulped in air.

Why was it so hard to hate this guy? If she could hate Hunter, it would help detract from the self-loathing pooling in her gut.

He was genuinely attracted to her. They'd both felt it from day one. And she could even believe he'd enjoyed her company. He'd wanted to laugh with her, to have her help him with the ridiculous string of problems he got himself into. These were normal, human wants.

Ani rose and paced to the back of her van, reminding herself of all the adventures it had brought her.

If she stayed, Hunter would expect her to keep amazing him at every turn. And when she ran out of surprises, he'd be left with a self-involved, stubborn woman who was out of her element.

A light knock startled her. She looked up to see Lacy peering in through the window in the passenger's-side door.

Ani pulled in a deep breath and wiped her tears away. She walked to the slider door and opened it, stepping back to let Lacy in.

"I have some good news, and a surprise," Lacy said, holding up her phone. "Which do you want first?"

"Hi. Um—"

"Or at least I think it's good news. I'm not entirely sure. One of the families you helped at the Mistletoe Festival wants to give their child riding lessons."

"Oh." Ani swallowed. She could read Lacy's expression. The family wanted *her* to teach the lessons.

Lacy glanced around the van then tilted her head. "Are you packing up?"

"Yes." Ani tried to sound cheerful, determined. "My battery arrived. Thank you so much for having me stay."

"It's been our pleasure," she said, confused but determined to see the good intentions Ani just didn't have. "You must be happy to get back in your van."

Ani glanced around. She loved her van but was in no way happy about leaving the cabin.

"You're welcome to park on our property," Lacy continued.

"Oh, thanks." Ani drifted over to brush nonexistent

crumbs off the counter. "I'm taking off, right after I clean the events center."

She glanced at Lacy to see how the declaration had landed.

Not well.

Lacy glanced down at her phone, the color draining from her face. Then her strong gaze met Ani's. "You're leaving Outcrop?"

Ani scrambled for an excuse. "I planned to be in Tucson weeks ago."

"What's in Tucson?"

Ani's mind went blank. *What was in Tucson? Cacti? Rock formations?* She looked up at Lacy, who was waiting expectantly for the answer to her real question, *What's in Tucson that could possibly be more important than my son and his small-town dreams?*

Ani drew in a breath and dropped her shoulders. She looked Lacy in the eye.

"I have no idea," she said. "That's why I'm going."

Lacy stared at her then turned sharply and looked back at Eighty Local.

Everyone wants something from you.

Even this perfect family.

Blood began to pound in her temples as her fears were confirmed. Lacy Wallace had never seen her as anything beyond someone who could help her son improve his standing in the community.

It was good to have her dreams shattered like this. It was going to make leaving so much easier and ensure that she never got stuck like this again. The Wallace family might spend their whole lives pretending they cared about others, but in the end, they only looked out for one another.

Ani didn't need them. She would take pleasure in experience, in the now. The only possible purpose of life was to learn. She would travel, experience and observe. And she would never *never* get herself stuck in another trap like this.

"Thank you," Ani said, realizing she sincerely meant it. "This has been a wonderful experience. Thank you for taking care of me and including me in your family for the holiday."

Lacy gave Ani an icy glare, reminding her of Bella.

"I'm not the one you need to thank," she said. Her lips tightened then relaxed as she saw Maia crossing the lot toward them. She nodded at Ani. "I think there's some-one else you should say goodbye to. Best of luck in your travels."

Lacy walked away. Ani couldn't help but follow her out of the van.

"Thank you," Ani called again.

Lacy didn't turn around but raised a hand as though to block the words. "Thank Hunter," she said curtly.

The crooked smile Maia had been wearing dropped as Lacy walked past her into the restaurant. Intuitively, Maia glanced at Ani.

"Hi, there." Ani faked bravery as she grabbed her gift for Maia. "How was Christmas?"

"We made spaghetti." Maia raised her right foot to show off a new pair of black Converse high-tops. "And Caleb gave me these."

"Awesome!"

Maia pressed her wrists together. "They're like yours."

Ani nodded, unable to force a response past the pain in her throat. Maia glanced nervously at the side door to Eighty Local where Lacy had entered the building.

Ani pulled in a breath. She had to leave Outcrop. That was nonnegotiable. And, yes, Maia would be disappointed, but that wasn't something Ani could control.

Ani swallowed hard and held up the bag. "I bought you a present too."

Maia's eyes brightened. She looked at the logo on the bag then met Ani's gaze. "This is where I thought my mural could go, Second Chance Cowgirl."

Ani pressed her lips together, determined to hold back her tears. Maia, always so good at reading other's reactions, glanced past Ani into the van. Her eyes jumped to Ani's face then down at the bag.

"Sweetie, I have to go."

Maia closed her eyes tightly and shook her head.

"I live out of my van."

Big tears began to drip down Maia's face. Her voice was barely a whisper. "You…you can park it here. Hunter said so."

"I'm not very good at staying in one place," Ani said.

Tears were washing across Maia's face now. The girl struggled to keep it together. "You wouldn't have to stay all the time. You could park here and then go visit other places."

"Maia, I'm so sorry."

Maia shook her head against the apology in a panic. "But didn't Lacy tell you about the surprise?"

"Oh, Maia, I'd be terrible at giving riding lessons. I'm not a good teacher."

Maia's huge eyes met hers, incredulous. A sob constricted her throat yet she managed to whisper, "You— you're the *best* teacher."

Tears covered Maia's face.

Ani closed her eyes, trying to keep it together. After years of hurting people by being mean, here she was hurting someone she'd tried to be nice to. Pain was clearly all she was capable of inspiring.

Ani took a shaking breath. "Here, take your gift—"

Maia shook her head, choking back a sob, then turned and started walking away.

"Maia?" Ani called, holding up the bag. Maia didn't turn around. She just shook her head and started walking faster.

And this is why you don't let yourself get attached.

Maia fled across the parking lot. When she came to the mural they'd painted, she paused then turned back. Ani knew the girl well enough by now to know she felt bad about feeling bad, and that made Ani feel even worse. Maia gave her a little wave and an unconvincing smile before skirting the restaurant and heading back toward town, leaving Ani holding her gift.

THE BACK DOOR OPENED. Hunter kept his focus on the task before him, even as his heart lurched into his throat.

"Honey?"

Hunter dropped his knife. Not the voice he'd been expecting.

"Hi, Mom."

"You doing okay?" Lacy came to stand next to him and rested her hand on his back, like she'd done when he was in trouble as a kid. Gentle hand on his back, firm words of discipline ready to spill.

"Not really." Hunter grabbed another kohlrabi and started peeling it.

"What happened?"

Hunter didn't want to look at his mom.

What happened? Such a loaded question. When she asked, it generally meant *How did you manage to mess this up?*

"Her battery arrived," he said. "That's all this was. A job. A layover on the way to the next spot."

"I don't believe that."

"You can believe what you want, but she's out of here." Hunter slid the julienned kohlrabi into a bowl of ice water and picked up another.

Lacy reached over and grabbed a slice of kohlrabi from the bowl. Hunter glared at his mother.

"This is a restaurant," he reminded her.

"I am your mother," she reminded him, and ate the kohlrabi. Hunter grabbed another kohlrabi and a knife and handed them to her.

"Wash your hands, and then I need these julienned as thin as you can get them."

"Sweetheart. I can't believe she's just walking out. You two have been an incredible team these past few weeks. Even your sisters are saying so."

"Yeah? Well, I'm struggling with it myself. But she doesn't respect this." He gestured to the restaurant. "She doesn't respect my vision for this place, or the fact that I'm willing to work for it."

Lacy glanced around the room. Of all he had done, Hunter felt like this room was the biggest monument to his work ethic. He'd transformed the greasy back room of the former restaurant housed in the building. It was now a clean, streamlined workspace, with foods from every corner of Oregon. He'd worked incredibly hard to build this space, in which he worked so incredibly hard.

"Why are you so driven?" his mom asked.

Hunter looked up from his task. They'd had the argument about his relentless work schedule so many times. Every argument ended with her asking the same question, and him refusing to answer.

Was it possible she honestly didn't know?

He swallowed, kept his eyes on his work. "I want this to be a nice place. I want everyone who walks in here to get a good meal at a reasonable price. I want everyone

who works for or with me to think they got a fair deal."
He paused. Then he finally said what he needed to. "I want
you and Dad to be proud."

"Honey, we are proud. So proud of you."

Hunter shrugged.

"You know that, don't you?"

Hunter shook his head. "I know I was a huge disappointment in school."

"You weren't a disappointment—"

"Mom, I couldn't sit still, I could barely pull C's."

"That never mattered."

"If it never mattered, why did we fight about it all the
time?"

Lacy set down the knife and stared at him. She looked
hurt, which had not been his intention. He'd wanted them
to be able to discuss the past honestly, and his failure was
a big part of that past.

"Mom, I know it was humiliating. You and Dad were
these legendary teachers, and your son could barely pass
his classes. You had all these great students, like Jet. And
then there's me."

Mom seemed to struggle for the right words. "Hunter,
it wasn't humiliating. We just didn't understand how hard
it was for you. We wanted the same doors to be open for
you that were open for us. College was a formative time
for your father, and for me."

Hunter shuddered. He had been so happy to get out of
high school; college would have felt like a jail sentence.

"You were so smart. We felt like you could do anything you put your mind to." She gestured to the restaurant around them. "And you have."

"I hated sitting."

"You still do."

"I made everything so hard for you guys. And what with Clara and everything—"

"Unconditional love is never a cakewalk. But it opens you up to new possibilities. Yes, I thought I wanted you and Bowman to go to college. But look what you've done. You have this fantastic restaurant and Bowman has done so much for the fire department here." She glanced up at him. "Honestly, I've been much more worried about Ash for the last ten years, and he got straight A's."

Hunter gave her a wry smile. "You happy about Violet?"

"That woman makes my gratitude journal every single day," Mom admitted. "When you have children, the world tries to sell you on certain dreams. You're supposed to want them to have the life you always dreamed of. The greatest joy of parenting for your dad and me has been to watch you become your true selves. Once we got out of your way, it got pretty fun. We just had to let go of expecting you to get straight A's."

"Or even straight B's," Hunter muttered.

"Passing, I believe, was the bar we all agreed on."

Hunter laughed.

"Once we let go, it was fun to be at school with you. You always had a knack for making everyone feel comfortable. If there was a tense social situation, you were the first to diffuse it. If a new kid showed up, you made a point to say hi and check in. You were a leader."

Hunter let the words sink in.

"No, school was fun. The hard part was having you in my kitchen."

Hunter looked up sharply. "What?"

Mom shook her head.

"Wait, I thought we loved cooking together."

"We did. We still do. But imagine coming home from work, there are farm chores to do and five kids to feed, and a fifteen-year-old pulls up a three-page-long recipe for paella on his phone and says 'Mom, let's make this!'"

Hunter laughed.

"Or think about this. You wrangle your children into cleaning the kitchen after dinner and finally sit down after a long day. You barely open your book when one of your sons goes back into the kitchen and starts messing around with Grandma's cake recipes. Then every three minutes for the next hour it's 'Mom, where do we keep the baking powder?' 'Mom, can you help me separate an egg?' and the most frightening sound to come from the kitchen, 'Oops!'"

Hunter wrapped his arms around his mom. "I had no idea. I always thought you loved having me in the kitchen."

"I did love it. And I wanted you to feel welcome there. But, seriously, that was way harder than the grades."

Something shifted in Hunter's chest at his mother's confession. He'd hung on to his failure for so long, allowing it to wash over his life like a sepia filter. He'd read disappointment into his parents' words, even when those words had been filled with pride and love. It was time to set that baggage down and move on.

"Thank you."

She squeezed tighter. "Thank you."

Hunter kissed the top of his mom's head then let his eyes travel around the room. It looked different somehow. Less like he was trying to prove something and more like he'd done a really good job designing and building it. A lot got done in this room.

His thoughts jumped to seeing Ani here, getting in his way, teasing him, using equipment she wasn't trained to use. Hunter's lungs constricted.

"What am I going to do?"

Mom leaned back and looked at him. "About Ani?"

He nodded. "This—" he placed a hand over his chest "—is so hard. It hurts."

"Her leaving?" Lacy asked.

"The whole thing. It hurts to care like this."

Mom's eyes softened. "I know."

"In a way, I'm glad she's going now. I couldn't stand getting any closer and having her take off."

"I don't understand," Mom said. "Why is she leaving?"

Hunter shook his head. "She doesn't believe in permanent connections. She told me everyone acts in their own self-interest and it's better to admit it and live with the fact."

"I hate to attack anyone's worldview, but that is unsubstantiated nonsense."

Hunter chuckled. "Wow, Mom. Judge much?"

"I'm sorry," she muttered. "And I should tell you I was a bit harsh with her just now."

Hunter stared down at the floor. He blinked against the tears blurring his vision.

"Look, sweetheart, I don't know what demons Ani is battling, but I think it's safe to say you shed light on whatever she's struggling with. If she has to go, that's not a reflection of you."

He nodded, but it wasn't true. If Ani felt anything close to what he was feeling, she'd never be able to leave.

"It's okay to love her, even if it's not going to work out."

Hunter struggled against the pain rising in his chest.

"Ani is extraordinary," Mom said. "And we may be a part of the journey that helps her realize she's worthy of love. She might be five years and fifteen thousand miles away before she's able to open up to someone else—"

"Please don't say that," Hunter begged. The thought of Ani ever having these feelings for anyone else made him sick.

"I'm sorry, sweetie. But you want her to be happy, don't you?"

He wanted Ani to understand this horrible pain. He wanted her to feel so connected to him she couldn't drive away without her heart being pulled from her chest.

He wanted her.

But she wasn't staying.

A flash of gray caught his eye. Hunter looked up and saw Maia backing away from Ani's van. He wasn't the only one who was going to be heartbroken at her leaving.

"Of course, I want her to be happy."

Lacy nodded. Hunter glanced around the room, seeing the scones Ani loved, her favorite soup bubbling on the stove. She'd be back to oatmeal and crackers when she left. If she was going to leave, she needed to know he still wanted her to be happy. He was angry, and hurt beyond measure, but that didn't mean he couldn't leave her with proof of how much he cared.

"Mom, can you help me with something before Ani leaves?"

CHAPTER EIGHTEEN

HUNTER WOKE UP on the cot in his office. He didn't remember lying down, but must have passed out sometime after 2:00 a.m. He'd stayed at Eighty Local working, waiting for Ani to come into the main restaurant. She'd been banging around in the hall most of the night, cleaning with some kind of vengeance.

And now she was gone. Hunter pressed his palm against his chest, against the dull, hollow pain.

It was almost seven. Everything was prepped for the gala, except for decorating the hall. Muscles ached as he stood and stretched. His head throbbed. He could do this. He could get through the day, get through the gala, get through a life without her.

Where should he start this morning? Hunter attempted a mental rundown of everything he needed to do in the next twelve hours.

Nothing came into focus.

He glanced into the parking lot. It was empty.

Hunter dropped back down into the cot, cradled his head in his hands.

She was gone, and she wasn't coming back. From the first moment he'd met her, she was an impossibility. A beautiful, creative, brilliant impossibility.

He never should have pushed her to stay. He should have just left this like she'd asked, a precious memory of twenty-six perfect days, rather than force her into an argument. She'd told him she could be mean. When he hadn't believed her, she'd dug in with the intention of hurting him. But what really hurt was that she felt like she had to release him by making him hate her. Like that was even possible.

He glanced at the clock again. Would she have found his gift by now? Probably not. More likely, she'd stopped at a truck stop for coffee. That was some satisfaction. She might not miss him, or Eighty Local, or Outcrop, but he was positive she'd never drink the weak brew at a truck stop without missing his espresso.

Instinctively, Hunter picked up his clipboard. There was the shortest list he had in years: decorate the hall, shower, change, assemble the hors d'oeuvres.

If she were here, she'd take the clipboard from his hands and argue with him about his priorities. If his pen were lucky, she'd chew on it.

What was it she'd said? *All of this could fold and he'd still live here, still have his family, still have people to feed.*

Hunter managed a smile. This was going to be so hard. He was pretty sure he would always miss Ani. But she was right, he had so much already. Hunter rubbed his hands across his face then picked up his phone and clicked on Clara's contact.

"Good morning, bro!" she chirped. Knowing Clara, she'd already had breakfast, matched up two or three clients, planned her future baby's wardrobe, and gone for a run.

"Hey. What's your day like?" He stood and grabbed his puffer vest off a hook.

"Literally the only thing on my agenda is to get dressed for the gala and show up."

"You're coming?"

"Um, yeah," she said as though this were obvious. "Jet and I bought tickets two months ago."

"Wait, Jet's coming?" Jet was a great guy, but fancy social events were not his thing.

"Of course, he's coming. And Piper. And Ash and Violet, and Maisy and Bowman. You know Bowman actually bought a tie for this event? Or rather, Piper bought it and then made Bowman pay for it and agree to wear it."

Hunter wiped his palm against the wetness on his cheek. He swallowed hard. "Thank you."

Her voice was soft as she said, "We wouldn't miss it. Now, how can I help?"

"I still have to decorate the hall."

"Sweet! I was so hoping you'd ask. What are you thinking?"

Hunter walked toward the events hall as he pulled on his vest. He hadn't put one thought into the decorations because he'd planned on doing it with Ani, who would know exactly what to do. He took a deep breath.

"I was thinking you could do the thinking and I'd move an extension ladder around the room and do what you tell me to."

"Perfect. Let me get changed and I'll be right there."

Hunter opened the door into the events center and stopped.

"Hunter?" Clara asked.

He didn't respond.

The events hall had transformed. Tall, curling willow branches had been gathered in antique pails throughout the room. Hunter fumbled for a light switch, and a thousand tiny white lights glowed in the willow branches.

He felt tears run down his face.

"Hunter?" Clara asked again, concern rising in her voice.

Soft greens and pinks capped the ends of some of the willow branches. Hunter moved closer to investigate. Ani had fashioned tissue paper to look like flower buds at the ends of some of the branches. The room was like a winter fairyland, with the promise of spring to come.

"I'm here," he said. "The room, it's…"

"Did she decorate?" Clara asked.

"Yeah." Hunter stood in the middle of the room and rotated in a full circle. "It's beautiful."

"Oh, Hunter. You know she loves you, right?"

Hunter looked around the room. It was stunning. Fancy enough for BES, but earthy, and completely Eighty Local. His heart hammered in his chest. *She did love him. She did care about his gala.*

"If she loves me, why did she leave?"

"She left because she loves you."

Hunter took in the decorations, the pine trim she'd installed, the bar she'd leaned across while challenging him, the illegal outlets she'd wired after an argument she'd won by making him laugh so hard he couldn't stop her from doing what she wanted. She was everywhere.

"I miss her so much already."

"I know." Silence hung on the line before Clara finally asked, "Can I please come help with something else?"

Hunter glanced at his list then back at the room. He didn't need his sister's help, but he absolutely needed her company.

"Feel like pulling espresso?"

"Yes!"

"Thank you. Then, as a relationship expert, can you tell me something about time healing everything and that I'm going to get over her?"

Clara was quiet.

"Oh, come on," Hunter groaned. "Would you just lie and tell me I'm going to be okay?"

"You are going to be okay. But you need to be prepared."

Hunter placed a hand on his tightening chest. He'd been prepared for every eventuality for years. But nothing could have prepared him for Ani.

"This is going to hurt. You will get over her, but it will take some time."

Hunter nodded. He knew it was going to hurt, but he didn't think there was enough time on earth to get over her.

ANI REACHED DOWN and fiddled with the radio dial as she ran out of range of another station. Nothing stretched out in all directions around her, only the flow of a brown and gray landscape. Two lanes, one human soul and hundreds of miles between her and Hunter Wallace.

A tune emerged out of the static. The beat and imperfect, soulful voice held her attention. Ani turned up the volume.

She had been driving since 6:00 a.m., making a brief stop forty miles out of Outcrop for a cup of subpar coffee. She was officially very hungry by this point.

The only problem with traveling alone was that no one could hand you a snack while you were driving.

The only problem.

A sign for Jordan Valley flashed by. Time to stop and restock. It would have been nice to take the day in Outcrop to ready herself and the van for traveling, but Hunter had made it clear he'd just wanted her gone. When she'd climbed into the van that morning, her heart had quickened when she saw an envelope on the front seat. But rather than a letter from Hunter, all it held was a check. A small beige rectangle representing all the time, energy and creativity she'd poured into Eighty Local.

The town appeared on the horizon. Did she really need to stop? Maybe she could plow through until she hit the state line. The song on the radio energized her. She had plenty of gas and she wasn't super hungry. A small farm flashed by, then another. The music tapered off and a perky voice came through the radio waves.

"That was Jeffrey Desoto with 'Turn Up.'"

Ani reflexively hit the off button. Of course, the *only* radio station that came in was playing Hunter's favorite musician. Was the whole state in cahoots with the Wallace family?

"I'm not going back," she told the radio.

The radio remained silent, because it was off.

An old brick building appeared and then a few houses. A little store stood bravely at the side of the road.

Ani weighed the advisability of stopping.

What was she afraid of? That if she hit the brakes, she wouldn't have the will to keep going?

It was absurd. She had power over her own actions. Ani slowed and pulled into the tiny lot. She parked, looking around at the miniscule town. Her hand reached for her phone to snap a picture then stopped. Exactly who was she planning on sending the picture to?

Ani stretched and headed into the back of the van. She scanned the shelves over the kitchen area. Coffee, oats, some crackers she'd bought over a month ago, salt, pepper and cinnamon.

None of it seemed particularly appetizing after a month of Eighty Local meals.

Ani knelt to the lower cabinets and opened a drawer.

She stared for several seconds, trying to make sense of the rolls in an Eighty Local take-out bag. She lifted them, only to find two scones and a jar of freshly ground coffee.

Ani tugged on the chest refrigerator. It was packed. Marinated salads, sliced brisket, chicken soup, everything she loved. Ani choked against her tears, but they began to flow anyway.

She sat back and leaned up against the slider door.

There was no note, no expectation, nothing. Just Hunter's gift. She stared at the cabinets and slowly became aware of a book tucked in with the food. She pulled it off the shelf. It was Lacy's novel that Ani had only gotten half-way through reading. The book dropped from her hands. Lacy would have had to bring the book to Hunter, after they'd argued. Hunter would have packed her van after she'd been so horrible.

Ridiculous Wallace family. Doing nice things even when she'd been the ultimate brat and left Hunter in the lurch right before his gala. It was like they saw something in her that wasn't even there. Or something she'd kept hidden.

Ani reached out and grabbed the jar of coffee. She un-screwed the top and breathed in. Tears fell heavy as she finally admitted the truth. She was in love with Hunter. She loved herself when she was in his company. For years, she'd been running from her home and competitive horse-manship because she'd felt they'd brought out the worst in her. Maybe it was time to set the past behind her, and ac-knowledge that she *had* changed over the last five years. She'd changed over the last four weeks.

She'd become the woman a man like Hunter Wallace could fall in love with.

Ani let a fantasy flicker. She could turn around now and get back in time for the gala. She could help Hunter with his big night, laughing with him as the women of the Bend Equestrian Society trotted around the events center in their finery.

But, no. If she walked into the gala, dressed appropri-ately for the situation, Shawna and Holly and all those other women would recognize her. She'd be Stephanie Blaisedell again. Stephanie, the center of attention, the unquestioned social leader in any situation.

Wait.

She'd be the unquestioned social leader. It had been years since she'd been one of those women, but wealth and horsemanship were their two primary values. If she showed up at the gala, she'd be in a position to comment on how perfect the events center was, how much she loved Eighty Local. She would definitely talk about how fantastic the decorations were.

Ani headed back to the cab of her van. She checked the clock; seven hours to make it back and get ready.

Her heart thundered in her chest. What did she need to do to pull this off? The right clothes, the right attitude and the help of a creative thirteen-year-old who was, hopefully, still willing to talk to her.

Ani tapped her phone then typed Second Chance Cowgirl into a Google search. The website loaded, and Ani scanned the page for the phone number. Christy Kessler would probably be willing to contact Maia for her, but Ani had hurt the girl so deeply. Would she be willing to forgive her? Would Hunter? Would either of them even be willing to talk to her?

Ani closed her eyes as the implication of her thoughts hit home. Before calling Christy, there was something else she needed to do. If she were going to ask others to listen to her apology, she needed to learn how to listen herself.

She opened her text messages and clicked on her mom's contact. Before she could think it through, Ani wrote:

Hi Mom. Christmas was wonderful this year. Really special. Talk later?

Ani's thumb wavered over the send button then connected. With an ordinary swoosh, the message was sent. She could imagine her mother's manicured hand picking up her phone at the ping of an incoming text, reaching for a pair of designer reading glasses.

Okay, she'd taken one step. That was all she was going to ask of herself for now. Ani clicked out of Messenger then called Second Chance Cowgirl.

She had a gala to attend.

CHAPTER NINETEEN

"This is a weird party," Jet said, turning back to Hunter at the bar.

"It is," Hunter agreed.

The room was beautiful. Hunter was certain there wasn't an event space in central Oregon that could top his. Objectively, the people were also beautiful. Every horse-woman in Deschutes County and her date were decked out in what Hunter knew to be expensive clothing. The food was outstanding, that was a given.

But the vibe of the gala was undeniably weird.

The night had begun with a few uninspiring comments, kicking off a tame silent auction. People milled about, uninterested in the auction items or each other. In a half an hour, the live auction would start, then dancing. People might be willing to pretend they were enjoying themselves.

Hunter wanted the horse ladies to be having a lot more fun. Not because he particularly cared about horse-lady fun, but because he wanted them to associate his establishment with positive memories.

"I mean everything you did was great," Jet said.

"Thank you. I agree. But I can't have fun for them. Beer?"

"That might help." Jet accepted the beverage with his eyes fixed firmly on the crowd. A low murmur rumbled around them, as though everyone had agreed to speak at the exact same volume.

Maia appeared with a camera. "Smile!"

Maia had drifted by Eighty Local that afternoon and asked to take pictures of the gala. Apparently, Christy had called Lacy with the idea. The BES had hired their own photographer, of course, and iPhones snapped like cicadas to document the evening for social media, but Lacy and Christy thought it might be nice for Maia to help out.

Not surprisingly, Maia turned out to have a good eye for photographs. What *was* surprising, though, was that Maia was in a good mood. Several times Hunter had caught her grinning, like she had a secret.

Other people, apparently, got over Ani a lot quicker than he did.

Hunter leaned toward Jet, not feeling particularly like smiling. "Think about good Yelp reviews," Maia said.

Hunter chuckled. Maia snapped the picture and examined it with a little grin. She'd dressed up in her own way, wearing high-tops, new black jeans and a long-sleeved black T-shirt with the Duran Duran top Ani had bought her over it. She looked more confident than normal and was in an awfully good mood for someone whose idol had just skipped town.

"Okay, these are like the strangest people on earth," Clara said quietly as she arrived at the bar.

"Tell me about it," Hunter said.

"It's like they don't know what to do."

Hunter noticed the door open at the end of the room. A small burst of conversation sprang up.

He filled a glass with soda water for Clara. "Lemon?"

"Please," she said, flashing a big grin. "Actually, can I have all the lemons? That sounds really good."

"You can have most of the lemons." Hunter dropped several slices into the glass.

A burst of laughter came from the far end of the room.

"Maybe the Madras Mules are kicking in?" Clara suggested.

Several people abandoned their tables and began moving toward the silent auction. Hunter noticed someone point, and everyone seemed to be focused in that direction.

He looked at Jet, who seemed as baffled as he was. Maia skipped off with her camera to document whatever was going on.

Holly Banks stalked to the bar and hammered her copper mug down on the counter. She flexed her empty hand at Hunter.

"Can we assume that means she wants another?" Clara asked.

Holly turned sharply. "It's not for me," she snapped. "Stephanie's here."

"Who?" Clara asked.

Hunter looked past Holly into the crowd. The guests seemed to jostle and shuffle around a central figure. He caught a glimpse of long, carefully styled hair. The crowd shifted and a flash of a cream-colored dress came into view. And then she stepped forward.

In the center of the room was a stunning woman. Her long hair fell in styled waves over her right shoulder. Careful makeup highlighted her huge almond eyes and full lips. She wore a rich, cream-lace dress out of another decade, and an extraordinary pair of boots.

"Stephanie Blaisedell," Holly said. "And if you had any idea who she was, you'd be a lot quicker with that drink."

Hunter wasn't in a position to be quick with anything. His hands were trembling as he stared at Ani.

Ani laughed with a woman then gave the subtlest nudge, sending the woman to up her bid on a silent auction item.

Another woman said something Ani didn't like and was quickly frozen out.

"What is she doing?" Clara asked.

"Drink, please," Holly demanded.

Hunter watched Ani move through the crowd, a group of women walked with her. Their husbands hovered nearby, wishing they could move closer, but none of them had been given the signal to do so. Hunter shook his head, smiling. He knew exactly what she was doing.

"Leading the herd."

IT WAS ALL so easy, so much easier than Ani had imagined. As planned, Maia had planted the seeds of her comeback, idly asking a few people if Stephanie Blaisedell had arrived yet. By the time Ani arrived, she was recognized within seconds of entering the party and fawned over immediately. The intimidating social dominance she'd learned from watching her mother kicked in. With the makeup and the dress, she could be Stephanie Blaisedell. The boots, which Christy and Maia had convinced her to wear with the dress, were a solid reminder that she was still Ani.

And she had to admit, it was kinda fun.

"Oh, my gosh! Stephanie? You look amazing!" was the first sentence she'd heard upon walking into the room. Shawna Hains had come running over. Ani had stilled herself for the hug then remembered that she was in charge. She'd relaxed her shoulders and looked past Shawna as she'd offered her cheek for an air kiss. No one had tried to touch her since then.

No, this was easy. It was the thought of seeing Hunter that had her heart storming inside her chest. Still, she would help make the gala a success. And if she managed to make him furious while trying to help out? Well, that wouldn't be a first.

Ani kept her eyes away from the bar. A camera snapped a picture and Ani turned to grin at Maia. "Still think the boots work?" she asked under her breath. Maia held out the camera so Ani could see the picture.

The boots definitely worked.

"I love the way you styled that T-shirt," Ani whispered. Maia shrugged one shoulder then grinned as she skipped off to take more pictures. Ani gave herself over to gratitude that Maia was willing to accept her apology, and her gift, and help pull this off. Then she waved her hand with condescending indifference and glanced around.

"What are we bidding on?" Ani asked a man scribbling his name on a silent auction list. His wife scurried over, explaining the vacation package she'd committed five hundred dollars to. Ani managed to look extremely excited about the opportunity of playing golf in Pendleton. Three more women put their name on the list, upping the bid each time.

"You have to try this." A woman pushed a cold copper cup into her hands. "We had it especially developed for the gala."

Ani looked up, straight into the eyes of Holly Banks.

"Did you?" she asked.

"The guy who runs this place is a bit of a savant."

Ani took a sip. The cold cup felt good against her lips. She closed her eyes and savored Hunter's concoction.

She opened her eyes and found her gaze had run to the bar.

Hunter's almost-too-long hair was neater than usual, but still scruffy. He wore a dark button-down shirt and slacks that had clearly been picked out by one of his sisters.

He was looking at her and grinning.

Ani felt herself blush; she looked back down into the cup.

"It's good, isn't it?" Holly asked.

Ani was tempted to brace her hands against the wall and deliver a quick kick to Holly, just like Bella would have. But that wasn't what she was there for.

Ani rolled her eyes up. "So good."

She snuck another look at Hunter. He was laughing. *Was there anything better than making Hunter laugh?*

"What are we raising money for, anyway?" Ani asked.

Holly spoke quickly, making sure her answer was the first and definitive one. "Walk On. It's a charity that gives kids the opportunity—"

Ani turned away from Holly as she interrupted her to finish the sentence. "Riding lessons for neurodiverse kids. Such a good cause." Ani reached out to grab a mini grilled cheese from a woman with a tray. The waitress stopped and stared at her.

"Ani?" Janet asked, squinting.

"Stephanie," Ani said.

Janet looked from Ani, back to Hunter, then to Ani again. She shook her head and started to walk away. Ani grabbed two more little sandwiches from the tray.

"I think this may be the best thing I've ever eaten."

"Right?" Holly agreed.

Ani looked past Holly to see Hunter still watching her, still smiling. Ani stuffed both sandwiches in her mouth and made a gesture with her hand reminiscent of Holly's request for the drink.

Hunter grabbed a platter from Caleb and started on her way.

Uh-oh.

The music cut and Shawna stepped up to a small dais. "It's time for our auction to begin," her voice boomed through the microphone. "But before we start, I want to thank each and every one of you—" she paused and looked at Ani "—for joining us. We could not do this without your support."

"We couldn't do this without these Madras Mules!" Ani responded. Shawna laughed along with everyone else.

"Tonight's main item is an all-inclusive ski vacation in Lake Tahoe. Let's start the bidding at one thousand dollars."

"Two thousand," Ani said.

"I hear two thousand. Is there—"

"Two thousand, one hundred dollars," a man offered.

Ani glanced over at the man and raised her brow. He blushed.

"Two thousand, five hundred," Ani said, keeping eye contact.

"Two thousand, six hundred," he said.

Ani pretended to be affronted. "Three thousand."

"Well, someone wants a trip to Tahoe." Shawna grinned at her.

"What someone really wants is another grilled cheese," Ani said. People laughed. The husbands quickly caught on that the way to get her attention was to bid, and the numbers started flowing. It never ceased to amaze her how wealthy people loved sitting in a room together yelling out how much money they were willing to spend on something.

The bidding spiraled, far past the worth of the trip. Probably time to put these guys out of their misery.

"Six thousand, three hundred," Ani proclaimed with a finality to stop the bidding.

Several men looked at her indulgently. She gave the room a hopeful smile.

"And the trip goes to number 108, Stephanie Blaisedell."

Ani jumped up as though she was excited and then asked, "Where's the trip to again?"

"Skiing in Lake Tahoe"

"Oh," Ani said, feigning disinterest. "I don't really ski anymore. Whatever. I don't need the trip. I just love the idea of all those kids on horses."

The room reacted as she wanted them to, getting all misty-eyed about her generosity.

"Who was right before me?" Ani looked at the man who had been bidding against her. "You guys, right? You should have it and I'll just donate the money." Ani opened her clutch and pretended to search for a bank card.

"I'd like to make a donation too."

Ani looked up at the words. It was Holly Banks. Perfect.

"Us too!"

And let the public display of wealth begin.

Satisfaction washed through Ani as she scanned the room. Money was flowing. Madras Mules were flowing. Walk On would receive a pile of money, as they should; it was a fantastic organization. The Bend Equestrian Society Gala at Eighty Local would go down as the most success-ful in history. And Ani had done this for Hunter, knowing full well that ship might have sailed forever.

Warmth emanated from behind her as a man stepped up close. Ani turned.

"Hey."

"Hey." She gazed into earthy brown-green eyes. "Do you have any more of those sandwiches?"

He moved closer, grinning down at her. "They're in the kitchen."

"Can I help you get them?"

"That's just what I was going to ask."

CHAPTER TWENTY

HUNTER'S HAND WAS on the small of her back before they cleared the door into the back room, and he was unable to stop his fingers from winding into hers as the door swung shut.

"Hi," she said, leaning against the oak table.

"What was that?" One hand ran across her hip, rough against the lace of her dress. His other hand braced against the table, pinning her in front of him. So much for playing it cool.

"Helping?"

Hunter realized he was leaning in to kiss her. He pulled back. But that gave him a better view of her in that dress and he found himself angling for a kiss again.

"Is this what Stephanie Blaisedell looks like?"

She shrugged her left shoulder. "Kind of. The hair and makeup definitely."

A shiny dark lock rested on her shoulder. Hunter's fingers drifted to it.

"Still pretty. Different, but pretty."

"The dress is on loan from Second Chance Cowgirl. Christy set me up. Maia met me there and we came up with this plan." She grinned, nodding her chin toward the events center. "I think it's working."

"Everything works when you're involved." He leaned in to kiss her.

"Hey." Ani sounded serious, reaching up to touch his

face. Hunter drew his gaze from her lips. "I'm sorry. Leaving like that right before your big night." She paused. Her eyelids slid down and she took a breath. "Leaving right after we…" She couldn't seem to finish the sentence.

Hunter helped her out. "Spent the best month of my life together, celebrated Christmas and shared an incredible evening in front of the fire?"

The start of a smile danced across her lips.

"Yeah. What you said." She placed her other hand on the front of his shirt. "I was wrong. I hope you can forgive me."

She smiled. Hunter lost it. He lifted her onto the table, falling into her kiss. His hands ran down her silky arms then wrapped around her. Nothing mattered outside of this kiss.

"Does this mean yes?" she asked, tilting her head up to look at him. He cradled her face with his hands and nodded. Ani glanced down, flushed with pleasure. That was all he needed.

"Take me with you." Ani started to speak but Hunter went on. "I mean it. When you go, I want to go with you. We can get a food cart. I'll make grilled sandwiches and we can sell them wherever you want to go. Please." Hunter settled his hand along her jaw.

"I'm not going to take you away from your restaurant, or your ranch."

"I don't want any of this unless you're here," he said. Ani's eyes filled with tears. "You know—" His voice caught. Hunter started over. "You know I'm in love with you. Without you, this is just work. With you, it's fun."

Ani's beautiful smile spread across her face. "I'm going to stay. I can learn how to stay."

"I don't want you to change."

"I won't change. I'll grow. I mean I'm still going to want

to travel. A lot. I'll never stop exploring. But that doesn't mean I can't have a home."

His heart began pounding against his ribs.

"Plus, I have to earn six thousand dollars to pay off the pledge I just made to the Bend Equestrian Society."

Hunter laughed.

"It's honestly a good cause. And, um, seriously, I need a job." She gave him a guilty smile.

Hunter let his hand rest at the nape of her neck. Everything seemed to spin around him, but Hunter remained firmly anchored to Ani as she smiled up at him.

"How does teaching riding lessons sound?"

"But you wouldn't be there to boss me around."

"Bella can take over for me." He kissed her cheek then her ear, whispering, "Welcome home."

THIS WAS WHAT home felt like.

Hunter threaded his hands through her hair again. Ani pulled his mouth to hers. Time disappeared as she lost herself in Hunter's kiss.

"I love you, Ani," he whispered against her lips. "I love everything about you."

Her gaze connected with his, and she felt it, his powerful, sustaining love. She felt free, and strong, and ready for this.

She stretched her arms around his neck and told someone how she really felt for the first time in a very long time. "I love you more."

He shook his head, eyes sparking. "Not possible."

"How would you know?"

"Why are you questioning me?"

"Why *aren't* you kissing me?"

Hunter laughed and pulled her closer.

"We need to be careful with this dress. It's on loan from Christy."

He leaned back, giving her an appreciative once-over before leaning in to kiss her again. "I am buying you this dress."

His lips met hers and Ani was pretty sure she'd be spending the rest of her life perched on the worktable in the back room of Eighty Local, kissing Hunter Wallace.

"Oh. Oh, wow. Hunter?" Ani looked up sharply at the new voice. "Stephanie? What?"

Holly Banks stood in the doorway, pure shock written all over her face. Hunter groaned and looked up at the ceiling. Ani bit the inside of her cheek to keep from giggling.

She looked at Holly and rolled her eyes.

"Oops!" she chirped. "Have I got my hands on the staff again?"

She patted Hunter's arm and made a show of squeezing his biceps. He flexed. Ani didn't allow herself to make eye contact.

"Such a bad habit." She stood next to Holly then crossed her arms and evaluated Hunter. "He's just so good-looking. Throw in those mini grilled-cheese sandwiches and…" Ani blew out a breath and turned to Holly. "I'm sure you understand."

Holly was still running several paces behind but managed to realize she was being treated like a good friend, and that was more than enough.

"Oh, absolutely," Holly said.

"We should get back to the party." Ani flashed a grin at Hunter. "Thank you!"

His brilliant smile broke out as he shook his head. "My pleasure."

Ani kept eye contact with Hunter as she adjusted the straps of her dress then strode toward the events center. At the door, she looked over her shoulder at him. "You need to wash your hands."

Hunter sputtered out a laugh.

"Twice," she instructed. "Or someone's going to have to call Captain Clean."

Ani led the way back into the events hall, her head spinning. Hunter loved her. Not despite her flaws, but with them. He wanted her, and this. She glanced up at the exposed wood ceiling then out at the party circling around her.

"I totally understand," Holly said in a low voice.

Ani startled. *What was Holly talking about?*

"Hunter's a total hottie," Holly said, glancing back at the kitchen as she masked her disappointment. "Planning this event was a blast, and the eye candy didn't hurt."

Ani planted her feet. Her chin rose. "No."

"What?" Holly stepped back.

"Hunter." Ani gestured to the kitchen.

"Oh, I just meant I completely understand why you would—"

"Dibs" was the only thing that came to Ani's mind.

God, who was acting like a hoofed mammal now?

Ani readjusted her shoulders. She leaned over to give Holly a peck on the cheek.

"This party is fantastic, thank you. You've done a terrific job," she said. "But the cowboy chef is mine."

Ani didn't look back as she walked away, as much as she was dying to see the look on Holly's face. The party swung joyously around her. People were laughing. Someone had put on a dance mix and the floor was swamped with tipsy horse ladies and their husbands. Bowman covered for Hunter behind the bar, prepping the Madras Mules people kept requesting.

A soft shoulder bumped against hers. Ani turned to see Clara.

"Can I act like I know you now?"

"Everybody else is." Ani instinctively reached out to hug Clara.

Piper scooched up on Ani's other side. "That was awesome!"

Ani wrapped her other arm around Piper. "You can see why I had to escape winding up like Stephanie Blaisedell."

"Totally," Clara confirmed.

A sly smile crossed Piper's face. "But it had to be a little bit fun to throw that down."

Ani glanced over at the bar. Hunter had returned. The sweetest, hardest working, most incredible man was busy keeping people fed and happy. Doing anything with this man was fun.

"I'm glad I could help out."

"Speaking of helping, Mom and Dad are renting an RV to take a trip to Mesa Verde." Piper flipped subjects, like Hunter's siblings always did.

Ani scrambled to keep up while Clara jumped right in. "They want to look at Ancestral Puebloan ruins. Apparently, there are whole cities built into the cliff side."

"But they can't just book a tour."

"They have to drive themselves."

"And we worry, because they are getting older, and they don't have any experience with RV travel."

"Lots of older people travel safely in RVs." Ani looked from one sister to the other. "In fact, almost everybody in an RV is over sixty."

"I know." Clara squirmed. "But we'd feel better if you'd talk to them."

"And then since Mom will be gone…" Piper continued.

"The guys need help with Bella?" Ani guessed.

"She's horrible. Except to you and Mom."

Ani glanced at the floor and caught the sight of her beautiful boots. She started to laugh.

"So, the mural isn't enough? You two need me to stay indefinitely."

"Please!" Clara said. She started to bounce on her toes. "He's so happy when you're here."

Ani looked up at the sisters. They had no idea. They couldn't possibly imagine what this was like for her.

But then again, they *were* matchmakers.

"My learning curve is going to be steep," Ani admitted. She glanced over at the bar. Hunter caught her eye. "Steep, but fun. I'll probably need…help." Ani pulled in a breath. "I'm going to need help. I don't know what a good relationship looks like. I'm going to need to learn how to stay."

Clara was now jumping up and down and Piper was clapping.

"That's our job!" Piper said.

"That's literally what we do! Our goal is to bring more beauty and joy into the world by helping people fall in love."

"We'll all be here for you," Piper said seriously.

Ani glanced from one sister to the other, anticipation fluttering through her. She felt brave and free. "Thank you."

"Oh, and has anyone told you about the horse?" Piper asked abruptly.

Because in this family you were talking about long-term relationships one second and equine the next.

"You mean Bella?" Ani was confused. She glanced past Piper at Hunter again. He grinned.

"Nooooo." Clara's cryptic response brought Ani's attention back to the twins. "Oh, wow. I get to tell her!"

"*I* get to tell her," Piper said.

"You show her the picture." Clara pulled Piper's phone from her bag.

"Is it Bella?" Ani asked.

Clara and Piper were buzzing with excitement, shaking their heads, grinning, like they had when they'd caught her with Hunter under the mistletoe.

"Do you remember at Christmas—"

"When Mom wouldn't put her phone down?"

"She was basically setting up the best surprise ever, for you, because you're amazing."

"What is it?" Ani asked.

Piper spun her phone around and they both crowded next to her to look at the screen. It was a picture of Bella, Lacy and the best friend Ani thought she'd never see again.

EPILOGUE

RABIANA PUSHED HER nose against Ani's neck then gave her hair a gentle tug. Ani laughed, letting the familiar gesture take her stress away.

"I should get back inside," she told the horse.

Rabiana didn't seem to think Ani had to do anything other than continue to shower her with love, but Bella trotted over and announced her presence with a nicker. She would take care of Rabiana, as she'd been doing for the past four months, while Ani met today's challenge.

Her parents.

"Everybody okay?" Hunter called, emerging from the barn.

What that man did to a T-shirt and jeans.

"We're fine." Ani pulled in a deep breath of cool spring air. She might be so nervous her heart threatened to hop in the van all on its own and bust out of town, but she was so much better than fine.

New, bright green grass had shot up across Hunter's property the minute spring hit. The oaks surrounding the old house were just leafing out and the hundreds of bulbs Hunter had planted sent up shoots. Everything felt fresh and new.

Except for maybe the house, which felt overwhelming and thrilling. She and Hunter had begun working on the dilapidated old house by tackling the least glamorous jobs first, like dry rot and crumbling foundation blocks. Once the condition had gone from critical to stable, they'd poured their time into the kitchen. From there they'd moved on to the dining room. The rest of the house would be finished as they found motivation and inspiration. For now, one place to cook and one place to gather was all they needed.

Hunter had cut back his hours at the restaurant, giving more responsibility to Caleb, who thrived with the challenge. There, they'd celebrated Maia's fourteenth birthday with a huge chocolate cake, fancy tea drinks and her first job at Eighty Local. With the new mural she and Ani had planned, Maia would have plenty to fill her time that summer. Watching her confidence grow had been one of the greatest gifts of staying in Outcrop for Ani.

The extra time and focus Hunter had went into the house and the ranch. He was experimenting with growing feed for the Canadian Horses, and Ani teased him about making sure that all living creatures in Outcrop could eat local products. She still worked with Hunter at Eighty Local from time to time but had started giving riding lessons at the ranch, as well, sharing her love and knowledge of horses with others.

Rabiana had been well taken care of over the years, and her present owners were more than willing to let her live out the end of her life at Wallace Ranch. While the horse was older and less agile, she still loved to run, and still loved Ani above everything.

Horses, endless engaging projects, delicious food and Hunter Wallace...who could possibly ask for anything more?

Ani trotted toward the barn. Okay, fine, technically she was trotting toward Hunter. He opened his arms and wrapped her in a hug, resting his cheek against her hair.

"Your parents won't be here for another hour."

Ani's pulse flooded her system, pounding in her ears and throat. She tightened her grip around Hunter.

"Not until four o'clock." Ani pulled in a deep breath.

"The visit won't last more than three hours. By seven o'clock, it will be over and done with." Hunter pulled back and cradled her cheek with his hand. "This is going to be good."

"Blech." Ani moved past him and headed back to the house. "What more do we have to do?"

"I've got the duck in the oven. Mom's working on the potatoes. Mostly, it's a matter of setting out the salads and finishing up the focaccia. I thought maybe we could take a—"

"Is this dress okay?" Ani pulled at the vintage calico dress Christy Kessler had set aside for Hunter to buy her. The woman knew a sucker when she saw one.

"You look beautiful."

Ani turned her head away from his.

"The boots aren't too much?"

Hunter drew in a breath and wound his fingers into her hair.

"The boots are good," he murmured. Ani tried to frown, but it was hard when he was smiling at her like he did. She hooked her thumbs into the back pockets of his jeans and drew him closer.

Hunter's family was all gathered in the kitchen. Ani's parents were on the road, expected at the ranch in less than an hour. She intended to plant herself here in Outcrop, and this was a vital step in becoming comfortable in the life she'd chosen to create.

She glanced past Rabiana's paddock to where the Sprinter van was parked. After a tearful conversation about commitment, and what was on record as the sweetest kiss of her life, Hunter had slipped out and bought a gift for the van: an Outcrop Eagle red bumper sticker that read "Local."

"Let's get it done," Ani said, stepping out of Hunter's protective embrace and heading into the kitchen.

Lacy stood at the vast wood-block island, chopping potatoes. "I love using the knives here," she said. "Always perfectly sharp."

Ani smiled at the compliment. "I'll come do yours next week."

"I thought you were taking a road trip next week?" Clara said.

"We're not leaving until Wednesday," Ani told her. "The deal is we all suffer through my parents, then Hunter and I get a billion things prepped at Eighty Local so Caleb will be ready in case of any disaster, then we take off."

"Where are you going?" Maisy asked.

Ani grinned. "I have no idea."

Hunter opened the door to the spice cabinet. His to-do list was attached to a clipboard he'd hung inside the door. He grabbed a pencil and checked off some chore on the list. Ani peeked over his shoulder.

"What'd we finish?"

Hunter started and slammed the cabinet door.

"Nothing."

"You checked off nothing?"

"No, it's just not important."

"Then why was it on the list?"

"Because I felt like writing down something meaningless and crossing it off." Hunter shook his head but he was smiling. There was something secret on that list. He crossed his arms and leaned against the counter, blocking the spice cabinet. "Nosy."

"Bossy," she replied.

"List Judger."

"Cabinet Slammer."

"Are you two going to do this in front of Ani's parents?" Lacy asked. "Or are we special?"

A wave of trepidation hit her with the words. "Yuck." Ani covered her face with her hands. "Why did we invite my parents again?"

"Because coming to terms with the past is an important step in creating your future," Clara reminded her.

"What are you afraid of?" Violet asked. "I mean, I don't mean to make light of this, but you're never afraid of anything."

Ani gazed around at the kitchen she and Hunter had poured their souls into, then up at Hunter. He ran his hand over her shoulders.

What was she afraid of? *So much.*

"I'm afraid they'll insult you," she said. "I'm afraid my mom won't eat Hunter's cooking, which she won't. I'm afraid they'll be sincerely sorry, and I'll feel silly for letting it go on for so long. I'm afraid they're not really sorry. I'm afraid you won't like them, or you will like them and think I've been foolish for not liking them."

"Ani." Lacy rested her hand on Ani's back. "We're here for you, no matter what happens."

Ani smiled weakly, glancing around the room at Hunter's family. They'd all come to meet her parents and support her as she saw them for the first time in five years.

"There's only two of them, right?" Ash asked, his back to Ani as he chopped rosemary for the potatoes.

"Parents?" Ani asked. "Yeah. I have two."

Ash glanced around the room then grinned at Violet. "Well, there's twelve of us. Thirteen, if you count the baby." He gestured to Clara's pregnant belly. He looked at Ani and winked. "I think we can take 'em if it comes down to it."

Ani laughed. The tension sitting like a gremlin on her chest seemed to float away. She wiped the tears from her eyes. "Thank you. Thank you, all of you. This is hard. And weird."

"It's okay," Clara said. "We've got your back."

"I'm sorry—" Ani started but found she couldn't complete the sentence. The situation was sorry, but Ani couldn't claim, or place, any guilt. This had to be as hard for her parents as it was for her.

They had behaved selfishly, and vindictively, but so had she. She didn't fit in with her family and, at twenty-one, she hadn't had the tools or resources to deal with them productively. She'd just left. But for the last five years, she'd continued to view her parents through the eyes of a teenager. She had changed, and it was possible they had too.

Ani would never share their values, but she could approach them with less judgment. She had no idea what was going to happen with her parents this afternoon.

But she had a pretty good idea of what she wanted to happen with Hunter.

Ani shuffled closer to the spice cabinet where his list was hiding. Hunter blocked her then wound his arms around her. She glanced up at him. She was going to get a look at his list, no matter how attractive and tall he was going to be in her way.

The back door banged open, fresh air blowing in with Piper.

"Piper, you okay?" Hunter released Ani and strode toward his sister.

"I'm fine," she snapped, rolling her eyes. "I'm just late."

Bowman, always protective of Piper, crossed to her and murmured something.

Piper studied the floor then looked up at Ani. Sadness tinged her eyes as she wrestled a bright smile into place.

"I brought some Pinot gris." She held out the bottle. "If your parents are cool, we share it with them. If not…well, we have a bottle of Pinot gris."

"Thank you." Ani took the wine then blinked back tears. She looked around the room at the Wallaces, all here, supporting her on this difficult day. "You guys are…" Her words trailed off. *Amazing? Incredible? The best?*

"Annoying?" Piper guessed.

"Noisy?" Lacy suggested.

"More like nosy," Bowman muttered.

"Ridiculous," Ani said, studying the flowers. "Ridiculous Wallace family, being nice and supportive and fun all the time." She shuddered dramatically. "It's not natural."

Piper glanced at Hunter then Clara. The sisters smiled at each other. "Speaking of family, Hunter, have you got everything crossed off your list?"

Hunter sent Piper a warning glance. "I'm working on it."

The door to the spice cabinet was ajar. Ani shuffled closer. Hunter leaned an arm against the counter, blocking her.

"We have everything covered here," Clara said. "Why don't you two go for a walk?"

"Good idea," Hunter said, sounding suspicious. "Ani, want to go for a walk?"

Ani tilted her head to the side and looked at Hunter. He hadn't left the house when preparing for a big meal in all the time she'd known him.

"Really?"

"Sure." He glanced around the room. This had to be killing him. "We'll take a short walk before your parents get here."

"What's still on the list?"

"Not much." Hunter placed his hand on the cabinet door.

"We never have 'not much' on the list."

"We should take it easy, relax before your parents arrive." Hunter was now leaning against the cabinet awkwardly, his palm firm against the wood.

"Um, okay." Ani held up her hands and backed away.

"Let's go for a walk," Hunter said for a third time, nodding toward the door.

"Yay!" Clara clapped her hands. "They're going for a walk!"

"O-okay," Ani said slowly. "A walk sounds great."

Hunter followed Ani to the door and grabbed his vest.

Ani calculated her timing. Just as Hunter began to push an arm into his vest, she jumped for the cabinet.

"Hey!" he yelled.

Ani giggled as she pulled the door open and scanned the list.

Hunter's upright letters marched across the page, spelling out commands. Most were followed by check marks.

Marinate duck. Check.

Sweep porch. Check.

Fill ice chest. Check.

Kiss Ani so she can forget her parents are coming. This was in her handwriting. Double check.

Set out grain salads to warm. Check.

Text Ash, ask him to bring rosemary. Check.

The list ran down the page, task after task, check mark after check mark. Hunter ran up next to her and started talking, but Ani focused on the list.

Her finger ran down the length of the page then stopped on the last item.

Ask Ani.

Her finger began to tremble against the list. "Ask me… what?"

"We made him put it on the list because—"

"He's been talking about it nonstop since January." Piper and Clara spoke over one another.

Ani looked up at Hunter. His brown-and-green eyes connected with hers in a question. She looked back at the list. This wasn't a joke. If Hunter put something on the list, he intended to get it done.

And there was only one ask she could think of big enough to make the list.

"I didn't want to scare you off," he said softly. Ani reached her hand out and took his. His brilliant smile broke free. "I also, really, did not want to ask you in front of the peanut gallery here." Hunter glared at his sisters.

"Then for heaven's sake, go take a walk!"

Ani wound her fingers into his. "I'm not afraid."

"Not even a little bit?"

"Not anymore."

Hunter's arms closed around her. His lips met hers and stripped away everything in the world, save Hunter Wallace.

But the family would not be ignored. Cheers and catcalls bounced through the kitchen. Hunter's arm slipped under her legs and he swept her off her feet, cradling her in his arms.

"Let's go!" he whooped. "I have a big romantic plan to convince you to say yes."

"I'm warning you now, there's no ring yet," Piper said.

"Enough!" Hunter turned on her. "This is not your proposal."

Clara ignored him and said to Ani, "We told him you should help design it. It's our fault there's no ring."

"It is also our fault that you're here right now, in his arms, because we hired you to paint a mural." Piper leveled a superior glance at them. "Just keep that in mind."

Hunter shifted Ani in his arms and looked down into

her eyes. The entire noisy, nosy Wallace clan evaporated. "I did want to design a ring with you. But there may be about a million proposal flowers waiting for my future wife in the barn."

Ani kicked her legs and wrapped her arms tighter around Hunter's neck. "Seriously?"

He paused at the door and looked down into her eyes.

"I can't wait to spend my life with you. Every day, every minute. I love building my world with you in it."

Ani felt herself surrounded by Hunter's love. This man, this house, this family, this life they would create together, it was unfathomably beautiful.

Ani kicked the door open with her boots, exposing the endless new spring grass, lit by the afternoon sun.

"Then let's go!"

* * * * *

Once Upon A Charming Bookshop

Heatherly Bell

MILLS & BOON

Bestselling author **Heatherly Bell** was born in Tuscaloosa, Alabama, but lost her accent by the time she was two. After leaving Alabama, Heatherly lived with her family in Puerto Rico and Maryland before being transplanted kicking and screaming to the California Bay Area. She now loves it here, she swears. Except the traffic.

Visit the Author Profile page
at millsandboon.com.au for more titles.

Dear Reader,

I have to admit, writing this book scared me a little bit. Let me explain. At the time I began to write this book, I'd just lost my father after a long illness. Later that same year, my husband lost his older brother quite unexpectedly and shockingly. I suppose it isn't any surprise that in 2022 I tackled the subject of grief. Writing, however, felt like a huge and agonising undertaking because it hit a little too close to home.

But as with everything, there is the other side of the coin. Even with a great loss, there remain friends, family and faith to get you through. There is a comfort and joy found in books. I know I'm not the only one who has closed a book and walked away filled with a sense of hope and inspiration. That's what I set out to have a reader feel in this best-friends-to-lovers romance. So, we have the *Once Upon a Charming Bookshop* in Charming at Christmastime, our quirky senior-citizen poetry group, a literary-character costume contest, lights, decorations and heartfelt gifts.

And finally, we have two best friends who have experienced a great loss together. Twyla, our heroine, and Noah, our hero, discover that friendship endures through grief and guilt, and at times it even catches fire.

I always love to hear from you. You can reach me at heatherly@heatherlybell.com.

Heatherly Bell

DEDICATION

For those who believe that books can bring you joy

CHAPTER ONE

TWYLA THOMPSON WAS thrilled to see a line out the door on the night of *New York Times* bestselling author Stacy Cruz's book signing. This was exactly what Once Upon a Book needed—an infusion of excitement and goodwill and the proverbial opening up of the wallet during the holidays for a book instead of the latest flat-screen TV. Even if Stacy's recently released thriller wasn't exactly Christmas material, the timing was right both for her, the publisher and certainly Twyla's family-owned bookstore.

The reading had been short due to subject matter—murder—and Stacy took questions from the crowd. As usual, they ranged from, "How can I get published?" To "I have an idea for a book. Would you write it for me?" To "My mother had a *fascinating* life. It should be a book, then a movie starring Meryl Streep." Stacy was a good sport about it all since the Charming, Texas, residents were her friends and neighbors, too.

Twyla, for her part, would never dream of writing a book. She barely had time to read everything she wanted to. Which was basically…everything. The heart of a bookseller beat in her and she recommended books like they were her best friends. Want an inspirational book? Read this. Would you like a tour de force celebrating the power of the human spirit? Here's the book for you. A little escapism with some romance and comedy thrown in? Right here. Want to be scared within an inch of your life? Read Stacy Cruz's latest suspense thriller.

The very best part of Twyla's day was getting lost in the worlds an author created. Her favorite books had always been of the fantasy romance genre, particularly of the dragon-slaying variety. She adored a fae hero who slayed dragons before breakfast. But honestly? She read anything she could get her hands on. Owning her four-generation family bookstore had made that possible. She'd grown up inside these four walls filled with bookshelves and little alcoves and nooks. She read all the *Nancy Drew* mysteries, Beverly Cleary and, when her grandmother wasn't looking, Kathleen Woodiwiss.

Twyla stood next to Roy Finch at the register as he rang up another sale of Stacy's latest book, *Vengeance*, that featured a serial killer working among the political power brokers in DC. Twyla had read it, of course. She could not deny Stacy's talent at terrifying the reader and making them guess until the last page. You'd never expect this from the married, sweet and beautiful mother of a little girl. She was as normal a person as Twyla had ever met.

"Nice crowd tonight," Mr. Finch said. "Too bad Stacy doesn't write more than one book a year."

Too bad indeed. Because while hosting yoga classes and book clubs, and selling educational toys had sustained them, it would no longer be enough. For the past two years, the little bookstore, the only one in town, had been in a terrible slump. Her grandmother still kept the books, and she'd issued the warning earlier this year. Pulling them out of the red might require more than one great holiday season. Foot traffic had slowed as more people bought their books online.

"I've got a signed copy of Stacy's latest book for you." Lois, Mr. Finch's fiancée, set a stack of no less than ten books on the counter by the register. "And I grabbed a bunch of giving tree cards."

The cards were taken from a large stack of books in the shape of a Christmas tree Twyla set up every season. Instead of ornaments, tags indicated the names and addresses of children who either wanted, or needed, a book for Christmas.

"We can always count on you, sweetheart." Mr. Finch rang her up.

It was endearing the way residents supported the Thompson family bookstore. They might have been in this location for four decades, but they'd never needed as much help as in the past two years.

Mr. Finch, a widowed and retired senior citizen, volunteered his time at the shop so Twyla could occasionally go home. For a while now they hadn't been able to afford any paid help. Her parents were officially retired and had moved to Hill Country. Their contributions amounted to comments on the sad state of affairs when a bookstore had to host yoga classes. But the instructor gave Twyla a flat rate to rent the space, and she didn't see *them* coming up with any solutions. They didn't want to close up shop. Of *course* not. They simply wanted Twyla to solve this problem for the entire Thompson family by selling books and nothing else.

"I don't know what I'd do without either one of you," Twyla said fondly, patting Mr. Finch's back. "Or any of the other members of the Almost Dead Poets Society."

Many of the local senior citizens had formed a poetry group where they recited poems they'd written. It had all started rather innocently enough—a creative effort, and something to do with all their free time. Unfortunately, they also liked to refer to themselves as "literary" matchmakers. Literary not to *ever* be confused with "literally."

They'd failed with Twyla so far, not that they'd ever give up trying. Last month they'd invited both her and Tony Taylor to a reading and not so discreetly attempted to fix them up.

You're both so beautiful, it's a little hard to look at you for long, Ella Mae, the founder of their little group, had said. *Kind of like the sun!*

The double Ts! Lois had exclaimed. *Or would that be the quadruple* Ts?

Quadruple, I think, Mr. Finch had said.

You won't even have to change the initials on your monogrammed towels! Patsy Villanueva had clapped her hands. *I mean if it works out, that is.*

But no pressure! Susannah held up a palm.

Twyla didn't own anything monogrammed, let alone towels, but she'd still exchanged frozen smiles with Tony. They'd arranged a coffee date just for fun. Unfortunately, as she'd known for years, Tony batted for the other team. He even had a live-in boyfriend that the old folks assumed was his roommate. It was an easy assumption to make since Tony was such a "man's man"—a grease monkey who lifted engines for a living. And he hadn't exactly come out of the closet, thinking his personal life was nobody's business. He was right, of course. But…

"You really *should* declare your love of show tunes, Tony," she'd teased.

"I'm not a cliché."

"Well, you *could* get married."

"I'm not ready to settle down." He scowled.

Still, they'd had a nice time, catching up on life post-high school. He'd asked after Noah Cahill, and of course she had all the recent updates on her best friend. In the end they'd decided she and Tony would definitely be double-dating at some point.

When Twyla could find a date.

This part wasn't going to be easy because Twyla had a bad habit. She preferred to spend her time alone and reading a book. Long ago, she'd accepted that she wouldn't be able to find true love inside the walls of her small rental. But accepting invitations to parties and bar hops wasn't her style. She wanted to be invited, really, but she just didn't want to go. An introvert's problem.

This was why she'd adopted a cat. But, she worried, if she didn't get a date soon, she was going to risk being known as the cat lady.

"That's the last copy!" Stacy stood from the table, beaming, holding a hand to her chest. "My publisher will be thrilled. I honestly can't *believe* it."

"I can." Twyla began to clear up the signing table. "You're very talented and it's about time people noticed. I just wish you'd write more books."

"So do I, but tell that to my daughter." Stacy sighed. "She's a holy terror, just like her father. Runs around all day, throwing things. I'm lucky if I get in a few hundred words a day."

"That's okay." Twyla chuckled. "We can't exactly base our business plan on how many books you write a year."

Stacy blinked and a familiar concern shaded her eyes. "Are you…are you guys doing okay? Should I maybe ask my publisher whether they can send some of their other authors here for a signing?"

As a bookseller, she knew everyone in the business was suffering, and publishers weren't financing many book tours. Stacy did those on her own dime, hence the local gig. Twyla didn't like lying to people but she liked their pity even less. She constantly walked a tightrope between the two.

"As long as we have another great holiday season, like all the others, we should be fine!" She hoped the forced quality of her über-positive attitude wasn't laying it on too thick.

But Stacy seemed to accept the good news, bless her heart.

"What a relief! We can't have a *town* without a bookstore."

"No, we can't," Mr. Finch agreed with a slight shake of his head. "It would be a travesty."

One by one the straggling customers left, carrying their purchases with them. Not long after, Stacy's husband, the devastatingly handsome Adam, dropped by to pick her up and drive her home. Everyone said their goodbyes.

Mr. Finch and Lois brought up the rear, wanting to help Twyla close up.

"You two go home!" She waved her hands dismissively. "I'm right behind you."

"I'll be by tomorrow for my morning shift promptly at nine." Mr. Finch took Lois's hand in his own.

"Are you sure you don't want to take a break? Take tomorrow off." Twyla went behind them, shutting off the lights. "You worked tonight."

"I'll get plenty of rest when I'm dead," Roy said, holding the door open for Lois.

"Roy!" Lois went ahead. "Please don't talk about the worst day of my life a second before it happens."

"No, darlin'." He sweetly brought her hand up to his lips. "I'll be around for a while. You manage to keep me young."

These two never failed to fill her heart with the warm fuzzies. Both had been widowed for a long time, and were on their second great love.

Which meant some people got two of those, and so far, Twyla didn't even have one.

Twyla arrived at her grandmother's home a few minutes later, having stopped first at the bakery for a salted caramel Bundt cake. She and Ganny usually met for dinner every Saturday night and she always brought dessert. Was it sad that a soon-to-be thirty-year-old single woman didn't have anything better to do on a Saturday night? Not at all. She had her gray cat, Bonkers, waiting at home. He was mean as the devil himself, but he'd been homeless when she adopted him from the shelter, so she was all he had.

Twyla also had at least half a dozen advanced reader copy books on her nightstand waiting for her. There were also all the upcoming Charming holiday events she'd agreed to participate in because that's what one did as a business owner. Ava had told her about a rare angel investor offering a zero-interest loan to a local Charming business. On top of everything else, Twyla had to prepare an essay this month to be considered. It wasn't as if she didn't have anything else to do. Too much, in fact.

"Hello, Peaches."

Ganny bussed Twyla's cheek. Occasionally she still referred to Twyla by her old childhood nickname. Once, she'd eaten so many juicy fresh peaches from the tree in Ganny's yard that she threw up. It wasn't the best nickname in the world.

"How was the book signing?"

"A line out the door." Twyla followed Ganny into the ornate dining area connected to the kitchen and set the cake on the mahogany table.

Ganny had been widowed twice and her last husband, Grandpa Walt, a popular real estate broker, had left her with very little but this house. It was too big for Ganny, but she refused to leave it because of the dining room. It was big enough to accommodate large groups of people, which she felt encouraged Twyla's parents to visit several times a year.

"It was a good start to the month."

"Good, good. Well, that's enough book business talk for tonight." Ganny waved a hand dismissively. "I've got a surprise for you tonight. An early Christmas present."

"You didn't have to get me anything."

But a thrill whipped through Twyla because her grandmother was renowned for her thoughtful gifts all year long. It could almost be anything. Maybe a trip to New York City, where Ganny had promised to finally introduce her to some of the biggest booksellers in the country. People she'd met over a lifetime of acquiring and selling books. Twyla had wanted to go back to New York for years. She could still feel the energy of the city zipping through her blood, taste the cheesecake from Junior's, and the slice of pepperoni pizza from Times Square.

"Why wouldn't I give my only granddaughter the best present in the world?" Ganny smiled with satisfaction. "He should be along any minute now."

All the breath left Twyla's body. Just the thought of another blind date struck her with a sadness she had no business feeling during the holidays. Everyone in town was conspiring to fix up "poor, sad Twyla who can't get a man."

She could get a man, but she wasn't concentrating her efforts on this.

Please let it not be Tony again. And yet there were so few single men her age left in town. Hadn't her grandmother always told Twyla she'd do fine on her own? If she couldn't find the right man, she didn't need *any* man? Twyla had embraced this truth. She wanted the perfect man or no one at all.

"Life with the right man is wonderful. But a life with the wrong man might as well be lived alone. So many things in life can replace a spouse. Work, travel and books, to start with," Ganny had said.

Twyla, then, *could* lead a happy and fruitful life without ever being married.

"Oh, Ganny." Twyla slumped on the chair. "You didn't fix me up with someone, did you?"

"Of course not, honey!" She patted Twyla's hand. "But speaking of which, you're not going to meet anyone special if you don't get out more."

"I'm just like you. Books are my family."

It seemed to have skipped a generation, because though her father, Ganny's son, had loyally run the family bookstore, it wasn't exactly his happy place.

"Yes, but keep in mind I made myself go out and meet people. It wasn't like it is today. Certainly not. I used to have three dates on the same day. No funny business, of course, but your mother already told me things are different."

Twyla couldn't imagine going out three times in one day. She'd be lucky to go out once every three years. Okay, she was exaggerating. But still. Men weren't exactly lining up to date her. One of them had said she'd look prettier if she'd stop wearing her black-rimmed glasses. Twyla refused to go the contact lens route because if glasses stopped a guy from being interested in her, it wasn't the guy she wanted anyway.

"Fine, I promise I'll go out! But please don't fix me up." Her friend Zoey had bugged her to go out with her and her boyfriend, Drew, and Twyla hadn't yet.

"No blind date. This is someone you actually want to see."

"I can't even imagine."

There was only one "he" she'd like to see, and he was all the way in Austin, at home with his girlfriend. Probably planning their wedding.

"That's it. I'm having dessert first." Twyla opened the cake box.

The doorbell rang and Ganny rose. "You stay here and close your eyes! Don't open them until I tell you to."

Oh, brother. It was like being twelve again. She clasped her hand over her eyes, but not before taking a finger swipe of salted caramel frosting, feeling…well, twelve again.

"Okay, fine. My eyes are closed."

Twyla heard the front door open and shut, Ganny's delighted laughter, but no other sounds from this "he" man. Nothing but the sounds of boots thudding as they followed Ganny's lighter steps.

"Can I open my eyes now? I would really like to have a piece of cake. Whoever you are, I hope you like cake."

"I love cake," the deep voice said.

Twyla didn't even have to open her eyes to recognize the teasing, flirty sound of her favorite person in the world. She didn't have to hazard a guess because she knew this man almost as well as she knew herself.

And Ganny was right. It *was* the best present.

Ever.

"Noah!"

Twyla stood and hurled herself into the open arms of Noah Cahill, her best friend.

CHAPTER TWO

THERE WERE FEW things in his life Noah enjoyed as much as filling his arms with his best friend. He held Twyla close, all five feet nothing of her. Her dark hair longer now than it had been a year ago when he'd left Charming. Today she was wearing her book-pattern dress, which meant the store must have had a signing. The outfit was a type of uniform she wore for those events. She had a similar skirt in bright colors with patterns of dragons, swords and slayers.

God, she was a sight. The old familiar pinch squeezed his chest. He almost hadn't come home this Christmas, thinking it would be easier. There was already so much he hadn't told her when he normally told her everything.

Almost everything.

Then he'd narrowly missed death, or at the least a devastating injury, and everything changed in the course of days. He would not waste another minute of his life doing a job he no longer wanted to do.

"I thought you weren't coming home this Christmas!" Twyla said, coming to her tiptoes to hug him tight. Her arms wrapped around his neck.

Automatically and before he could stop himself, he turned his head to take in a deep breath of her hair. She always smelled like coconuts. He set her down reluctantly, but he was used to this feeling with Twyla. It was always this way—the push and pull always resulting in the distance he'd created due to guilt.

And loyalty.

"Things have changed."

"Noah isn't just *visiting*," Twyla's grandmother said, sounding pleased. "He's come home to stay."

Bless Mrs. Schilling's kind heart. She'd always been pulling for Noah, against any and all reason, even if he could have told her a thousand times it was useless. He was destined to pine after Twyla forever. What he wanted to have with her would never work and the door had been slammed shut years ago. Now the opening might as well be buried under rubble. Like the roof that nearly fell on him.

"You're here to stay?" Twyla brightened. "But what about your job in Austin?"

"I quit." He held his arms off to his sides with a shrug. "It's not for me. Not anymore."

"It's *exactly* you. You've been an adrenaline junkie since you were a boy. How is it not for you?"

Yeah, best not to tell her about the roof that fell inches from him during a building fire. His entire squad had been lucky to escape with no fatalities. Three had wound up with minor injuries.

Noah could have sworn something, or *someone*, had shoved him out of the way. In that moment, with the heat barreling toward him and unfurling like a living thing, he'd felt his brother, Will, there in the room with him. Will, shouting for him to get out of the way.

His long-dead older brother was telling Noah, in no uncertain terms, to stop trying to be a hero. To, for the love of God, stop rescuing people and start living his own life. Noah had first worked as an EMT, and then later a firefighter in nearby Houston for the past few years. He'd saved some people and lost some, but "imaginary Will" had called it. No matter what Noah did, he'd never get another chance to save Will.

And he was the only save that would have ever mattered. Now it was high time to honor his life instead. Noah may have always felt second best to his much smarter and accomplished brother, but that feeling wasn't one encouraged by Will. His older brother had always had Noah's back. Even on their last day together.

"It was good, for a while, but it's time to move on."

"But—"

"Let's have some of that delicious cake." Mrs. Schilling urged them to take a seat at the table. "We have plenty of time to discuss all this."

"I never say no to cake." Noah took a seat, avoiding Twyla's gaze.

If he looked too directly at her, she'd see everything in his eyes, so at times like this he had a system in place.

Don't make eye contact.

Three serving plates were passed around and Twyla sliced off generous pieces.

"No matter what, we're glad you're home," Mrs. Schilling said. "Aren't we, dear?"

"Yes, of course. It's just such a surprise. So…unexpected." Twyla took a bite of cake.

Using an old trick, he purposely looked at her ear, to make it look like he was meeting her eyes.

"It's a career choice. I have a really great opportunity here."

"Where are you staying?"

It was a fair question since he'd given up his rental when he'd grown tired of the memories that haunted him here and moved to Austin to start over.

"I rented one of those cottages by the beach. Just temporary until I find a place. The place where I'll be living is far less important than what I'll be doing." Noah winked.

This was his biggest news: the culmination of a long-held dream. He'd squashed it for so long after Will's death that he'd nearly forgotten it. But in that fiery building, he'd *remembered*.

"What *are* you going to be doing?"

"Taking over a business here in town." He'd start with the easy stuff first.

"Wonderful!" Mrs. Schilling clapped her hands. "Obviously, I have always loved the entrepreneurial spirit. Why, it's the reason the Thompson family started Once Upon a Book."

"What kind of business? Fire investigation? Teaching safety? You would make a *great* teacher." Twyla smiled and took another bite of cake.

He hoped the news wasn't going to kill her like it might his own mother. But he couldn't live the rest of his life in fear. Or worse yet, accommodating the fears of others.

"No. I'm taking over the boat charter. Mr. Curry is retiring, and he's been looking for a buyer for a year or more."

When his news was met with such silence that he heard Mrs. Schilling's grandfather clock ticking, he continued.

"He actually wants someone local to take it over, so he'll work terms out with me. I have enough hours on the water, so I'll be taking the USCG test for my captain's license. I've obviously already had first aid training and then some. Until I get my license, I'll have Finn's help and he already has his license. Mr. Curry said he'd be around awhile longer, too, if we need help." He filled his mouth with a big piece of cake.

Twyla sucked in a breath, and Mrs. Schilling's shaky hand went to her throat. Other than that, Noah thought everything here would be okay. Nothing to see here. Sure thing. They'd all get used to the idea. Eventually.

Just give them a couple of decades.

"Are you serious?" Twyla pushed her plate of unfinished cake away.

Only he would fully understand the significance of the move. For Twyla not to finish a slice of cake meant that in her opinion, the world just might be ending.

"Yes, I'm serious. Ask yourself whether if anyone else said the same thing, you'd have this kind of a reaction."

"That's not even funny. You're *not* anyone else." She took a breath and whispered her next words. "You're Will's brother. You…you almost died out there, too."

"Now, Twyla…let the man finish." This from Twyla's grandmother, thankfully, the voice of reason.

She didn't let him finish.

"If this is my surprise, I don't like it." Twyla stood.

With that she walked right out of her grandmother's kitchen.

"Twyla!" her grandmother chided. "Oh, dear. Noah, I'm sorry. She's had a rough year. The bookstore isn't doing well, and—"

"Let me talk to her."

"Noah? Are you sure about this? If Twyla reacts this way, you can only imagine how your poor mother—"

"I know. *And* I'm sure."

He found Twyla outside on the wraparound porch's swing, bare feet dangling as she stared into the twinkling sky. Without a word, he plopped himself next to her and nudged her knee.

"Hey."

"Hey." She leaned into him, and he tamped down the rush of raw emotion that single move brought. "I'm sorry. I may have…overreacted."

She couldn't stay angry at him for long. Neither one of them could. Not since they'd been kids.

"You think? It's not that I don't understand the concern

but everyone seems to forget I grew up boating. Will and I both did. I'm going to be careful and follow all relevant safety practices. Probably go overboard with them." He chuckled and elbowed her. "See what I did there?"

"Funny man."

"I just…can't pretend anymore."

Starting over had served its purpose. He'd lived in a city in which no one knew him as Will's younger brother. A new place where he'd excelled and never been second best. He'd tried to settle down into a stable relationship with Michelle. But he hadn't been happy even before the roof collapse.

"What are you pretending?"

"That I'm okay living someone else's life. I don't want to live in Austin. I want to live here. You do realize the ocean is not the only danger in life?"

"Sure, I'd prefer you do something normal like… I don't know, real estate? You'd make a killing. *Everybody* loves you."

Wind up the only surviving brother after a boating tragedy and you're bound to get a lot of sympathy. He was tired of that, too. Another reason he'd left town.

He grunted. "Real estate is not going to happen. Too much paperwork."

"Why now? Did something happen?"

While he could tell her, letting her realize that it wasn't only water that could kill a man, this didn't seem like the right time. Later, he'd tell her about the roof collapse. Later, he'd tell her about Michelle.

And everything else. Someday. Just…not now.

"I think Will would want this. And I want this. This was our dream when we were kids. We'd wake up every day and go fishing. Every day would be like a vacation."

"I know he would want you to be happy."

"*This* is going to make me happy. I'm tired of living for other people. You only get one life. This one is mine."

They both sat in silence for a beat. Will had been only eighteen when they'd lost him in the accident that nearly took Noah's life, too. Their family had never been the same. When Noah's parents divorced, his father left the state and now rarely spoke to Noah. His mother still lived in Charming and had never truly gotten over the loss of her oldest son. She'd laid her dreams at Will's feet, who had done everything she'd ever asked of him. He'd been the good son, the strong academic. Noah had been the classic bad boy, unable to live up to the impossible standard that Will set.

"Remember when you, me and Will would lie under the stars at night?" Twyla pushed her legs out to start swinging. "And Will renamed the Little Dipper 'Noah Dipper' after you, and the Big Dipper was 'Will Dipper'?"

"Yeah, even if 'Bill Dipper' would have sounded better."

Noah smiled at the memory. Will believed in the power behind words and used to play around with letters all the time. Mixing them up, creating new words. Like Twyla, he was a bit of a book nerd. The valedictorian in his graduating class of Charming High. He and Twyla had been so much alike it was no wonder that though Noah met Twyla first, it was Will who wound up dating her. His courtship with her might have been short and sweet, but at least he'd had one.

"He used to like renaming stuff. Combining two words together, shifting letters. Word play."

"Mine was easy. Twilight was hereafter renamed Twyla for short." She chuckled. "Totally made sense."

It had been a long while since they talked about Will. Remembered. He was that silent spot between them, keeping them apart but making Noah wish for nothing more than those good times.

"He had the biggest crush on you."

Of course, Noah had been the first to have the crush, except *crush* might not have been the right word. He'd been astounded. He recalled literally gaping when he first laid eyes on Twyla helping her mother at the bookstore, dressed in a pink dress and matching shoes. Pushing her horn-rimmed glasses up her nose and giving him a shy smile. She looked like an angel to an eleven-year-old boy.

"We should do that again sometime," Twyla said. "Lie under the stars together."

He almost jerked his neck back in surprise. She'd never suggested anything like this before. It amounted to doing something together that they'd only ever done with Will.

It was like…reinventing it.

"Why?"

"Why?" She spoke just above a whisper. "Because they're still there. Still twinkling. Is it okay with you if I want to look at them again and see them in a different way?"

He reached to lighten the moment. "Rename them, you mean?"

"Anything. Of course, maybe Michelle wouldn't like it. You and I spending so much time together."

Ah, that's why she'd brought it up. She didn't know about his breakup with the woman he'd dated while in Austin. He'd brought her to Charming once, where she'd met Twyla and the family. She thought Michelle was still there between them, a safe buffer from getting too close to him. There was no point in telling her the truth. Let her relax in her false belief. Their guilt had kept them apart this long. What was another decade?

Noah would throw himself into work. His dream. He'd live his life the way he wanted to and reach for happiness wherever he could find it. Around every blind corner. Behind every rogue wave. Fake it till he made it. He was excited about the future for the first time since he could recall.

Life was too short and if Will hadn't taught him that, then certainly the roof collapse had.

"No, probably not. She wouldn't like it," he lied. "But I don't care."

Twyla took off her glasses and wiped the lenses on the edge of her shirt.

She didn't say anything to that—probably because they didn't usually talk about any of his girlfriends. It was better that way.

He changed the subject. "Is it true you're having problems with the bookstore?"

Twyla sighed. "Why do you think I want to lie under the stars like when I was ten? Yes, we're having trouble. What else is new?"

"I thought everything was better after the last holiday season. You always say December counts for ninety percent of your business."

"Welcome to the book world. A lot can change in a year. The ground is constantly shifting under my feet."

"Well, you can't close the bookstore."

"Everyone says that."

"We grew up in that museum. Reading dragon slayer books in those cozy corner nooks filled with pillows. I'll help. Just put me to work."

She smiled. "You're going to be busy if you insist on this madness."

"I'll figure out a way."

"Hey, does this mean you'll be at the tree lighting ceremony tomorrow?"

"Wouldn't miss it."

"Wait until you see the little book shaped ornaments we have for the tree."

She sounded excited and like her old self for the first time tonight.

"Let me guess. Dragon slayer books?"

"Among some others, of course. We can't ignore *The Night Before Christmas* and the other classics."

Sometimes, Noah could still see himself and Will sitting among the shelves of dusty books. They'd read quietly every afternoon after school because Twyla's parents didn't mind being an unofficial after-school center. It wasn't until much later, when he and Twyla had been in the depths of their shared grief, that they'd found "the book." The one that had defined the years after Will. They'd take turns reading chapters. One week the book stayed with Noah and he'd read three chapters, and one week it was with Twyla. He'd write and post stickers in the margins of the book, which had technically belonged to Twyla.

Noah would comment: *That idiot deserved to be killed by the dragon.*

And Twyla would answer: *Sometimes the dragon chooses the right victim.*

They'd mark significant parts, but almost never the same ones. Noah was far more impressed with dragon slayer tools while Twyla loved the mushy stuff about love and sacrifice. The book came to belong to them both, since they'd literally made it their own. Noah had never done this with any other book before or since and he'd venture she never had either. For reasons he didn't quite understand, they'd made this particular book, *A Dragon's Heart*, their own. They shared the words until the day Noah stole the book from Twyla. There was just no other way to put it.

He'd "borrowed" the book without returning it.

That, at least, was something he'd never tell her.

CHAPTER THREE

THE NEXT DAY, having risen before dawn to drive to the docks, Noah watched the sunrise while he waited for Mr. Curry to arrive. The view was calming and soothing in the way a Gulf Coast native could appreciate. Gold mixed with shades of blue and painted the sky with morning. Noah found little more beautiful than a Gulf Coast sunrise other than a sunset accompanied by fireflies. Over the years, he'd been seeing less of them lighting up the coastal nights.

"You're early." Mr. Curry emerged from his brightly detailed pickup truck.

The truck itself was practically a Charming landmark. Granted, it had seen better days and could definitely use a paint job. But the etching of two dolphins meeting half-way, blending into sharp blue and purple hues still grabbed attention. The letters spelled *Nacho Boat Adventures* and the phone number. Boat tours, fishing charters, diving excursions, water skiing, rentals. Group rates available.

A walking advertisement. Not that Noah would need to take out an ad because the business, decades old, was practically the apex of Charming tourism.

And if Noah was early, it was because he couldn't wait to get started.

He handed Mr. Curry a coffee cup. "Will you throw in the truck, too?"

"Let's talk inside." Mr. Curry put his key in the door of the unimpressive A-line shack on the pier.

Weather-beaten and somewhat battered, the outside could also use a makeover. So could Mr. Curry, for that matter, who had grown his white beard down to his chest and looked older than his sixty-five years.

"Are you doing okay?" Noah asked, watching him hobble inside.

"Ah, it's the arthritis. Makes me a grump most days. Don't take it personal." He took a swig of coffee, then held it up. "Thanks for this."

"No problem." Drinking from his own cup, Noah took in the shop he hadn't been inside of for years.

A handwritten schedule of boat tours hung on a whiteboard behind the register. Surf boards were propped against the rear walls, hung near boating equipment like ropes and clips. The smells of wood and salt were comforting. Noah inhaled and took it all in. It was his burden to have never had a healthy fear of the ocean. And even after all he'd been through, he still didn't shy away from the memories of long summer days boating. Their father had taught both of his boys everything he knew, and they'd manned the captain's wheel from the time they were thirteen and fourteen. Two boys, a year apart. Irish twins, his mother called them.

"You should know. I'm moving." Mr. Curry interrupted Noah's thoughts.

"I know. That's why you're selling."

"Me and the Mrs. We're headed west to Arizona."

"Landlocked?" Noah raised his brow. This he had not expected.

"Hell, yeah. They got lakes. Need the dry and hot weather for my stupid arthritis." He went behind the counter and seemed to be fiddling around back there. "That's all to say that while I want someone like you to take over, I also need someone who's going to stick around. Do I make myself clear? I can stay on awhile and take some of those boat tours we've already scheduled for the real die-hards, but there's no turning back. No second thoughts. Of course, you could sell, but you see how long it's taken me. This isn't the greatest moneymaker in the world."

"I figured." Noah had some ideas of his own to increase business but best not interrupt the man's flow of thoughts.

"You won't get rich owning this business, but you will also never be poor."

"I'm in this for the long haul. I picture myself a grand-father, like you, finally retiring someplace dry because I have arthritis." Noah reached for some other older per-son's ailment and came up with nothing. "Or something."

"That's what I want to see. You, growing old in this town. Safe. Giving tours. Teaching. Because, well, you know…"

Noah let the silence hang between them for only a mo-ment. He knew where this would be going. Knew it far too well.

"I know," Noah completed the sentence. "And the ac-cident still doesn't define who I am. Never did."

"My wife is going to kill me twice when she finds out who I sold to. I told her I had an offer from a local. That I'd offered financing to help the young man out. She thinks the idea is great. But she doesn't know it's *you*."

Noah sighed. He'd felt the protectiveness of this town come over him like a choke hold. It no longer felt like pro-tection. It felt controlling. Unreasonable.

"It's time for all of us to move on."

"*If* you're sure." Mr. Curry crossed his arms. "Then this…is a done deal."

"I'm absolutely one hundred percent sure. I'm never going back to firefighting again. One roof nearly falling on me is enough."

Mr. Curry gaped. "Hot damn, son. You might be the luckiest man I've ever met. All right. Welcome aboard."

He chuckled, then went on to give Noah the speed version of the business he'd managed for two decades. It was all written down, of course…somewhere. Though good help was hard to find, Noah would have two staff members staying on through the transition. They were both part-time workers—teens who loved boating and were willing to be paid a microscopic salary for the pleasure of working for the new boss.

Concern hit Noah like a hot spike, but he forced himself to shake it off. Teenagers near water did not *automatically* mean danger.

"What do they do around here?"

"As little or as much as you want. Diana answers the phone and takes the bookings. Sells the little equipment we have for sale and the surf boards." He waved his hand in the air. "Tee, that's the ridiculous nickname he goes by, is working on a boating license. You can fire them both as far as I'm concerned but they're good kids and for a while they'll know more than you will about how we run things."

He had a point.

"Be at the bank tomorrow morning and we'll sign the papers. Owner financing the first year. It's all in the contract." He then reached under the register and came up with a small box. "May as well take these with you since you're here."

Noah accepted the box. "What's all this?"

"Christmas."

Indeed, dozens of tree ornaments in the shape of boats announced "A Merry Christmas from Nacho Boat." They were for the tree lighting ceremony tonight. This meant a couple of things. After tonight, almost everyone in town would know Noah was the new owner of Nacho Boat Adventures.

He was on borrowed time before his mother heard about the contract he'd sign tomorrow morning.

But he told himself one more day wouldn't hurt anything.

JUST BEFORE THE tree lighting ceremony, Twyla closed up shop and drove her sedan the short drive to the boardwalk. She carried her basket full of ornaments for the lighting of the Christmas tree. This had always been the first Charming event at the start of the month, which kicked off the season's festivities. This never failed to make her heart buzz with anticipation, even if the excitement was dulled tonight due to Noah's unexpected news. She didn't like the idea of him taking over Nacho Boat any more than his mother would. But, more than anyone else, she understood what it was like to live under the heavy weight of opinion.

Charming was a small town and its residents were similar to an extended family you loved to hate. Even if more than a decade had passed, she was still thought of as "Will's girl." Even though she and Will barely dated for a year before he broke up with her because he'd be going away to college. Of course, that never happened. He'd never made it to college. She was Will's *last* girlfriend and some people, Noah's mother included, saw her forever frozen in the tragic role. The reason, she understood, was that Will himself would remain forever eighteen.

Twyla, on the other hand, would be twenty-seven this year. Like Noah, who'd been trying to escape his role as town hero responsible for the biggest water rescue in Charming history, she'd been trying to move on from the role of grieving ex-girlfriend. She'd signed up for some of the dating apps and forced herself on the occasional date.

She'd even expressed her interest in Adam Cruz when he'd arrived in town over a year ago. He'd been single for about two minutes, however, and then there went that opportunity.

Over the years, she'd dated men here and there that Noah interestingly always found fault with. Yet he'd never even tried to fix her up. Not even with his best friend, Finn. Noah would sing the guy's praises all the live long day but whenever he was single, Noah stopped talking about Finn. She and Noah had never been on dates together, keeping that part of each other's life separate. She never complained about guys to him, and he never complained about women. But as far as she could tell, Noah never had any issues with the female population, other than the fact that he'd never seemed ready to settle down. Michelle, someone he'd met in Austin, was simply the latest and Twyla wondered how long they'd last long distance.

Walking toward the boardwalk along the seawall, Twyla took in the holiday scene. As usual, the decor on the boardwalk was already in full swing. Many of the vendors would stay open through their mild winter, their shops decorated to the hilt with snowflakes, trees and more lights. Sounds from the roller coaster on the amusement park end of the boardwalk were as loud as on any summer night, only with residents and not many tourists. Families were out having fun, creating memories. She strolled along accompanied by the sound of seagulls cawing and foraging for food in the sand. Aromatic and delicious scents of fresh coffee, hot cocoa and popcorn competed. She would need some hot cocoa sooner rather than later.

Despite the lower tourism rate that tended to hit every business, winter in Charming was her favorite time of the year, when temperatures hovered in the low sixties and, on a good day, reached the high fifties. She loved sweater and boot weather. Finally, she could haul out her cowboy boots and wear them without anyone teasing her.

She waved as she passed the Lazy Maisy kettle corn store, selling their classic peppermint-flavored, red-and-green popcorn as they did every December, each worker dressed like an elf for the entire month. Strands of white lights hung from every storefront. A plastic model of Santa and his sleigh guided by a reindeer were suspended across one side of the boardwalk, cheery signs everywhere announcing a "charming" Christmas. Yes, thank you. Twyla would have a charming Christmas indeed.

Noah was back. Christmas would be even better now.

She had to keep telling herself that. Nacho Boat had a great safety record. Noah was bright and intelligent. He'd take all necessary precautions because he'd never want his mother to hurt again. For so long, they'd all walked on eggshells around Katherine Cahill. Twyla included. The woman had suffered enough, but Noah did have a point. His career as a firefighter wasn't exactly a desk job. At least here, they'd all be able to keep an eye on him. Keep him safe. Yes, she'd do that. For Will and for Katherine. But mostly, for herself.

"Hey, Twyla."

She turned to find herself face-to-face with Valerie Kinsella, a third-grade teacher and wife of one of the three former Navy SEALs who ran the Salty Dog Bar & Grill.

"Check these out. I think the ornaments are amazing this year. I found a specialty shop in Dallas with a great price." She handed the box to Valerie, who would mix it up with the others.

"You've outdone yourself as usual." Valerie smiled.

Baskets filled with all donated ornaments would be passed around to the residents, who each got to choose at least one to put on a branch. People were already gathering around the huge tree in the center. Ava Del Toro, president of the Chamber of Commerce, climbed up the temporary risers hauled over from the high school.

Meanwhile, this year's Santa walked through the crowd, handing candy canes out to kids as the ornament baskets made the rounds. Twyla glanced in the crowd for Noah, since he'd texted her that he'd be there early and she should come and find him. At first, she didn't see him at all, and then noticed him talking to Sabrina, one of his old girlfriends. Most of his life, Noah had never failed to get the attention of girls, and later, women. It was the whole bad boy thing. He'd surfed, driven fast cars and even had a motorcycle for a nanosecond. Twyla hated motorcycles but she loved those boots Noah got to wear when he rode one. Even teachers liked Noah. He wasn't a stellar student, but he was funny and kind.

When he'd been hospitalized after the accident, there had been so many flowers in his room that it resembled a botanical garden.

Twyla watched now as Sabrina leaned into Noah, touched his broad shoulder and tossed back her long red hair. The familiar and unwelcome pinch of jealousy, this time on Michelle's behalf, burned in Twyla's stomach. Then Noah turned, saw Twyla and his smile brightened. He gave a little "see ya later" wave to Sabrina.

He walked over to Twyla, hands stuck in the pockets of his blue denim jeans. "Hey, Peaches."

She grinned, ready to tease him. "Um, I'd be careful. You're going to make Michelle jealous."

A flash of guilt crossed his eyes. "Yeah, about that—"

But he was interrupted by a loud Ava nearly yelling through the bullhorn in her hands.

"Welcome, everyone! It's time for the lighting of the tree! So! Fun! This year our tree is donated by Tree Growers of Bent, Oregon. Another Douglas fir. Before we hit the switch and light up the night sky, you'll each get to place an ornament on the tree. Just reach in the baskets we're all passing out. Find an ornament in there and put it on the tree! And don't forget the upcoming Snowflake Float Boat Parade, followed by the first annual literary costume event at Once Upon a Book. Come dressed as your favorite literary character and support the giving tree! One of you could win a gift card worth hundreds of dollars, which ought to help with all that holiday shopping."

Many turned to Twyla and smiled, giving her a thumbs-up. She'd love to claim the idea as her own, but it had been yet another one of Ava's creative brainstorms. The woman was a marketing genius when it came to town tourism and supporting local business. Before Noah's return, the costume event would have been the most excitement she'd have all year. She'd been planning for months, her own ideas swinging between Elizabeth Bennet and Hermione Granger. She hadn't yet decided, but she already had the long Jane Austen-style dress she'd found for a deep discount on eBay.

"Literary character." Noah winked and tipped back on his heels. "Does dragon slayer count?"

Her heart raced at the memory. Their favorite book. She'd misplaced *A Dragon's Heart* about a year ago, just before the move into a smaller rental to save money. Books tended to get swallowed whole in a bookstore and half the time she expected to come across it on a shelf. So far, she hadn't. Everyone, including Mr. Finch, was on the lookout. This particular copy was unlike any other, and even though the genre had grown out of popularity with most readers, Twyla liked to read the book once a year. She'd ordered another copy for that reason alone, but it could never take the place of the one she'd lost. Noah's handwriting was in the margins of that book, along with her own.

"You can come as anything you'd like. I'm just happy to have you."

She nearly corrected herself but then let it go. He knew what she meant. She didn't *have* him. Michelle had him. And though she wondered with every moment that passed what he'd meant when he said, "About that…" she refused to ask.

"I kind of look like a dragon slayer and I'm sure I can find a cool sword."

She chuckled. "You do *not* look like a dragon slayer and I'm fairly sure you already own a plastic toy sword."

"Are you calling me an overgrown child?" He narrowed his eyes, filled with humor and mischief.

"Maybe."

"Got to say, it's tough to hang out with someone who knows me so well." The basket came around to them and Noah dug for several long seconds, causing even Valerie to quirk a brow. "Ah, yeah. Here we go."

He held up the ornament depicting the cover of *Where the Wild Things Are*. "My favorite book. Still read it every night before bed."

"Bless your heart," Valerie said and waited while Twyla dug through the basket.

She picked out an elf from the Lazy Maisy store and together she and Noah went forward and placed the ornaments. Side by side like they'd done for years. Just like old times.

A few minutes later, the lights slowly went up the giant tree, starting from the lower half and scrolling slowly to the top until bright lights beckoned.

Noah turned to Twyla. "Let the wild rumpus start."

CHAPTER FOUR

THE NIGHT WAS clear and bright, not socked in with fog like the Gulf Coast could get on some nights. Twyla and Noah strolled along the seawall. She should go home soon and feed Bonkers, even if he was the most antisocial cat on earth. Also, she looked forward to changing into her favorite jammies and curling up under the covers with her book.

But she kept hoping Noah would restart the conversation from earlier without any prompting.

About that...

"I'm signing the contract tomorrow morning."

Noah went on to explain how he'd managed to get Mr. Curry to agree to owner financing and then cashed out all of his savings to invest. He'd now be the proud owner of a catamaran, rental equipment and big plans to grow the business. Twyla swallowed hard at the thought of how fully invested Noah was in this new venture. Now she'd have no choice but to be his cheerleader or stand by as he lost...everything.

"I'm all in."

"Have you told your mother?"

Twyla could only imagine how that conversation would go over.

"Not yet."

She walked next to him as he ambled onto a pier and sat, his long legs swinging over the edge. It was on the tip of Twyla's tongue to ask how Michelle felt about him moving back to Charming and whether or not she'd be joining him. But she simply let Noah take the lead as he asked questions about the bookstore and drilled her on the finances until she asked him to drop it.

"But I'm worried," he said.

"Don't be. If we have to, we'll sell. It was a nice run."

He snorted, understanding her words betrayed how difficult it would be for her to let go. "And what will you do then?"

"Ganny always promised me a trip to New York City to introduce me to some of the booksellers she'd met over the years. Last night, I thought that was going to be my surprise."

"Sorry to disappoint."

She playfully slugged his shoulder. "You never could, Noah. Stop it. You are always the best surprise."

He turned to her then, so close she could breathe in his delicious scent. The moonlight made his dark eyes shimmer and her heart tugged with the familiar warmth. *Noah.* She didn't think she'd ever love anyone quite the same way she loved her best friend.

"Yeah. Something you should know about me and Michelle. We're not together."

Poor Noah. Weren't they a pair? He had about as much luck as she did in the relationship department. "What happened?"

"I told her the life she wants to lead is not my life. Then she accused me of having commitment issues. Commitment-phobe, I think she called me." He whistled. "It was ugly. It wasn't great to admit to myself that she's probably right. But I wasn't going to ask her to come along with me on this new adventure. This is my thing, my dream, and I won't answer to anyone."

She linked her arm through his. "When you're ready, the Almost Dead Poets Society likes to play matchmaker."

"Um, no thanks."

Twyla chuckled. "Last month they set me up with Tony."

"That would never work. For obvious reasons."

"It was better than Zoey, who fixed me up with Gus."

Noah's neck jerked back. "*That* loser?"

"He's a bit handsy but I wouldn't call him a loser."

"Did he *try* something with you?" Noah narrowed his eyes.

Her cheeks flushed. "No, and never mind."

They sat quietly for another few minutes as the waves lapped against the wood piles of the pier.

"Do you think you'll leave town if the bookstore closes?"

"I don't know, but I might need to leave. At least for a while."

"Why? I just got back."

"Noah, you're not the only one that thinks it might be nice to start over somewhere else." She swallowed hard. "Do you realize I still occasionally get referred to as Will's girlfriend?"

"You mean by someone other than my mother?" Noah shook his head. "If you want her to move on from your tragic love story, you need to give her something else to talk about. Give *everyone* something to talk about. Learn from my experience. Life is too short to please other people."

"You must really mean it this time. Breaking up with another girlfriend is going to make your mother pretty unhappy."

"Yeah, well, so is buying Nacho Boat."

"That one's going to worry a lot of people."

"Don't you be one of them. I'm going to stick around for a long while. Long enough to make sure you don't get fixed up on any lousy blind dates. Everyone is going through me from now on." He thumped his chest.

"Really? You're not going to find something wrong with every date I have? That's kind of your thing."

"It's only *been* my thing because of the men you've picked."

She bristled at the memories, because she had a truckload of them. "How was I supposed to know Jimmy Lee was engaged to be married?"

"You couldn't have known. That's why you have me."

But she also had him to stop her from dating some of the better-looking guys in town.

"Well…what about Finn?" she asked.

Noah blinked. *"Finn?"*

You would have thought she'd asked him to fix her up with Chris Hemsworth.

"Is that so crazy? Isn't he single again?"

"Finn is going to be busy. He's my partner and is helping me get this business off the ground. He won't have quality time to spend with you and that's what you deserve."

She hesitated from stating she wouldn't be that picky with the right man. For reasons she didn't quite understand, Noah did not want her dating his other best friend. To her, it was further confirmation that, in his mind, she'd never belong to anyone but Will.

"Fine." She stood, frustration spreading through her like a wildfire. "This lonely spinster is going home now."

"Hey." He followed her, coming within inches of her before he stopped and reached to slide a warm palm down her arm. "Don't be mad."

His touch, the warm timbre in his voice when he apologized, never failed to squeeze her heart with a powerful ache.

"I'm not *mad*. Just…tired of being lonely. I don't need

forever but I refuse to spend another Christmas alone. This might be one of the few times when you're single at Christmas, but it's not new to me."

"Great. If that's really what you want, I'll ask Finn if he's interested in dating someone again." He grimaced, like the thought of the two of them together made him sick. "What's so great about Finn, anyway? I don't see it. He's tall, sure, but so am I."

She nearly rolled her eyes. *Tall* had never been on her list of qualities for the perfect man.

"What do you mean? He's a nice guy, and he's got one fantastic quality. He's available."

THE NEXT MORNING, Noah left the local bank as the proud owner of Nacho Boat Adventures. He drove the truck Mr. Curry had indeed thrown in as part of the deal straight to the docks. A few residents honked when they saw him driving down the road in the painted truck, giving him a thumbs-up.

Today, he'd called for a meeting of his staff to discuss the transition. Noah had a running list of things to do started on his phone app and he glanced at it now.

1. Staff meeting
2. Inventory
3. Boat inspection
4. Check the ledgers
5. Make plans for grand opening
6. Join the Chamber of Commerce
7. Talk to Finn about Twyla (maybe next week)
8. Call Mom

Nope, he hadn't called his mother yet. For all she knew, he was still on the job in Austin. No harm done. The fact that he'd listed talking to her below talking to Finn said it all. The problem was that Noah was like many men in his generation. He hesitated to disappoint women until the last possible second.

It was the primary reason his relationship with Michelle had gone way past its natural expiration date. He'd tried to fall in love with Michelle with everything he had, agreeing it was time to settle down and have a family. He wanted that, too—children and a wife to grow old with. Someone who made him feel good about himself every day, someone who loved him unconditionally. Someone he looked forward to *seeing* every day and not out of obligation. Someone who looked just as good without makeup and perfect hair.

Someone like Twyla, but…*not* Twyla.

Noah opened up shop, and as the morning progressed, he set up, pinning a scrolled red banner Ava had handed him this morning after his signing at the bank: *Under new ownership.*

The first staff member to arrive was Eddie Pierce. He had a Mohawk and wore board shorts, boat shoes and a black T-shirt that read: *I hate it when the voices inside my head go silent. I never know what they're planning.* According to Mr. Curry, he was the one working on his captain's license. Well, he'd be working on it for a while longer if Noah had anything to do with it. He intended to keep everyone on his staff safe.

"Call me Tee, Bossman." He fist bumped with Noah.

"Tee?"

"I like to wear T-shirts year-round. It's kinda my thing."

His other staff member, Diana, arrived just behind Tee, the girl who booked appointments and answered the phone.

When he greeted her and introduced himself, she barely looked at him.

"What do we call you?" Tee said. "Mr. Cahill? Can I call you Bossman? Head honcho? Captain? Nacho Man?"

"Nacho Man is my favorite of those, but just call me Noah."

"Chill. Dude, that's super easy. I had a lot of other great names but that one works, too."

The girl had still not looked at Noah, but she made an agreeable sound.

"I know Mr. Curry has given y'all a lot of freedom here, but I'm a stickler for rules. Regulations. Safety first and foremost. Got me?"

Jesus, he sounded like a drill sergeant. Tee's neck jerked back slightly, and Diana continued to study her shoes.

He pulled back some, clearing his throat. "Of course, we're going to have fun here, too. No doubt about that. This is a great part-time job and I appreciate your dedication. I'll be hiring some others as time passes and we grow the business like I plan. But first things first. Let's take a look at the inventory. Today, I want a list of everything we own in this shop and how many we have."

"Um, we did inventory," Tee offered.

"A year ago," Noah said. "I have to believe there might be some changes."

"He's right," Diana said, looking up for a second. She caught Noah's gaze and blushed a thousand shades of crimson.

"Yeah, I guess." Tee shrugged.

"Inventory is not fun, I know, but it's necessary to a solid business plan. I'll start ordering right away if we're short on anything." He offered Tee one of the laptops he'd invested in to bring the business into the new millennium. "Everything has to reconcile with what we have listed on the master spreadsheet."

Tee not so discreetly passed the laptop to Diana.

"Also, all boating excursions are on hold until I personally inspect every inch of the catamaran. I have to prep it for the Snowflake Float Boat Parade."

"But—" Diana began.

"Shouldn't take me long." He pointed to Diana. "You can reschedule. Blame it on the switch in ownership and the fact that the new boss is a hard-ass."

She flushed an interesting shade of purple. "Um, yes."

Noah scrolled through his phone notes to see if he'd missed anything. "Any questions?"

"Can we have Pizza Party Saturdays?" Tee said, scratching the side of his Mohawk. "Mr. Curry said that'd be up to the new owners."

Far be it from him to ruin all the excitement around here. He remembered the fun of being a teenager far too well.

"Sure. Let's see how we do this week, and then we'll talk."

CHAPTER FIVE

"THEY'RE HERE!" TWYLA ran to the shop door and threw it open for the delivery guy to come inside.

At Once Upon a Book, receiving day was a bit like celebrating Christmas once a month, all year long. For December, Twyla had ordered extra copies of the children's books on the giving tree wish list. But as usual, there was a mix of everything. The latest *New York Times* fiction bestsellers, a little bit of mystery, fantasy, romance and women's fiction. She'd also ordered several copies of the latest nonfiction number one bestseller in the country—a memoir from a cervical cancer survivor. And the special orders for poetry books, at the request of her staunchest supporters, were also arriving. They always sold out within a day.

"Look at you." Carlos, the UPS guy, grinned as he hauled one box in over his shoulder. "I love book day."

"Even if these boxes are the heaviest?"

"Nah, why do you think I work out?" He set the box down, then curled his arm, showing off biceps. "Months of weight lifting all to prepare for the holiday season."

He left, waving with a wink and a goofy smile. Twyla went to opening boxes and shelving. She had to remove some of the older books that hadn't sold, always causing a heavy ache to form in her throat. *Books without homes*. But though most of the publishers had a good return policy, Twyla usually donated them to organizations like the women's shelter and the local library, of course. Probably not the best business practice, come to think of it. Next year, if they made it through, she'd have to start returning unsold inventory.

Using her X-Acto knife, Twyla carefully sliced through the top of a box. The wonderful scent of paper and ink immediately filled her with memories. Twyla had an e-reader like everyone else, but there was nothing like the feel of a book in her hands. She turned it over and admired the cover, then read the synopsis on the back of the book and all the author endorsements.

Sliding a heavy box down the aisle, she moved over to the children's section. The same throw pillows Ganny had bought on a trip to India with her second husband years ago were scattered cozily in a nook. Twyla smiled at the *Where the Wild Things Are* tapestry that hung on the wall nearby. Leave it to Noah to mention Christmas as a wild rumpus. He wasn't wrong. But she wished she could have people knocking her doors down like they did at the big-box retailers in Houston.

Maybe instead of donating these books, she should line them up outside and offer a two-for-one discount. Something to think about even if she hated discounting books. It seemed criminal, like she was somehow devaluing them. But every book deserved to find a home. She'd just finished making shelf space for new additions when the familiar bell chimed as someone swung open the doors. It was wrong to hope for Noah, of course, because he'd be busy all day. But she hoped for him anyway.

"Hey there, girlfriend!" Zoey Lambert, Twyla's good friend who ran Glamtique, walked inside.

The boutique was the perfect place for the always-fashion-conscious Zoey. Gorgeous and statuesque, she was often mistaken for a model. Her black corkscrew curls framed her flawless latte skin.

"I'm back here." Twyla waved from the children's section. "It's delivery day."

Zoey appeared around the corner, her eyes narrowed in concern. "Oh, no. That also means books-go-away day. You want to go have a drink after work? Drown your sorrows? Is there a book I can buy before it goes bye-bye?"

"It's just business. By now I should realize I order too many in anticipation of a book's success. But—"

"No one can guarantee any book's success." Zoey completed the sentence. She understood the book business nearly as much as Twyla did—the casualty of being the best friend of a bookseller.

"I don't want to go anywhere, but why don't you come over? We'll watch a movie and I'll make cupcakes."

It had been a while since they'd had a girl's night because Zoey was spending much of her spare time power dating a kickboxing trainer from Houston. She'd gone in for lessons and left with a boyfriend. This was always the way with Zoey, who never seemed to have any trouble in the romance department.

Zoey took her phone out and started swiping. "If you don't go out sometimes, you'll never meet anyone."

"Ugh. Yeah, I guess that's true. But I don't want any more of your fix-ups!" Twyla pointed her finger. "And I mean it!"

Zoey's face fell almost comically because apparently that was exactly her intention. "I was just texting Drew that I wouldn't be available for our usual, um, session tonight."

Twyla flushed when Zoey smiled wickedly. She unfortunately heard too much about their sexual "sessions" which seemed to verge on acrobatics.

If nothing else, they were both in fabulous shape.

Zoey followed behind Twyla, pushing boxes she could probably lift with one hand. "So, I heard about Noah. Your grandmother told me."

"Yes, that was my Christmas surprise."

"But did you hear he and Michelle broke up?"

"*Yes*. Of course, he told me."

"I heard from Betty that it was ugly."

"Ugly?" This didn't sound like Noah at all, and Twyla resented the implication.

She didn't want Betty floating around rumors that put Noah in a bad light. When he'd broken up with girls in the past, they'd always remained friends. Zoey was a perfect example. She'd also dated Noah for a time.

Really, who hadn't?

Twyla. Twyla hadn't. That would be a big fat no for her. But there were several benefits to that, one of which was that at least she'd never be one of his exes.

"I heard she accused him of being in love with someone else!" Zoey huffed in outrage.

"That doesn't sound like Noah at all. And if there was someone else, I would know!" She thumped her chest.

"That's what I thought, which is why I'm here."

Twyla paused shelving to plunk her hands on her hips. "You're *not* here to commiserate with me over 'the book has to go away' day?"

"I actually *forgot* that was today." Zoey grabbed a book from the children's section and flipped through the first pages. "I'll get this one for my nephew."

"If that's your guilt talking, get another one for the giving tree."

"Okay, *fine*." Zoey grabbed another one. "Are you just going to ignore this latest development?"

"I've actually reformed my vision around that. All positivity. There's probably no one better to take over Nacho

Boat if Mr. Curry is set on retiring. Noah will be super safety conscious and I've seen the way Tee pushes limits. That won't happen anymore. Not under Noah." She drew an imaginary line in the air. "Poof! Another teen safe from his own stupidity."

"What? He bought Nacho Boat?" Zoey gaped.

"I'm surprised the news isn't everywhere by now."

"He just got back, didn't he?"

"Apparently he's been planning and talking to Mr. Curry about this for a while."

"Well, then that's probably the real reason those two broke up. Long distance wouldn't work."

"If you weren't talking about Nacho Boat, what development *were* you talking about?"

"Duh. Noah is single again, and so are you."

"Well, maybe not for long."

"You're not kidding. Sabrina is already moving in. She said she's all about second chances. You've got to work fast. Check me out with Drew. You have no idea how many women were swooning for him. I locked that down the first day." Zoey held up her fist in triumph.

"I meant *me*. I might not be single for long."

Zoey blinked. "Who is he? Why don't I know about this?"

"Because *Noah* is going to fix me up."

"Um what? With who? When? How? Why?"

"With Finn." Twyla smiled with satisfaction. "He's single, too."

Zoey clutched her chest. "Finn? Finn *Sheridan*?"

"The one and only."

"I've had a crush on him for ages." She fanned herself. "But Noah. He's even better than Finn. What about *Noah*?"

"Noah is unavailable—" When Zoey made an exasperated "I give up on you" face and threw her hands up, Twyla went on, "To me."

"Bull hockey! Why don't you just grab the bull by the horns and *tell him* already?"

"What is it with you and bulls?" Twyla shook her head.

She did not understand Zoey's obsession with getting her and Noah together. Twyla loved him, sure, but it was a different kind of love. A deep friendship. She just didn't feel that way about Noah.

"I'm serious now. All you have to do is stare at his lips and wait to see what happens."

"He'll just ask me if he's got something on his mouth."

"You're hopeless. Stare at his mouth while you lick your lips. Like this." Zoey did just that and looked ridiculous, quite frankly.

Twyla gaped. "And men go for this?"

"Yes! You can't just wait for the man you want to show his interest. Sometimes they're waiting for you. I'm telling you. Noah has the hots for you."

"No, he *doesn't.*"

"You're just scared to realize it, which is totally normal."

"You don't understand. We're close in a way no one else seems to understand." Only someone who had been through the grief she and Noah both shared would know. "We have a friendship that means everything to me."

So many things in life changed and evolved, and for someone that loved quiet, solitude and the comfort of routines, she loved what she had with Noah. After the accident, he'd been a shell of her friend. Recovering from the accident that had nearly killed both of them.

Dealing with his grief over losing Will, over feeling responsible because he'd been driving the boat when it hit a sandbar and threw both of them out. She'd simply been there for him, as his best friend and someone who also loved and missed Will. She'd sit and read to him, eventually finding *A Dragon's Heart*, which she read for the first time when he was in the hospital. He'd loved that book.

After leaving the hospital, Noah had gone out of town for some extensive rehab on the leg he'd injured in the accident. When he'd returned weeks later, they went back to their easy friendship. They moved on without changing a thing. And now that she'd seen Noah through so many girlfriends, she'd grown accustomed to feeling nothing but friendship.

"I mean, how can he even know you're interested? You just asked him to fix you up with Finn!"

"You don't get it. That's just the thing. I'm not interested in Noah."

Zoey snorted. "Please, girl."

"Look, I can see why you and everyone else mix up our friendship with something else. But it is possible to simply be friends, and that's all we are. It's all we'll ever be. Now, if only *you* would understand this."

Twyla went to the register and rang Zoey up, then placed the two books in individual Once Upon a Book gift bags. It had always been their special touch.

"See you tonight?" Zoey handed over her plastic.

"Sure. What kind of cupcakes would you like?"

"No cupcakes. Come with me to the Salty Dog. Please."

"Oh, Zoey. I don't know. There will be people there."

"Exactly. And how are you supposed to get a date for New Year's Eve if you don't ever leave the house?"

"I leave the house all the time!" She made a sweeping motion around her shop.

"You know what I mean," Zoey said, hand on hip.

"Fine! But just one drink and then I'm going home."

Because Zoey did have a point. She wouldn't meet anyone unless she put herself out there.

FOR THE NEXT few days, Noah skillfully avoided everyone. He even managed to hold Twyla off, telling her he was "working" on Finn, that they were busy with inventory and a dozen other things, and he'd let her know when he had a free moment.

Right now, he had surrounded himself with seaworthy tasks and was settling into his new reality. If now and then he had flashbacks to the day of the accident, he was dealing with them.

He and Will had been on a motorboat when the accident happened. It had been such a bright, clear summer day and Noah had begged his older brother for a ride. Will, having just received his license, drove them at high speeds. They'd had an argument over, of all things, Twyla. Will had broken up with her and Noah pointed out he was an idiot.

You have a thing for my girlfriend, don't you? Will had winked.

No, of course not.

He'd never admitted that he pined away for Twyla. She was his brother's girlfriend and that was the end of it.

Now, Noah pulled his attentions back to the matter at hand. He'd been to the store to buy more lights for the parade tonight. He had Finn's help, which made this all go much faster. Finn, who was an expert diver, and one of his best friends. Finn, who Noah was supposed to fix up with Twyla.

He didn't want to, so he kept stalling.

Noah threw a strand of lights toward Finn, who stood at the stern. Tonight was the Snowflake Float Boat Parade, an annual Charming event.

"I still think this is a ridiculous custom." Finn grumbled as he picked up the lights and began to wrap them around the hull.

"Bah humbug. What's your beef? Electricity and water? C'mon, live a little." Noah chuckled.

They worked together in silence for several more minutes. This would be the perfect time to suggest he ask Twyla out. But then, Diana came out with a light-up wreath, green garland and fake tree. She handed them over to Noah and indicated their placement. She tried directing them for a bit, coming out of her shell more than he'd seen so far. But then she had to head back inside when the phone rang.

Noah felt his heart race. This was so ridiculous. They weren't in eighth grade, were they? He should be able to fix Twyla up with a date. Even if he never had before, there was a first time for everything. If she didn't share the feelings Noah had for her, and she clearly did not, he'd rather see her with someone he approved of. Like Finn.

"So, I guess I should fix you up with a woman," Noah grumbled.

Finn snorted. "No, you *shouldn't*."

Yeah, he wasn't any good at this. "No, really. You'll like her and you already know her. She's super sweet with a good personality."

"Oh, Jesus." Finn groaned.

"Okay, never mind, that came out all wrong. It's *Twyla*, okay? Tell me now how you feel."

Finn blinked and dropped the strand of lights. Yeah, of course. Because this was Twyla. Gorgeous, smart, kind and, for reasons he'd never understand, still somehow available. It was the eternal mystery of the cosmos. Where do we go after we die, and why is Twyla still single?

"You know what? I *should*, just to shake you up." Finn crossed his arms and scowled.

"She asked me about you, okay? So that's why I'm going through with the insanity. Believe me, I know you can get your own dates without any help from me." Viciously, he wound the lights around the tree and strapped it tight to the mast.

"I'm never stepping into that mess of a triangle so forget it. Just go for it. Tell her how you feel and be done with it. You know you want to."

"I can't. It's complicated for us. She had a thing for my brother, or did you forget?"

"How could I forget? It's all anyone around here talks about. You're going to hate yourself when she winds up with some other guy who doesn't like you as much as I do. Who won't care what you think. Then, it's going to be too late."

"It's already too late."

Noah had fallen second best with his own mother, so to say he never wanted to be in that position again was an understatement. From the beginning, in their family the alliances had been Will and their parents. Noah the second child, feeling at times like an afterthought. He'd rather not wind up second best with Twyla, too. But it went far beyond pride.

After everything they'd been through and had invested in each other, he wouldn't cross the line. No matter how much he wanted her, no matter how deeply he needed her, he had to be smart about this. There was too much to lose.

"It isn't too *late* until one of you is married. Don't wait until she's finally happy with someone else to tell her how you feel. Don't be an idiot. I hate idiots."

And as if he wanted to confirm the state of his idiocy, Noah leaned over to tie a light on the bow and promptly fell overboard.

Even from under the water, Noah heard the deep sound

of Finn's laughter when he leaned over and offered a hand. It
was like the universe giving Noah a hard slap. A heavy jolt.
He was once again reminded that when it came to Twyla,
he was indeed a one hundred percent, certified dummy.

CHAPTER SIX

TWYLA STOOD NEAR the seawall where she could get the best view of the Snowflake Float Boat Parade. The evening was cold and brisk for Charming, the skies a bit cloudy, but she loved this time of the year. Though she'd never move anywhere where the weather suited her clothes, it had occasionally been a passing thought. In New York City, for instance, she could wear boots in autumn and all through spring. Oh, she understood she tended to romanticize New York. But after a steady diet of Nora Ephron books and movies, it was only natural to dream.

As usual, families had come out early and already staked the best places to view, setting folding chairs out hours in advance. Twyla didn't plan on staying too long, but because Ganny loved this kind of thing, she'd driven her out and scouted an available seat with a good view. Only one, but that was okay. Twyla would stand for the thirty or so minutes it would take for all the boats to glide by.

"I'll get you some hot chocolate," Twyla said to her grandmother. "Sit tight."

"Don't be gone too long, dear, or you might miss Noah."

On her way to the Salty Dog, supplying hot chocolate just outside their doors, she ran into at least a dozen people she knew. Ava and Max cuddling, Adam and Stacy walking with their little toddler, Valerie and Cole with their baby. And there was Zoey, too, cozy under a Dallas Cowboys blanket with Drew. Couples everywhere cozying up to each other on a brisk night. Sigh.

Zoey was right. She hadn't met anyone in her rental or at the bookstore. Two places, unless you wanted to count the grocery store, so the odds were low.

Two days ago, Twyla watched Finn walk by with barely a nod in her direction. So, it looked like yet another Christmas of being single. That was fine. She had so much to do when it came to work, and romance would only take her attention away from her real problems. Which was, of course, exactly what she'd wanted. An escape of sorts. A moment to know everything would be all right whether the bookstore survived or not.

She didn't want to be the Thompson forced to hang up a sign that said that after forty years, they would have to close their doors. Flashback to Meg Ryan, sadly closing the doors to her family bookstore in *You've Got Mail*. It didn't help that Twyla had remodeled the shop to resemble the one in the movie.

When Twyla got back with two hot chocolates, some members of the Almost Dead Poets Society were hovering over her grandmother. Every year at this time, they tried to talk Ganny into joining their poetry club.

"We can't lose our bookstore!" Patsy Villanueva fretted, obviously on another subject now.

"We won't," Mr. Finch assured her.

"Of course not! My granddaughter is on it," Ganny said. "She has so many wonderful ideas."

"The literary costume event!" Patsy clapped her hands. "I can't wait."

"How will you be dressing?" Susannah asked.

"Scarlett O'Hara, of course!" Patsy fanned herself and pretended to spin a parasol and hold it over her head.

The others were planning to be Jo March and Hester Prynne, "Lest anyone forget!"

"The poetry books y'all ordered arrived," Twyla interrupted. "I've got them behind the counter for you."

"I'll be in tomorrow for mine," Ella Mae said.

"Would you pick mine up, too?" Patsy asked. "I'll vemma you the money."

"What's a vemma?" Ella Mae wrinkled her nose.

"I don't know, but Valerie will do it for me." Patsy waved a hand dismissively. "She does this all the time and people never complain."

"Oh, thank the good Lord, here come the boats and not a moment too soon," Lois said. "I'm shivering."

"Why in the world didn't you say something, darlin'?" Mr. Finch removed his suit jacket and placed it over Lois's shoulders.

The night was cold by Gulf Coast standards and Twyla snuggled into her sweater. The boats sailed by, all decorated with colorful bright lights, which lit up the dark sky. First came the Santa boat hosted by the Salty Dog Bar & Grill this year, with a chubby Santa dressed in full regalia, waving to the crowds. There were blinking patterns of fairy lights, boats filled with flashing stars, wrapped presents, a tiny sleigh, plastic reindeer and trees. Another was filled with characters from *The Nightmare Before Christmas*. A Texas-themed boat sailed by, complete with an inflatable horse and a large lone star blinking brightly enough to be seen from outer space.

And bringing up the rear came Noah's boat, decorated with wreaths, trees and plenty of twinkling multicolored lights. Nacho Boat Adventures, his sign read. He received the biggest cheers of the evening as Noah and Finn waved to the crowds.

"Yay, Noah!"

"Way to go, son!"

"We're here for you!"

On the way back to the car, Twyla did a double take. A woman looking very much like Michelle was strolling toward the Salty Dog Bar & Grill. But that couldn't be because she was in Austin, probably fuming over Noah's imagined interest in someone else. There were plenty of tall willowy women with long blond hair in Charming and this didn't have to be Michelle.

"Isn't that Michelle?" Ganny asked, still as sharp as ever.

Well, it looked like a distinct possibility now.

"No, maybe just someone who looks like her?"

"You're probably right." Ganny buckled into her seat belt. "What would she be doing here anyway?"

"Trying to get Noah back?" It was an obvious answer to Twyla.

Some days, she didn't honestly believe they were done. Michelle was a practicing attorney and a smart woman. If she threw her support behind Noah and his new business, he might actually consider taking her back. After all, he never said he'd stopped *loving* her. He'd been, in fact, very vague about the whole breakup and she hadn't pressed for details. She attributed this to the fact that they didn't normally share all the gritty details of relationships and she'd like to keep it that way.

She'd never told Noah that her most recent ex-boyfriend of two months, Alex, had broken up with her because he was tired of coming in second to Noah. His timing couldn't have been worse. Shortly afterward, Noah had moved to Austin, and it became a nonissue. Still, she was so tired of needy and insecure men. If Alex had been worried about Noah, he could have upped the stakes and thought to also bring her chicken noodle soup when she was sick the way

Noah always did. But no, all he wanted was for Twyla to be at *his* beck and call.

Twyla had pulled into the circular driveway leading to her grandmother's front door when her phone buzzed. An incoming text from Noah.

Movie night tomorrow? I'll bring the popcorn. We're watching Die Hard.

A smile came quickly to her lips because some things never changed. She and Noah would have the annual argument over whether *Die Hard* could be called a Christmas movie. He'd say he was bringing the popcorn but then forget. She'd make it and he'd complain the kernels were too brown, the way *she* liked them. Then, he'd *really* piss her off and proceed to hog the remote control. But in between all that there would be a lot of laughs. There would be touching because when wrapped up in a movie, that tended to happen. They'd sit on the floor, and she'd lean against him to get comfortable. They forgot themselves, too involved with the movie. She called it snuggle time and it had never been anything more than that.

She might not have a Hallmark movie romance, but she had Noah.

And sometimes he was all she really needed.

AFTER THE PARADE, Noah texted Twyla. Then he and Finn docked the boats and unstrung the lights. They headed out for a cold beer at the Salty Dog to celebrate the end of this particular holiday event. The way Noah looked at it, he only had obligations for one more. The literary costume event at Twyla's bookstore. Then maybe he could focus on the plans he had for the business and plan their grand opening after the first of the year.

He swung the door open to the sounds of cheers and waves from some of the locals. Obviously, many had made their way inside after the parade. In the year since Noah had been gone, the bar had undergone some changes. Mostly the staff. Bartenders and a few waitresses he didn't automatically recognize on sight. The former navy SEAL owners were hit and miss these days. Noah wanted to connect with Cole at some point and ask his advice on surfboards since the dude was an expert. He'd simply have to give him a call or drop by the renovated lighthouse where the lucky man lived.

"Noah," came a soft voice from behind.

Every muscle in him tensed. *No, no, no.* Not this again.

He whipped around to confirm his suspicions. Michelle stood behind his stool, wearing her barracuda "I'm going to win this argument if it kills me" smile. And to think he'd once found the smile wicked in a *good* way.

Noah exchanged a look with Finn. He shook his head and downed the rest of his beer.

"What are you doing here?"

She placed her hand on her hip. "Making sure you don't make the biggest mistake of your life."

"And on that note…" Finn stood and clapped Noah's back.

Michelle gave Finn a grateful, non-barracuda-like smile and took his place on the stool next to Noah's.

"You're wasting your time." Noah gripped the neck of his beer bottle.

"It's never a waste to try to salvage something real."

Something real. If that were true, he'd have never left Austin—even if a roof nearly fell on his head. Something real was worth fighting for. With something real, he'd have never walked away.

"It's time to face the truth. We can work this out, but

you need to explain to Twyla that she should give up on you. Then we can try to put the pieces back together."

Noah nearly choked on his beer and swallowed, then thumped his chest. "Um, what?"

"Twyla has a thing for you and please don't be a stupid guy about this. I'm going to assume she was behind your decision to come home. I know you feel responsible for her because of Will, and it makes sense. She's safe. Familiar. Twyla won't ask anything more of you. She won't demand that you stretch and grow to become the best man you can be."

Noah groaned. "We've already talked about this, and I won't do it again for the hundredth time. That's a common misconception about me and Twyla. But she does *not* have a thing for me. You're one hundred percent wrong."

"I'm not, Noah. You're the one who refuses to see it."

It wasn't the first time one of his girlfriends had mentioned Twyla's obvious "crush" on him. At one time, it had reached such a fevered point that he'd been within two seconds of asking Twyla if any of that was true. He remembered the day and time because she'd told him about Alex, a guy she'd met at a book convention and was so happy to be dating.

No, Twyla had plenty of opportunities to tell him how she felt and never had.

"You have misled poor Twyla at every turn so of course she pines away for you. Every time she called, you would leave the room to talk to her. You've encouraged her. It's like you two have something going on that you won't let the rest of the world in on. When you had an issue at work, you confided in her. Not *me*."

"She's been my best friend for more than half of my life."

"And she would like to be so much more than that."

"You're wrong. She just asked me to fix her up with *Finn*."

Michelle blinked. "That's surprising."

"You don't know her. Stop trying to make excuses for what happened between us. It didn't work, even though we tried."

"Noah, what did happen?" Her hand rested on his forearm. "I thought we were doing okay."

"I'm sorry," he said, shaking his head. "I care about you, and I realize that I wasn't being fair."

He'd wanted to love her, desperately, but couldn't give her the words she wanted to hear. It was his deepest regret because he'd never intended to hurt her, and now he had.

"If you cared about me once, you can't turn it off that quickly. I'll be patient."

"No, I can't ask you to do that. It wouldn't be fair. Your life is in Austin."

"My life can be anywhere I want it to be. Law firms are everywhere. Even here in Charming."

The words shocked him, and he wouldn't be lying to admit she'd flattered him. He'd never expected this development. No one had ever given anything up for him. No one had ever rearranged their life for him. Michelle was an attorney at a prestigious law firm in Austin and now she was willing to forgive him for being an idiot. Willing to move here so they could work it out.

In the meantime, Twyla had asked him to fix her up with Finn. It was time for Noah to stop dreaming.

One woman wanted to fight for him. The other had loved his brother, and Noah could hardly compete with that.

"Okay. Good to know."

Michelle smiled and Noah's phone buzzed in his back pocket. "Excuse me. This could be important."

He was hoping for Twyla, but no. His mother's voice

greeted him and the moment she spoke, Noah knew it wouldn't be an easy conversation.

"Noah Michael Cahill! You bought Nacho Boat? Are you *trying* to kill me?" his mother said.

He held up a finger to Michelle and walked outside for some privacy with his mother. "Who told you? I want names."

"Never mind who told me. Why didn't *you* tell me?"

Noah rubbed the spot between his eyes, feeling a headache coming on. "Listen, I planned on telling you everything when I came over for dinner."

"Well, in the future, if you could tell your own mother before everyone in town knows, I'd appreciate it!"

If he thought he'd catch his mother at the Snowflake Float Boat Parade, he would have told her by now, but she hadn't attended for years. Hadn't even stepped foot near the docks since the accident.

"Sure. Yeah, and I'm sorry."

"Fine, I'll see you at dinner and don't be late this time."

"I was late once—"

But he didn't get to finish that sentence as his mother insisted on the last word.

Noah went back inside to see that Michelle was already being hit on by one of the men at the bar. A beautiful blonde, she never failed to get attention from the opposite sex. Noah didn't know if he should feel jealous or relieved. At the moment, he was a mix of the two.

Unfortunately, he fell far more on the side of relieved that he should.

CHAPTER SEVEN

WHEN NOAH CAME to movie night this time, he actually brought the popcorn.

Twyla clapped her hands. "Oh, my God, you remembered!"

"What do you mean?" He shrugged off his windbreaker after he handed her the bag of kettle corn. "I said I would bring it."

"But you always forget." When he gave her a blank stare, she waved her hand in the air to jog his memory. "And then I make some in the microwave and burn it a little?"

"Glad we're avoiding that." He scowled.

He seemed to be in a mood, but Twyla's spirits were buoyed the moment she'd spied the big bag of salted caramel kettle corn from the boardwalk. In the kitchen, she grabbed a big bowl and poured some from the two-foot-long bag. He'd brought her the extra large one. This could last all week if she rationed, but she'd bring in some for Mr. Finch tomorrow. It was good to feel almost as if she had a real coworker. It brought back the times both she, her mother and Ganny ran the bookstore together.

Bonkers slunk out of the bedroom and gave Twyla his usual disgusted look.

"Hang on, I have to feed Bonkers."

"You still have that cat?"

"I sure do, and you know what? I think he's really starting to like me."

Noah groaned. "You're way too good to him."

But Noah was a dog person so what could she expect? She had originally adopted Bonkers in hopes he'd also make a good bookstore cat. Customers could pet him as he sat calmly in his box near the register. Sadly, on the first day she'd taken Bonkers to work, he'd hissed at a child who'd made the unfortunate mistake of petting him.

And that was the end of Take Your Cat To Work Day.

Bonkers tended to look at her as if she was a five-foot can opener, but hey, things were getting better. He'd even let her pet him without hissing.

"There you go."

Twyla set his bowl down and backed away because Bonkers didn't like to be watched while eating. It was one of his many quirks.

On the couch, Noah had already spread out his long legs and taken control of the remote. Little cat, big cat.

She sighed. "It's on the DVR. I recorded it."

Twyla placed the bowl between them. Noah worked the remote, all the while grinding his jaw like something, or someone, had royally pissed him off.

"Okay, tell me what's wrong."

"What makes you think something's wrong?"

"Um, the clenched jaw?"

"Someone told my mother about Nacho Boat before I could."

"It wasn't me!" She brought her hand to her chest.

"I know." He slowly shook his head. "Anyway, I got read the riot act. She's not happy, but what else is new? I never fail to disappoint her."

Twyla tried to put herself in Katherine's position. Were Twyla a mother who'd already lost one son, she'd feel the same kind of fierce protectiveness over her only remaining child. She'd worry every day that something would go wrong somehow. Just as it had for Will. How could Katherine simply trust that the universe would allow her to keep Noah? Twyla thought for many years that Katherine needed the type of grief counseling they'd given all students after the accident.

"It must have been a tough conversation."

"Yeah." Noah ran a hand over his jaw. "Not much of a conversation, though. Pretty one-sided."

While Noah always wore a well-trimmed beard, tonight he looked almost…unkempt. The guilt had to weigh on him because he'd always felt as though he owed his mother something. He claimed he'd never been her favorite but was the only son she had left. Twyla didn't disagree that in those early years, Will had clearly been Katherine's favorite. He had been the people pleaser, the one who toed the line with her authority. Noah never had.

Too many times, Twyla had wanted to step in and say what everyone else was thinking out loud: *Noah lost a brother, too. He could use your attention as the only son you have left. He might not be a straight-A student headed for medical school, but he deserves your love.* Still, over the years, no one had the guts to tell Katherine that she had to be strong for Noah and not the other way around.

She took the opportunity to grab the remote. "Well, let's fast forward and watch evil Hans fall off the Nakatomi building. That's your favorite part."

"*Great* special effects. He actually looks like he's falling."

"I know. He was such a great actor."

"But we're starting from the beginning." Noah reached for the remote and lowered himself to the floor with his back leaning against the couch, then pressed play. "Hey, do I...um..."

There was a pause. Too long of a pause. "Do you what?"

"Confide in you too much?"

"What's too much? We're best friends. I've known you for over half my life."

"Okay. So, it doesn't bother you?"

"Why would it *bother* me?"

There were already lines they wouldn't cross. She and Noah were both private about stuff you wouldn't necessarily share. They had achieved, in her opinion, the perfect balance. Were there times when she shared more with him than a partner? Sure, yes, but that was only reasonable given their closeness.

"I had a feeling I was wrong about this."

But rather than seem happy, he looked disappointed.

"Wrong?"

Twyla felt a pinch of dread squeeze between her ribs. Since the moment he'd returned, she understood on a bone-deep level that he wasn't telling her something. This thing, whatever it was, was bigger than his breakup. Bigger than a decision to go after his dream.

And every time she saw him it felt like that tiny thing had grown larger between them.

"Don't worry." Noah patted the empty space next to him. "Some people are trying to mess with me."

The movie had started, and Bruce Willis now carried an enormous teddy bear off the plane and met his driver. It was difficult for Twyla to focus.

Something had rattled Noah.

She plopped down and grabbed a handful of popcorn. "Who's messing with you? Finn?"

"No." Noah scowled. "Why are we talking about him?"

"Did he say you and I are too close? I shouldn't have asked you to fix me up with Finn. That was stupid."

"You're right. That *was* stupid."

"Why was it *stupid*?"

He cocked his head, observing her as if studying a strange phenomenon. "You just said so."

"Well, I can say that. But why would *you* say it?"

He closed his eyes and rubbed the middle of his forehead. "God, help me."

"Honestly, is there something fundamentally wrong with me? Why is it so stupid that me and Finn could be a thing? He's single. I'm also single."

"It's because…" Noah's eyes were strangely focused on her now, as if there was nothing else in the room. No TV on in the background with Bruce Willis making his way into his screen wife's boisterous office Christmas party. "Well, Finn…is… He's still hung up on someone."

"Oh."

"Yeah, so it wouldn't work because he can't stop thinking about this other woman."

"Well, that's a good reason."

"He thinks about her all the time. Day and night. It's… ridiculous." Noah rubbed between his eyebrows and looked genuinely worried for Finn.

"Gosh, don't be so hard on him," Twyla whispered. "It happens."

"Yeah. Okay. I won't be." Noah squeezed her hand, like he always did. A little pat of reassurance.

But this time, his hand lingered on hers even as he put his attention toward watching the movie.

Twyla lost what little focus she had, though she tried to follow along. Easy to do since they'd watched this movie dozens of times.

She was afraid to speak or even breathe.

Noah practically recited certain lines verbatim. Twyla winced when the elevator doors opened, and a dead man appeared wrapped in lights and wearing a Santa hat.

"This is not a Christmas movie," she said, shaking her head.

Noah smiled, but even after she spoke, he didn't seem to notice they were basically still holding hands. The popcorn bowl sat between them, and she took handfuls with her left hand though she was right-handed. Letting go of his hand to take some might be easier, but if she let go there were no guarantees they'd get back to this moment.

Which was…nice. This didn't mean anything. It didn't have to. She was with her best friend, and he needed extra comfort tonight. But she could almost see Zoey's deadpan expression if Twyla told her about this.

After the movie ended, she walked him to the door and this was different, too. *Awkward* different. Instead of casually giving her a quick hug before leaving like he always did, he gave her a long look. He behaved like he'd never even *seen* her before.

Oh, hello, nice to meet you. Who are you again?

Have we met? I feel like we've met before.

Honestly, it was surreal.

She leaned on the door frame while he lingered just outside, checking his pockets, finding his phone, then pulling out his keys. He seemed so…out of sorts.

"Well…call me tomorrow?"

"Yeah. Okay, good night."

Then he was gone, concluding their strangest movie night in history.

TWYLA WAS HELPING a third grader find the perfect book just after the incident happened. Valerie had brought her class in for a field trip right before the long holiday break and she was in the middle of breaking up a disagreement between two boys.

"Apologize to Jackson," Valerie ordered.

"I'm sorry I shoved you, but you called my sister dumb. She's not *dumb*. She's smarter than you'll ever be!"

Valerie rolled her eyes and pointed to the other kid. "Jackson, apologize for calling Naomi dumb."

"I loved this one when I was a girl," Twyla said louder, to distract the girl the boys were fighting about. She handed her *A Wrinkle in Time*. "My mother used to read it to me every night before bed."

Naomi sweetly cradled the book to her chest. "Reading is my favorite thing in the world."

"Me, too."

She was so cute, dressed in the school's uniform—a blue skirt and tan top with matching windbreaker. Her dark hair was coiffed into two perfect braids, and she wore wire-rimmed glasses. It was like Twyla going back in time and helping little Twyla. She'd been the bookworm that had never been cool. Later, both Will and Noah became her pseudobrothers, ready to punch anyone out that called her an ugly name.

"I bet you fall asleep reading, too."

She pushed her glasses up her nose the same way Twyla did at least once a day. "My mom won't let me. It gets past my bedtime, and she says, 'Lights out.'"

"I bet you would if you could."

She nodded. "Yeah."

Twyla bent low and met her eyes with a conspiratorial smile. "When you're a grown-up, no one can stop you. I do it all the time."

Of course, that often meant staying up until two o'clock because the book was too good to put down. Adulting 101:

you have to pay for your mistakes by getting up and going to work anyway.

A few minutes later, Valerie was gathering the class and, with the assistance of her parent chaperones, herding the kids into the line to pay for their chosen book.

Thirty-five sales later, Twyla wished every teacher brought in the children for a field trip. As an independent bookstore, her prices were steeper than ordering online, or from a big chain store, so she appreciated every sale.

"Thanks, Valerie," Twyla called out as they were leaving.

"See you soon." Valerie waved.

And at that moment, Michelle held the door open for the class as they followed their teacher outside.

Michelle.

So, she hadn't been a mirage. She was here and Twyla had no idea why. But if she was going to accuse Noah of cheating, Twyla would set her straight. That could never happen. Noah was too loyal of a person. She'd defend him till the last breath left her body.

"Hi, Michelle."

Twyla waved from behind the counter and tried to plaster something resembling a smile on her face. Now, with the children gone, she and Michelle were alone. Completely.

"Hey there," Michelle said, sauntering up to the counter. "We need to talk."

"Well, I'm working right now. Can I help you find a book?"

Relationship Rescue?

Moving On After Heartache?

"Gosh, I wish I had the time to read *fiction*. You must have such fun. Meanwhile, I have legal briefs to read. Very boring intellectual stuff. If I had enough time, I'd give my brain a break."

"Uh-huh."

Twyla wished she had a smart-aleck reply to the obvious dumbing down of fiction books. She could explain that she both read and sold nonfiction but that wouldn't be snappy and snarky. She'd likely think of the perfect comment lying in bed tonight when it was far too late.

"Well, you've probably heard all about Noah and me by now. He tells you everything."

"Not *everything*."

"Right. Would you do me a giant favor and meet me for lunch at the Salty Dog? My treat. I have something to discuss with you."

"I brought my lunch." She fished under the counter and held up her paper sack. PB&J for the win.

"Adorable. Bring it with you if you insist."

"It will all depend on if Mr. Finch gets here before noon. Otherwise, I can't leave the store."

"Surely you can afford to close up for an *hour*."

"I really *can't*. Not at this time of the year. My busiest season."

She glanced around the empty shop. "I don't see the crowds. You'll miss one sale, if that."

"And I really can't afford to miss a single sale."

Only a moment later, with the timing of a metronome, Mr. Finch arrived. "Good morning, ladies."

"Perfect timing." Michelle greeted Mr. Finch with a smile and strolled toward the door. "See you at noon."

"You have a lunch date?" Mr. Finch came behind the counter and made himself at home.

"I suppose I do." She sighed. Then as soon as the door shut, she thought of the perfect snarky comeback to Michelle needing to give her "brain a break."

Well, it sure sounds like you could use one.

"Ha!" Twyla snort laughed. "Good one."

"You all right, dear?" Mr. Finch said.

"Yep!"

Twyla pulled out her phone and texted Noah:

Your ex is here and wants to take me to lunch.

She waited for the bubbles to appear indicating he was composing a reply. Nothing.

Hello? Noah? A little help here?

With Mr. Finch here to take care of customers, Twyla busied herself in the back, folding up cardboard boxes. Her mind drifted back to last night and all the hand holding with Noah. She hadn't actually held hands with a guy since possibly seventh grade. But there was such a sweetness to holding hands simply to keep the connection. The whole thing had also been so confusing, so unexpected. It was likely because Noah was lonely after his breakup, seeking some kind of comfort. She wouldn't make too much out of it.

Twyla glanced at her phone. Still no reply from Noah. As the hours wore on, Twyla cleaned and dusted every nook and cranny. She rearranged shelves and stocked some of the new educational toys. Finally, she could avoid it no longer.

Lunchtime.

"Don't rush," Mr. Finch said, as he read a book behind the counter. "I brought a sandwich."

"I won't be gone even thirty minutes. You and I need to go over the plans for Literary Character Day when I get back."

It helped to put her mind to something far more pleasant and with less of a root-canal-like appeal. She drove her sedan to the boardwalk and found a parking space close to the Salty Dog. Inside, she found the usual holiday frivolity and spotted Michelle almost immediately. She waved from a booth near the back. Okay, so this is how they were going to do it. Privacy, so Michelle could trash talk Noah without any judgment. Uh-uh. Not going to happen on Twyla's watch.

"Thank you for coming." Michelle set down the menu. "I've lost my appetite, but please, you go ahead and eat. I'm still treating."

"Um, I'm not hungry, either." She *was* hungry but damned if she would eat while Michelle stared at her chewing.

Debbie dropped by, and they both ordered diet sodas.

"What's going on?" Twyla made a show of glancing at the clock above the bar to send a message. "I only have thirty minutes."

"I'll get right to it. I want Noah back and I'm wondering if you can help me."

CHAPTER EIGHT

"HELP NOAH SEE that he will never have a chance with you as more than just a friend."

"Huh? What?"

"I'm sure you see that on some level he feels responsible for you because of Will. But I talked to him the other night and I know we can make things work. I'm willing to move to Charming to do it."

"You…you are?"

This shouldn't surprise Twyla. She wasn't sure how Noah was still single, frankly. Over the years, he'd had plenty of women fall for him. Hard. Many had come to cry on Twyla's shoulders afterward, in fact:

I miss him so much. You're so lucky, Twyla. He'll always be a part of your life.

And Twyla had listened, agreed and commiserated, knowing they were right. Noah would always be in her life. She couldn't imagine life without him. Eventually, his exes had moved on. But now here was Michelle, back to fight for Noah. She wanted Twyla to help. How could she say no? She would have to consider this because there had to be a way to say no without being mean.

"I'd like to help, but I don't know what I can do. We're best friends, but Noah hardly takes relationship advice from me. Not that I've ever tried giving it."

"Maybe it's a good time to start."

"I wouldn't know what to say." Twyla studied her hands. She'd never been in this position before.

"As I told him, feelings like the ones *we* had for each other aren't ones a person can just turn off like a light switch. There's still something there, a little spark, and I'm willing to work on it."

"That's...amazing. I know he must appreciate it."

Michelle smiled and Twyla noted that she really was a beautiful woman.

"Sometimes, in order to get what you want, you have to swallow your pride, take a risk and put yourself out there. That's what I'm doing. Noah means a lot to me. Listen. I apologize for hitting you with this now. Especially during the holidays with how busy you are. But Noah is quite obviously struggling after the accident, and I'm concerned he's making a mistake leaving everything he built in Austin behind."

"Wait. What *accident*?"

Twyla's hands shook. An accident he hadn't told her about. Maybe this was the thing between them.

Michelle's neck jerked. "He didn't tell you?"

"I told you that he doesn't tell me *everything*."

"Probably because of how protective he still is over you. This is exactly what I mean. He's still thinking of *your* feelings when a roof nearly collapsed on him in a fire. And that's when everything really changed. He said he needed time, but we were trying to work things out. After the accident, everything got much worse. The secret phone calls to you increased. The plans to move to Charming and buy the business formulated, and nothing I said could talk him out of it."

"I didn't know about those plans, either, until he showed up. It was a surprise to me, and I thought he was just visiting for Christmas, not that he'd moved back."

"It's a confusing time for him. Anyone who cares about Noah should be concerned. He could be making a big mistake."

But all Twyla could think about was one more accident in which Noah came close to death or injury. It had to have brought back some of those old memories and nightmares. Maybe Michelle was right and he'd had a knee-jerk reaction when he'd broken up with Michelle.

"I didn't like the idea of the charter business, but I trust Noah. He'll be safe. The dream means too much to him to treat any part of this recklessly."

"Here's what I think." Michelle folded her hands together as if preparing for closing arguments. "Noah moved back for more than one reason. You need him. After all this time, Noah feels responsible for you and *your* happiness. That's why we had zero chance of success from the start. I know you're a strong woman and don't want his pity, but until you let him go, he won't be free to have a serious relationship."

Twyla ground her teeth and fisted her hands. "I am not stopping him from having a serious relationship."

"I'm sure you're not one hundred percent aware that you are, but he and I could still have a chance at something real. Something lasting. It will be up to you to cut the unhealthy ties he still has to you. You were Will's girl, and on some level, now that he's gone, he feels responsible for you."

Unhealthy ties. Feeling responsible for Will's girl.

Noah, thinking he owed her something because of Will. All of it hit Twyla at once, making her stomach burn. She did not want to accept that Noah felt *obligated* to her. She would not accept that his relationships with other women had never worked because he was reluctantly tied to her. She got enough of the "poor, sad Twyla" comments from other people, and she expected Noah to know better.

But maybe…maybe her heart and mind had overre-acted to this suggestion because on some level, she knew it to be true.

A SALTWATER FISHING expedition had already been sched-uled with a group of folks that Noah hated to disappoint, so after he passed the USCG test, he chose not to cancel. Mr. Curry would have pitched in if he'd asked, because he and his wife were still trying to decide where in Arizona they would move. But Noah didn't want to bother him. Re-tirement should be enjoyed fully and without feeling any leftover obligations. Finn was otherwise busy at his cur-rent place of employment since Noah couldn't offer him a salary yet. Of course, he had Tee who was on a school break and looking for all the hours he could get. Today Noah's assistant wore a T-shirt that said, *In my defense, I was left unsupervised.*

Note to self: never leave Tee unsupervised.

"Hey, Noah. Should we call you Captain?"

Terry, the organizer of the group of avid fishermen and an old friend of Noah's father, climbed aboard. There were three of them on the hunt for flounder. Since fishing was good year-round in the Gulf Coast of Mexico, they were bound to catch something.

"Call me Noah, Terry. I've known you all my life."

"You got it, son. Hey, Rick? Have you met Noah Ca-hill?" Terry made the introductions.

"Are you the one on the plaque?"

Noah was bound to come across this and he was pre-pared. He simply nodded and gave a hand to the next fish-erman. This man seemed older than the others and a little wobbly on his feet. Noah would keep a close eye on him, because Terry had the whole story regarding the plaque that hung on a spot on the dock, and was retelling it now.

Noah readied the boat with Tee and half listened as Terry rehashed the story.

Boat capsized on the bay…young driver…little experience…heroic rescue…nearly drowned. Of course, the way everyone told the story, Noah had been driving the boat. That's what he'd told everyone when the coast guard rescued him after several hours of treading water. No one ever questioned the story because it made sense. Noah was the wild card. Will was the good son. He'd screwed up once. Once. And Noah would not let him be remembered as anything other than the good brother he'd been. It had been a small price to pay. The people who loved him before still loved him afterward.

If anything, they understood he'd paid the ultimate price and sympathy for him grew and never waned. He hadn't been charged since there had been no drinking. Simply a terrible unforeseen accident when they hit a sandbar at high speeds and lost control. And Noah did feel responsible because he'd been the one to beg Will to go on a ride on that late summer day.

He understood the residents of Charming wanted to remember. On some core level, they *needed* to remember. A few years ago, he'd felt differently. Now, he realized with the benefit of some maturity that their discussion of the accident was no different than the remembrance of historical events in the larger scope. They couldn't forget, lest they risk repeating.

The only thing Noah wanted to forget was the constant reminders that he hadn't saved his brother. It didn't matter that he'd tried. He'd *failed*. That was the point no one but him seemed to fixate on. Him and his mother, that is. He doubted she'd ever forget only one son had walked away from that disaster. Probably not the right one.

For a while, every news media outlet in Texas covered

the story of the two Cahill brothers. Photos of the capsized boat graced the covers of the local paper, *The Charming Times*. Pictures of Noah being airlifted to Houston for his injuries. In later weeks, a photo of him and Twyla had been on the cover. He'd been holding her tightly in his arms, his head lowered to her head.

Surviving brother and girlfriend united together in grief.

Tragic and dramatic. Will would have hated every part of the attention and coverage. Especially the tragedy of it all. He'd had an almost gallows-like sense of humor and would have hated the tragic tone.

Noah accepted the role of a cautionary tale. The part he'd chosen for himself. He'd never wanted Will's memory to be reduced down to an eighteen-year-old who'd made one stupid mistake.

Finally, they arrived at the fishing spot on the bay. Tee anchored the boat, and everyone cast their lines. He and Tee went around helping the others and Noah constantly checked their navigation and reports of any weather changes. But after a while there was nothing to do but kick back and wait. Sooner or later, someone would get a bite and Noah and Tee would render assistance if needed.

"I didn't know that was you with the rescue," Tee said, cracking open a soda.

"It was a long time ago."

"Yeah." Tee shook his head. And then, quite unexpectedly, he threw his arms around Noah in a bear hug. "My dude."

Noah shook him off, suppressing a chuckle. "I'm your *Captain.*"

"Oh, Captain, my Captain." Tee saluted.

"Got a live one!" Terry called out and Noah and Tee went to offer encouragement and stand by for help if needed.

By the time they headed back, after all fishermen had a catch, the sky had turned a striking yellow with hints of blue and deep purple. The figure of a woman stood at the pier and as they drew closer Noah saw Twyla. Dressed in her usual skirt with thick stockings, boots and a sweater, she had a hand cupped to her forehead. For a moment, she looked like a figure from the past, watching and waiting for her sailor to return.

A lump formed in his throat at even the thought that he could be the one she waited for.

He waved to her as they drew closer to the boat slip.

Noah docked the boat. Tee hopped out to tie the ropes. After a fishing expedition, there was much to do, and Noah first busied himself helping the men with their catch.

"I'll be a minute," Noah called out to Twyla. "Anything wrong?"

"Nothing," she said in a tone that meant, *everything*.

Fantastic. Maybe Mom had put a bug in Twyla's ear to get him to stop this nonsense. They were still close, and Twyla dropped by from time to time.

He took his time unloading the boat, not wanting to face another argument, but it all went a lot faster with Tee there to help.

Finally, Tee took off. "See ya tomorrow, Captain!"

Noah hopped off and briefly balanced between the stem of the boat and the dock, and Twyla slid him a look he couldn't quite decipher. A moment later, he read it clearly enough. He almost heard her thoughts, the way he did when she couldn't hide them. She was…hurt. Had Finn said something to her? Turned her down? Embarrassed her in some way? That didn't sound like Finn. He'd let her down easy and he had enough experience turning down eager women.

He walked to meet her at the edge. "Got your text but couldn't reply. We were on the boat all day."

"I couldn't get out of it, so I went to lunch with Michelle."

"She shouldn't involve you in what's going on with us. Yeah, she wants to get back together. I have to admit, I'm surprised she would move here. She'll have to find another job if she leaves her law firm."

"I think you really hurt her when you left."

"I never meant to."

"No, you never mean to hurt any of them, but you just do."

The words were quiet, but they hit him like little bombs.

Guilt spiked through him, because he thought he might know exactly why he'd hurt so many people, thanks in large part to Michelle's words. She was right that he felt responsible for Twyla, but not entirely because of Will. He'd taken this on himself, wanting to keep her close even if she'd never return his deeper feelings, and keeping her safe the way he hadn't managed with Will.

It didn't matter. She would never love him like she'd loved Will and he wasn't about to compete with the ghost of a first love. Either way, Noah had been careless and he'd hurt enough people for a lifetime. From now on, he would be the perfect angel. He'd stay single and work on the business until he made it the successful venture he envisioned. That would require all his focus and energy. After all that was in place for his future, if there was time for romance, well, he'd *think* about it. For now, he felt done with women and all the expectations. He would answer only to himself.

Michelle would either have to wait for him, or just give up.

"Did you have an accident at work?"

He shut his eyes, anger piercing him. "She had no business telling you any of that."

"You're right because *you* should have been the one to tell me."

"I didn't want to worry you. Since I was okay anyway, it was a nonissue."

"That's not a nonissue. It must have been terrifying for you."

How could he explain? No one but the people who were in that fire with him would understand. The hard crackling sounds consuming everything in its way, the darkness of the moment filled with smoke, the sounds of the building falling all around them. The sense that something or someone had shoved him out of the way.

"It *was* terrifying. Want to know the scariest thing about that roof nearly falling on me? The fact that I might have lived the rest of my life worrying what other people thought of me. Yeah, the fire changed me. I realized that I don't care anymore whether people blame me for the boating accident."

Her eyes were wide like she'd never considered this.

"Noah! No one blames you."

"Well, maybe you don't. The residents see me as the hero of this story which is dead wrong. You don't know how many times I've wanted to pull that plaque off the wall and throw it in the ocean. And my mother? That's a different story. My father left us because he couldn't stand looking at me anymore."

This was the truth and something he hadn't even spoken out loud until this moment. It was as if he thought if he didn't say it, maybe it wasn't true. But it was. He'd heard his parents arguing late at night after the accident, their despair mixed with anger. They'd blamed Noah and how couldn't they? He blamed himself.

"That's not true."

He hated the sorrowful and pitying look in her eyes. She'd been the one person who also loved Will but didn't blame Noah. And this was even though she still believed he'd been driving the boat.

"Yeah, don't feel sorry for me, Peaches. I don't deserve that or want it."

"Do you feel sorry for *me*?" she interrupted him, her voice nearly a whisper under the sound of the waves.

"What? No, I don't. What's this about?"

The sun set over the horizon and seemed to frame Twyla's form. "I thought we were friends because we love each other but I never thought it's because you feel *sorry* for me."

"Why would I feel sorry for you?"

"The same reason everyone else does." Her lower lip quivered, and she didn't have to say more. "Like I had my chance and now I'm going to wind up like old Mrs. Havisham living in her wedding dress."

He quirked a brow. "No, I do *not* feel sorry for you."

Instead, he fought the overwhelming urge to take her in his arms, pull her against him and take all the hurt away. But especially now, he couldn't afford any more risks. He'd already lost a brother, and somehow come back from that.

He'd never survive losing Twyla.

"Michelle thinks you feel obligated to take care of me, to watch over me because of Will, and that's why none of your relationships have ever worked."

"Victim blaming?" He snorted. "That's all on me and not on anyone I've ever dated. She's looking to blame someone else because she can't accept my decision."

"She must really love you." Twyla twisted her hands together.

He shook his head because he no longer believed this to be true.

"No, she doesn't. She just can't stand losing."

"You tend to underestimate the way people feel about you. Nobody likes the idea of losing you."

He tapped her nose. "You're not going to lose me."

"Is this…is this why you were being weird on movie night?"

He hesitated a beat. The oddity of movie night had been Noah forgetting himself. He'd allowed that door between them to open a small crack, because of the shock when he realized Twyla wasn't going to shake off his hand and tease him about it. Honestly, he hadn't watched much of the damn movie and simply stared at the screen, wondering when she would finally notice he wasn't letting go.

He hadn't replied and Twyla wanted an answer.

"I can stand a lot of things, but I can't stand your pity."

"You don't have it," he said slowly.

"Good. Please be honest with me. Because… I don't want to hold you back from being happy. Whatever it takes. I'll help Michelle understand, maybe give you some more time and space so you can eventually… I don't know. Get back together with her if that's what you want. You know I'd do anything for you."

She met his eyes and gave him her sweet, heart-stopping smile. Something inside him cracked open and slid into place like a key.

But then, she took a step closer, running her hand down his arm. "Okay?"

He swallowed and only his willpower kept him from crushing her in his arms and kissing her fiercely.

"Peaches, you and I are *always* okay."

CHAPTER NINE

BOTH TWYLA AND Ava had determined the rules of the literary character costume contest months ago. The costume itself would be each person's entry. The giveaway, for one lucky person, was five hundred dollars in gift cards donated by local vendors. The entire point of the contest was a fun way to get more customers inside her brick-and-mortar store. People were far more likely to buy a book when they actually stepped inside.

Twyla's grandmother, dressed as Jessica Fletcher from the mystery series, brought her famous peppermint squares. Others had contributed candy canes, hot chocolate and cookies in the shapes of stars, trees and reindeers. "All I Want for Christmas" by Mariah Carey piped through the speakers, and the room was filled with the spirit of the holidays.

In the end, Twyla went with the classic Elizabeth Bennet costume. Wearing a long brown dress with pockets, she'd drawn her hair up into a historically appropriate bun. The dress was a little long for her frame and she hadn't taken the time to hem it. She should have worn heels but considering she expected to be on her feet for hours, that hadn't made sense. All night long she'd had to raise her hem slightly in order not to step on her own dress. In addition, in order to remain a purist to the character, she'd set her glasses behind the register. This made her squint a lot, but she'd put them back on when she had to drive home.

"Good evening, Sherlock." Twyla greeted Mr. Finch, wearing a tweed trench coat and carrying a large magnifying glass.

Next to him, Lois had dressed as Mrs. Marple from the Agatha Christie mysteries, complete with a gray blazer and hat.

"You two are adorable." She pointed to the table with the clipboard. "Make sure you enter your names into the giveaway."

She could always count on her senior citizens. Patsy dressed as Scarlett O'Hara as promised, Susannah as Daisy Buchanan and Ella Mae as the accused Hester Prynne, with a huge scarlet *A* stitched over her modest period dress. Books had come alive tonight with people dressed as everyone from the Cat in the Hat to Harry Potter. Max and Ava had coordinated their costumes to be Peeta and Katniss and looked intriguingly dangerous. Valerie was another Elizabeth Bennet, this one with her own Mr. Darcy. Stacy had on an obscure costume no one recognized, and she promised to give the first person who guessed a second entry. Adam, dressed like Eeyore, carried his daughter on his shoulders, dressed as Winnie the Pooh.

And a few minutes later, Zoey and Drew walked in as Bonnie and Clyde.

"Give me all your money and nobody gets hurt," Zoey said.

Twyla put her hands up. "You look great, but that wasn't a *book*. So, it can't be a *literary* character."

"They made a movie from the book," Drew said.

"They were real-life people." Twyla studied the ceiling to locate her misplaced patience. "Nonfiction."

"Such a stickler for detail! Did someone write a book *about* them?" Zoey placed a hand on the hip of her flapper-style dress.

She wasn't fooling anyone. Zoey wanted to look dangerous and sexy for Drew. She very much doubted this was her favorite literary character from a book she'd actually *read*.

"Um…well…"

"I rest my case."

Zoey had her. She'd found a loophole. Quite a stretch. Nonfiction, yes, but Twyla would allow it.

"Fine. Go ahead and enter your names for the giveaway."

All night, she searched for Noah, turning and squinting every time the door opened and more characters stepped inside. None of them disguised enough to be unrecognizable. And still no Noah. After the other night and learning how responsible he still felt for Will's death, she hadn't slept more than four hours a night.

She'd tossed and turned, reliving the day she'd learned from a classmate that both Will and Noah had been in a terrible accident. One brother had died, but no one was sure which one. To her shame, for a brief moment, Twyla had prayed it wasn't Noah. *Please not Noah, with his sweet smile, and lock of hair that perpetually fell over one eye.* In the midst of one of her nightmares, she'd jerked awake, bathed in a heavy sweat, certain Noah was gone and she'd lost them both.

She hadn't been able to get back to sleep until it was late enough in the morning to text him and wait for his reply.

The event had given her a good excuse. She'd already told him she was dressed as Elizabeth Bennet, but he still hadn't made up his mind.

You are coming tonight? she texted.

Try and stop me.

Now, she grabbed her phone, squinted and texted him again, Are you here and hiding in plain sight? Who are you? Where are you?

On my way. Be there in five, he answered.

This meant he had to be close since the boat docks were a good fifteen minutes or more from the boardwalk. Twyla busied herself with matching books to their owners. Someone wanted to read a particular book but could only remember the cover was blue. A few months ago, after the third time Twyla had a similar request, she'd created an entire display of blue books. They ranged from romance to science fiction, but hey, they were blue. She'd put up a display sign that read, The cover was blue.

"If it's not here, I probably don't have it." Twyla pointed to the sign. "But I can order it!"

The children were always her favorite. Their eyes widened when she told them about dragons, magic and sorcerers. The twins, Naomi and David, were here with their mother. Amy was dressed as Glenda the good witch from The Wizard of Oz. Of course, Naomi was Dorothy, complete with red and shiny shoes. David was the scarecrow. What an adorable family. Their father traveled for work, so he wasn't here with them tonight.

"I'm afraid I'm going to hate you after tonight," Amy said. "Or at least my wallet will."

"This one, too, Mommy!" Naomi put another book on the pile her mother carried.

Twyla bit back a smile. There had to be close to a hundred dollars' worth of books in their pile.

"She is probably my best customer." Twyla patted Naomi's head.

"Either way, I'd rather buy books than video games," Amy said with a sigh. "C'mon, kids, let's get out of here, go home and read these books."

"Have a peppermint square or two before you go," Twyla said. "I'm not taking those home with me."

She helped others find books and made more recommendations. By her calculations, it had been more than five minutes and Noah was still not here. Something must have gone wrong. Maybe Michelle had intercepted him. Either way, she couldn't dwell on Noah. He showed up or he didn't. The bookstore was having a great night and Twyla began to think they might pull out of this slump. She'd ask Ganny to see the ledgers after tonight. Maybe she wouldn't have to give the speech at the Chamber of Commerce that had her in an almost constant state of panic. They wouldn't need the angel investor loan, after all. Leave it to the citizens of Charming to save the bookstore and prevent Twyla from public speaking. She was one of those people that would rather die.

When someone dressed as Professor Dumbledore, completely with cape and long beard asked for a rare special edition, Twyla couldn't turn him down. She pulled out her rickety ladder and pushed it to the back of the store. It was old but still did the job.

"Are you sure you have it? I don't want to bother you if you don't," the customer said. "I can always order online and have it shipped home."

But that's precisely what Twyla wanted to avoid. People could always buy books at home, but what she wanted with Once Upon a Book was a sense of community. A place to belong. Everyone spent far too much time behind their screens. It wasn't healthy. She wanted the days back when kids hung out after school like she had, when avid readers haunted the bookstore or came in just for that unique book smell. You couldn't bottle the scent of a freshly printed book or one with weathered pages. And like so many other small-town places, the bookstore brought people together.

That's why she was still here and not giving up. This place still meant something to her that went far beyond books or making a living. It was about people.

She made a note to put some of these thoughts into her speech if she was forced to make it. So far, she'd struggled to put her ideas into a structure that made sense. She worked on it every day behind the counter but frankly, she'd rather be reading.

"I'm sure I have it. Sometimes I send books back if they're returnable, but I kept a few copies of this one. It's the reissue of a classic for a reason."

She climbed up a few steps to the top shelf. Here, she had a somewhat blurry bird's-eye view of the entire store and as she found the book and pulled it out, she took a moment to soak this in. Characters from all the books she'd enjoyed as a child and adult were crowding her little store. The sensation was one of books literally coming to life, the way she'd always hoped for as a child. She saw Valerie, the other Elizabeth Bennet, holding her baby boy. She was standing between what appeared to be two Mr. Darcy's. Twyla hadn't seen the second one come in. They both had their backs to her, but then Valerie handed Wade to the Mr. Darcy on her left. The other one turned, and it was… Noah. Or was it? She squinted hard.

Noah—or whoever—smiled, then held up his walking cane and bowed. The regency tailcoat, the Victorian ascot necktie with a white shirt…this guy was the image of a classic romantic hero. When the errant hair fell over one eye and he pushed it back, she knew. This was her Noah. Noah, like she'd never seen him before.

Her pulse quickened and a sharp sting of awareness slammed into her. Prickles of desire sliced through her, blood rushing too fast to her head. In that moment, a blindfold was removed. The mask that said "friend and not lover." The one that refused to see what had maybe always been there. A weight pressed on her, heavy and warm like a blanket. All those tender emotions for him over the years. The longing. She'd told herself all those feelings were normal for someone she knew so well. Understood and, yes, loved.

Now, for the first time, the thought came fully formed: *I'm in love with Noah.*

Dear *God.* She wobbled on the ladder and had to right herself. No. No, it couldn't be true.

Noah headed toward her now, with a determined gait. Mr. Darcy, wielding his cane, made his way through the crowd.

"So…you have the book?"

Oh, yes. She was up here to find a book.

In a somewhat stupefied daze, Twyla bent to the customer's outreached hand and handed him the book.

"I knew I had it."

"Super." The customer turned it over to glance at the back cover copy.

Twyla headed back down, picking up her dress as she went down every rung, careful not to step on it. Then, for reasons she could not explain, the next rung on the ladder disappeared beneath her. She heard a loud crack, then a gasp, before everything went dark.

WHEN TWYLA OPENED her eyes again, the faces of characters from books surrounded her. She was in a dream. Sherlock Holmes fanned her with a book while Eeyore ordered everyone circling her to back up and give her some breathing room. Bonnie was crying into Clyde's chest.

And her aching head…was in *Mr. Darcy's* lap. He had his fingers wrapped around her wrist yelling at everyone to stand back. His haunted expression made her wonder if somehow, in the past few seconds, she'd been told she only had months to live.

The last thing she remembered was Noah, in his collared shirt, looking so handsome that her equilibrium had been upset.

Had she literally *fainted* over Noah dressed like Mr. Darcy? Really, how embarrassing.

"W-what happened?"

"I've told you to stop using that ladder," Ganny said. "It's older than I am, and my brittle bones creak every morning. What on *earth* were you thinking climbing that ladder?"

"It's not her fault," Noah said, but it sounded more like he'd yelled.

"Of course, it's not," Scarlett O'Hara said.

Oh, it was Patsy. Next to her was Rhett Butler, who Twyla assumed was her husband. What a cute couple they made.

"It's *my* fault," Professor Dumbledore said, hand to his chest. He was the customer she'd been helping before she fell. "I should have waited for the book. I could have ordered it online and had it delivered right to my house. Then none of this would have happened. She climbed the ladder to get my book!"

"It's not your fault, either. It's nobody's." Twyla sat up, loosening Noah's grip around her wrist and wiggled her hands, to demonstrate she still had control and possession over all of her limbs. "Look, I'm fine. I just lost my balance. And it's an old ladder."

"You were out for a few seconds," Noah said. "The longest seconds of my life."

"It rather seemed like hours," Sherlock Homes said. Oh, Mr. Finch. That's right.

"You of all people know how clumsy I can be," Twyla said to Noah.

Someone handed him a pillow and his hand gently pushed her back down. "You need to get checked out."

"I agree," Mr. Finch said. "There's no mystery here."

"Very funny, Mr. Finch."

Former paramedic Noah would naturally want to put her through the paces and make sure she wasn't dying. She had started to argue her case again when the EMTs arrived.

"Who called the ambulance?" But she didn't really have to ask, did she?

Twyla groaned. "Oh, Mr. Darcy. What have you done?"

He smiled and flashed a single dimple. "Be quiet, Miss Bennet. You swooned."

NOAH GOT A few strange looks in the Houston emergency room waiting area.

"Costume party?" a lady sitting nearby asked.

Noah nodded.

"Who are you supposed to be?" the kid next to her asked. "You look like an old-timey guy. And…kind of *weird*."

"Damon!" his mother chided. "Don't be rude."

Noah swirled his walking stick. "I was going to be a dragon slayer, but then…well, Mr. Darcy is a character from *Pride and Prejudice*. You know that book?"

Damon wrinkled his nose. "You should have been the dragon slayer."

"Tell me about it."

After all, Twyla had expected him in the dragon slayer costume. Maybe if he'd worn it, she wouldn't have looked at him with such surprise in her eyes right before the ladder rung broke. He'd wanted to impress her—that was the ridiculous truth of it all—wanted to see her eyes widen, the brightness of her smile show the colors only he saw in her. But he hadn't wanted to *stun* her.

She fell, and for one moment, it was *his* life that flashed before his eyes. Enough. He was tired of losing people he loved.

He stood and walked over to check in with the receptionist. "How much longer?"

"Five less minutes than the last time you asked me."

He couldn't sit any longer, so he paced the hallway, occasionally getting too close to the automatic doors so they swung open when nobody was ready to leave. Except for him. He'd been ready hours ago and he resented being kept away from all of the medical information he would understand. Possibly yeah, he had too much knowledge, and it had forever been an issue with his loved ones. One year, his mother complained of a slight pressure in her chest after a large dinner. He'd rushed her to the ER worrying about full cardiac arrest.

She'd had a bad case of gas, but one could never be too careful.

Finally, eons later, an orderly wheeled Twyla out. She sent him a scowl.

"Hospital procedure," Noah answered her unasked question. *Why am I in this wheelchair when I can walk?*

Funny how in some instances he could hear her thoughts. He'd parked nearby, so he ran outside and pulled up his truck within seconds. The orderly wheeled her to the passenger-side door.

"Thank you, good sir," Twyla said in full character. "I am forever indebted to your kindness."

"What's the name of that book again?" the orderly said.

"I'll write it down for you." He handed Twyla a pen and she ripped off a piece of what must be her discharge instructions. Great. "You're going to love it."

Always the bookseller.

Noah leaned over and clicked her seat belt into place. This was quite possibly overkill, and his suspicions were confirmed when she slid him a look that said, *I'm not a child.* Unless he got that one wrong. She might also be thinking, *Not how I planned to spend my evening.* Sometimes hearing her thoughts wasn't much fun. It seemed at the moment that she might be quietly listing how many ways she could hurt him without killing him.

"What did the doctor say?" He took the papers from her. "Let me see."

"He said I'm fine, but he understands how I would want to be checked."

Reading over the discharge instructions, he saw the usual warnings of watching for symptoms of extreme headache, nausea or dizziness. There was the standard recommendation for observation and quick action if anything changed. Call 911, in other words, and don't wait.

"You have a mild concussion."

This was fairly standard and what nearly everyone who arrived at the hospital with a bump on their head was told, but if he said that she'd shrug it off as nothing.

"I should get back to the store now. This was definitely not on the schedule tonight."

"Don't worry. Ava chose the giveaway winner, and your grandmother closed the bookstore."

"And I missed it all." She slumped down in her seat.

"You were busy getting your brain checked." He turned onto the highway and headed for Charming.

"Wasn't it wonderful tonight?"

She'd moved on to earlier in the evening. Good deal for him.

"It was a great turnout."

He'd been late, having spent too much time on the accounting ledgers, and then been irritated to find the entrance blocked. People were packed in too tightly. After a brief discussion with others as to why the doorway had to remain clear for fire safety, he told himself not to worry about whether they were exceeding capacity. He wasn't an employed firefighter any longer. His new modus operandi was to stop saving people.

Then Twyla fell and everything stopped. The world just...froze.

"I might not even have to make my speech now. We should do it every year." She leaned back in the seat now, relaxing. "You make a very handsome Mr. Darcy, by the way. But why Mr. Darcy? I thought you were coming as a dragon slayer."

"Too predictable. I wanted to surprise you, and I did."

"You don't think I...? That's *not* why I fell."

"I know. One of the ladder rungs broke because you're still using one from the regency period apparently. I'll get you a new ladder, the highest-rated one for safety. The old one is going to be scrap."

He swung by his rental to grab a change of clothes. A few minutes later he'd pulled in front of Twyla's small cottage downtown not far from the bookstore. She'd moved to this neighborhood sometime last year to save money. The area was a mix of business and residential zones, with all the homes from the post–World War II era. Charming didn't have a dicey or questionable part of town, but if they did, this would be it. He hated the fact that she'd been forced to move here to save money but had no say in the matter.

Tonight, at least, he had a voice. He shut off his truck. "I'm staying with you tonight."

She met his gaze, eyes cool and assessing.

"No, you're not. I know this is you feeling that you

should have done something to stop me from falling off that ladder. But listen carefully—it was an *accident* and I'm fine. You can go home now. You've done your duty."

"You think this is about *duty*?"

"Because this is what you do. You try to fix things and rescue people. Well, I'm here to tell you I don't need to be rescued."

"Who said that? I didn't." He reached for the discharge instructions and read the section about observing slips out of consciousness and having someone wake the patient every few hours.

"I'll set an alarm clock."

"Which would work well as long as everything is fine. And defeats the entire purpose of when something is suddenly *not* fine."

"You want to stay here all night dressed as Mr. Darcy? What if I ask you to walk around the living room?"

He hadn't read *Pride and Prejudice*, granted, so he was a bit confused. "Why would we walk around the living room?"

"Well, because I don't have a garden."

"This is something from the book, isn't it?" He narrowed his eyes.

"You should have read it years ago, when I first suggested it, and then you'd know what I'm talking about now."

"I prefer *A Dragon's Heart*. At least it's not written in old English." He snorted.

The mention of the book spiked his anxiety. He still had the damn book, packed away in a box, and at some point, he should really confess. Confess and give it back to her. Okay, but maybe later.

"Honestly, Noah, you can stay with me if you insist. But don't be surprised if I force you to dance the Boulanger with me. It's a circle dance with other couples but we'll fake it."

"I don't dance."

"The tango? Waltz?"

"No."

"Slow foxtrot? Quick step?"

"No dancing."

She drew her hand over her forehead, as if she'd swoon again.

"With me as Elizabeth and you as Mr. Darcy it will be inevitable, I fear. We must dance or die."

"You're such a smart-ass sometimes."

He chuckled, the joy of the moment almost unrecognizable. But Twyla never failed to make him laugh. Twyla, who always had his back, whether he was in Charming or Austin.

Too many times, he'd failed to be there when she needed him.

Tonight would not be one.

CHAPTER TEN

BEST FRIENDS WERE annoying sometimes. Particularly when they were over-the-top alpha dogs like Noah. The way he dressed tonight, as the genteel and well-heeled Mr. Darcy, was totally incongruous with the real Noah. No wonder she'd been so surprised that she fell. The real Noah Cahill occasionally wore motorcycle boots and leather and had often run into burning buildings.

But damn he looked fine as a regency-era gentleman. Fine enough to knock her off a ladder, apparently.

"This isn't up for discussion." He climbed out of the truck.

All she wanted now was to go inside and put an ice pack on her head. It still hurt, not that she would tell him that. He'd probably phone 911 again when all she needed was some Tylenol and a little sleep. She also wanted to change out of this dress which, while it had pockets, wasn't exactly her style. The next time she wound up at the ER, she would not be dressed as Elizabeth Bennet. In the bay, the nurses' teasing over Mr. Darcy driving Elizabeth to the hospital seemed to never end. At least she'd introduced one new reader to *Pride and Prejudice*. Everyone else had seen the movie, and not read the book, and said Noah was better looking than the actor.

She didn't disagree. Not for the first time, she felt the pinch of having a gorgeous looker for a best friend. She supposed it was better than having a girlfriend who continually outshined her, but then again, she had one of those, too. And speaking of Zoey…

"I should really call Zoey, or should I say 'Bonnie'? She seemed really upset."

"And call your grandmother. She made me promise."

Bonkers met them at the door and greeted her with his usual mix of disgust and apathy. He hissed his welcome, then turned his back to her as if he couldn't be bothered.

"Hey, Bonkers." Noah bent to pet him before Twyla could warn him.

"Don't tou—"

Bonkers made the guttural sound of a cat possessed, baring teeth, and arching his back.

Noah straightened and frowned. "I thought you said he was doing better."

"And he is doing better, but still a little temperamental. We understand each other. See, I have to act like I don't care. As soon as he relaxes, and sees I'm not terribly needy, he'll curl up at my feet or jump in my lap, purring away. But the trick is he has to *think* I'm not interested." She tapped a finger to her temple.

"So…you play hard to get. With your cat." He sent her a look from under hooded lids.

"You wouldn't understand. You're a dog person."

"I'll pretend I don't care. See how that works for me."

Noah ambled into the kitchen, and Twyla went to her landline to call Ganny. She reassured her that she'd been thoroughly checked out, and that Noah was doing his usual over-the-top thing and staying with her tonight.

"Thank God for Noah," Ganny said. "You do as he says, young lady. He's a professional."

"Yes, he is. A professional pain in the neck. How do you think we did tonight?"

"I'd say it could be a record December if we go by to-night's extraordinary sales."

"Fantastic!"

"But."

"There's a but?"

"I still think you should still try to get the angel inves-tor. Do the speech and see what happens. It won't kill you."

"Won't it? I don't like people, much less a room full of them staring at me. I don't know if I can do this."

"You *can* do it. You're a Thompson through and through, made of strong stuff."

"I haven't got a clue what makes you think that. I'm a reader and I have a big imagination but even I can't imag-ine myself making a speech to all those people."

"Practice with Noah."

"No way. He'll throw spitballs at me and make me laugh."

"Oh, you two act like you're still in third grade."

Except that the feelings she'd had for him tonight were not at all childlike. Watching Noah tonight made her body do things. Almost unrecognizable things. She'd never been one to have bursting, hot sexual chemistry or attraction with any man, but tonight her body seemed to house a furnace.

Twyla said her goodbyes, then went into her bedroom to change out of her frock. She found her standard uni-form of black yoga pants paired with a long-sleeved T-shirt. With some welcome privacy from Noah, she phoned Zoey to assure her she only had a mild concussion. With only a smidge of sarcasm, she told Zoey she would live to read for another day.

"It happened so fast," Zoey said. "What do you remem-ber?"

"Not much. I was coming down the ladder when I saw Mr. Darcy. I mean Noah. He smiled and…"

She recalled the sweaty palms, the racing pulse. Heart pounding against her rib cage. But that had to have been excitement at the success of the evening and the surprise at seeing Noah in a whole new way.

"I guess I did hear the crack of the ladder rung and felt myself slipping."

"Noah tried to catch you. He ran so fast, like a cheetah or some other wild animal. Just one second quicker and he might have broken your fall. He was kind of amazing, even if he yelled at everyone to get away from you, which startled me so much I started crying. Then Adam and Max got everyone to back up and give you some air. After that, you woke up and told us you were fine. Thank you. It was quite the end to a dramatic evening."

"I honestly think calling 911 was a little over-the-top but what do I know."

"Well, it was the first thing Noah yelled at us and he sounded so scary. No one was going to argue with him. I think at least three people called."

"Something happened and I haven't had a chance to tell you."

"Oh, my gosh, spill the tea!"

"Michelle wanted to talk. She came to the bookstore and wanted to take me to lunch. Which I thought was so mean because then she wouldn't eat. So, of course, I couldn't eat."

"What did she want, anyway?"

"She wants me to help her get Noah back and she thinks all I have to do is tell him I don't need him anymore. She says he feels sorry for me and feels an unnatural attachment because of Will." Twyla took a breath. "Do you... think that's true?"

"No. But what did Noah say? I assume you asked him."

"He said no, of course. But even if it's true, I mean, he wouldn't want me to feel bad."

"I don't think it's true if it helps. You and Noah have your own relationship now."

"Sure, but I…" Twyla couldn't say it out loud.

Surely she was wrong about this. She couldn't be in love with Noah.

"What happened with Finn, anyway?"

"Noah said he's hung up on someone else. He can't stop thinking about her."

"What a shame. I mean, if you and Finn could get together, that would make sense. Then you and Finn can double date with Noah and Michelle. That will cure her of thinking he needs to take care of you."

The thought made Twyla sick, which was plain weird. Since when did the thought of Noah with someone else make her sick?

Maybe since the moment she realized she'd started to fall for him.

Oh, this was impossible!

"Unless…that bothers you."

"She said Noah always leaves the room to talk to me."

"Wait. He does? Just to take your call? I mean, why? That's really suspicious behavior."

"I don't know why, but maybe he wouldn't have done it had he known the way it bothered her."

"Maybe. But honestly, c'mon, I thought Noah was smarter than that."

"With any other woman he would be. But it's *me*."

"Yes, you. A very attractive single woman his age. I can understand why anyone who had her sights on Noah would feel threatened. Can't you?"

"But… Noah doesn't think of me that way."

"Before tonight I might have agreed with you. Now, and with this brand-new information, hmm. I'm not so sure."

"You just think that way because you've never had a man be a close friend."

"Noah is pretty unique. I don't think many men can keep those relationships completely separate." She called out to Drew. "Hey, babe, do you think a man and a woman can be good friends and nothing more?"

"Zoey!" Twyla hissed. "Do not bring him into this."

"If they're not attracted to each other," Drew could be heard responding, "then of course, it's totally possible."

"Did you hear that?" Zoey said.

"Yes, and I'm worried Noah heard it in the next room."

"What? He's still there?"

"He's staying the night. Because of the concussion thing."

Zoey whistled. "Oh, my God."

"It's nothing, just Noah's over-the-top concern. He'd do it for anyone."

"Well, I doubt he'd shove people out of his way to get to *me* if I was falling." Zoey paused and it sounded as if she'd moved into another room when TV sounds faded into the background.

"You might ask him why he always left the room to talk to you. Keeping your conversations private was not a good way for him to reassure her, you have to admit."

"This is something I should stay out of. Bringing it up now sounds like asking for trouble."

"Maybe trouble is what you need right now." She hesitated a beat. "Trouble of the fun kind. I mean, how off base is she? Aren't you even the slightest bit attracted to Noah?"

"No, I—"

"You're not being honest, Twy. I mean, hell, even *I'm* attracted to him. He's a good-looking man, charming, fun. If you're not attracted to him, I guess I can't understand why."

"You know me. Sexual magnetism, the stuff that happens to you daily, almost never happens to me. And… I've repressed it."

"Oh, okay. Kind of like me and my college calculus teacher. Man, that guy was hotter than a jalapeño pepper. And married. It was never going to happen." She sighed. "But Noah isn't married or too old for you. You two would actually be kind of perfect together. I'm not sure why it never happened."

"You know why."

"Honey, you haven't been Will's girl in over a decade."

"He still thinks of me that way. Maybe he always will. You know how loyal Noah can be."

"So, that's it? *Will* is the reason you two have stayed apart? That's getting old. If that's all, it's not enough."

"Look, even if he's interested, which I highly doubt, maybe I don't want to take the risk. Noah has a lot of ex-girlfriends in his past. I don't ever want to be one of them. Ganny adores him and he's like part of my family already. And Noah needs family."

She peeked into the living room to see Noah had plopped down on the couch. He'd changed into a pair of jeans that were hung loose on his hips and a faded blue T-shirt that read, *Surf's Up*.

"Anyway, I'm fine. I'll talk to you tomorrow."

"Be sure to thank Noah for me. He didn't just save his best friend, he also saved mine."

Twyla hung up and the first thing she saw as she walked into the living room shook her to the core.

Noah sat stretched out on her couch, a purring Bonkers in his lap. And Twyla could tell he was there by choice.

"I did what you said and played hard to get. He's half in love with me now."

Twyla plopped down on the couch beside Noah and gaped.

"He's a Benedict Arnold. I should change his name. Do you know it took me *two months* to get him to jump on my lap? Some days I had to pretend he wasn't even in the room. I'd put his food dish down and leave."

She reached to nuzzle Bonkers between his gray ears and noticed something else entirely. She and Noah sat close together, hip to hip, knees brushing against each other. They'd sat close before, but it was only that now this felt...*different*. Something had indeed shifted for her in the store when, for one moment, she'd seen Noah in a different light. She saw him as she had the very first time. This time it wasn't the crush that she'd suppressed for so long from the moment she'd met both brothers and only one of them had stolen her heart. This felt like falling in love. The feeling was so rare that she might be mixing it up with some other deep emotion. This *had* to be wrong.

She *couldn't* fall in love with Noah Cahill. It would be the dumbest thing she'd ever done. When she glanced up, he'd cocked his head and continued to study her with... what? Concern? Yes, of course, worry that she'd hit her head. Nothing to see here.

"*What?* I'm fine, don't give me that look." Self-consciously, she touched her head.

"What look?"

"The one that says you're concerned. It's the same look the doctor gave me and I'd appreciate it if you didn't."

"And how *is* your head?"

"My head is fine. Let's talk about something else, shall we?"

He continued to pet Bonkers, who may have actually sighed, but didn't offer up a subject change, so she did.

"It looks like I'm going to have to make that speech for the Chamber of Commerce, after all."

"You said you'd rather walk barefoot over hot coals."

"And that's still true, but no one is going to give me an angel investor loan for walking over hot coals. I wish they would."

"Okay, let me hear it. Give me the speech."

"You? What for? You'll only make fun of me."

He sent her an easy smile. "Nah. I promise to be good. No spitballs."

"Well…"

"C'mon, be brave. It's just me. I'm a good person to practice with."

He might be right. At least she was comfortable with Noah. But it would also be different because she was here in the comfort of her home, the place where she felt safest. She went to her notebook and the speech she'd been working on about books and community. It was pretty good, though she wished she had the nerve to ask Stacy to write it for her. Though that would probably be cheating.

Speech in her hands, she read the first few lines she'd memorized to herself, then faced Noah. His earnest dark gaze pinned her, and all thoughts seeped out of her like wind through an open window.

"Stop looking at me! I'll lose my place." She pointed, hoping to look threatening. "Just…turn around and face the other way."

"You might as well get used to it the way you'll have to do it." He hooked a thumb to his chest. "It's just me."

"And you're a person."

"A man waits his whole life to hear those words." He quirked a brow. "Just picture me naked."

She swallowed hard, nearly choking on her own saliva. "I... I don't think that will help me."

Picturing Noah naked might send her into cardiac arrest. Which might help, because then everyone would give her a pass on the speech.

"It's what they tell everyone who's giving a speech for the first time. You're supposed to picture everyone in your audience naked. You never heard of that?"

"Maybe. But why? What's the point?"

"To make you laugh and realize you shouldn't take it all so seriously." He shrugged. "People are all the same."

"I don't think that's going to work for me." She very much doubted that any man would look the way Noah did naked. Which meant, again, she had a fantastic imagination.

"Look, let's go slow with this. You're a novice. Think of me in my underwear."

But that was almost worse. She thought Noah wore boxer briefs because once, his shirt rode up as he stretched and revealed a taut and tanned hint of bare skin. It was just the small peek at the elastic band of his underwear. Black. Picturing him wearing those now tantalized her and would not accomplish anything but making it hard to sleep tonight.

Now she couldn't *stop* thinking about Noah naked!

He sat up straighter and Bonkers hissed, disgusted that anyone would move his current resting place.

"What's wrong? Is it your head? You look a little pale."

Maybe because all the blood had drained from her face.

She threw her notepad on the couch and covered her face. "At this rate, you won't have to wake me up, because I won't be able to sleep tonight thinking about this stupid speech."

Yes, that was her story, and she was sticking to it. It

wasn't because she'd suddenly developed a keen awareness of Noah. And it couldn't be because her cheeks warmed when he said *naked*. He'd always been handsome but now she noticed it a lot more. Noticed the stubble that darkened his cheeks and chin. The long, hard body. For almost as long as she'd known him, Noah hadn't grown a beard— and as a firefighter, he hadn't been allowed to. He'd had to remain clean shaven and now…he was not. It gave him a roguish, almost dangerous air about him.

But she wasn't *attracted* to Noah because she one hundred percent refused to be.

Nope. None of that.

IF TWYLA BIT on her lower lip one more time, Noah would lose his ever-loving mind. She was already dressed in a white nightshirt so thin he could see through the cotton to her plunging pink bra. He wasn't trying to, honestly, but he couldn't look away. Or wouldn't. Whatever.

"Let me show you how it's done." He picked up the notebook she'd thrown down and took her place.

"Now you're good at giving speeches, too?" Her eyes widened. "Perfect."

"I'm not going to do it *for* you, so stop looking at me that way."

She shook her head sadly, pouted and curled up on the couch. "No, they wouldn't allow it."

"At least once a year, it was my turn to give the fire safety speech at the local elementary school, so I got used to it." He glanced at the few sentences she had written down. Not long enough to be a speech, but they'd worry about that later. Knowing Twyla, the writing was the easy part.

"Just picture me naked," she said, coming up on one elbow.

"I don't need to do that."

Besides, he already had. Countless times. Both naked and wearing sexy lingerie, which is why he knew it would not help him.

"Eyes on me," Noah began.

"Why do I feel like you're about to tell me where I can find all the fire extinguishers and exits in the building?"

He snorted but ignored that. "This is how you do this— Good morning, everyone. I'm Twyla Thompson and—"

She burst into laughter and threw a pillow at him. "No, you're not. You're not *Twyla.*"

"C'mon, Peaches, you gotta suspend disbelief. That's what you told me about the dragon books. Yes, there's a shaman who can chant a few words and turn a dragon's fire into ice. I totally buy it. So, here we go." He glanced down at her notes, then straightened. "The trick is not to read it all but to try to look up and make eye contact every few seconds. Bookstores are important to a community."

Noah read a few lines, then glanced up. And was promptly hit in the head with another pillow.

"Hey!" But he couldn't help but laugh with her as she threw every pillow and hit her mark each time.

"It's not fair that you're good at everything! I have to stop the insanity! You must pay!"

He could protest that he wasn't good at everything. Far from it. That had been Will. But instead of arguing, he returned fire. That was a hell of a lot more fun. The pillows became missiles and he showed zero mercy, but neither did she. Her glasses fell off and she scrambled to both put them down and get another pillow. Bonkers, who had been hanging out, hissed and arched his back.

When Noah ran out of pillows, he chased her around the couch, ducking shots. God, it felt good to laugh like this again. To play. His mother once accused him of never wanting to grow up, and that had been true at one time.

But no one ever saw this side of him anymore. Just Twyla. Reaching her, he grabbed her from behind, his arms around her waist and lifted her. She squealed and continued to laugh when he threw her on the couch. It might have all stopped there but then she reached to tug at him, and he not-so-accidentally fell on top of her.

Then all the laughter abruptly stopped, and they simply stared at each other for one excruciating moment. He fixated on her full bottom lip and wondered if she would taste like caramel. Her blue eyes widened and appeared larger with her glasses removed. She was a woman who wore little makeup and her lashes were still dark and long. But more than anything, holy God, she felt good under him. Soft and sweet. He wanted her so badly that he couldn't think straight. The last time they'd been in this compromising position they'd been fourteen, joking around, and back then Noah had quickly jumped off her. *Will's girl.* He'd told Noah countless times that he had a thing for her, that he'd ask her out when he got the courage. Will hadn't asked Noah to stay away from her, but of course he had. Of course. Will was his older brother and he looked up to him. Adored him as much as a teenage boy could adore anything or anyone.

But there was really nothing keeping them apart right now other than the status quo. Which could change. Maybe he only had to make the first move.

Bonkers suddenly hissed and pounced on Noah's back. The timing was impeccable because only an interruption like this would have stopped Noah from kissing Twyla.

"Ouch!" He stood, censoring himself. There were a few other choice words rolling on his tongue.

"Bonkers! You bad, bad cat!" Twyla chased him out of the room. "Noah, I'm so, so, *so* sorry. I should have him declawed. Are you okay?"

The cat's claws were the least of his problems. "Yeah, I'm good. I'm good."

"Let me see. Did he take some skin?" She came closer and he really should let her check but for the first time in longer than he could ever recall, Noah felt...vulnerable.

And not because of the cat's claws.

"No, I'm good. He barely touched me." That wasn't quite true, but he was having second thoughts about everything. He'd just decided he would stay away from romantic entanglements and what had he almost done? "I think you need to actually work on the speech. It's not long enough yet."

"Yes, I just started writing it."

"That's what I thought. Once you have it all written down, you can practice on me." He faked a yawn. "I'm tired. Think I'll hit the sack."

"Oh. Yeah, okay. You must be tired, getting up so early." She left the room and came back with a spare pillow and blanket for him. "I'm only doing this because you insist on staying here and I want you to be comfortable."

"And don't worry about the speech. You've got this."

CHAPTER ELEVEN

Twyla tossed and turned until midnight. Noah was *sleeping* in the next room. On *her* couch. He wasn't naked, but he didn't have to be. Thanks to a few glimpses and her active imagination, she almost *knew* what he looked like. *Stupid imagination.*

Despite what had to be scratches on his back, he'd simply gone to bed as if this was any other day. Now, she glanced in the living room and saw him curled up on the couch, an arm slung over his face. Carefully, she tiptoed close and pulled the blanket to cover him up to the neck. She could deal with a lot of things in life, but tonight she did not want to deal with noticing Noah's naked, perfectly sculpted chest. It was practically a work of art. Not that she was all that familiar with said works of art, but she watched Netflix, after all. And, one day, a little bored at the store, she'd created an entire display she'd labeled, *guys missing their shirts.* Some of the best books she'd ever read. And, well, let's just say that Noah could easily model for one of those covers.

She really needed to get her head screwed on straight. Slipping into the kitchen in the dark, she was careful not to wake Noah. What she really needed was a shot of whiskey to knock her out cold so she could endure this torturous night. But she could almost hear paramedic Noah's voice in her ear: *Um, no. Bad idea. Mixing alcohol with a concussion?* Well, even she realized that could be risky. She went for the milk since she was probably the least exciting person on the planet. Milk was boring. She poured some into a cup and warmed it up in the microwave.

Funny new things to note? Noah didn't even snore. And apparently, Bonkers didn't hate him. He sat at the edge of the couch like a sentry, guarding Noah's feet. Occasionally he took a swipe but always missed. Bonkers never missed. He didn't hate Noah!

Right now, Twyla desperately needed to think of one thing that was very wrong with Noah. Just one thing, please, other than the fact that he hadn't even let her attend to his cat scratches. That was irritating, sure, but it could be said he didn't want to bother her. She was at a loss, other than his often unnerving need to rescue everyone. And she could be more irritated by that if she didn't realize exactly what had caused it.

She turned and blinked when Noah's chest appeared in her line of sight.

"Hey," he said from under hooded lids. "I was just coming to wake you."

She tried to ignore the way he rubbed his eye with the back of his palm. And suddenly, she had it. The one thing that irritated the hell out of her about Noah.

She pointed her finger at him. "That's it! I have it now. Want to know what your problem is? You're stealthy and sneaky. It's no wonder Bonkers doesn't hate you like he hates everyone else."

"Huh? He attacked me."

Right. He had, in fact, pounced on Noah's back, which was the kindest thing he'd ever done to a guest.

"I didn't hear you there, right behind me."

"Sorry, I wasn't trying to sneak up on you."

No, of course he wasn't. Regret pulsed through her. He

wouldn't understand why she suddenly had to come up with something awful about him.

"You look tired. Do you want some coffee?"

He slid her a blank stare. "It's after midnight."

"Oh, so you're going back to sleep?"

"I was planning on it. You seem to be firing on all cylinders. Can't say I'm worried." He scrubbed a hand across the beard bristles on his jaw.

"Good. Nothing to see here."

Except her suddenly wild and raging crush on Noah Cahill. All those years spent quietly pushing her emotions down and one Mr. Darcy costume had them roaring back to life.

The timer to the microwave dinged and Noah reached past her, brushing his hand against her waist when he did so. He pushed the button to the microwave, and it clicked open.

"You're having warm milk?" He sent her a slow smile. "What a classic."

For several long seconds, she simply stared into his eyes. "That's me. Boring and classic."

Twyla Thompson, bookworm and faux Elizabeth Bennet. Not even the real thing. Even for her time, Twyla could probably take lessons from the regency-era lady. The woman had loved books and reading, but she had chutzpah, too. Then again, *her* Mr. Darcy was rude and a complete stranger.

"You're not boring, Peaches. Far from it."

Twyla was locked in a staring contest with the only man she'd ever truly loved. Of course, theirs was a philia type of love—a deep friendship. Except at the moment, with the darkness surrounding them and the utter quiet of the night, they were like two different people. They weren't Twyla and Noah who had known each other for years. And now she wondered what it would be like to meet him for the first time. What it might have been if she hadn't said yes to Will about that first date. If she'd have waited for Noah to ask. Would she have waited forever, or would he have eventually asked her to be more than friends? It was long ago, and she'd never know. They had all this history buried between them, and it would require a wide and sturdy bridge to get across all the years.

His eyes were the deepest shade of brown she'd ever seen. Like dark chocolate. Like melt-in-your-mouth brownies.

Okay, stop this right now.

"Guess I'm going back to bed now that you say I'm okay." She turned but then stopped midway out of the kitchen.

Maybe she *would* like to change everything. It wasn't like her love life was something to be envied. But changes like this couldn't be made on a one-way street.

"I think… I'll go." It was almost as if he'd read her mind. "You definitely are okay."

"I tried to tell you that, but thanks for listening." Twyla might not want Noah to go, but she did not want him to stay with her out of obligation. As her caretaker. Given that, it was best to say good-night now and not wait until the sunrise.

She followed him into the living room where he pulled his shirt over his head in about two seconds flat.

"If you feel nauseous, if anything happens at all, you call me. I'm as close as the phone."

"What if I see a spider?"

"Yes, smart-ass. Even a spider."

"Thank you, Noah, I'll be fine."

She walked him to the front door where he hesitated for a moment and turned as if to do one last triage on her.

Eyes? Check. Color? Check. Alertness scale? Double check. They'd done the same thing to her in the ER.

"I'm *fine*."

Then with little warning other than the sudden shine in his eyes, he hauled her by the neck to him and kissed her, square on the lips. It was a deep and long kiss that didn't seem to have a beginning. Nor did it have an end. He pulled her tight and they were hip to hip, belly to belly. Even through the shock of the totally unexpected, she kissed him back. She sunk her fingers into his hair and kissed him with everything she had in her. With every last inch of longing wrapped up in her, saved over the years and packed away where the raw intensity of the emotion couldn't destroy her.

She fisted his shirt. She ran her hands up and down his back, feeling the muscles tense and bunch.

It was over just as quickly and then they were both panting, staring at each other.

"I'm sorry." Noah took a step back, leaving a healthy distance between them. "Yeah, I shouldn't have done that. That's wrong."

Wrong?

"It's okay," she stammered because she didn't know what else to say in the moment.

Yes, it was wonderful, please kiss me again, because I think maybe I've always loved you?

"It's just…that was wrong of me. I don't feel that way about you."

Oh, God. There went her heart, pierced and sliced into tiny bits.

I don't feel that way about you.

No, he was right. This *was* wrong. And if he had regrets then damn it, so did she.

"Me, neither. I don't feel that way about you."

"I know."

The certainty in his voice broke her heart a little. How could he be so sure she wasn't straight-out lying, trying to save her pride?

She chewed on her lower lip. "So, let's just forget it. Pretend the kiss never happened."

"But…we're okay?"

Worry and regret filled those dark puppy dog eyes. Not long ago, she would have understood. But now she knew what it was like to be kissed by Noah and her heart shattered to think it would never happen again.

"We're okay. You're probably right, huh? Bad idea."

"Yeah, I just don't want to…you know…" He ran a hand through his hair, looking desperately vulnerable, like a man searching for a lifeline.

And what kind of friend would she be not to throw one to him?

"It was just, well, okay, maybe we're both lonely. And it's after midnight. I…got um, confused." She had no idea what she was saying but it sounded good, and he seemed to be receptive.

"Yeah, so did I."

"And I've got a date tomorrow night so that could be awkward."

Now she'd lied to her best friend, but she'd also kissed him within an inch of his life, so either way she was in brand new territory here.

He quirked a brow. "You have a date? Who is he?"

"Some guy."

"Some guy? Does 'some guy' have a name?"

"Of course he has a *name*, Noah. He's some guy I just met." She crossed her arms. "Weren't you leaving?"

He scowled. "Yeah. I have an early day tomorrow."

"Bye." She closed the door before he could say another word.

Now she was going to have to find herself a date.

NOAH SPENT THE rest of the day irritated with everyone. It wasn't fair to Tee or Finn, who had dropped by to help with inventory, otherwise known as the job that never seemed to end. Every time he thought they'd finished, they found another box of ropes or T-shirts or boat shoes.

Last night, once again, Noah had taken what he wanted without thinking or caring what anyone else thought. Not thinking of what he could risk. Of what he could lose.

He'd kissed Twyla and felt an intense pull that tugged him under.

I'm sorry, he'd said to Twyla, like he'd accidentally stepped on her foot.

Now he'd probably screwed up his friendship with Twyla, and he didn't know how to move forward. Worse, he'd lied to her when he said he didn't feel anything more. But this was one lie that would stay in place. She deserved someone better. Noah couldn't give her everything she deserved. And whether right or wrong, he did not want to come in second.

And besides, Twyla had a *date* tomorrow night.

"Are you going out tomorrow night?" he now asked Finn.

Were Finn to have asked Twyla out, he would have surely said something to Noah first. Considering Finn knew Noah had a thing for Twyla, he'd sounded pretty negative about the whole thing.

Finn glanced up. "Why? You want to hit up the bar for a cold beer or two?"

"I meant whether you have a date with a…a lady."

"I'm taking a break from 'the ladies.'" Finn held up air quotes. "But hey, thanks for caring."

"Hey, boss," Tee said. "I'm not seeing anyone."

"So?" Noah barked.

"In case you've got someone you're trying to fix up. I'm available." He held his arms out. "Just sayin'."

Finn chuckled and shook his head.

"A cold beer actually sounds like a good idea," Noah said.

It was highly likely someone there would know Some Guy. He couldn't believe she wouldn't even give him the name of the dude. All he could say was Some Guy better be a saint. A man just as good as Will would be today. Nothing less than Twyla deserved.

Later that night, Noah headed to his mother's house for dinner as promised. It was nothing less than he'd earned after the stunt he'd pulled. He'd once more be reminded of Will, the perfect son, and Twyla's first love. Just in case being in his mother's house wouldn't remind him enough, there were the photos she still displayed. Photos of Twyla and Will, even if their romance had been a short-lived one.

His mother's oldest friend, Ella Mae, answered the door with a huge smile.

"Is that my son?"

Noah could hear his mother's voice calling from the kitchen.

"Yeah, it's me, Ma. The prodigal son returns."

"It's so good to see you, Noah," Ella Mae said. "Please talk to your mother about joining us at the Almost Dead Poets Society meetings. I think it would be so good for her. Poetry is an escape for me, as you know. There's so much to say and now I have a chance to say it. I think Katherine would greatly benefit from the creative expression."

He followed Ella Mae into the kitchen. "Absolutely. I couldn't agree more."

"We have a lot to talk about, young man!"

Despite the fact that he never seemed able to please her, Mom still greeted him with an all-encompassing hug. She held him a little longer than normal this time, almost as if she was remembering. She seemed to do a lot of that these days.

Even though she was barely in her sixties, her life had changed so dramatically that to Noah, she'd aged twenty years in a decade. Her once red hair was now completely white, and she'd never regained the weight she lost ten years ago when she wouldn't eat and rarely left her bedroom. She looked feeble and felt small in his arms as he squeezed her tight.

Dinner, it appeared, was the usual tuna fish casserole, which Noah detested. She never seemed to remember that it had been Will's favorite and never Noah's. Either way, some days it gave him some comfort to indulge her in these small rituals.

"I'm on my way out the door," Ella Mae said. "But I brought dessert. Please enjoy it even if you don't eat anything else."

She said the last words in a half whisper as even she remembered that Noah was not fond of tuna casserole.

"Thanks, Ella Mae." Noah bent down to buss her cheek.

The senior citizen had acted as a pseudo-older sister to his mother for all these years, doting on her and checking in on her frequently. He had particularly appreciated this after his father left them. And during the year Noah had been gone, he could relax knowing that his mother always had a friend even if she didn't particularly do anything to encourage Ella Mae's devotion.

Katherine did not have many friends because she'd chosen to isolate herself. Her oldest friends remained the women she'd known as a Dallas cheerleader. Yes, his mother had been a cheerleader in her twenties. She'd returned to Charming after college but despite the years and distance, the Dallas connection used to mean that she'd visit the city. She hadn't in at least a decade.

"I don't understand, Noah. What happened with Michelle? She's such a great girl, such a wonderful girl."

"I know she's great. She really is. Just not for me."

"But why Noah, *why* won't you settle down? No one is going to be perfect."

And neither were Will and Twyla a perfect couple. What would his mother say if she knew what he'd done with Twyla last night? He'd kissed her and felt an ache grow and spread in his chest. For one sweet and carefree moment he had lost control and taken what he'd wanted for so long.

"I know I won't ever find anyone perfect. You're going to have to understand that when the time is right it will happen and you'll accept the woman I love, no matter who she is."

She bustled around the kitchen, then leaned over and served him a huge helping of tuna casserole. Noah tried not to gag.

"I *would* like some grandchildren before I'm too old to enjoy them."

"It's going to be a bit longer for that." He helped himself to dessert first—an apple pie.

Silently, he thanked Ella Mae as he took a bite.

"I know what the problem is. You're just frightened. And I can't say that I blame you when you look at what happened between your father and me. But what you have to understand, honey, is that sometimes tragedy brings people together and they're even closer than before. It's an unbreakable bond. Maybe that didn't happen for us, but God forbid if you go through something tragic and terrible again in the future, you and your wife should be able to work through it. Stay together."

Funny thing, he did understand this far better than she realized. He supposed his mother could not see that he *had* already bonded with someone in tragedy and that connection never seemed to wane. It was Twyla, of course, the one girl who knew him almost better than he knew himself. And if he didn't do something to stop the insanity of last night from happening again, he supposed he'd risk losing her friendship, too. And that was one thing he could never bear. Almost unconsciously, he glanced at the framed photo nearby of Will and Twyla on their first date.

Next to that were plenty of photos of Will and Noah, and also of the three of them in earlier years. One was taken at the boardwalk at the Fourth of July celebration. Twyla was sandwiched between them and both he and Will had an arm slung around her. Noah swallowed hard at the photos of him and Will fishing and boating. The pit in his stomach grew.

Mom noticed him glancing at the photos and smiled.

"How *is* Twyla doing, the precious girl? I'm sure you've checked in with her. I think of her all the time. I keep meaning to invite her over to dinner."

"She'd love that."

But Noah wasn't sure Twyla liked coming here anymore, even though she was very fond of his mother. She'd once told him she felt like the daughter-in-law that never was. That would never be.

"Mom, you do remember Will broke up with Twyla because he wanted to be free to date whoever he wanted and whoever he met in college?"

"Yes, of course, but I believe he would have quickly changed his mind. Don't you think? He would have never found someone better than Twyla. There's just something about first love, I guess…"

"Yeah."

Noah felt the familiar pinch in his chest. That feeling that no matter how hard he tried or how well he did he would never be good enough.

He pointed his fork at her. "Hey. Think about the poetry group. I think it would be good for you."

"That group is scandalous." She plopped in the seat across from him and helped herself to some tuna casserole. "I heard Patsy Villanueva's poetry is verging on erotica."

"I'm sure that's not true." He shook his head, biting back a laugh. "And anyway, what's a little erotica between friends?"

"Noah Cahill! I am your mother, young man. Do not mention that word at my table again."

"You brought it up." He scowled.

It wasn't like he relished the word mentioned anywhere near his mother, which said something about how much he wanted her to join the club. She'd get out of the house once a week.

"Mr. Finch's poems are about the history of Texas. And I know how you love Texas. Besides, they meet at Twyla's bookstore. Two birds, one stone." He made a shooting motion with his thumb and finger.

"I support my sweet girl's bookstore. I order my books online through a system that lets me assign the sale to Once Upon a Book."

"That's great, but Twyla mentioned something about community. People can get their books anywhere now, but a bookstore is a lot more than a place to buy books. It's a place to get together and talk about important things. Check in with each other."

"I've been so busy organizing. There are still piles and piles of papers to go through." She sighed.

After ten years, she still hadn't adjusted to life in the much smaller house she'd moved to after his father left. Do-

nating or recycling was a four-letter word to her. She'd had
a difficult time letting go of anything that belonged to Will,
naturally. Anything from kindergarten drawings to book reports. She kept Noah's cards, drawings and homework, too.
Even if he'd begged her to get rid of it all. Who in the world
cared that he'd drawn a red fire truck when he was five?
He'd rather she care more about what he was doing *now*.

"I'll help you. Anytime you'd like. We can go through
it all and make piles. Stuff to donate, stuff to keep."

"I tackle a little bit every day."

Noah knew the subject was a touchy one but he would
ask anyway. "What about a tree this year?"

"I…don't think I'm ready for that. Besides, it's so much
work for such a short time."

"Some people get started earlier for that reason."

"Well, it's too late now."

"No, it's not. What if I do it for you?"

She quirked a brow. "Do you even have a tree of your
own?"

"No, but I will." The other night at Twyla's house, his
spirits were lifted considerably by all the decorations.

"Well, maybe when you get a tree, I will, too."

Yeah, she didn't believe him. Noah got it. Christmas
was a tough time for the Cahill family and had been for
a while.

"I'm not kidding," Noah said. "I'm *getting* a tree."

His mother glanced at him, quirking a brow, shaking
her head. She had her doubts. But finally, it was time to
move on and it was up to Noah to lead by example. Will
would want it. He would hate that they'd stop celebrations
because of him.

Now, Noah would simply have to prove that he meant it.

CHAPTER TWELVE

As it worked out, it had been much easier to find a date in one day than Twyla had ever thought possible. The trick? One couldn't be too picky. So, she'd agreed to let Zoey fix her up. This wasn't always a great idea. In the past, Zoey had introduced Twyla to a drug dealer, a gorgeous actor with an anger management problem and a man clearly not over his ex. He'd sobbed through the bruschetta appetizers because they'd reminded him of her.

"I hope tonight will be different," Twyla had said over the phone just before she grabbed a seat at the bar inside the Salty Dog Bar & Grill.

She'd given Zoey a small list not long ago: no drug dealers, no anger management problems and no criers. But she was already way out of her comfort zone among all these…people in the bar.

"His name is Paul. He's Drew's cousin and they look like they could be brothers."

Drew was a good-looking guy, so this filled Twyla with some hope. Either way, she wasn't really interested in a long-term relationship. She just wanted someone for the holidays. It would be nice if she could tell Noah about a new relationship so he wouldn't think she was pining away for him and another kiss. Even if she was. Whatever. All she wanted was someone to kiss at midnight on the thirty-first. If the guy wasn't a face-sucker or a drooler, she'd be happy. Clearly, she wasn't asking for the moon.

"Are you sure about this? I mean, Noah kissed you! He *kissed* you," Zoey said.

"And regretted it the moment that he did."

"That's only because you've crossed a boundary. He must feel weird about that. I mean, don't you feel weird?"

"Yeah, sure, of course."

But she didn't.

It hadn't felt strange at all, which should be disturbing on some level. How long had she secretly fantasized about him and ignored her feelings? Or was this something new? If this was new, she couldn't afford for it to be transient. Maybe Noah was right in that it would be best to forget about their kiss. If she could manage to do that.

"He said it was a mistake and he doesn't feel that way about me."

"Liar."

"It doesn't matter because I have to forget about it. I don't like him as anything more than a friend, either. So, we're even." An extremely handsome man walked inside and waved in her direction. "I should go. He's here."

Now, this was more like it. He was, if possible, even better looking than Drew. Clean-cut and clean-shaven and dressed in a double-breasted suit, for crying out loud. He was taking this seriously, or maybe he worked as the VP of a company. Maybe they'd marry, have beautiful children and he'd help her run the bookstore in all his free time.

"Hello, Twyla. What a pleasure." He reached for her hand and kissed it.

"Oh." Gosh, was this guy royalty? Nobody kissed hands anymore. "It's nice to meet you, too."

They ordered appetizers and drinks and within minutes, Twyla learned that Paul was a great conversationalist. Most of the conversation had to do with him, of course, but she was here to get to know him. They'd never met before so it was only natural that he would discuss all of his many achievements at length. She simply nodded in places, trying to look interested when he recited his college football stats. Currently, he worked as a car salesman. That seemed to be a bit of a jump in careers, and she asked the question.

"What made you settle into sales after your college career?"

"Good question. Mostly, I'd have to say it's the money. And fast cars. I love fast cars. And fast women." His gaze slipped down and admired what little cleavage she was showing tonight.

Okay, he was coming on a little strong but nothing she couldn't work with. Maybe he was nervous. She shifted the conversation away from fast *anything* and toward her own life. The bookstore, how much it meant to her and her family for generations, and books. She, of course, tended to ask men what they were reading. She felt it told a lot about a man.

"What would you say is your favorite book of all time?"

"The Bible." He nodded.

That seemed to be a bit of a canned response, especially after the comment about fast women. He might be trying to form a different connection with her.

"How about fiction?"

"I don't have time to read fiction. But I do love bookstores. They're actually a great place to meet women." He put an arm around her shoulder. "So, tell me. Is this bookworm-sexy-teacher thing something that works for you?"

"I'm sorry?" Twyla pushed her glasses up her nose.

He slid her a knowing look. "The moment I walked in here, I knew you were someone I wanted to get to know a *whole* lot better. What's your favorite fantasy?"

"Oh, definitely a house with a floor to ceiling library—

kind of like Belle has in Beauty and the Beast. Have you ever seen the movie? I assume you have."

His neck jerked back a little in surprise and he gave her a strange look. "That's not the kind of fantasy I was referring to. I mean, do you like to be tied up? Handcuffs?"

She blinked. "You know what? You're coming on a little strong. I'm not interested in either of those two things."

"You mean this whole Little Miss Perfect vanilla thing isn't an act?" He circled his hand around her.

The doors to the Salty Dog swung open and in walked Finn, followed by Noah. Both were dressed like they'd just come off the water, wearing their windbreakers and well-worn jeans. They strolled in casually, shaking hands with some of the regulars and going up to the bar.

Twyla stared longingly at the man who had never once mentioned ropes and handcuffs to her, nor lost his temper, cried over a former girlfriend or tried to sell her a bag of weed.

And she'd bet he never would.

"You know what? I don't think this is going to work out. Maybe we could just be friends."

"Me?" He snorted. "Friends? With a woman? It's not possible. Not possible because I'm always thinking about how I can—"

"You don't need to finish that sentence."

Looked like she had one more item to add to her list for Zoey. No more men like Paul, Drew's cousin.

"Hey, I'm sorry. Why don't we just start over? Let me order you another drink. What do you say?"

"Well, I suppose it couldn't hurt."

At least, in this way, Noah might notice her here with someone else. It didn't hurt that Paul was definitely handsome even if he was a little icky. But Noah didn't have to know that, did he? All he had to know was that she was here with a date, as promised. No lie.

Paul ordered their drinks, then turned to her with an apologetic expression on his face.

"Look, I'm sorry. I didn't mean to come on so strong. I can go slow if you'd like. I mean, I have a sister, so I understand."

How nice. Maybe she could reform him. Stranger things had happened. She smiled and accidentally met Noah's eyes. He'd been looking in their direction. She didn't know for how long. He smiled back, then went back to chatting with Finn.

"I'm sorry for the misunderstanding, too. You see, I really haven't been out with anyone for a while. I have to confess I'm kind of a homebody. My perfect night is a good book, a bag of salted caramel popcorn and my cat. If he's being nice."

"Hmm," Paul said, and took a pull of his beer.

"It's not easy to get back into the dating scene. Don't you think?"

"No, I kind of love it. I love the adventure. I love the start of something new each time. Endless possibilities ahead."

"I wish I could feel that way."

"Maybe you just need to loosen up a little."

"No, I doubt that's the problem."

It happened so fast that Twyla almost didn't see it coming until it was too late. Like a slithering snake, Paul's hand slid under her skirt, up to her behind. Her eyes widened as she stood in a state of semishock and then met Noah's gaze. *Help*, she said via mental telepathy.

Noah's eyes narrowed and his brow furrowed. And then without words he understood. A few things happened in quick succession. She slapped Paul and Noah stood right behind him.

"Do we have a problem here?"

"Apparently, we do. Look, Twyla, you're very nice but I'm really not into violence. At least not this kind. This isn't going to work out." With that, he threw a few bills on the bar and stomped out.

Noah's gaze followed him out the door, his jaw tense. "Was that Some Guy?"

"Yeah, and I won't be seeing him again."

"Do I want to know?"

"No, you don't. I guess I'll get myself home. Hey, at least he paid for drinks. I'm still going to have words with Zoey. That's the last time I let her set me up, so help me God!"

"I'm going to hold you to that, Peaches. And you deserve a lot better than a guy who pays for *drinks*."

"I don't know what I deserve anymore." Twyla glanced in Finn's direction, who now chatted amiably with a beautiful brunette.

"Is that her? Is that the woman Finn has a thing for?" Twyla didn't automatically recognize her. But she might be a tourist or possibly new in town. They were very cute together. She'd have to say that.

"Yeah, I don't know. I guess., I think she's... That might be. I don't know." He lifted a shoulder.

"Tell him I think it's sweet that he can't stop thinking about her. I'm rooting for them." She slid off the stool. "And now, I'm going home to change into my pj's and read."

IT WAS SUPPOSED to have been a carefree night, but for Noah it had quickly segued into the seventh circle of hell when he saw Twyla with Some Guy. Irritation and something resembling jealousy spiked through him, and he slammed the first beer down.

He met Twyla's gaze and she smiled back, looking happy. Happy with that jerk? What was *wrong* with her?

Noah jutted his chin in their direction and snorted. "Check out that loser."

Finn followed his gaze. "You mean the one wearing the double-breasted suit? Yeah, he looks like he just crawled out of his tent."

"Ha! I see right through that whole presentation. He's trying to *prove* something."

"By dressing nicely for a date with a beautiful woman?"

"Overcompensating." Noah actually sounded like he knew what he was talking about.

He'd read a lot over the years, a casualty of having a best friend who wanted him to read a book so they could discuss it later.

"His mother probably didn't love him enough." Umma, the new part-time bartender, set another beer in front of Noah. "He might be handsome, but he lacks character."

"Exactly. I don't think he's handsome, but you know what I'm talking about!" Noah said, finding an ally. "She could do so much better."

Finn moved his hand to Umma in the universal "cut it out" gesture. "Don't get involved in this. It's a whole thing he does."

"What thing?" Umma said.

"He acts like he doesn't care who she goes out with, but nobody ever seems to be good enough."

"Especially not this guy." Noah nudged Finn's elbow. "Check out the way he's looking at her, like she's a piece of meat."

"I wouldn't know." Finn rolled his eyes. "I've never done that."

Umma threw a look in their direction, then wiped the bar. "The guy *might* be a vegetarian and you're wrong about the piece of meat thing. Maybe she looks like a tasty avocado."

"You don't understand. Twyla isn't the kind of woman you treat casually. And that guy has 'temporary' written all over him."

"Here we go," Finn said.

"Am I boring you?" Noah turned on Finn.

Finn shook his head slowly. "I wish you'd get on with it. Just get over yourself and admit you're in love with her. Save us all a bunch of time."

Umma gasped and held a hand to her chest. "Oh, my God. I didn't see that coming."

"You didn't see it coming because it's not true. She's my best friend."

And it was precisely at that moment when he glanced over to find Twyla, eyes wide, and Some Guy busy groping her so blatantly that Noah could see it from where he stood. He didn't process any other thoughts but moved to their side of the bar so fast it was like he'd been beamed over there. He stood behind the guy at the moment Twyla slapped him, and Some Guy reared back, taking his filthy hand with him. Twyla quickly smoothed down her skirt.

Noah's hands had curled into fists, and he heard himself growling in a voice he barely recognized.

Less than a minute later, Some Guy was gone with his ridiculous excuse of not condoning violence. Good riddance. Noah hated that Twyla was desperate enough to date someone clearly not good enough for her.

Is there anyone good enough?

Finn would say that Noah didn't believe anyone could be.

Before she could go, too, he grabbed her elbow. "If you

really want to go out with someone, I'll find a decent guy worthy of you."

She cocked her head. "No *thanks*. I don't want to date the reverend."

There went his best idea, the closest he would ever get to a real-life saint. "Fine. Not a reverend. I promise."

He walked her to her car and tapped the hood before she drove off. Then he headed back inside where Umma, Finn and the brunette he'd started chatting up turned to him.

"You're going to fix her up?" Umma deadpanned.

"I don't want to talk about it," Noah said, throwing his hands up.

"What a mess," Finn chuckled.

Noah hated to admit it, but in this case, Finn was right.

CHAPTER THIRTEEN

THE NEXT DAY at work, Twyla decided that if Noah ever found anyone he believed was good enough for her, she'd turn the guy down flat. It didn't matter if he was the Second Coming of Henry Cavill. She was done. Done! Maybe she'd become a nun. Nuns could own bookstores, right? First, she'd have to convert to Catholicism but that sounded a whole lot easier than her love life these days.

Zoey had apologized profusely about Paul, excusing his behavior by the fact that he'd mixed alcohol with over-the-counter medication. Really? This was going to be his excuse. At least she had the Almost Dead Poets Society coming in today. They were all such a breath of fresh air. Ironically. Old as the hills and still bright with fresh, new ideas. She hoped she'd be that way in her old age, still running the bookstore, encouraging her young grandchildren to read. *Grandchildren*.

For that, she'd need some children first. Plus, a husband would be nice.

Mr. Finch had already been working a shift today so as the time approached, he helped Twyla set up the chairs in a circle. First to arrive was Lois, early so that she, too, could help. Susannah arrived with Patsy and bringing up the rear was Ella Mae. But utter surprise hit Twyla when Katherine Cahill came through the door behind Ella Mae.

"Look who I found," Ella Mae said. "We have a new member, folks."

Katherine shook her head. "Let's not get ahead of ourselves. I'm here tonight and I'm not promising anything. Y'all know that I don't like *clubs*."

"Oh, we're not a club." Lois waved her hand dismissively. "We're a *society*."

Twyla went into Katherine's arms because she hadn't seen one of her favorite people in months. Her always slender figure was even more so now. Katherine Cahill had once been a knockout, a former cheerleader, and still had those great legs.

"How are you, my darling girl? I want to have you over for dinner sometime. I think the last time you were over was with Noah."

"Has it been that long?"

"Noah was just over a couple of nights ago." She turned to the senior citizens. "I'm actually here tonight for *him*. For reasons I don't understand, my son is worried about me. He thinks I should get a hobby." She held up air quotes.

A few of them laughed. Patsy elbowed Lois, seated next to her now. "And my granddaughter would love nothing more than for me to stop this particular hobby."

"If I'm joining this society, then your grandmother should as well," Katherine said to Twyla.

"I've been saying that!" Ella Mae called out.

"You know her. She prefers people come to her and she loves to entertain. But I'll keep bugging her."

"We need to talk later." Katherine patted Twyla's hand and went to find a seat.

As the senior citizens read their poetry, Twyla stood in the back, their eager audience. Here and there, customers would stroll in and listen. The seniors always brought in their fans. Twyla would then lead prospective customers to the shelf they needed. Even if they hadn't heard them before, customers naturally gravitated to listening to the

old folks. As usual, Mr. Finch spoke of Texas, and everyone clapped at the end of his poem, which today fixated
on the rolling hills of San Antonio.

Susannah had a new poem about Doodle, her poodle,
now getting older and far less active. As she spoke about
growing old together, Ella Mae wiped away a tear.

Ella Mae's poem was about the power of friendship,
and several times she met Katherine's eyes. Katherine observed all of them curiously as if they were a strange lab
experiment. But she nodded and clapped in places until
Patsy came up. Tonight's poem wasn't nearly as seductive
as many in the past, but she still discussed the special romantic love between two people.

"Some of us are done with romance." Katherine clapped
politely at the end of Patsy's poem.

"Oh, no," Patsy said. "You must never be done with romance, not until they put you in the ground."

The whole "put you in the ground" comment seemed
to freeze Ella Mae's face. She reached to pat Katherine's
hand.

Patsy covered her mouth. "Oh, I'm sorry. I didn't
mean—"

"No, we know you didn't," said Mr. Finch. And he
turned to Katherine, his very old-school stately demeanor
dripping compassion. "We're so happy to have you here
tonight, dear."

"Thank you."

Now and again, Twyla believed they all tiptoed around
Katherine's grief in an unhealthy way. All the books she'd
read on grief claimed there were stages. Katherine had
been through all five of them in the past decade, maybe
even twice. In some ways, she seemed stuck in the depression cycle. She had a wonderful son in Noah, who she had
never failed to compare to Will. Noah, somehow, seemed

to come up short. As a friend, it had been painful to watch. It wasn't anything Katherine did with intention, but now she did not seem able to move on and Twyla wondered if, somehow, they all were enabling her.

She could not imagine the pain of losing a child, but Katherine had another son who needed her, too. He needed her to love him unconditionally and without judgment.

At the end of their poetry session, everyone wandered around the bookstore as they tended to do, looking for something new to read.

Katherine found Twyla. "I think our boy is in trouble. You know how he struggles sometimes. He's making some bad decisions."

Twyla remembered the other night with Noah and the kiss. Perhaps she was also a bad decision.

"The boating worried me, too, but we have to trust in Noah. He grew up on the water. And I think being back there again must remind him of Will. It could be a good thing. Maybe he feels closer to him."

"I'm not actually talking about any of that right now. My concern is that he's ended things with Michelle. She was his best chance to be happy—finally settled down—and have children."

"I'm sorry to hear that," Twyla said, pretending she didn't already know.

"He won't listen to me, of course, but you're his best friend. When you talk, it's almost as if Will is talking to him."

It wasn't anything like that. But Twyla stayed quiet, simply nodding.

"Maybe you could talk to him? Help him reconsider things with Michelle."

From somewhere deep inside her Twyla found the courage to say something she'd waited a long time to say.

"I think people need to make their own decisions about relationships and, if things don't work out, move on without them. Life goes on. Even when we love someone, if it doesn't work out, we have to accept this."

Katherine did not seem to read between the lines.

"Noah has always had a very strong head, always the most stubborn child. If he'd just listened to me long ago and understood he couldn't have everything he wanted right when he wanted it…well. Maybe things would have been different."

Twyla prayed Katherine wasn't going to bring up the boating accident. Not now. She really could not stay silent if she did or deal with that tonight. Inside her shop, fairy lights were blinking and her little artificial tree in the corner was finally decorated. Outside, she could hear Christmas carols as people walked by, carrying their purchases. Life went on.

People made mistakes, but they should not have to pay for them for the rest of their lives.

Yes, Noah had asked Will if he could drive the boat on that awful day. But he hadn't seen the sandbar they hit. He'd been the one to try to pull Will out of the water but hadn't been strong enough to do it. Still, he'd nearly died trying.

And all Katherine had seemed to focus on was that it was Noah who had wanted to drive. Noah who had begged his older brother.

"I don't think Noah…"

"Just talk to him, please. I want him to be sure before he moves on that this is truly what he wants."

"Of course, Katherine. You know I will."

"All I want is for him to be happy and finally settled. He's the boy that survived. He can't throw his life away."

So now he was throwing his life away if he didn't re-unite with Michelle?

Ella Mae came to the rescue with a book she placed in Katherine's line of vision. "You need to read this book. One of my all-time favorites this year. A wonderful escape. It's about a woman who starts over in her sixties. She buys a ranch in Wyoming and falls in love with a local beekeeper."

Katherine rolled her eyes. "Well, *that* sounds realistic."

"And there's always this one." Ella Mae held up another, far less exciting book. The book was titled, *Moving on from an Endless Cycle of Grief.*

Twyla stiffened over the absolute and direct honesty coming from Ella Mae. But wasn't that what friends were for? Someone who could tell you when you were screwing up because you were too wrapped up in yourself to see it? Twyla had once told Zoey that she had to stop going after unavailable men. She found and bought her a book and forced her to read it. They even did the exercises together in a workbook. And shortly after, Zoey went into therapy and discovered she was going after unavailable men because she was dealing with abandonment issues with her father. Problem solved. Well, maybe not completely, but at least she was aware of it.

Should Twyla really be forced to do this kind of thing for Noah? Should she get him a book on commitment issues? She couldn't help but think that he'd laugh. He'd make light of it, but that was his go to response when faced with the uncomfortable.

"If I had to pick between those books, I'll take the ranch." Katherine grabbed the book from Ella Mae. "I'm fine, and I wish you would all stop worrying about me."

"I would, but what are friends for?" Ella Mae winked.

After everyone had left, Twyla took in the cozy stillness

of the shop. She had the best job on earth, one in which she could almost be paid to read. Last week, she'd finished another rom-com on the *New York Times* bestseller list. And now, unable to resist another moment, she went to her copy of *A Dragon's Heart* and pulled it from under the register where she kept it hidden. To think that once she'd thought a man could slay her dragons. But that was fiction. A myth. She'd learned to slay her own dragons. So, yes, this meant she'd been lonely for years, but she'd undergone a lot of personal growth during that time. She'd learned she wasn't responsible for other people's happiness. And she'd learned, through the fog of grief, that happiness was a choice. One she made every day because the other option was unthinkable.

Her heroines—those in the pages of the books she'd loved so long that they'd become a part of her—never gave up. Neither would she.

Flipping off the lights as she went, Twyla took her book, and locked up the shop.

NOAH BEGAN TO feel the pinch of loneliness like he did every Christmas. It always hit him late in the evening when it was time for bed, the feeling large and crowding. Suffocating. Christmas in the Cahill home used to be an event. The biggest tree they could cut down. Decorations galore, both on the lawn and anywhere they had an empty space indoors. Not anymore. Not for years.

He drove to the boardwalk and wandered up and down the stores. The only gift he had so far was Twyla's. Like most men, he wondered what to buy the women in his life. His mother claimed every year since he and Will were ten that she wanted something handmade with love. He didn't draw stick figures and hearts anymore, so he'd pressed her for something else that he didn't have to make.

"A framed picture of you."

"Ma, I'm not going to get you a picture of *me*. Who am I, Narcissus?"

He hated to cheat with a gift card so usually he tortured himself doing the shopping thing twenty-four hours before Christmas Day. This meant he used to wind up with batteries and car air fresheners. Practical gifts.

One Christmas, he'd given Twyla AAA batteries and a car air freshener that he thought smelled like her. Like fresh apples, though he'd never told her this. He'd given the same to his girlfriend at the time, and she'd yelled and broken up with him. Not that he blamed her now. The gift was lame and showed the little thought he'd put behind it.

But Twyla laughed so hard she nearly fell off her chair.

What? he had said, laughing, too.

He loved how they always laughed together. It was the best part of being with her and always had been.

Oh, my god, Noah. You're so bad. Was this all they had left at the gasoline station?

How did you know? I waited too late, as usual.

Just so you know, for me, chocolate is always a good choice. How hard is it to find chocolate?

He'd pulled a bag of M&M's from the drugstore out of his pocket and handed them over. This time she laughed so hard she had to run to the bathroom.

When he was smart, he remembered to buy the women in his life chocolate.

Tonight, he couldn't face going home to his unfurnished, barely decorated cottage. He didn't have to be alone. Michelle kept calling, inviting him to a party with a law firm interested in her. It sounded like she was staying, and he wasn't any more excited about it. He'd never moved past the flattery that someone, anyone, would re-arrange their life for him. Even though he'd refused her invites, she just wasn't getting the message.

Now it was ten days before Christmas, and Noah suddenly wanted a tree. A tree, and possibly some lights. Although he had no idea if he could find anything at this stage of the game. What he did know for certain was Twyla would help because she loved the holiday. And this might be a way to get over the awkwardness between them.

He texted her:

Need help. Now. Christmas emergency.

Rather than text, she phoned him.

"Noah! What's wrong?"

Damn, he hadn't intended to *spook* her.

"What's wrong is that I'm completely clueless about decorating and I really don't want to sit in this place another day without having a tree or some tinsel inside."

"*That's* your emergency?"

"Yeah, I figure all the decorations have to be gone by now. Where am I supposed to find a tree? I checked and the lot only has Charlie Brown trees left."

"There's nothing wrong with that, but I actually have an artificial one you can have. It was too big for my new place once I moved, and I already have one for the bookstore so I'm not using it. You can have it."

She had an *extra* Christmas tree. He was not surprised.

"When should I pick it up?"

"I'll be over in a little bit."

This was far better than he'd hoped. They were going to get over this little bump in the road and things would go back to normal. Whatever that meant. If it was *normal* to pine away for your best friend, that is. This was the kind of normalcy he'd come to live with, however, and he'd like it back thank you very much.

Twyla arrived a few minutes later with not only a tree in a box but several bags filled with string lights, ornaments and decorations. She wore an elf hat, and a long-sleeved blouse that said *Merry and Bright*.

"Hey there!"

"What in the hell is all this? Did you buy out the store? I don't think I need all *this*."

She gazed at him from under hooded lids. "You *said* it was an emergency and I took you at your word so don't even think you're going to back out now."

She was right, of course, as usual. He'd asked for all *this*. So, he hauled a huge box inside and all the rest.

"Tell me you didn't buy all this."

"No these are just some of the things I had left over. I got some new decorations donated to the bookstore, so I decided to switch things up a little. But there's still some good stuff in here."

It was his job to unbox the tree and put it together, which he did, linking the pieces easily. The mechanics of it were easy and in his wheelhouse. But then Twyla glanced in his direction and brought her hands to her hips.

"That's sad. You think that looks okay?"

He cocked his head and viewed it from another angle. "What's wrong? All the pieces fit together."

She walked over and began to spread out the fake branches and pine needles. "It's not going to look like a real tree unless we do this to every single branch."

"Jesus, we're going to be here all night!"

"I thought you wanted your house to look like Christmas."

"Fine, okay. Let's do this thing."

The best thing about having a task like this was that

they avoided talking about anything else. And he mostly avoided looking at her in that cute getup—the skirt with red leggings. He worked on one side of the tree, and she worked on the other. After what seemed like hours, she finally stepped back to observe it, like a judge at a contest looking for the best in show. She walked around it, inspecting.

Noah snorted. "Does it meet with your approval?"

"I think it will do. Now, time for the ornaments."

"Right, can't forget the ornaments." And then an idea occurred. A way he could make this night last longer and do some good in the process. "After we're done here I have an idea. What if…what if we take Christmas to my mother's house?"

Twyla gaped. "She hasn't had a tree in years."

Not since his father left them but even before that. The holidays hadn't been enjoyable for years. All three would simply sit staring at each other, not knowing how to do this without Will. Noah had waited for his father to lead, which in hindsight was a mistake.

"But if *we* do the work…"

"Maybe you're right. There's something about the colorful lights that have a way of cheering a person up. It does seem sometimes like she's still, I don't know, depressed. But she did come over last night to the poet society meeting."

"Great, I asked her to just try it out."

"Don't get too excited. I'm not at all sure she'll be back but I'm proud of her for trying."

"She isn't getting out of the house much these days. Even less than before I left for Austin."

They were both quiet for a moment, knowing this wasn't anything new.

"She did ask me something. She wants me to talk you into giving Michelle another chance."

"I'm sorry she bothered you. I know it's that she just wants me to be happy and she doesn't see that I already am. Why do I have to be married?"

"No, you don't. But, let's face it, it comes down to the fact that she'd like grandchildren."

"Yeah, and I'm the only way she's going to get any." He reached to place the star on top of the tree. "I guess by now Will would have a whole gaggle of kids. He always did whatever she asked."

The quiet between them stretched, tight and strong. It was still tough to talk about him.

"And you never have," Twyla said, breaking the thick silence and turning it around. "You're stubborn."

"Look in the mirror sometime."

"I'm *not* as stubborn as you are. You take the prize."

"As long as it's first place." He chuckled.

"I think we're done here." Twyla rubbed her hands together. "Now, on to your mother's house. We're bringing Christmas to her!"

Noah attempted a smile, but emotions were swirling through him, heavy and raw.

He only wished this would go over as well as they both hoped.

CHAPTER FOURTEEN

"This one!" Twyla pulled out the last fresh tree on the lot not under three feet tall. "It was hiding all the way in the back."

Noah hauled it out. "From now on, I need you with me when I go shopping."

"I'll be goldarned! Women find all the things. I didn't even know this was back here," said the tree lot guy.

They paid and, within minutes, were on the road to Katherine's house. Once, she'd lived in a much larger home, the place where she'd raised her family. But after the divorce, Katherine had been forced to downsize. To say that downsizing had been difficult for the former Dallas cheerleader was an understatement. The last time Twyla had been over, there were still boxes of mementos that she struggled to find a place to display. It no longer seemed possible for her to get rid of anything.

For the first time since they'd had the idea, Twyla worried this could be a mistake. Katherine might resist the idea or be upset by the realization that yet another holiday had arrived, and she still hadn't unpacked. It was as if she thought maybe if she waited long enough, her situation would magically get better, and she'd be able to afford to move to a larger place. It wasn't optimism so much as delusion.

"Are we doing the right thing?" Twyla turned to Noah

when he pulled into the driveway of the small residential home.

"We're cheering her up and this is what she needs whether she realized it or not."

"Christmas is always hard for her." But Twyla wanted, more than anything, for Katherine to start celebrating again.

She'd privately told Twyla once, *It doesn't feel right to be happy.*

And while her depression wouldn't be lifted in one swoop with decorations, or in one holiday celebration, maybe she'd at least enjoy their company. It would take her mind off her latest disappointment in Noah at the least. Maybe it would remind her she had a wonderful son who might have at least partially moved back to be near her.

When Katherine threw open the door, she glanced first at the tree, then Noah. Finally, Twyla. "What's all this?"

"We brought you Christmas." Noah brushed by her, then bent to kiss her cheek. "You said it's too much work to set up so we're doing it for you."

"But I don't have the room." She waved around the cluttered living space.

Surrounding them were unopened boxes still stacked one on top of another—labeled *office*, and *den*—stacks of paper both loose and in an accordion-style file. After they dragged the tree and decorations inside, Twyla set about moving boxes around almost immediately. With Noah's help, she simply moved them, giving them more space.

"This is just temporary," Twyla said.

"I'm *not* getting rid of anything. I still have to go through these boxes. I'm not quite ready to let them go," Katherine said, setting her hand on a box labeled *Boys' homework*.

"I understand," Twyla said. "And we're not throwing anything away. We're just making a little room."

Without Noah here, Twyla doubted she'd have ever had the nerve to take the initiative, but somehow the three of them being here together gave her added strength. Surprisingly, Katherine went along with it for the most part, admiring the fresh tree's scent.

"You know what? It's been years since we had a fresh tree for Christmas. Somewhere, possibly in the garage, I have an artificial tree."

"Sometimes you just need a fresh tree, right?" Noah said.

"I'll go get you two some eggnog."

"Spike mine with some rum and we've got a deal," Noah muttered under his breath as his mother walked away. "I'm sorry I suggested this. This is a lot of work, and I didn't mean to drag you into this mess."

"You didn't drag me. I love Christmas, remember? I'm happy to be here." Twyla elbowed him. "Let's get to work."

Meanwhile, Katherine observed, directed and gave some input while they carefully set up the tree in the stand they'd bought. She would chip in now and then, bringing them the eggnog, then a pitcher of water for the tree.

Noah pointed to the basin. "Remember to water this tree every day. Otherwise, it's a fire hazard."

"I'm surprised you're even letting her have a fresh tree."

"Living dangerously. You have a way of doing that to me, Peaches. If the guys at the station could see me now."

Still, Noah had made certain they placed the tree nowhere near any vents or sources of heat. They'd placed the tree in front of the picture window so that it faced the street and when the curtains were open, it would be a bright display.

After they were done, not only did Katherine bring eggnog—the unspiked version—and cookies, she also brought out a photo album. This was not surprising, as nearly every time Twyla visited Katherine, the albums made an appearance.

"I don't think I've seen this one before," Twyla said, admiring the cover of a happy family of four. *The Cahills*, established 1989.

"This is why I don't throw anything away until I can go through it. I found this one in a box I had yet to unpack."

Katherine sat wedged between them and turned the pages, admiring the family photos, many of which included Twyla. Will, Noah and Twyla. Photos of them when they were children, on the first day of school. Then later, in their teenage years. Twyla had seen photos like these dozens of times in the past, but tonight, she caught something she'd never noticed before. There—in a photo of all three of them, Will with his arm over her shoulder—she caught a look in Noah's eyes she'd never seen before. Unless she was imagining it, it was a kind of wistfulness and longing as he looked at Twyla.

She glanced over to Noah but if he'd noticed this, too, he gave her no clue.

How had she ever missed this? Noah, his eyes on her as if *she* were the prize. The prize he'd lost to his older brother. How was that even possible? She'd never even seen a clue of it in those years. But now, she saw it in nearly every photo where there were three of them. In one photo of her and Will on the beach in which he was playfully giving her a piggyback ride, Noah stood in the background. With a gaggle of girls behind him, his gaze followed Will and Twyla.

Later, after the eggnog had been finished and the photo albums put away, Katherine hugged both of them tight.

"You were right. I needed this, and I feel much better now."

"That's great," Noah said, bussing her cheek.

"You two are all that's left of my favorite trio in the world. You're both very special to me."

Katherine cupped Twyla's chin in her small hand. "And you, my dear, brought both of my boys such happiness. But especially Will. Oh, how he loved you. Who knows? You might have been my daughter-in-law."

Twyla swallowed the raw pain in her throat. This was the opposite of moving on.

On the way back to Noah's place to get her car, Twyla sat huddled in the passenger seat, resentment and guilt filling her. Her thoughts were sprinkled with a heavy dose of sadness so complete that she nearly couldn't carry the weight. Some time ago, she'd relegated Will to good memories and happier times. But his mother would never let him go. It made sense. As a mother, Twyla never would, either, and sympathy carved another hole in her heart.

"That was tough."

"But necessary. Thanks for agreeing to it."

"I'll do anything for you. Nothing has changed." She reached and squeezed his hand briefly.

These tender and affectionate gestures no longer felt as friendly and chaste as they once had. At least, on her part. Noah had said that he didn't feel anything more than friendship for her. But those photos she noticed tonight showed her that at least at one time Noah might have felt more. Either way, they were both possibly better off forgetting.

"You want to come inside for a minute?" Noah asked.

"No, I should really get home. Tomorrow morning is the Chamber of Commerce breakfast where I'm giving the speech."

"You've written the whole thing?"

"I don't know if it's any good but yes."

"It's probably fantastic."

She smiled. "It's our only chance to get the angel investor. I never like to miss the holiday meeting anyway. Ava goes all out as you know. I heard the gift bags have a Tiffany item in them this year."

"I won't keep you. Just come in for a few minutes."

"Why, Noah?"

"Why?" He tipped back on his heels. "I wasn't aware I needed a reason. Never did before."

"Sure," Twyla said. Never let it be said that she wouldn't give in to Noah. "For a minute or two."

Noah got her a bottle of Cheerwine, turned the switch on for the lights and together they stood quietly admiring the twinkling lights on his tree.

"We did good tonight," Noah said.

"We spread the cheer." Twyla held up her bottle to his and they clinked. "So, any luck finding me a date for New Year's Eve?"

"I have until New Year's Eve?" Noah scowled.

"Or sooner but you're running out of time." She sighed. "Or, you could just forget all about it. I've been thinking maybe it's not a good idea to allow you to select a date for me."

"Why, since you've already explained the reverend is off the table? I understand that." Then he turned to her and there was a gentle softness in his gaze. "But you're right, I don't think I should fix you up with anyone."

"Why bother? Everyone is taken. Some Guy was a dud and Finn is pining away for a woman."

And you're still not available, even after that smoldering kiss.

"I have to confess. Finn doesn't have anyone." He took a step toward her, closing the tiny distance between them.

"Why would you make that up?"

"It was easy to do. I know what it's like to think about one woman all the time."

"Michelle?"

"No." He shook his head. "I think if there's any man in your life, it should be me."

She blinked at the shocking words. He'd already said he didn't feel that way about her.

"What are you saying?"

He set his bottle on the nearby table, then took hers out of her hand and set it down next. "I mean, you and *me*."

The words didn't sound real. She had to be imagining this. It was too perfect. Too wonderful. Maybe she hadn't imagined seeing all those longing glances in the photos. Noah was the kind of brother who would have stepped aside, after all, no matter how he felt about Twyla.

"You and me? You and me. Y-you?" She stammered. "But you *said*—"

"Don't listen to me, or anything else I said that night. I lied to you because I was terrified. But look, after being forced to go through that album tonight, I'm reminded of how much you loved Will. It's in every photo we took. And that's okay, I get it. I would have never interfered with that. But a lot of time has passed. Tonight, I thought maybe, just maybe, now there's a chance for you and me—"

She didn't let him finish the sentence but met his tender gaze. Simply the thought that Noah saw himself as second best, even with her, made her ache.

Slowly, she slid her hand down the slight scrape of razor stubble on his cheek.

"I did love Will. But I never loved him the way I love you."

Noah tugged her the rest of the way to him, flush against his rigid body. He took her hand from his face and pressed a kiss on the palm of her hand. Then they were kissing, their mouths moving against each other in a crazy and fierce moment. They weren't tender or slow. Their kisses were desperate and deep, filled with explosive emotion. Her skin was too tight, her heart too full. She slid her hands down his back, feeling the taut and firm muscles bunching under her touch, the heat spiraling from his skin and emanating through his shirt.

They broke the kiss, his hand still cradling the back of her neck, warm and strong.

She pressed one finger gently to the hollow of his neck and sensed the steady thrum of his heart. "It's almost… too much. I'm going to explode."

He chuckled. "Good."

She reached for him and fisted his shirt in her hands to tug him close. Kissing and panting. Losing herself. It was freeing, the only kind of release that mattered. She was his and he was hers. Finally.

She wanted and needed his hands touching her everywhere, tenderly and with amazing skill. He moved from her sensitive earlobes to the column of her neck, taking his time with every nibble of her skin, every touch of tender flesh.

In one skilled swoop, Noah removed her top and it fell to the ground.

"You, too," she said, not wanting to be alone, and helped him remove his shirt.

His chest was a thing of beauty—soft, dark chest hair and sculpted muscles like those of a man who did physical work. His skin was taut and tanned and a little windburned in places. He kissed her bare shoulder, and the feel of his stubble against her skin gave her a full-body tingle. When he lowered his mouth to her nipple and drew her into his mouth, she moaned.

"Let's go," he said, cupping her ass and lifting her.

They rolled onto the bed, clothes discarded like flower petals. His warm bare skin pressed to hers, he slid her a slow smile. He threaded his fingers through hers and then braced her hands above her.

"I got you. You're mine."

"I'm not going anywhere."

She heard the sound of a condom packet ripping open and he slid into her, making them both gasp. He moved inside her with firm and unrelenting thrusts, as if certain of what he did to her. How he slayed her with every single touch and every single hot kiss. She could never trust anyone else the way she trusted Noah. Would never love anyone like she loved him. He had her heart. Always. This was it, finally, all she'd ever wanted.

Noah Cahill. Her person.

There had never really been anyone else. Not for her. There never could be.

"Twyla." Noah groaned and dropped his forehead to hers. "So good."

She wrapped her legs around him and arched her back, taking him deeper. Good was an understatement. Great didn't quite get there. Fantastic. Terrific. Nothing fit.

Maybe, just maybe, there was no one word big enough for this feeling.

CHAPTER FIFTEEN

NOAH HAD DREAMED of this moment once or twice before. Okay, many times. But the reality, as it turned out, had been far better than any of his horny teenage fantasies about Twyla. She was incredible and worth waiting for. Soft, tender and all the best kinds of wild. Their kisses were slow and lazy. Like making up for lost time. They'd languished and rolled around in bed for hours, napping briefly, then waking to reach for each other again and again.

"We should have been doing this all along. All that wasted time." He pressed a kiss to her temple. "What have we been waiting for?"

He'd waited for a guilt he hadn't deserved to subside. He'd waited to believe the lie he'd told everyone else about who'd been driving the boat.

Waited for the longing for her to go away but it never had.

"I was waiting for you." She whispered this softly into his neck. "I was hoping for you."

"Funny, because I was waiting for you. I mean, how could you not know?"

"Know what?"

"That I was crazy about you from the moment we met." He threaded his fingers through her silky hair.

"Easy. You never said anything. And I was too afraid

to think it could be true." She hesitated. "Until I saw us in the photo albums tonight."

"That was my well-kept secret. I wanted you for myself."

He kissed her again and again and made love to her.

Later, he slept fitfully, waking only when rays of light gave way to the sunrise. Still, he didn't wake her as she lay quietly in his arms. *Just a little bit longer*, he told himself, feeling selfish for the first time in a decade and allowing himself to be okay with that.

He'd dozed off again when Twyla woke with a start and sat ramrod straight.

"Oh, my God! What time is it?" She rolled out of his arms, off the bed and bent to reach for her clothes. "The Chamber breakfast. My speech!"

"Oh, crap."

She rubbed her face and widened her eyes when she read the numbers on his digital clock. "I have to be there in half an hour."

Damn. He knew there was something she was supposed to do this morning. Of course, he also liked an early start at the wharf, but there were some benefits to being your own boss. With no scheduled tours today, he could go in whenever. But Twyla didn't have the same luxuries with a floundering business that depended on the community. That reminded him, he should probably join the Chamber of Commerce. This was something Mr. Curry had encouraged Noah to renew under his new ownership.

Noah flew into action, pulling on his jeans and rushing to the coffee maker. When Twyla hopped out after a quick shower, then dressed, he had a cup ready for her. Just the way she liked it with cream, no sugar. Never let it be said that he wanted her to regret a moment of last night. She would be at this meeting on time, or he'd die trying to get her there.

"Thank you." She met his eyes, then almost shyly glanced away. She seemed to really see him for the first time this morning. "Okay. I'm off."

"I think you'll be there on time. Don't drive too fast. Promise me." He tugged on her elbow.

"Of course. Please don't worry."

She turned, then stopped herself midway. Setting the coffee down, she threw herself into his arms. He gave her a long, deep and warm kiss that he hoped encouraged her to be back in his bed soon. Maybe happiness was really this simple. It came down to taking a risk at the right time.

"I can't believe this. We... Is this really happening to us?"

"It is. We crossed the friend zone."

"And it was glorious. I wish I could—"

"No. You told me about this last night, and I should have remembered to wake you. I don't want to be the reason you miss this meeting."

"If it wasn't for the angel investor and my speech, I'd forget the whole thing even with the Tiffany gift bags."

"That's high praise. Are you saying I'm better than a Tiffany bag?"

"You're better than one thousand of them." She then picked her coffee up and strolled to her car.

And he caught her smiling the whole way.

NOAH GOT HIMSELF ready for work in record time and had just pulled into the harbor's lot when he had a call on his cell. Glancing at the ID, he saw the caller was Tate, his old crewmate at Station 80 in Austin. The bonding that happened at a fire station was real and lasting but the bonding after a near disaster was in another category. This crew would be with him and have his back for life. Since he'd retired and moved here, they checked in on him at least once a week.

"Miss me yet?" Tate said.

Noah would be lying to say he didn't miss the constant adrenaline rushes and the camaraderie. Mostly the camaraderie. For someone who'd lost a brother, the attachments had meant everything. He considered he now had roughly five brothers for life. It didn't make up for Will, nothing ever would, but it was something.

"Can't say that I miss your ugly mug," Noah chuckled.

"You doing okay, though?"

"Yeah. It's all good here. Things are going just like I planned. Better than I could have even hoped."

"No reminders?"

"Plenty of those, but it's okay now."

"If you need to talk…"

"I know, I know."

After their accident, the rotation crew that had narrowly missed devastating injury was assigned to therapy. Noah had sailed through his, because after what he'd been through as a teenager, the roof collapse was a blip on his radar. A blip that had him making some important changes, but still…a blip in the overall scheme of things.

"Man, what I wouldn't do to get up every morning and go fish."

"You're welcome anytime. Get yourself down here on your next vacay."

"I think I will. And what about Twyla? How's she doing?"

"Yeah." Noah sighed. "She's great."

Unfortunately, Noah had a bad habit. Dangerous. He talked in his sleep. He was really going to have to do something about that. Fortunately, he no longer had to bunk with men. One night, Tate had heard him calling out Twyla's name. When he tried to tell Tate she was his best friend back home and his brother's first girlfriend, he'd simply quirked a brow.

I don't believe you. It was the way you were calling out to her.

Noah remembered the dream, or rather, the nightmare. Instead of being unable to save Will, it was Twyla this time. Twyla whom he'd lost forever.

He'd endured some relentless teasing, but for the most part he didn't talk about Twyla. She was a part of him that he protected. And until the day he had impulsively kissed her, and she'd kissed him back, he'd never been sure she felt the same way about him. The day of the costume event at the bookstore, when she'd met his eyes and given him a look like she'd never seen him before. Well, now she had seen *all* of him. If he was lucky, really lucky, he'd be able to hang on to her.

After pushing the subject off to Tate's romantic woes, Noah eventually managed to hang up.

He had work to do, even if some days it did not feel like work.

"AND IN CONCLUSION," Twyla said. "I want to thank the Charming business community for supporting your local bookstore. My family has long believed that bookstores serve communities. And communities serve bookstores. Books mean love and learning, and bookstores are yet another place to gather and express ideas. We're like a town watercooler. And I want to welcome you all to my watercooler, and to the irreplaceable beauty and importance of books. Thank you for your support."

With a round of applause, Twyla headed back to her

table. She could no longer feel her legs, but she somehow made it back anyway.

The most wonderful part was she'd been too busy last night to stress about the speech. Then, she'd been too focused on making it to the meeting on time to worry about the actual speech. But the moment she'd stepped up to the podium after Ava's heartfelt introduction, her anxiety returned. A pebble lodged itself in her throat and her palms were sweaty. She adjusted and readjusted her glasses—a nervous habit pushed into overdrive. Faces of local business owners were trained on her and she swallowed. Zoey waved to her from the back, giving her a thumbs-up. So did Ava, then Max.

When all was said and done, she'd given a speech even she could be proud of. Plus, she'd walked back and forth to the podium and hadn't once tripped. The fact that she wore yesterday's clothes, her *Merry and Bright* blouse, red skirt and green tights didn't seem to bother anyone here at all. Apparently, she was "festive."

"That was amazing, girl," said Zoey. "I thought you were going to be nervous and shy."

"I *was* nervous and shy. You couldn't tell? I kept staring at my notes and thought I'd lost my place once."

Reading, and even writing, was so much easier than talking.

"Nobody could tell and wow, va-va-voom. It's like you've got this whole new look about you. You practically strutted up to the microphone." Zoey leaned forward, squinted and examined Twyla's pores. "What kind of skin product are you using? Something new?"

It wasn't skin product. It had to be love. But this wasn't exactly the right place to mention this, especially when Twyla caught Michelle coming in her direction. Twyla could not deal with this right now. What on earth was Michelle doing here?

"Um, okay. I have to go to the restroom." When Michelle turned to greet someone, Twyla stood and practically ran all the way to the ladies' room praying Michelle hadn't noticed.

She shut the stall door and put her back against it. Maybe she could stay in there awhile before anyone noticed. But it wasn't long before she heard the distinctive high-heeled clicking steps of Michelle coming to the sink and turning it on. A moment later, she shut it off. But she wasn't going anywhere. To her utter shame, Twyla dipped under the door and spied Michelle's black stilettos pointing in her direction, crossed at the ankles, as if she intended to stay awhile.

Okay, this is it. Just face her. It's not going to kill you. Honesty is always the best policy. Really, was it her fault that she loved Noah? How was she ever to know he felt the same way? She hadn't a clue until the first impulsive kiss. And he'd asked her to forget about the kiss. Told her he didn't have those kinds of feelings for her. Liar, liar, pants on fire.

Look who's talking.

Twyla threw open the door and pretended she'd just noticed Michelle. She blinked a couple of times for good measure. "Oh, hey there. It's you. I didn't see you."

She went to the sink next to Michelle's and turned on the faucet to wash her hands.

"That's funny, because I'm pretty sure you did when you ran in the other direction."

"You thought that was for you? Listen, I drank a lot of water while I waited for my speech. What are you doing here? Joining the Chamber of Commerce?"

"I'm thinking of opening up my own law firm and wrangled an invite."

"You're officially moving here?"

"Yes, this way when it doesn't work out for you and Noah, I can consider taking him back. *If* he grovels." She crossed her arms. "Is there something you want to tell me?"

Damn, did she have surveillance on them? Otherwise, how would she know?

Twyla stalled for time and checked herself out in the mirror, pretending to dot her lips. Because she hadn't taken her makeup bag with her this morning, she wasn't wearing a stitch. Not that she wore much on any day—usually just a hint of mascara, a little lipstick and some blush. Interestingly, she didn't have her usual ghostly washed-out look. She noticed the pink cheeks Zoey had referred to. Twyla did look rather fresh and new today.

"I guess I haven't been completely honest with you."

"Yes? Go on."

She tossed her hands up. "I'm in love with Noah. I probably have been for a very long time, but I swear to you, nothing *ever* happened between us while you two were together. I wouldn't have done that, and neither would he."

"An affair of the heart is just as important." She quirked her perfect brow.

"I don't know if it could be called that when I wasn't aware I felt this way. I tried not to love him. I swear. I've always just wanted him to be happy, and I still do. No matter what happens."

Michelle simply stared at her for several long seconds from under those incredibly long lashes. Her expression was fairly blank.

"Besides, weren't you the one that told me love is worth taking a risk?"

Michelle's eyes narrowed, and she turned to the mirror

to fluff her hair. "Thank you for being honest with me. I wish you both the best and I hope it works out for you. Even if Noah has a commitment phobia, you never know. You might get lucky."

Michelle turned and strutted out of the bathroom. Zoey was wrong. Twyla didn't strut. She'd never strutted a day in her life.

Now Michelle? *That* girl had a strut.

For a few minutes, Twyla imitated the walk. She gauged her progress in the mirror as she walked by, swinging her hips. Nope. Not happening.

When she got back to her table, Zoey had already opened her gift bag.

"It's a Tiffany headband which, if I put it on, looks a little bit like a tiara."

Twyla dug through her bag to find a similar gift. Ava had excellent taste. "Me, too."

"So, what happened? I saw Michelle following you into the restroom."

"She just wanted to make me feel guilty."

"About what?"

"Now please don't gloat."

"Who, me?" Zoey held her hand to her chest.

"You're right and I don't know why it took me so long to realize."

Zoey's eyes widened. "Oh, my God, are you finally going to start wearing heels?"

Twyla had to laugh. "No, I'm on my feet all day. Zoey, how many times do we have to discuss this?"

"Well, what is it then?"

"It's Noah."

"What about him?"

"It's *me*, and Noah." She slid Zoey a significant look until she gaped.

"You mean, finally? Finally! Really?"

And then Twyla told Zoey everything, censoring the more intimate details.

Zoey squealed and held up her palm for a high five. "Way to cross boundaries, girl. I wonder how many were technically crossed in one night?"

Twyla explained how she and Noah had brought Christmas to his mother's house. How they'd put up the tree and spent some time looking through old albums. And what she'd seen in those photos that rocked her to the core.

"Oh, my gosh. Come on. All that time pining over you. But of course he felt guilty. He wanted what his big brother had, and then he failed to save him."

But the thing of it was, Twyla had loved Noah first.

She remembered the first time she had ever seen him— his wavy dark hair falling over one eye as it never failed to do. A smile that always brought one out of her. She wouldn't have called it love then, but what she felt for him had always been more intense than what she'd felt for Will. Her personality had been far better suited to Will, who was also the quiet type. Not quite as handsome or charming as Noah, he was still a good-looking kid. Twyla had been flattered when he asked her out. She'd said yes because Noah would never ask.

After the Chamber breakfast, and finally disentangling from Zoey's many questions, Twyla headed home to change and feed Bonkers. She opened the door to the sounds of mewing. If a cat could give the finger, Bonkers would. His eyes were tiny slits of utter disgust. His human servant hadn't been home to feed him last night.

"I'm so sorry, but it's not like you're going to starve." Her cat, according to the vet, was overweight.

She opened up a can of wet food and set his bowl down. Tonight was the regular meeting of the poet society, and since even Katherine had attended once, Twyla thought her grandmother should make an appearance as well. She brought it up after the last poetry meeting, pointing out that even Katherine had now attended, so surely Ganny could as well.

"Poetry has never been my thing, and you know it."

"You could at least show up and support your friends. Be their audience. Art is a medium that needs an audience, after all. Poems are not meant to be spoken into the void. They just want to be heard."

"Well, you can do that. I did go to a meeting *once*, about a year ago."

"Then I think you're due."

"I don't have anything to wear."

"That's a lousy excuse. I'll find something for you to wear. Just watch me."

"Okay, okay! I'll go. Unless I feel sick that day."

Twyla had been checking on her daily just to make sure she couldn't fake it at the last minute.

Later that afternoon, Ganny, who got a ride with Mr. Finch and Lois, strolled through the doors of Once Upon a Book for the first time since the costume event.

"I'm just here to support y'all," she said. "My grand-daughter doesn't think I spend enough time at the place where I worked all my life."

"Don't you miss it?" asked Lois.

"I do sometimes, but the world is a different place now. What with the e-readers and audiobooks, too many people have forgotten print."

"Not us!" the seniors said in unison.

"Print is actually making a comeback, Ganny," Twyla said. "And among young people, believe it or not."

Earlier today, she'd arranged a new display of print books that were bestsellers thanks to a new popular social media site. *As seen on...* the sign read. At least two teens had picked up one of those books.

"I'd love publishers to carry more large print books." Patsy sniffed. "If anything, the print gets smaller."

"And who wants to read with a magnifying glass?" Susannah said. "If you would tell the publishers, Twyla, that would be so helpful."

Yes, because publishers did exactly what Twyla said they should.

"I'll give it a try."

Finally, they were all settled in their circle and began to share their poems. Twyla applauded after each one, because honestly, they were all getting so much better. Mr. Finch's poems were verging on literary fiction, especially with the one tonight he'd titled, "When Texas was Young." But Twyla was suddenly quite partial to Patsy's romantic poetry.

Noah had texted her earlier today that he wanted to grab dinner, and he'd be by later. She already missed him in new ways that had her both giddy and anxious. It occurred to her that if they were able to save the bookstore as it looked like they were doing, and she could be with Noah, she might actually be too lucky. Did she deserve this much happiness? She wanted to believe so, but good people who meant well and worked hard did not often get what they deserved.

The poetry reading over, a few seniors were standing in a corner discussing the latest memoir on the *New York Times* bestseller list. In another corner, a couple of people were trying to understand a plot point in a book where the ending seemed to be in flux. Did she kill him or not? And if she did do it, then *how*?

Twyla usually eagerly added to the conversation, but as she stood back and listened in, warmth spread through her at the community they'd created here. Maybe it had taken selling educational toys, too, so a person could buy a toy for their nephew's birthday and the latest bestseller in the same place. Even the yoga classes meant someone lingering. The teacher had recommended many books in the health and wellness section. They had something special here and weren't going to lose it. It wasn't just a line in her speech, it was the dream, and it was here. Maybe not always bright and shiny and glowing, but nonetheless precious in the way the best things in life are. Not perfect, but real.

Force of habit had her glancing up when she heard the ding of the shop's bell and her heart tugged with sweetness when Noah walked in. He sent her a slow smile, then quirked a brow when she beckoned him to the back of the store. It took him a few minutes, but he finally joined her in the fantasy section. *Their* section. She wanted to pull the book out and read with him just like old times, this time knowing he had tender feelings for her.

"I got here as soon as I could, but the old folks sure know how to talk an ear off."

She went into his arms, threading her fingers through his soft wavy hair. "I thought you were going to meet me for dinner."

He pulled her flush against him. "I was, but I couldn't wait."

She loved hearing those words. They'd waited long enough.

"I forgot to say something earlier today. I hope you'll forgive me."

Oh, boy, here it comes. The one thing that might ruin everything. She almost didn't want to hear it because this moment was too perfect.

And the world tended to take perfection and squash it to bits.

"I don't want any more misunderstanding between us. I'm going to be one hundred percent honest with you."

She tensed. "Do I want to hear this?"

"I hope so." His voice was soft. "Last night? This morning? I forgot to tell you that I love you. And I have for as long as I can remember."

"Oh, Noah."

Her heart was too full. It was going to spring a leak any minute because it wasn't big enough yet, but it was already changing. Growing and stretching to let everything new inside.

"Is that okay with you?" He smiled, like he knew.

Then he pulled her in by the nape of her neck and kissed her. Like all his kisses, it was intense, long and deep. She almost forgot where she was, until the rather pronounced voice of Patsy Villanueva spoke, or rather squealed, right behind them.

"Oh, my God it's happening again! How long has *this* been going on?"

Before long, the fantasy nook filled with the senior citizens, elbow to elbow.

"Was it Patsy's poem or mine?" Ella Mae asked, hand to chest.

"Well, both were truly wonderful," Twyla said, lowering her hand from Noah's chest to his abs.

"Well, my poem was about kissing, and Ella's was about a garden. So…" Patsy said.

"Love grows in a garden! Remember the seed I mentioned? What do you think I was talking about?"

"A seed," Patsy said with a straight face.

"It's a *metaphor*." Ella Mae sniffed.

"I didn't hear either one of your poems but I'm sure both poems were great." Noah nodded.

"Of course, all of our poems are wonderful and that's not news," Susannah said. "But if you could give us some direction, we would love to be a little more hands-on with our matchmaking."

"That's true," Patsy said. "I want to know if I should get spicier or tone it down some."

"Do you young folks get the seed metaphor, or should I perhaps be more direct?"

"Ladies." Mr. Finch cleared his throat. "Time to admit a few things. We're lousy matchmakers. It's all been accidental. We've simply been lucky."

"Maybe we should rename ourselves the Accidental Love Poet Society," Patsy said. "It's a better fit. I don't plan on dying soon so I hate the 'almost dead' part."

"It is kind of morbid," Lois agreed.

There was some argument about renaming the society until Susannah reminded everyone the name was tongue-in-cheek and not to be taken too seriously. And also, they had already ordered business cards and it was too late to change now.

"I'm sorry, ladies, but Mr. Finch is right. At least about these two." Ganny muscled her way to the front and now waved her hand between Twyla and Noah. "*This* isn't new."

Twyla glanced up at Noah.

They were both brand new and old.

"What do you mean? She was Will's girl." This from Lois. "Wasn't she?"

Twyla wasn't imagining Noah tense beside her. His grip on her tightened.

Ganny shook her head. "A long time ago. But in my opinion, she's loved Noah for just as long, if not longer. And I for one, couldn't be happier for them."

CHAPTER SIXTEEN

NOAH BELIEVED HIS own mother would be just as happy about them as Twyla's grandmother. If he got lucky, Twyla would one day soon be his mother's daughter-in-law. But he better not get ahead of himself. He already felt like someone who'd won the lottery—lucky and possibly undeserving. Even if his privacy had been violated, the knowledge these "accidentally matchmaking" senior citizens approved of him filled him with hope.

Instead of taking Twyla to a restaurant for dinner, Noah drove to his favorite stand by the wharf and picked up bread bowls of clam chowder, fried calamari and shrimp cocktails. After tonight, and the unexpected unveiling of their new romance, he wanted to take Twyla somewhere special. Meaningful.

He would take her to the one place in the world he felt most at home.

They sat on the bench seats of the catamaran and watched the sunset while they ate. Funny, but before the accident, he'd never paid much attention to color. He'd listen to girls talk about the sunset and all the fancy descriptions of ribbons of red and gold. Once, when he and a few friends had missed the sunset, Noah had tried to lighten the disappointment by saying, "There will be another one tomorrow." It had been a while since he'd believed that.

Tomorrows weren't promised to anyone.

Will would be happy for them. Noah liked to think he

would be, since he'd once thanked him for stepping aside. He'd give anything to have his brother back, and he didn't know that Twyla and Will would have wound up together anyway. Will claimed to be moving on to college and a new life.

Privately, just between brothers, Will couldn't wait to get away from their parents. Always being the good son hadn't exactly been *his* choice. Just like being labeled the stubborn one hadn't been Noah's. He'd walked around in a state of perpetual guilt for both what he had done and what he hadn't. Now, he could release the guilt. He'd tried to save his brother and failed. It was the biggest regret of his life, but Will had a part in the accident. He'd driven at high speeds, scaring Noah, laughing maniacally.

If our parents could see us now! Will had laughed.

Stop, Noah said. *You're going* too fast.

What's too fast?

It just wasn't fair.

Will had just been a kid, a teenager on the cusp of a new life in a town where he might not be labeled as perfect. For a moment, Will went against the rules in a complete break of character. And it had nearly killed them both.

"You're quiet. What are you thinking?" Twyla bumped his knee.

He pulled her into his arms, and her head settled on his shoulder. "About us."

"Yes, us. My favorite subject."

"Did you know I was going to ask you out first, before Will did?"

"No," she said quietly.

"To the junior prom."

"You went with Sabrina. I was *so* jealous."

"You would have been my first choice. Anyway, Will

told me he really liked you. You remember that Will didn't date much and I…well, I did."

"Mr. Popularity."

"My popularity was based on the fact that I cared too much because I needed everyone to like me. I wasn't particularly intelligent and all I had was my personality. It was important for others to like me because Will… He was always my parents' favorite."

"That's not true." She clung to his neck. "Please don't say that."

But she more than anyone else understood because she'd witnessed it. Will was the kid eager to please his parents. The older and dutiful son, always doing what was expected. Schoolwork had come easily to him, while Noah always struggled. Will behaved, while from day one, Noah couldn't sit still.

"Just promise me one thing." Noah brought her hand to his lips and spoke through it. "Don't start treating me any differently. When I'm a stupid guy, and I will be, try to see me through the best friend lens. Know that whatever I fail to do, or forget to do, it isn't because I don't love you."

"Yes, okay. I can do that. You do the same for me. The best friend thing. Except… I will still talk to Zoey about you. She's also my best friend. I tell her stuff I can't tell you."

"What can't you tell *me*?"

She went still for a moment, and he got concerned. He didn't want to accept that she kept anything from him, which he realized was selfish. He already kept something huge from her.

"Like what I'm getting for your birthday or what I might get you. And I have to do the girl-talk thing. I have to tell her all the wonderful things you do to me in bed and how it makes me feel."

"Tell me that stuff, too."

"But I wouldn't want you to get too conceited."

"Fine. Just make sure you always talk me up. Make me sound even better than I am." He chuckled but the laugh died within seconds. "There's also...something I've kept from you all these years."

"I know. You liked me."

He swallowed the pebble in his throat and cleared it. "Yes, but not...not that."

"Noah, you can tell me anything. I don't want any big secrets between us."

"I know, but this... I never told anyone. It was better that way."

She stilled in his arms. "Maybe, if you can't tell me, you can tell someone else."

Such a sweet gift, giving him the permission *not* to tell her. There was such trust in that one sentence. Trust that he'd make the right choice.

"On the day of the accident? The thing is, I *wasn't* the one driving the boat."

She froze and met his eyes. "But...you said you were the driver, and the police investigated."

"Not very well. They believed what I told them and why wouldn't they when I took blame? 'Will let me drive the boat and I hit a sandbar going too fast.' It made sense to them."

"*Why*, Noah? Why would you take the blame?"

"Because I loved Will. Idolized him. He had one bad moment and paid for it with his life. I didn't also want him to lose his reputation. It was hard enough on my parents, and they were used to my being the one to blame. Used to Wild Noah, breaking the rules once again. I hoped their unconditional love would get my family through this, but my father never looked me in the eyes again."

"Oh, Noah." She buried her face in his neck, tears flowing now, wetting his skin.

"Some days I thought you were the one person in the world who knew it wasn't me. I thought you'd see right through my lie. You didn't and yet you still loved me."

"I will always love you. And your father loved you, too. Some men are not strong enough to show their love through the tough times. To stick it out, for better or worse. He was a weak man."

"Hey, didn't mean to make you cry." Noah reached to tip her chin. "But I didn't want the lie between us anymore."

"You should at least tell your mother. She doesn't blame you, but she does have Will on a pedestal."

"He might deserve to be. I lost a brother, but she lost a child. Maybe she has the right to do whatever she wants. It's easier to blame me and she needs to put the blame somewhere."

They sat quietly for several minutes, simply holding each other tight.

Noah closed his eyes and listened to the sounds of the water lapping against his boat, the woman he'd loved for half his life in his arms.

"Oh, my God, Noah! Look."

When he opened his eyes, fireflies danced just off the stern of the boat. Fireflies such as he hadn't seen in years, a shimmering display of lights.

"How many do you think there are?" Noah said.

"Hundreds!"

They stood and drew closer to them.

"Did you know that this is their mating call? Fireflies light up this way to find a mate," Twyla said.

"I thought it was to ward off predators."

"That used to be the case, but they've evolved over millions of years. They're near extinction now." She reached for his hand. "And a group of them are called a light posse…or a sparkle."

"Sparkle. That's perfect." He pressed a kiss to her temple and pulled her in front of him, wrapping his arms around her waist.

Noah wasn't one to believe in magic or fantasy other than in the books he and Twyla liked to read. But if he did, he'd think the sparkle was Will's doing, giving them his stamp of approval. After all, he had loved them both. Noah sensed in that precious moment that Will would want nothing more than their happiness.

They stayed and watched the sparkle for a very long time.

THE CLOSER THEY drew to Christmas Day the more anxious Twyla grew to give Noah her present. She'd been working on it for nearly a year now and had simply planned to ship it to him in Austin. But this would be so much better, so she could see his face light up at the book that had meant so much to the two of them over the years. It had added significance now, years later, because the grief had lifted and that had given them the possibility of a much brighter future than she could have ever dreamed.

Finally, five days before Christmas, she removed the book from behind the checkout counter where she kept it to add notes here and there as they occurred to her. Opening to the first page, she wrote the inscription:

For Noah, my whole heart. It feels like I've loved you for one hundred years.

It was the other copy of *A Dragon's Heart*, and though it would never be quite like the first—in which they'd honestly expressed their grief through a story—she had a feeling this, too, might serve a purpose. While "Silent Night" piped through the speakers and customers wandered around for last minute purchases, she carefully wrapped the book.

Tonight, she'd give him the gift early because she couldn't wait another minute. She was sure that like her, he'd missed the book which, in some ways, forever cemented their connection to each other. And what better book for two confused and hurting young people to read than a fantasy in which even dragons who breathed fire could be slayed?

So busy wrapping that she hadn't even noticed someone at the counter, Twyla looked up. "How can I help you?"

The man who looked vaguely familiar held out his hand. "I'm William Hart."

"Nice to meet you. I'm Twyla and my family runs this store. Can I help you find something?"

He shook his head. "I thought I'd drop this by instead."

He reached inside his jacket pocket and pulled out an envelope. "I wanted to personally deliver this check. I heard your speech at the Chamber breakfast and though I was leaning toward you anyway, those beautiful words clinched the deal for me. You should know that I'm a different kind of angel investor. I don't ask for anything in return. I want you to keep this bookstore around for many years to come."

Twyla stared at the closed envelope, then back to Mr. Hart. William.

Will.

It could be the coincidence of a very common first name, but delight pulsed through her anyway. First, after Noah's heartbreaking confession, the fireflies just *had* to have been sent from Will for both her and Noah. They couldn't see him, but he was still with them. Always.

Now this.

"Have we met before?"

"I don't think so, but I've been around." He patted his chest and smiled. "Merry Christmas."

"Thank you."

Twyla turned the card over in her hands, not wanting to open it in his presence. She would be grateful for any amount he'd given from the kindness of his heart.

"This means so much to my family. I want you to know—"

When she glanced up, the man was already gone. He had moved so quickly, and she'd been so engrossed, that she hadn't even heard the door chime as he left. And when she ran to the sidewalk, there were so many passersby that she didn't catch a glimpse of him in either direction. He'd melted into the crowd.

Walking back inside, she opened the envelope and took a look at the check. She blinked when more zeros than she could have ever hoped for followed the comma.

In the memo portion of the check, William Hart had written:

Books are forever.
Just like love.

WHEN SHE GOT HOME, Twyla phoned Ganny to give her the good news.

"I knew if anyone could pull us out of this slump, it would be you."

"Well, it was actually Mr. Hart. *William* Hart. Did I mention that?"

"Yes, you did. And, honey, I don't believe in coincidences. That was a message."

Twyla's eyes were suddenly wet. "You think so?"

"I do. Am I to assume you'll be bringing Noah to my annual Christmas party?"

"Of course."

"Make sure Katherine comes, too. We'll have a big crowd this year. Dana, the yoga teacher, and all of the Almost Dead Poets Society members. Ava, of course, and Max. Valerie and Cole. Stacy and Adam may show up, too, if they can get a babysitter. Everyone who has gone out of their way to support us."

"You'd have to invite the entire town," Twyla said.

Twyla hung up and carefully placed Noah's book under the tree along with a few of her other presents. Definitely on a budget this year, every single one of her gifts had been handmade. For Ganny, she'd put together an album filled with memories of the bookstore. Old newspaper articles going back to four generations when the store first opened. A photo with her parents and grandmother at the book signing of the first bestselling author they'd ever hosted. Photos of family and friends and books.

Bonkers came running out from wherever he'd been hiding today, stopped short when he saw her, then give her a dirty look and stalked away, his tail high in the air.

"That's fine. Go be in your bad mood. I know you like me, even if you act like you don't. What would you do without me? Huh? Yes, you'd starve, that's what."

She poured the dry food and set the bowl down. Bonkers sniffed it, then decided he'd rather starve.

The doorbell rang. "That will be my boyfriend."

Yes, her boyfriend. Noah Cahill.

Tonight, she'd give him the book and he'd know without words how much she loved him. She opened the door to a tired-looking Noah. His cheeks were ruddy and wind-burned, his gorgeous dark hair its usual tousled and wavy look. She took his arm and pulled him inside.

"What's wrong? Rough day?"

"You could say that. Tee got ahead of himself and took the dingy out without asking me. I would call that an offense worth firing him for, but Finn talked me off the ledge."

"Leave it to Finn. Does Tee know what he's doing?"

"Finn assures me he does. But Tee is going to have to prove to me that safety is more important than impressing girls."

"I almost forgot to tell you. You're never going to believe this!" She went to her purse and pulled out the check. "The angel investor came through for us, and his name is William."

She told him the entire story and handed him the check to see. Even Noah's eyes widened.

He took her into his arms, then pressed his forehead to hers. "I'm so happy for you. He's right, you know? Books are forever."

Just like love. She'd loved Will as an innocent young girl, and she would forever. But Noah. The love for him was different and always had been. Deeper and wider.

And she'd like to think she and Noah were a forever kind of love.

"Come here. I have something for you." She tugged him toward the tree and pulled out her present. "It's a few days early, but I just can't wait another minute. I've been working on this for almost a year."

With a smile tugging his lips, Noah tore into it with the excitement of a little kid. But she couldn't miss the blank look on his face when he turned the book over in his hands.

There was almost a hesitance there. A flash of regret?

She felt the need to explain. "Remember? I lost our book and felt so bad about it. When it didn't turn up, I decided I would just recreate it. Of course, it's not the same but—"

She didn't get to finish the sentence because he grabbed her in a fierce kiss.

"Wait until you read the inscription," she gasped, a little out of breath.

"I love this, baby. But I'll read it later. *Much* later if you don't mind." Then he carefully tossed the book on her couch and hoisted her into his arms, carrying her to the bedroom.

"I don't mind at all."

FRESH AND RAW new guilt pierced Noah. He could only imagine the hours Twyla had spent recreating the book. The one she should have never had to replace. The one he'd taken and kept from her. It should be a simple thing to return now, to let her know the reasons he'd taken it. They'd be better received now. He hoped. But the lie, such as it was, or omission of truth, wouldn't go down as easy. He'd lost count of how many times Twyla had asked him whether he'd seen their book, and when and where he'd last seen it. She'd apologized to *him* for losing it. Apologized!

He'd almost broken down then and told her he had the book, and would she mind if he kept it? Hindsight being twenty-twenty now, he knew she would have understood. But she might have also *understood* that he'd loved her for years but didn't know how to tell her. That he loved her but had allowed an unnatural guilt to build a wall between any possibility of having more. And yes, she would have been disappointed to hear it, which was the risk he took now, too. He would still give it back to her, because now the original book would again be something they could hold between them. Their shared history.

A FEW HOURS LATER, Noah woke to the delicious scent of coconut tickling his nose. Wait. Was he on a beach in Hawaii? In a hammock on an island somewhere under a palm tree? When he opened one eye, Twyla's gorgeous dark locks were fanned over him, just below his chin. She'd burrowed into the side of him like a rabbit. Funny how he didn't mind, not in the slightest. It took great effort to disentangle himself from her sweet soft skin, but he heard scratching sounds right outside the bedroom. He climbed out of bed, pulled on his boxers and, as he drew closer to the door, identified the sound on the other side.

No surprise, he opened it and found Bonkers midswipe.

"I like you, dude, but you're not getting in here with us." Noah softly shut the door.

The cat probably needed to go outside and perhaps this was a regular nightly ritual. He and Twyla had been a little distracted for the last two hours. The kitchen digital clock flashed the time. Midnight. Come to think of it, Twyla had mentioned that her cat roamed the house all night and mostly hid during the day except for feeding time. He didn't seem like much of a pet to Noah. More like a vampire.

He walked to the back door, and Bonkers followed him, rubbing up against him and winding between his legs so Noah nearly tripped on him.

"What's wrong with you? You like me, and I don't really care much about you. But you don't like Twyla, and she's one of the kindest people I've ever known. She loves you, though I can't imagine why."

He held open the back door, and Bonkers slipped outside.

Now he could take another look at the book that had thrown him back into a guilt cycle.

He read the inscription, feeling his heart slam against his chest like a wild animal trapped inside. Love shouldn't be this easy. He should have gotten over his damn self years ago and they could have been happy together instead of miserable with other people. A colossal waste of time and he didn't want to waste another second.

Noah crawled back into bed, pulling Twyla, who had rolled over on her side away from him, back into his arms. She made a soft sighing sound, then began to burrow herself against his body once again. Look at him, cuddling. He never thought it possible he would enjoy anyone invading his personal sleeping space, but leave it to Twyla to turn him into a cuddler.

"And I've loved you for a hundred and five years, and probably more," he whispered into her hair just before he fell asleep.

The next morning, disappointment clouded his senses because he didn't smell coconut anymore. He no longer had a gorgeous woman trying to physically attach herself to his body. So, he was alone. He'd spent the night, and he was alone in her bed. Great. Then he heard steps rushing back and forth outside the door of the bedroom and eventually the door swung wide open.

Twyla began to search through dresser drawers and under her bed.

"Lose something?" Noah rubbed his eyes.

"Bonkers! I can't find him anywhere. I used the can opener this morning and usually he comes running out of whatever place he's been hiding in at that sound. Maybe he's trapped somewhere? But I've looked everywhere."

Noah went up on his elbows and tried to shove away the layer of fog from his brain. He remembered letting Bonkers out last night and must have forgotten to let him back in?

"Could he still be outside? Did you check?"

"*Outside?* He never goes outside. He's terrified."

"Terrified? That little monster? What on earth is he terrified of?"

"I don't know, but he never got used to outside so he's just an indoor cat. I'm so worried!"

Oh, crap. Realization cut through him like a knife. He'd let an *indoor* cat outside. It was a wonder he hadn't scratched at the door all night. Or maybe, just maybe, Noah hadn't *heard* him. Noah jumped out of bed and pulled clothes on. Great, now he'd lost her cat. First the book, now the cat. Before long she might learn to hate him. One he'd stolen and the other he'd apparently lost out of idiocy.

Time to confess and beg for mercy. "I thought Bonkers wanted outside. I heard him scratching at your bedroom door last night and when I opened the door, he went right outside like he knew what he was doing."

Twyla gasped. "He could be anywhere now. There's also a very mean cat a couple of houses down. If he gets to poor Bonkers, I don't know what will happen."

"Don't worry. I've got this. Do you have any idea how many calls I've answered for stranded kittens and trees?"

"Is that still a thing?"

On a slow day maybe.

If he was lucky, really lucky, Noah would find Bonkers, and he'd find him uninjured and possibly shivering behind a bush somewhere. Horrified to be set out into the wild. First, Noah went outside the back door in the direction he'd let Bonkers out. But for a scaredy-cat, it appeared that Bonkers had strayed from the roost. He wasn't in Twyla's small fenced-in yard, or behind any bushes or shrubs. And yes, he checked the tree.

He walked down the street asking any neighbor he saw outside whether they'd seen a gray cat, mean and with a lot of attitude. Noah went all around the block and was headed back when he noticed ruffling on the higher branch of a tree two houses from Twyla's. *Bonkers*. This should be easy. A no-brainer. The cat liked him, last he heard, which gave him an advantage. Shouldn't be too difficult to wrangle him out of that branch and back down the tree. Then, he and Twyla would carry him inside and laugh about this later, maybe even go back to bed for a little morning sex. His very favorite kind. Which he had notably missed this morning.

Noah started to climb the tree and scaled it quickly. The Fire Academy had taught him to endure both tight spaces and heights. He was fortunately afraid of neither. Yes, this would be a piece of cake. Or, it should have been, but just then the Texas skies opened up. They tended to do this at times without much warning so everyone could have a good old-fashioned drenching.

The cat, disgusted by the water, screeched and jumped from one branch to another, seeking better cover. And Noah got it. The branches were offering some shelter but, hell, Bonkers needed to be inside. Twyla wanted him and she would get him. The water fell hard enough that he wished he had windshield wipers for his eyes. Or at least a ball cap. With one hand, he reached for the cat, who should have been happy for the rescue. Instead, he retaliated with the only weapon he had.

"Ow. Oh, hell." Noah drew back his hand. Bonkers had claws.

Guess what? So did Noah.

"Come here, you idiot."

Then, in a death-defying stunt, the cat jumped to the ground and ran off. That's when Noah noticed a blur of black. Black, not *gray*. He might have had the wrong cat in the first place. Who could tell in this torrential rain? Noah headed back inside for a ball cap to resume his search.

When he opened the front door, there sat Twyla, Bonkers in her lap.

"Did you hear me calling you?" She stood. "What *happened*?"

"I think I got attacked by the wrong cat." He ran a hand through his damp hair. "But all's well that ends well. I see you two are getting cozy."

"He came home almost as soon as you left. And you know what? He's been pretty affectionate. I think maybe all he needed was a good scare to know he has a good thing going here."

"Looks like he missed the downpour." Meanwhile, Noah had been through a shower with his clothes on.

Twyla came close. "Why didn't you come in out of the rain, silly?"

"I had to get Bonkers. It's my fault he went outside in the first place."

"Oh, Noah." She framed his face. "Rescuer of cats and damsels in distress. My hero."

"Well, he's no dragon and you sure as hell are not a damsel in distress."

"I love you." Then she kissed him so deeply that he *wished* with everything in him that he'd slayed a dragon.

"Don't you know I'd do anything for you?" He took her hand and brought it to his lips to kiss the inside of her wrist.

She shook her head. "I didn't know, but I'm starting to believe you."

Later they'd find he had fresh scratches torn through his long-sleeved Henley. Twyla used antiseptic on each one and kissed the spot before she applied a bandage.

And as it worked out, he got his morning sex.

Twice.

CHAPTER SEVENTEEN

WITH THREE DAYS before Christmas, Noah realized his timing could have been better, but nonetheless this had to be done. He'd been a coward when he'd left Austin with the excuse that the roof collapse had forced him to reevaluate his life. That was true, but only to a point. The real truth was that he wasn't running from something. He was running toward the only person he'd ever truly loved.

Michelle had followed him here, which meant he hadn't been clear enough. He hadn't made a clean break. And yes, he'd been flattered by her actions, but now it was time to be brutally honest. Even if their relationship had failed, Michelle had been a good friend when he was far from home and missing the person who'd always been at the center of his heart. The person he told himself he couldn't have. Now, all that was in the past and he was moving forward.

He asked Michelle to meet him at the Salty Dog and now sat in a booth near the back of the bar for a little privacy. He couldn't discount the fact that he wanted to meet in a public place to avoid any big scenes, even if Michelle wasn't known for them. He also didn't want to lead Michelle on even in the smallest way. If he'd asked her to come over to his house to talk, she might have assumed things.

The moment she met his eyes, her whole face lit up and he realized he'd miscalculated. Meeting with her at all was misleading. He had never been any good at this.

Will was the one with the silver tongue that always had all the right words.

He studied his hands and sent up a little prayer. *Mind helping me out a little here, buddy? I feel like I'm about to blow this and hurt someone I care about.*

"Noah," Michelle said a little breathlessly.

Maybe something in his gaze brought her up short because she blinked and then sat across the booth from him.

"Well, I'm thinking whatever this is, it isn't going to be a good thing for me."

Michelle wasn't a top-notch attorney in Austin for an inability to read social cues. She was an expert.

"Listen. You were a good friend to me when I was struggling. I didn't know anyone when I got to Austin, and you were good to me. I tried—I really tried—to make a go of this."

"But your heart was always with her. I just wish you'd been honest with me all along. *Both* of you."

"I wish that, too. Most of all, I wish we'd been honest with ourselves. I wasted a lot of time letting my guilt rule me. I'm not going to do that anymore."

"I don't think it's going to be as easy as you expect. Obstacles don't just move out of the way because you want them to."

"That's clear, but sometimes there are things worth fighting for. People worth fighting for."

Michelle lowered her gaze to the table and when she met his gaze, her eyes were damp.

"I wish you both luck. You deserve happiness. I'm just sorry I couldn't be the one to give it to you." She reached for his hand and squeezed it tight. "Don't let anyone ever put you in second place. Not even her."

The words surprised him, because he didn't realize Michelle had been so in tune with his own feelings of inadequacy. She was good. He'd give her that.

Over Michelle's shoulder, Noah saw Finn as he walked inside the bar. He quirked a brow in Noah's direction and his entire body became a question mark.

Is there a problem? Do you need me?

Thank God Noah had come back home. He'd forgotten how many true friends he had here. People he'd grown up with who saw him as more than someone who'd failed to rescue his brother. He had an entire "found family" in town, including Twyla.

Especially Twyla.

Noah gently shook his head in answer to Finn's unspoken question. Yeah, he was good.

And finally, for the first time in over a decade, he believed maybe he was worthy.

ON THE NIGHT of the Thompson family's Christmas party, Noah drove his mother. He'd been the first to tell her the good news of the angel investor that had rescued the bookstore. As usual, the Thompson family's beautiful ranch-style home had been decorated to the nines. Bright lights flashed from the oak tree and the shrubs, and they outlined each window. A Santa with his sleigh and reindeer was the lawn's focal point. Candy canes lined the pathway to the front door.

"Honestly," his mother said. "Look at this display. She's had so much loss in her life. Perhaps she shouldn't be celebrating."

Noah wasn't going to touch that remark anytime this year. It was that time of the year when he grew especially protective of every remark he made around his mother. Some days, it was like walking on landmines, afraid one word would set her off and she wouldn't leave the house for days.

Inside, they were greeted by Twyla, who hugged them both warmly. She led them toward the kitchen that was perfect for entertaining. Along the granite countertops, dozens of glistening crystal tumblers were set out around a tub of eggnog. Noah hadn't been to the Thompson family party in a few years, as the party often fell on one of his forty-eight-hour rotations. And as much as he'd loved being part of the emergency medical system, one of the things he'd never miss was answering calls during the holidays.

Roy Finch and Lois, along with their friends, were seated on couches watching the football game. Well, Mr. Finch was watching the game, along with Max and Adam.

Ella Mae stood and patted the seat beside hers. "Katherine, come sit beside me."

Noah walked his mother over to the gang and greeted everyone.

"At last, some more young people," said Patsy. "Valerie and Cole can't be here tonight. They have a thing out of town."

"A thing?" Ava laughed. "Valerie made teacher of the year and they have a ceremony."

"Yes." Patsy straightened, pride flashing in her dark eyes. "I wasn't going to say anything, but my Valerie won an award."

"Congratulations," Noah said.

Trays of hors d'oeuvres were passed around and Adam appointed himself as bartender, mixing drinks behind the bar.

"Everyone," said Ava. "We have an announcement to make."

She stood in the center of the room, beaming, Max beside her with an arm snaked around her waist.

"We're pregnant!" Ava announced happily, clapping her hands.

Stacy went to Ava. "Congratulations, sweetie."

"We wanted to wait until I was ready. And I thought I wouldn't be ready this quickly, but you know what? I am. Well, I'm going to be."

"Nice holiday surprise." Adam flashed a knowing grin. "There's just something about Christmas and babies, isn't there?"

"And to think we were in the room when Max wrote and recited a poem for Ava. And now we're here when they announced their precious child is coming," Patsy said. "I'm telling you, we need to rename our society. Something about love should be in the name."

After the conversation further evolved into babies and names, and all the equipment needed to make it happen, Noah thought it a perfect time to exit stage left. He whipped his head around, searching for Twyla. She was nowhere to be found, though a few minutes ago she had been tending to the food under heating lamps and she'd waved at him.

Honestly, with all this talk of babies, he remembered how much he loved the process behind making them. He realized for the first time that he wanted children. He hadn't before Twyla changed all that for him. If they had a boy, they'd name him William and Will would always be with them, but no longer something wedged between them. This time he'd be just one more thing that pressed them together into a deep and settling kind of love. A forever love.

He strolled through the rambling ranch house, peeking into open rooms, and, of course, the grand library. No Twyla. And then he heard the whispered sound of his name. The door to the guest room was open and Twyla beckoned to him. He followed her into the room where everyone had laid their sweaters and purses on the bed.

He winked. "What are you doing in here, Peaches? And did you lure me here for a reason?"

"Yes, of course." She moved closer and went up on her tiptoes, easing his jacket off. "I want you to take your coat off and stay awhile." She tossed it on the bed with the others.

"I don't plan on going anywhere."

"Good, see that you keep it that way." She fisted his shirt and pulled him to her, then kissed him with a deep and longing passion that matched his own.

The kiss quickly grew a little wild, him lowering his hands to her behind and tugging her against him. He lowered her onto the bed on top of all the soft jackets.

"Noah," she whispered, her breath warm on his neck. "What are you doing?"

"Don't worry. I'll remember my manners. I like looking at you sometimes. Just like this." He rose over her, bracing himself, looking at her sweet face. The girl he'd loved for half his life. "I love you."

"I love you."

He'd waited years to hear those words and, more to the point, to feel worthy of them. It was perfect, too perfect, and then the door to the bedroom opened softly, letting in the sounds of Christmas music, glasses filling and people chatting.

He winced. "Okay, this is a little embarrassing."

Then he noticed Twyla's expression, wide eyes and crimson tinged cheeks.

"Noah! Twyla! What on *earth* are you two doing?"

It was the shrill voice of his mother. One he would recognize anywhere. Noah knew before he turned around that he would not be getting a warm reception when he saw his mother holding her jacket.

Noah rose, offering his hand to Twyla to help her up. "Sorry, Mom, there's a time and a place. I know. This is not it."

He'd been worried about coming off like an unruly teenager all over again, who simply wanted to shock his parents into noticing he was alive. But instead, he saw a much deeper problem. There was more than disappointment in his mother's eyes. He witnessed pain and shock, and the kind of fresh heartbreak he'd hoped never to see again.

"How long has this been going on?" she asked, waving a hand between them.

Noah and Twyla glanced at each other, both coming up short with words. Noah wanted to say, "About fifteen years," but thought it best to take the fifth now.

I refuse to answer the questions on the grounds the answer might incriminate me. Yes, I've been in love with "Will's girl" for over a decade.

Because she's not "Will's girl." She's her own girl.

His mother shook her head, obviously not waiting for the answer.

Noah winced. So, apparently, she would not be as happy as Twyla's grandmother had been. Then again, it had to be embarrassing to have walked in on them. It wasn't exactly his finest moment. He decided that alone was the issue. She was disappointed in his timing, though maybe she shouldn't have been. It had been decided long ago in their family hierarchy that he was the son who would disappoint.

Dinner was tense, with Katherine barely speaking to anyone, acknowledging only Ella Mae and her husband. She wouldn't make eye contact with either him or Twyla. And not surprisingly, she wanted to leave early, thanking Twyla's grandmother and wishing her a Merry Christmas.

"Do you have to go so early?" Ella Mae asked.

"Oh, yes. You know me. I'll probably be in bed by eight o'clock."

"I'll call you," he said to Twyla as he followed his mother out the front door.

While he drove, Noah imagined the entire ride would be tense and quiet if he didn't try to explain. "I'm sorry that my timing was so bad. It was awkward for all three of us."

"It wasn't the best way to tell me. You're my main concern, Noah. I don't want to see you hurt."

"I'm prepared for that, and for anything that might happen. But I think I've loved Twyla for a long time. I tried to stop."

"Is that why you left for Austin?"

"Not the only reason."

He could tell her that he'd left because he was so tired of seeing the plaque. Tired of the reminders everywhere that he'd failed. Tired of seeing the pain in his mother's eyes. He was so tired of the lie that he'd told for so long, it seemed almost true some days. It had felt like the right thing to do in the beginning and instinct made him protect his brother. But the lie had settled on him like an armored suit he couldn't take off.

"All I want is for you to find a girl who will love you and put you first. Twyla has been your friend for so long and I've never seen the slightest bit of interest on her part. You're my only son and I want you to be happy. But Twyla? Won't she always compare you to Will? I know how much your father hurt you when he couldn't forgive you. When he left, it felt as though he was saying you and I weren't enough reason to stay." She closed her eyes. "That's why I thought the move to Austin might be good for you. Somewhere where no one will blame you for the accident. No one knows your past. A clean slate."

Whether or not she loved him and was loyal, she did blame him. And why not? He'd given her every reason. It was just the two of them left now. Half of a family once whole. The truth mattered. It mattered because he'd sacrificed a memory for his own happiness. The lie had festered until it was ugly and painful. Slowly killing him.

"There's something I think you should know about the accident."

CHAPTER EIGHTEEN

THE PARTY WENT decidedly downhill after the awkwardness of Katherine catching Noah and Twyla kissing. And it definitely hadn't been the world's best timing, but it also wasn't the worst thing anyone could do. It wasn't like they'd been naked and rolling around on top of everyone's coats.

Even when Ava started to sing Christmas carols, starting with "Jingle Bells," the mood had lost its shine. Or maybe that was just all coming from her. She wished Katherine would have just looked at her across the table.

It wasn't that Twyla wanted to forget what amounted to her first puppy love. She wanted permission to move on. She firmly believed she'd been granted that grace. Not Noah. Poor Noah, caught between the past and the future he wanted. He was far more sensitive than anyone wanted to give him credit for. A good son, he did not want to hurt his mother, and Twyla believed he had never imagined he would by simply choosing to love her.

But this could change everything. Twyla wanted Katherine to accept her and Noah together, but she'd been foolish enough to think she didn't need her approval. She went back to the party, forcing herself to be happy. It wasn't any different than the way she'd lived the past ten years, so it came easily to her. Eventually, their guests left one by one, those with young children leaving first.

She and Ganny finished drying the dishes and putting away all the festive platters.

"Maybe you should spend the night," Ganny said. "I miss our sleepovers."

When she'd been a little girl, Twyla loved nothing more. There had been comfort in Ganny's soft cotton sheets and fluffy pillow. But somewhere along the line, she'd created all that warmth and familiarity in her own space. Now, she only wanted to go home to her own bed and slide under the covers. She wanted to read and fall into a world where she and Noah would be together with zero complications. If she could, she'd rewrite their story and he would have been her first love. Because whether true or not, it felt that way.

She got home and opened the door to a highly annoyed Bonkers who hissed and swiped at the air.

"I know, I know. I'm late." She removed her jacket and laid it on her living room couch.

Opening up a can of food for Bonkers, she set it down and watched as he circled it, as if he thought she might actually poison him.

"You need therapy," she said to her cat. "But I love you anyway."

Not long afterward, Noah texted her, I'm coming over in a few minutes.

Thank goodness. She needed to see him and be assured that he'd smoothed everything over with Katherine. They'd all be okay.

Twyla stepped outside into the brisk night and sat on the front stoop. Waiting like she had so many times before. For Noah. For Will. For both of them to show up together, wind-and sunburned from a day on the boat, ready to tell her all about the day's catch. She longed for easier days when love was simple and chaste. When love wasn't this giant boulder to carry everywhere.

Those days were gone. Love and loss were intermixed now and forever.

But anyone who'd ever lost someone could say the same. It didn't mean one couldn't love with all their heart and strength. Sometimes love was even stronger.

By the time Noah pulled up, Twyla had located both the Noah Dipper and the Will Dipper. She would look at the stars more often. Name new constellations. She'd see things in different ways all over again. She didn't have to go to New York to see something exciting. All she had to do was learn to notice everything around her, as though it was the first time.

Noah met her eyes as he walked up the porch steps to the stoop. His own eyes were slightly red. Not a good sign.

"Hey," he said, bumping her knee like old times.

"Hey, yourself."

He turned to Twyla and the utter pain in his eyes took her breath. All she'd ever wanted was to see those eyes shimmer with joy again and she had...for a little while. She knew in that moment he'd told his mother the truth of the accident. She held her breath and then asked the question.

"Did she believe you?"

"Yes."

Thank you, God.

"But I shouldn't have said anything. Not tonight, or maybe ever. She's already been through so much loss and now she's got even more to work through, knowing Will was to blame for everything. She made me sit down and hash out every moment of the accident. What Will said that day, what he did and how the accident happened. I didn't want to relive it again, but she asked for it." He rubbed his temples. "And then she sobbed and begged me to forgive her for blaming me. Because yes, she had. Even though she loves me and I'm all she has."

"It's okay." Twyla rested her hand on his thigh. "Now she knows."

"Even if the accident wasn't my fault, I always fell short when it came to my brother."

Her heart twisted because she heard the unsaid words. "Noah, you have *never* been second for me."

He seemed to ignore that.

"I'm going to find her some real help. Some counseling. Even if I have to drag her out of the house myself. I shouldn't have ignored her pain this long. I shouldn't have acted like it was normal to refuse to throw anything away. Grief is normal but she's…something different. She can't let go."

"Guilt can make it hard to let go, too. Not just grief."

"What does she have to feel guilty about? *None* of this was her fault."

"She must know on some level, Noah, that she failed you. She wasn't healthy enough to be the mother you needed. You suffered, too."

"I don't need to be mothered. I just need to fix this so she can be well. And happy. Somehow. If it's at all possible." Noah covered his face with his hands. "I don't know what else to do."

Every cell in her body hurt to see him in this position. She wanted to tell him it wasn't his fault, that he'd also lost someone he loved. Then he'd been left in charge when even his own father abandoned them. She wanted Noah to know he wasn't in charge of anyone's happiness but his own. But Noah, the rescuer, wanted to save his mother.

"I think we just need to…" Noah began, and then his own voice drifted and mixed with the sounds of the night.

"Break up." Twyla spoke through the sob in her throat. Why not make this easier for him.

"Right," he said, and took her hand in his, threading their fingers together. "We'll always be in each other's lives."

"Sure," Twyla said. "You take care of her. She comes first."

"I'm pretty sure she'll be ready to see you again soon."

"She…doesn't want to see me?"

Noah looked stricken. Maybe he'd meant to keep that tidbit to himself. "She's upset tonight. The news of us, the truth about the accident… It was too much for one day."

"Yes, sure, that makes sense." Still, the thought that Katherine had turned against her, even for a moment, was enough to cause fresh tears to form in her eyes.

She'd been like a second mother to Twyla for all these years. They might never be able to talk freely again. They might never just pull out a photo album and laugh and have cookies and eggnog and remember. It made no sense, but grief didn't have to make sense.

Noah stood and pulled Twyla up with him. "I'm going to spend more time with her. Get her some therapy. Maybe Finn will help more with the charters, so I don't have to spend all my time there."

He didn't have to add that he'd talk to Twyla every day, and he'd text. For a while, though, it wouldn't be the same. Not the wonderful way it had been for the past week when she'd literally had it all.

The world tends to take perfection and squash it to bits.

No. Turns out she didn't actually believe that. She did understand, however, that some people were incapable of seeing the beauty in brokenness. Once, she'd been one of them.

Twyla would no longer be that person. Not ever again.

Noah kissed her and held her tight for several long minutes, like he was trying to memorize the way they fit together. He might not realize he'd made this feel like a genuine goodbye.

Goodbye to the way he'd kissed her; goodbye to the way he'd made her feel loved and whole again.

CHAPTER NINETEEN

IT WAS THE end of the day on Christmas Eve, and Noah and Finn were tying up the boats.

Once they'd finished, they all headed inside for the "all persons on deck" meeting.

All afternoon, Noah had been a grump and needed to apologize. He'd scared Diana and Tee was staying out of his way because the kid was far smarter than he looked.

Today, he wore a T-shirt that said: *It seemed like a good idea at the time.*

Not a good message for your captain if you wanted to be trusted with more responsibility. Then again, nothing was funny to Noah anymore.

"I want to thank you all," Noah said. "I'm sorry if I've been a grump, or a little distracted the past few days, but I couldn't ask for a better crew. Next year, Saturday pizza day is back."

Tee pumped his fist in the air. "Yessss!"

Diana smiled but studied the floor. She still hadn't met his eyes but at least she spoke to him occasionally.

"Yay." Finn gave a wry smile and leaned against the counter.

"And, well, Finn knows better than anyone that I leave shopping until the last minute—"

"I don't need any car freshener, thanks." Finn held up his palms. "And I'm full up on batteries, too."

"Ha ha, smart-ass. I've moved into the new millennium

along with everyone else." He reached in his jacket and pulled out envelopes. "They're called gift cards. I hope y'all like books. And if you don't, it's time to change that."

They were all to Once Upon a Book. Approximately two hundred dollars' worth. Noah handed them out.

"Thanks, nacho man!" Tee had decided to call him by the ridiculous nickname and Noah had stopped correcting him. "Hope you don't mind, but I'm going to take my girlfriend to the store and let her go wild!"

Ah, another girlfriend who liked to read. Flashes of Twyla came back to him, curled on a pillow reading, but willing to drop the book for him. His chest tightened.

"Thank you, Mr...nacho... Captain, um," Diana stammered.

"Noah," he said.

"Noah." This time she met his eyes and in them he saw something...familiar.

A shy kind of sweetness that reminded him again of another girl, and of another time. Twyla had given him the same kind of bashful looks. Rarely meeting his gaze. He'd never imagined back then that she'd actually liked him as more than a friend which said something.

Maybe he'd put himself second before anyone else ever had.

"Okay, Diana. Let's get going if I'm going to give you that ride." Tee held the door open for Diana and when she went out, he turned to Noah and silently mouthed. *She has a wicked crush on you.*

Finn snorted, arms crossed. "Figures. They *all* have a crush on you."

"Shut up," Noah said and shoved him.

"Go have fun with your lady and I'll lock up."

"Nah, you go. I'm going to be here awhile longer."

"What the hell for?"

He may as well tell Finn now. "Twyla and I... We broke up."

"You're an idiot," Finn said, shaking his head.

"Tell me how you really feel."

"You asked for it." Finn scowled. "Who's good enough and who isn't? Nobody is good *enough*. We tend to think the women we love deserve better because we're not perfect. They deserve perfect but, brother, that's never going to happen. Twyla loves you. That makes you perfect the way nothing else ever will. You're perfect for *her*."

"I don't feel like I am. I've made too many mistakes. Too much baggage."

"I can't believe I have to tell you, of all people, but none of us have the time we think we do. The point is, we don't know how much time we have left."

"Twyla understands me. This breakup is a mutual thing. She's always going to be there for me."

"She will, as a friend. There's no denying that. But I don't know how you can be so sure about the rest of it. She's not going to wait around for you forever. If you want her, you're going to have to *choose* her."

Choose her.

It wasn't that simple. He already had but it didn't change the facts. She was too good for him. He would always be second best to someone who'd been better for her in every way. The last thing he'd ever wanted to do was take his brother's place. No one ever could. Maybe someday, someone else would come along and he'd find a way to be happy for her. The way he'd been happy for her and Will even when he loved her, too.

He and Twyla hadn't talked or texted much since the party, but they were still okay. Noah needed to believe that. He already missed her so much that his heart cracked every time he thought of her. Ridiculous. Once before, he'd stepped aside and lost Twyla to someone else. But he'd been someone Noah had loved almost more than he loved himself.

Will Cahill was good. Perfect. *He* deserved her.

But Noah still didn't believe that anyone else did.

Except maybe a reverend.

Finn was still yakking. "You've already had so much loss. I don't want to see you lose the best thing that's ever happened to you."

Noah swallowed hard. He really wanted to stop talking about this. He'd moved straight from the guilt of loving his brother's girl to the acceptance that he could never be good enough for her.

Eventually, Finn got tired of talking, which may have been around the time that Noah shot him a glare that indicated he'd had enough.

"Merry Christmas, idiot." Finn tossed up his hands.

"Don't let the door slam your ass on the way out!" Noah shouted.

But he followed Finn out and caught him before he'd gone too far. Noah didn't want to leave things like this. Not on Christmas Eve.

Not with Finn, one of his oldest friends. He'd been like a brother.

"Hey, but seriously. Sorry for being a damn grinch. Merry Christmas."

"Yeah," Finn said and pulled Noah into a man-hug.

They clapped each other's backs, and Noah lingered outside, watching Finn drive away.

A cool wind on the coast had turned the night chilly and Noah was glad he'd worn his jeans, long-sleeved shirt with a jacket and boots. He was about to go back inside when a beam of moonlight showed a string of Christmas lights they'd forgotten to remove from the night of the Snowflake Float Boat Parade.

"Guess I have to do everything around here," he muttered.

He was single, obviously, and had no one waiting for him at home. He didn't have to worry about his mother tonight, because Ella Mae and her husband were dropping by for a gift exchange. They were also bringing her dinner. He didn't know if his mother realized what a friend she had in Ella Mae, but Noah was grateful. Slowly, his mother was letting her friends know the truth. It hadn't been Noah driving the boat. It was as if saying it made it real to her, made it acceptable. She kept telling Noah the truth was important and she refused to live a lie. They'd get through this difficult time and on the other side of it. Someday.

Grabbing a flashlight from inside, Noah put it between his teeth and climbed the mast. He reached the top and worked the wires around. Funny, this had been much easier in the bright light of day when the wind wasn't rocking the boat. The mast swayed. Noah felt a wave of apprehension. He began to assess the situation. Worst case scenario stuff. No, but this was fine. He was good. Really, what could happen? He *could* fall and hit the deck. It would hurt his bum leg, but no serious harm. Noah had a good grip on the mast and just had to get this done faster. He wound the wire around, frustrated when it caught. Then he dropped the flashlight and it fell to the deck, making a cracking sound.

"Damn it!"

Now he'd have to shimmy back down and get the light. Halfway down, his weight must have upset the equilibrium and when a larger wave hit the boat it moved sideways.

Noah lost his balance. He was airborne for seconds before he hit the water and went under.

His first thoughts under the dark murky water were of the fire. Similar to this moment, he hadn't been able to see a damn thing in the thick black smoke. But in the fire, he had equipment to help guide him, oxygen to sustain him. Still, the terror he'd felt had been far too real. It wasn't natural walking into a building fire when everyone else was running out. But it had been his job, and he'd done it to the best of his ability. Roofs falling could not always be predicted or avoided. But to this day, Noah could swear he'd been pushed out of the way. Now, he felt Will with him again, reminding him it was his job, and his gift, to live.

And damn, how he wanted to—and be forgiven for surviving.

Noah nearly swallowed a lung full of water but came up kicking with every ounce of strength he had left. On the way down the mast, he must have nicked his leg on the side of the hull. His bad leg. It was hard enough to swim to the boat wearing all his clothes and boots, but now he had an injured leg to deal with.

How ridiculous would it be to drown only a few feet from the dock? How ironic?

For one moment, he doubted he'd get back as he struggled against the weight of his boots. Noah hadn't been the strong swimmer that Will had been, which was why he hadn't been able to save him. With strength he didn't even realize he had, Noah managed to get himself back to the dock and somehow pull himself up into the boat. He fell to the deck, lying there sopping wet. Hands splayed behind him, he looked up at the stars.

This is ridiculous.

He was so tired of playing it safe with his heart, so tired of trying to minimize the risks since that day over ten years ago when he'd been shattered with grief. A memory came back to him, clear as a bright day in June.

I can't do it, Noah had said, an eight-year-old treading water and trying to beat his own record of sixty seconds.

Yes, you can, Will said, his legs dangling over the dock as he kept time. *All you have to do is try. Remember, you just have to beat your last record. Not mine.*

And it was true, Noah might have competed with everybody else, but he had never competed with his brother. He used to think it was because he could never measure up. But from the beginning, Will told Noah that as brothers, they would never compete with each other. And neither one would ever be better than the other. Funny how Noah had forgotten this. But the words had come straight from Will, and it was like a Christmas gift to remember them now, solid and real, like they were floating to him on the light fog.

He scrambled off the boat and grabbed a hammer and pliers. There was one thing he'd been dying to do for years, and he'd waited too long to do it. Soaking wet and mostly alone out here, he stalked to the plaque stuck to the entrance of the dock.

In honor of the heroic actions of Noah Cahill.

Slowly, he pried the damn thing off and threw it in the bed of his truck.

TWYLA HAD CLOSED the store early on Christmas Eve, but once she'd fed Bonkers—and he'd gone back to ghosting her—she had nothing else to do. Normally she'd spend the evening with Ganny, getting ready for the big celebration held at her home tomorrow. But everything had already been prepared. And surprisingly, because at the time she assumed Twyla would be busy with the Cahills tonight, Ganny accepted the invitation by Patsy Villanueva to an annual party held at the lighthouse. Twyla refused to allow her to change her plans.

She'd see Ganny and the rest of the family tomorrow for the Thompson family's white elephant gift exchange. Twyla's gift was always a book she'd read that she wanted someone else to enjoy, too. Her parents were flying in tonight and staying in a hotel by the airport, and they would drive to Charming early tomorrow morning. Ganny would have her annual pancake breakfast, one in which she invited all the people that didn't have family in town. Tomorrow would be great, and her spirits would be lifted to see everyone together again. One more year completed with their family bookstore. All signs appeared they would be around for another forty or so years, if Twyla wanted to continue the tradition. And she'd found that she did, because though New York City sounded wonderful, Charming was home.

Zoey was spending time with Drew's family this year, which meant things were getting serious. Noah, of course, would be with his mother as he should be. Finn? She had no idea, nor did it matter. He was a handsome guy and might have been fun to spend a little time with during the holiday season. But he'd never replace Noah in Twyla's heart. She was beginning to worry no one ever would.

When she couldn't sit still another minute, and didn't know what to do with herself, she headed back to the store.

She wanted to be in the one place where her heart had first healed, among the stories of amazing worlds created in an author's gifted imagination. It was more than any single book to her, but it had now become all of the books. All those spines lined up together, feeling a little like a family, bathed her with comfort. She unlocked the shop doors, turned on the lights and when a few passersby scurried by wondering if they might grab a last-minute gift, she relented and let a few of them inside. This led to another, and then another.

"I can't believe you're open on Christmas Eve," the young man who worked with Noah said. Tee? He wore a silly T-shirt again as seemed to be his custom.

"Well, I couldn't sleep, and my family celebrates tomorrow, so I figured I'd just come here and hang out for a bit."

"Dude, lucky for me you're open. I leave my shopping till the last minute. And this year, I had no idea what to get my girlfriend. But then my boss gave me this gift card and the decision was made. This is perfect."

His boss would be Noah and she wasn't at all surprised he'd given bookstore gift cards to his staff. Twyla flashed back to the Christmas when Noah, always a helpless, last-minute shopper, gave her car fresheners and AAA batteries. She'd used some great mileage on that, teasing him over it for years. Eventually, he'd learned to be a more thoughtful giver, with a little help from her. Now he never failed to impress her. Last year, he'd sent his gift through the mail. A necklace with a pendant designed in the cover of *A Dragon's Heart*. If something could be made from one of her favorite books, he'd find a way to buy it.

Tee wanted recommendations. Twyla took care of the kid, then helped a couple of other shoppers find the perfect book for a loved one before she realized that her own purpose for coming here tonight was not to sell more books. She wanted some solitude to contemplate the end of another year. To plan how she would handle the rest of her life without Noah as a lover and only as a best friend.

After all the last-minute shoppers were gone, Twyla made sure the sign was flipped to Closed and shut off the front lights. She made her way to the back of the store and the fantasy section. Grabbing a pillow, she curled up in the nook, cracked opened a copy of *A Dragon's Heart*, and began to read.

She'd flipped to her favorite chapter, where the hero and heroine finally get together, when she heard the pounding on her shop door. More desperate last-minute shoppers. *Note to self: leave the store open later next year on Christmas Eve.* By then, shoppers knew it was too late to have anything shipped. Perfect chance to get their business. What else did she have to do? Bonkers didn't even want anything to do with her and she doubted a year would change that.

"I'm closed!" she shouted, but the banging continued, this time followed by yelling.

Someone was calling out her name and it sure sounded an awful lot like Noah. He was supposed to be at his mother's tonight. He told her that in an earlier text which had been short and sweet. It simply sounded like someone who felt guilty he'd suddenly cut off most of their communication.

Curious, she walked to the front of the shop and flipped on the light. What she saw there shocked her. Noah stood, hair wet, holding a wrapped package. One glance and her heart swelled with love. She let him inside.

"Hi," she said, trying not to look at him again.

"I dropped by your house, and you weren't there. I would have been here sooner, but I fell off my boat and had to go home and change."

"Wait. You fell? How did that happen? You're okay?"

"I'm fine, leg hurts a little but it's nothing serious. Still, I had to get your gift because I've waited too long to give it back to you." He handed her the wrapped present.

"Give it *back* to me? Is this a white elephant present? Noah, are you regifting?" she teased him.

Twyla wasn't going to lie. She'd made the lighthearted

comment to distance herself from the emotions quaking through her. She didn't want to hope, but hope was this irrepressible wave rising inside of her.

She blamed it on books.

"You'll see when you open it. Go ahead." Noah cleared his throat, looking positively boyish.

She tore open the paper to find he'd given her the same book she gave him.

"That's funny. Great minds think alike."

"It's not just another book, it's The Book."

When she took a closer look, Twyla saw it was the copy she'd lost a year ago when she'd moved to her smaller rental.

"How did you...how did you find this? When? I've been looking all over."

She flipped through the pages, finding all the places where they'd written notes to each other over that first difficult year when the book was their escape.

"This is the embarrassing part, and I have to apologize in advance. Please forgive me, but I took the book when I left Charming. I'm still sorry I never told you—still sorry I kept it from you for so long. For a long time, I didn't know why I'd done it. Then I realized, it was because as long as I had the book, I still had a part of you, a part of us, that I could never lose."

"Noah, no matter what happens, you will never lose me. I love it. It is the perfect gift."

She held the book tightly to her chest. It was nice that if they had to break up, at least she had the book back with her now. And now *she'd* always have this part of Noah with her.

Noah pointed to the book. "Read the inscription."

Twyla turned the cover and flipped through to the beginning where Noah had written on the empty page:

I will slay every dragon for you.

Her finger traced the words and her eyes filled. "Do you mean it?"

He stepped closer and his big hand rested on the nape of her neck, pulling her to him.

"Finn said something that finally made sense to me. He said if I wanted you, I'd have to *choose* you. The thing is, I can't remember a time when I didn't choose you. I just never thought you should choose me back. I always felt like someone else could make you happier. Someone better. Someone…without all my baggage."

Twyla made a whimpering sound but didn't trust herself to speak against the sob in her throat.

He took her hand and brought it to his lips. "And then I remembered something else when I was kicking back to the boat wearing all my clothes—so what if I'm not the best man in the world? I'm only in competition with myself and doing the best I can no matter what. And if you say that you love me, then I'm the luckiest man I've ever met."

"I love you." Tears slid down her cheeks. "I always have."

"For a hundred years?" He winked. "Because I swear, I've loved you for at least a hundred and five."

EPILOGUE

Six months later

THE GRAND OPENING of Nacho Boat Adventures was delayed until May—partly because of the weather, but mostly so that Noah could have more time to hire a full crew. Finn's brother, Declan, had joined their new and fledgling company. And when Noah's buddy, Tate, grew tired of running into burning buildings, he did, too. Tee and Diana were still with him, learning as they went. The company grew so quickly that Noah had forced himself to slow things down. A business could crash and burn if they took on too much and too soon. He'd joined the Chamber of Commerce and was getting plenty of business advice from people far more experienced than he was.

And besides, he'd wanted to spend time with Twyla and achieve the delicate balance of both work and family. He'd made one major decision just after last Christmas. Though the name of the company would remain the same, Noah took the unusual step of renaming a boat. He'd gone through the entire process. Though he wasn't the superstitious sort, many nautical types were. When they saw the new name, they'd be surprised she wasn't named after a woman—a normal custom. Not named after a goddess of protection, not after his mother and not after Twyla. He'd chucked naming conventions to the curb this time.

And on this bright, early spring day, they were officially christening her with the new name.

A small group of business leaders, residents and friends had gathered along the dock to watch and celebrate this new beginning.

Ava Del Toro, belly huge with child, stood in the crowd with Max. Nearby were Adam and Cole, fellow business leaders and people Noah relied on more and more. But Noah had his eye on only one person today. He only cared to see her face, wearing the sweet smile he now woke to every morning. Twyla stood sandwiched between her grandmother and his mother.

The past few months had been challenging ones for his mom. Between the knowledge and eventual acceptance that Will had been the one driving and understanding that she would have to accept Noah and Twyla as a couple, it hadn't been easy. But after the past two months, she'd finally turned a corner. The online grief therapy group she'd joined with Twyla's grandmother helped.

"Thanks for being here, everyone," Noah said. "As y'all know, this has been a labor of love from the moment we took over Nacho Boat. I have a lot of memories here, and plenty of them are even good, too."

Laughter from the crowd.

With a nod in Finn's direction, he communicated it was time to lower the sheet that covered the new name.

The Will Dipper.

Private little joke.

Not everyone here would understand, but Twyla did. And so did his mother, because while applause followed the unveiling, she dabbed at her eyes.

Love never dies, Twyla's grandmother had said to him shortly after Christmas. *It just changes form.*

Noah appreciated the sentiment and on days when his

thoughts inevitably turned to his brother, he felt less alone. Someone else made him feel less alone. Twyla reminded him every day that true love was worth taking a risk. They were still friends, because they'd never lose that, but now they were lovers, too. Rather than change their relationship, they'd simply enhanced it. He was the luckiest man to be in love with his best friend. He understood that not many people were that fortunate.

Noah broke the champagne bottle over the ship's hull and on Ava's insistence, gathered his crew together, smiled and faced the photographers.

Finally, he and Twyla could head home. For now, they were living in her small rental. It suited the two of them and Bonkers, of course. He'd broached a friendly truce with the cat, who was going to help Noah today. He'd practiced this over the course of the past few weeks, every time Twyla was working late at the bookstore. Today, everything would be perfect. He had the second bottle of champagne chilling. He'd written the speech, with some help from Stacy. Words were important to Twyla, so rather than speak from the heart, he'd wrangled words into submission. Beat them into shape. But Stacy refused to write it for him, unfortunately, so this wouldn't exactly be worthy of publication.

He could have done a loud and splashy proposal in front of everyone at the ship's christening. But Twyla would prefer something private and intimate. He'd wanted something, too, that would be clear, distinct and separate from the boat's renaming. One was a nod, a memory and an honor to the past.

This would be the start of their future together.

"Where's Bonkers?" Noah bent, as if that would encourage the cat to appear. "He always meets us at the door."

"Maybe he's hiding."

Bonkers would pick today to be the one day out of approximately one hundred days that he didn't greet them with his usual hiss. Very inconvenient. The ring box was tied to his collar along with his speech, rolled up like he was delivering the paper. Noah wanted to make this memorable and for reasons he couldn't fathom, Twyla loved this cat. God only knew why.

"You don't think he got outside again?" Twyla's eyes were a mix of horror and confusion, but they didn't match the fear churning in *his* gut.

His ring? Outside? With a pissed off cat?

What on earth was he thinking?

"No!" Noah shook his head. "I mean, how could he get outside? Now that I know he's an indoor cat, I never let him out. That only happened once."

Twyla rubbed Noah's shoulder. "Don't worry. He's in here. Somewhere."

And Noah had to find him. Now.

"Bonkers! Where are you, buddy?" Noah bent under the couch, searched in cupboards—which Twyla left open for him—and in closets. "Come out, wherever you are."

"You really like him now, don't you? I knew he'd grow on you, just like he grew on me. He's not mean, just misunderstood."

"Yeah."

Noah smiled through gritted teeth. If Bonkers didn't show up soon with the ring, not only would Noah hate him, but the cat's days would be numbered. He'd leave the back door open…just in case he wanted to stalk into the great outdoors. Maybe this time he'd go farther than the shrub.

Noah bent under the bed when a streak of gray went flying past him. He followed Bonkers into the kitchen, where Twyla stood near the can opener.

"This always works."

Why didn't I think of that?

Food, a powerful motivator for the beastie. The box, barely hanging on, fell right at Twyla's feet. Not exactly the plan, but mission accomplished.

Twyla blinked, then stared wide-eyed at the ring box, then at Noah. Back to the box. She picked it up, and Noah dropped to one knee. He had a speech prepared, which might be lying in tatters somewhere in this house, so he'd have to go from the heart. It wouldn't be perfect, but neither was he.

And she loved him anyway.

"Twyla, I've loved you for at least half my life. And I—"

"Yes!" She tackled him to the ground and now lay on top of him.

Noah was vaguely aware of Bonkers swiping near his head after getting a full meal in him.

"You didn't let me finish," he chuckled.

"Oh, no. Did I get it wrong?" A look of fear crossed her gaze. She hadn't even bothered to open the box, after all. "Is it a necklace? Or earrings?"

Now, he laughed. "No. It's a ring. You read me right."

"Thank God!" she said, covering her eyes with one hand.

"I had this whole speech I wrote and rolled up in a scroll. Bonkers had the ring box and the paper attached to his collar. He always greets us at the door." He looked behind him and caught Bonkers midswipe. "What the hell is *wrong* with you, man?"

"You wrote something? For *me*?" Twyla's hand went to her chest.

"I know how much words matter to you."

"Oh, Noah. You don't have to be a *real-life* hero." She smiled and lowered her lips to his. "That's why we have books."

* * * * *

WESTERN

Rugged men looking for love...

Available Next Month

A Temporary Texas Arrangement Cathy Gillen Thacker
Grace And The Cowboy Mary Anne Wilson

....

An Uptown Girl's Cowboy Sasha Summers
Hill Country Home Kit Hawthorne

....

Wrangling A Family Kathy Douglass
Second Chance Deputy Alexis Morgan

....

 LOVE INSPIRED

A Haven For His Twins April Arrington
A Country Christmas Lisa Carter

Larger Print

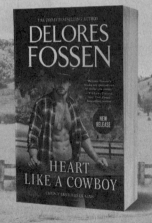

Subscribe and fall in love with a Mills & Boon series today!

You'll be among the first to read stories delivered to your door monthly and enjoy great savings.

WE
SIMPLY
LOVE
ROMANCE

MILLS & BOON

JOIN US

Sign up to our newsletter to stay up to date with...

- Exclusive member discount codes
- Competitions
- New release book information
- All the latest news on your favourite authors

Plus...
get $10 off your first order.
What's not to love?

Sign up at **millsandboon.com.au/newsletter**